VANISHED

VANISHED

A SAMANTHA STARR THRILLER, BOOK 5

S.L. MENEAR

ePublishingWorks!
love what you read.

Book and cover design by eBook Prep
www.ebookprep.com

October, 2020
ISBN: 978-1-64457-218-4 (Large Print)

ePublishing Works!
644 Shrewsbury Commons Ave
Ste 249
Shrewsbury PA 17361
United States of America

www.epublishingworks.com
Phone: 866-846-5123

For Dorothy Metz Littlefield

MY AUTHOR MOTHER

My mother's eyes are a deep
    turquoise-blue
They glisten and sparkle like crisp
    morning dew

Her face has a beauty that is timeless
    and bold
She has seen many years, but she'll
    never look old

Her mind is a garden of childlike
    delight
Where magical creatures live and
    take flight

Iridescent fairies with gossamer
    wings
Pearlescent unicorns and fanciful
    things

Inhabit a world filled with
    fluorescent flowers
Where songbirds serenade pink
    bunnies for hours

And sweet honey flows from gold
    combs in the trees

Made for the populace by
   purple-green bees

Waterfalls rain into luminous
   streams
Where willow trees weep for a
   mermaid's dreams

All of the wonders the author's mind
   can see
She records in her stories for you
   and me.

Soon her fairytales will entrance one
   and all
And then she will dance at the Fairy
   Queen's Ball.

ONE

June 3, 4:00 p.m.

Adrenaline surged through me, and swirling air whipped my long ponytail into my face as the 1939 biplane corkscrewed inverted ever closer to the ground. The spinning terrain seemed to rush up to meet us. If I didn't do something fast, the airplane would become a dirt dart, and we'd be splattered across the wreckage like two gallons of spaghetti sauce.

My student, harnessed into the front tandem seat, had frozen with his hands gripping the control stick and his feet locked on full left rudder. A windshield and instrument panel separated us, the back of his head and shoulders visible through the Plexiglas.

Shouting into the intercom hadn't worked. My

heart jackhammered my chest as I tried reaching over the windshield to smack him on the head, but my girly arms were too short. I couldn't unbuckle the seat harness without falling out of the open cockpit, which was upside down and spinning. The last resort would be reaching through the narrow space along the sidewall and stabbing him in the thigh with my great, great grandmother's giant hatpin.

But first I tried a less violent solution and belted out a few jarring lyrics from *The Phantom of the Opera*. My voice-activated microphone blasted the Phantom's chilling words into his headset as we plunged toward the ground with alarming speed.

Just as I reached for the hatpin, Kent snapped out of his trance, and I remembered to exhale.

"Holy hell, Sam, if that song was supposed to calm my nerves, it didn't work." He relinquished the controls and wiped his sweaty hands on his pants.

I neutralized the stick, let the nose fall through, and applied rudder opposite to the spin. Once the rotation had stopped, I gently pulled out of the dive and added power to recover our altitude. The world was right-side up again, and my heart rate had retreated from the terror zone.

As the roaring engine propelled us higher into the clear, late-afternoon sky, the South Florida sun erased my fear-generated goosebumps, and warm wind caressed my face.

"You said you wanted to learn spin entries and recoveries in my Bücker Jungmann." I throttled back as I leveled off at three thousand feet. "When you froze, I sang gruesome lyrics to jolt you from your death grip on the stick."

"Your singing was scarier than the inverted flat spin."

"*Funny*. The words seemed perfect for the situation."

"Perfect for dying!"

"Don't be so dramatic. I had to do *something*, and it was better than stabbing you with a huge hatpin."

"So, if plunging into hell wasn't bad enough, I'd also be gushing blood?"

"Geez, Kent, you sound like a drama queen."

"I didn't realize spins would be so terrifying. I'm too young to die."

"I'd never let that happen, especially since I have a hot date tonight."

"Ooh, is Mr. Tall, Dark, and Scottish back in town?"

"If he wasn't sent on an emergency mission, he'll arrive late tonight for a five-day visit." I paused. "I'm hoping I'll get his text soon because I have seven days off until my next airline flight."

"Lucky you. He's hot, but he's not my type—too scary."

"And too straight. Ross is a captain in the UK's Special Air Service. That's why he's so intense."

I banked over sugarcane fields and turned us

back toward the Atlantic Ocean, sparkling like a sea of blue diamonds in the brilliant sunshine.

"Well, girlfriend, I think we're done for today. I need to go home and change my underwear."

"Don't feel bad. Not everyone is comfortable with aerobatics. Next time, we'll focus on approaches to stalls and spins and how to avoid them."

"Avoiding death sounds good to me. Sign me up."

"Good. Now take the controls and fly us home."

The moment he took the stick, the airplane shook.

His voice tightened. "Where did that turbulence come from?"

"The flight controls on the Jungmann are so sensitive that if your hands are trembling, the airplane will vibrate. Try to relax."

"Well, that's not going to happen until I've downed half a bottle of chardonnay. Better take the airplane, Sam."

"Okay, I've got it."

As we neared the uncontrolled airport, I announced my intentions over the UNICOM radio frequency and entered the empty traffic pattern for a landing to the east. After cutting the power, I sideslipped down the final approach to keep the runway in sight. The soft whisper of air flowing over the wings was music to my ears as I eased the swept-wing biplane onto the pavement and turned off onto the broad ramp. Soon my baby was safe inside its hangar.

"Same time next week?"

"If I don't lose my nerve. I'll text you the day before." Kent waved and climbed into his silver Lexus sedan.

Straddling my red Ducati Diavel, I pulled on the full-visor helmet. Wearing it was hot in the blazing sun, but it was better than becoming an organ donor. I cranked up the almost-silent engine and zipped out of the parking lot.

Ten minutes later, I crossed the Southern Boulevard bridge to Palm Beach, turned left past Trump's Mar-a-Lago estate, and cruised up A1A to my beachfront condo. I had several hours before I needed to pick up Ross at Palm Beach International Airport around midnight.

I breezed into the top-floor apartment, stripped, and stepped into the shower stall. Warm water from the nozzle massaged my shoulders and back, relaxing the muscles. My mind went blank as I enjoyed the shower's caress.

That feeling changed in an instant.

The room darkened, and I experienced a vivid vision of muscular, dark-skinned men punching and kicking Ross's four-man SAS team, helpless with their wrists and ankles tied. Blood covered my handsome boyfriend's face as he lay on muddy ground in what looked like a jungle at night.

As I watched the brutal beatings, bile rose in my throat, and my stomach twisted into a knot.

I heard screams.

Mine.

I sucked in a deep breath and tried not to cry.

The violent vision vanished in an instant.

Somalia, Eight Hours Ahead of Florida Time

Captain Ross Sinclair gathered his black parachute and stuffed it under a bush. Soaking wet, he crouched behind thick jungle foliage and waited for his three Special Air Service teammates to join him. They had done a high-altitude-low-open jump at midnight and landed two miles west of a brutal warlord's encampment in Somalia.

His best friend and second-in-command, Lt. Derek Dunbar, and Chris MacDonald and Ian McShane joined him. A sudden downpour from the final month of Gu, the season of long rains, drenched them.

"Nothing like diving through a rainstorm to add excitement to our HALO jump." Derek wiped his night-vision lens.

Ross squinted through NV-binoculars. "Satellite infrared reported one hundred people in the camp."

"Let's hope the men are asleep so we can rescue the kidnapped schoolgirls," Chris said as he checked his rifle.

Ian glanced at his waterproof watch. "Ready."

"On me, lads." Ross slogged through muddy ground and heavy vegetation, his approach to the enemy camp masked by pounding rain.

His SAS predecessors, the feared Shadow Warriors, had been the first Special Forces in the world. Ross's elite soldiers, like Tier-One SEALs, were sent on the most dangerous missions, and this one was no exception.

Fifty yards from the target, he held up a fist, the signal to halt. They crouched behind a derelict truck overgrown by vegetation and scanned the camp.

"The children are probably in there." Ross pointed at a square tent in the camp's center surrounded by many smaller ones. Guards were stationed on every side of the canvas structure.

Derek focused his infrared scope. "Lots of warm bodies lying on the floor. Could be the fifteen girls, but no way to be certain with them so close together."

Ross studied the scene. "They could be guarding the girls or some corporate prisoners."

"Or maybe they're protecting Axmed Khalif and his lieutenants." Chris surveyed the camp.

Derek turned to Ross. "What's the plan?"

"Take out the sentries simultaneously with silenced head shots. Then we'll slip inside."

"Sounds good." Derek rechecked his rifle's magazine. "I'll take the east guard."

"I'll take the one on this side, and Chris and Ian will go north and south." Ross glanced at his men. "Call me when you're in position."

The men slipped away while Ross waited.

Minutes later, each man reported via radio, "Ready."

Ross took aim. "Three, two, one, fire," he commanded via his throat mike.

All four guards collapsed at the same instant.

Ross whispered, "I'm going in. Meet me at the target."

He crept up to the large tent's entrance. Crouching, he pulled aside the flap and peeked inside. Even with night-vision gear, Ross couldn't see the occupants. Their heads and bodies were covered with sheets.

He waited until his team joined him outside. Ross motioned for Chris to guard the entrance while he eased inside with Derek and Ian. He lifted a corner of the nearest linen.

A wide-eyed young girl about twelve years old lay atop a burly man. He held a blade to her neck and clamped his other hand over her mouth. The brute yelled, "Now!"

The sheets were thrown back, revealing men holding knives to the girls' throats.

Khalif, the militia leader, sat up. "Surrender or we slit throats."

The terror in the children's eyes made Ross's gut churn.

"If you hurt them, I'll put a bullet in your head." He aimed his weapon at Khalif. "Order your men to drop their knives and let the girls go."

Derek and Ian aimed at two men nearby.

"It only takes a second to slit throats." Khalif tightened his grip on the girl. "If you shoot me, my men will kill all the girls, and their shouts will alert my army. Give up. You have ten seconds before we start cutting."

Ross hesitated. He and his men had risked their lives many times, but he wouldn't be responsible for the deaths of fifteen young girls. There was no way they could kill all the captors before some of the girls were murdered.

Chris yelled from outside, "They've got us surrounded."

Khalif grinned, showing three missing teeth. "If they hear us yell, they'll fill this tent with lead. Time's up."

Ross clenched his jaw and dropped his weapons. "We surrender."

Derek and Ian followed his lead.

Ross called to Chris, "Stand down and surrender your weapons."

Khalif stood, a gold lion medallion hanging on a heavy chain around his neck. "Outside."

The Brits joined their teammate, and Khalif's soldiers bound their wrists and ankles.

"Time for football practice." The six-foot muscular leader sported a shaved head and a bushy beard. He grinned, shoved Ross onto the ground, and kicked him in the head.

Pain shot through him, and his vision blurred, but he kept silent.

The soldiers took turns kicking and stomping on him and his teammates, who were helpless with their wrists and ankles bound.

Bruised and bloodied, Ross gasped for air when he felt his ribs crack. Blackness replaced consciousness and brought him relief from the intense pain.

In seconds, the pain returned and doubled when militiamen doused his team with buckets of water, waking them and rinsing off their blood. He knew what was coming and was powerless to stop it. If his men resisted, the girls would be slaughtered.

Filled with regret, Ross glanced at his comrades. He'd failed his team. What had he missed? How had they been set up? And Sam—his heart ached at the thought of never seeing her again.

Militia thugs roughly rubbed towels over their wet, wounded heads.

"Must have clean faces for videos." A soldier holding a long, curved blade sneered at Ross.

Palm Beach

I took a deep breath, trying not to hyperventilate, and grabbed my cell phone. My twin brothers were two years older and serving in the US Navy. Matt was a fighter pilot, and Mike was a Tier-One SEAL. I called Mike.

He answered on the first ring. That never happened.

"Sam, I was about to call you." He hesitated. "Are you sitting down?"

I bit my lip so I wouldn't cry and launched into a high-speed recap. "I just had a vision of Ross. It was horrible. Please tell me you know where he is."

"He was on an emergency mission in Somalia when all contact was lost." He paused. "Tell me what you saw."

I took a moment to replay the vision in my head. "They were in a jungle at night, and it was raining. Ross's wrists and ankles were bound, and dark-skinned soldiers in shabby fatigues were punching and kicking him."

"Can you give me more details on the attackers?"

"I only saw one face clearly—a bald black man with a bushy beard and bulging muscles. He was missing three front teeth." I thought hard. "He had a gold lion medallion on a heavy gold chain around his neck. Could've been the leader."

"The Somali warlord. Makes sense. He's the guy who kidnapped fifteen schoolgirls."

I paced across the tiled bathroom floor. "Have the Brits launched a rescue mission?"

"An assault group deployed soon after contact

was lost. My team is on standby to assist the UK forces. We're waiting to hear—hold on."

I continued pacing into the bedroom, stopped at the balcony, and stared out at the Atlantic Ocean. "Come on, Mike." I gripped the silent phone.

"Okay, I'm back." He hesitated. "My team was just ordered to stand down."

"What does that mean?" My heart rate sky-rocketed.

"Nothing good."

"What about Ross?" I tried not to panic.

"No news on him or his team." His voice soft-ened. "I'm sorry, sis. Hold it together. I'll check a few sources and get back to you."

I had a sudden urge to vomit.

Somalia

Ross sucked in his breath as Khalif glanced at his gold watch and grinned at the prisoners. "Ready for the big show? Just in time for late news in London and early evening news in Washington." He mo-tioned to the guards. "Take them inside."

Beefy men dragged the captured soldiers into a tent where floodlights and cameras faced a cloth backdrop. For the girls' sakes, the SAS team didn't resist. Khalif's image, superimposed over crossed rifles, formed the banner's centerpiece. Four young captives cowered in the corner.

"The world will see what happens when foreign

soldiers interfere in our affairs." Khalif motioned for two of the girls to kneel in front of the backdrop.

The terrified children trembled and stumbled forward. Tears ran down their sweet faces as they were shoved into kneeling positions side-by-side in the center. Urine pooled under them.

Ross exchanged glances with his teammates. His mouth went dry and his breath caught as he focused on the scimitars two soldiers held. The saying: "Live by the sword—die by the sword," had never been more literal to him than it was at that moment.

Khalif pointed at Chris and Ian as the children sobbed. "Them."

The guards dragged the men into kneeling positions flanking the girls.

Khalif waved at the laptop. "Check the Internet feed. Are we live?"

The man handling the camera and computer nodded.

Ross swallowed hard as he looked into the eyes of his teammates for the last time. Chris and Ian were resigned to their fate, knowing any resistance would result in more girls being killed. They showed no fear as they faced the camera.

Two men holding sharp, curved blades stepped behind the kneeling prisoners and grabbed the girls' hair. The children screamed just as a satellite phone rang.

Khalif held up a hand. "Wait." He snatched up the phone and stepped outside the tent.

Tense minutes ticked down.

When the leader returned, he stared at Ross and Derek and then tapped commands into the laptop. Pictures of them filled the monitor. "Put these two in the truck."

Khalif followed as guards dragged Ross and Derek outside. He barked orders in his native language to the truck driver, and the guards pulled black bags over their captives' heads and tossed them into the canvas-covered truck bed.

The truck's engine rumbled to life, and Ross felt what he hoped was Derek beside him. The vehicle began moving, and pain shot through his cracked ribs as every pothole in the primitive road added to his agony. Ross wondered where they were going and what fate awaited them when they arrived.

———

Khalif swatted mosquitoes as he watched the truck disappear into the dark jungle. He dialed a number on a satellite phone. When his call was answered, he said in Arabic, "Ismail, your package is on the way. Transfer funds."

"Understood. Funds will be transferred, my brother. *Allahu akbar.*"

Khalif took a moment to relieve himself on a bush. He stroked his beard, thinking about the two million dollars that were being transferred into his bank account. He'd check it before he continued with the live videos.

He entered the video tent, typed commands into the computer, and waited. Nothing. "What happened to our Internet connection?"

"Sometimes heavy rain interrupts service." The cameraman checked the laptop's battery and the gas-powered generator's electrical output. "Okay, the Internet is back on."

Khalif tapped in commands. It took a few minutes for the response. The funds had been transferred as promised. He grinned.

"Now for some fun." Khalif stood facing the kneeling prisoners and glanced at the executioners. "Ready?"

They nodded.

He glanced at his videographer. "Everything set?"

The man rechecked his camera and then stood behind it.

"Do the girls first. I want these infidel soldiers to see the result of their foolish actions."

The executioners yanked up on the girls' hair, exposing their necks, and raised their blades high for maximum force as their victims' high-pitched screams filled the tent.

Khalif's emotion changed from glee to confusion. Soft pops preceded the executioners' deaths a nanosecond before his brain exploded, covering the kneeling captives with blood spatter.

Palm Beach

I pulled on jeans and a T-shirt and grabbed sneakers from under the bed. My long hair would have to air dry while I packed a suitcase. When Mike called back, I didn't want to waste a minute. Jeans, cotton cargo pants, and light, long-sleeved shirts would be best for buggy areas in Africa. My free week might not be enough, but I wouldn't stop looking until Ross was rescued. If only the visions would return and help me locate him.

I tried to push my worries aside and focus on packing. On the edge of panic as bloody images of Ross invaded my mind, I stumbled to my walk-in closet. Grabbing my best hiking boots and heavy socks, I thought about weapons. How would I sneak them into Somalia?

My cell phone trilled, and I snatched it up. "Mike, give me good news."

"Sis, the Brits sent in four SAS teams. They got there just in time to save Ian and Chris and all the girls."

My mouth went dry. "Ian and Chris? What about Ross and Derek?"

"His men said they were driven away in a truck about fifteen minutes before the teams parachuted in and attacked the camp. The cloud cover was too low and heavy to use a drone for overhead views. By the time the nearest satellite was tasked, the truck was long gone."

"Did the Brits find out where they took them?" I resumed pacing.

"Khalif was about to have Chris and Ian be-headed." Mike paused. "They had to put him down."

My voice shot up two octaves. "There has to be someone there who knows where Ross and Derek were sent."

"Sorry. The few survivors were foot soldiers. Khalif didn't share his plans with them. Your visions might be our only hope of finding them."

"I have no control over what I see or when I see it, so I'm hoping I'll get another vision when I'm in Africa. I'm catching the first flight to Mogadishu."

"Whoa, Sam, forget it. If they found you alone in that dung pit, a beautiful blonde like you would be a prime candidate for the sex-slave trade. Besides, I need you on my team."

"You want me on your SEAL team?"

"Well, not exactly. I volunteered us for a covert joint-forces mission tasked to rescue Ross and Derek. You know everyone on the team."

"Really? Who's going?"

"Banger will be the other SEAL with me, and we'll have SAS Lieutenant Bryce Manning and MI6 Agent Lisa Atwater from Great Britain."

"I've been in life-threatening situations with all

of them. They're extraordinary people, but how did you manage to get me on the team?"

"I recommended you because of your psychic abilities. They already know from past experiences that your combat skills are adequate." He paused. "Are you in?"

I punched my fist in the air. "Where do I meet you?"

"Pack sensible clothes and good boots. They're expecting you to fly into NAS JAX. Banger will be waiting. You have three hours to get your butt up there and hop a C-17 to Somalia. I'm already in Africa."

"No problem. I'm almost done packing. One of our corporate jets can take me."

"Good. I'll have all the gear and weapons ready when you get here."

"Thanks, Mike. See you soon." I rushed to my desk and grabbed my passport. My next call was to the Starr Corporation's flight department. The company had been founded by my late father, and my mother was the majority shareholder, so their corporate jets were always available to our family.

Captain Hiller answered on the first ring. "Hello, Sam, what can I do for you today?"

"Hey Bill, I need a ride to the Naval Air Station in Jacksonville. Any chance you can have a jet ready to go in thirty minutes?"

"Let me check." He paused a moment. "I can have a Lear 35 fueled and ready by the time you get here. I've got a pilot who lives nearby on short call."

"Thanks. See you in thirty."

I opened my wall safe for the first time in a month and pulled out a square gold medallion with a trident and a pyramid-shaped diamond embedded in it. The medallion was a unique key that had opened hidden doors for me in Petra. Maybe it would aid me in Africa. I hung it around my neck and concealed it under my shirt.

About to close the safe's door, I felt a strong urge to put my hands on the huge power diamond I had carried out of an obsidian pyramid in the submerged city of Atlantis. Two feet long and shaped like a rhombus, the gem had been an integral component of Poseidon's Sword, a weapon of mass destruction housed in the enormous pyramid. Now it was enclosed in a thick velvet sack, and it barely fit in the back of my safe. Only a handful of trusted people knew I had it.

Reaching inside, I loosened the drawstring and pulled the sack halfway down the diamond. The moment my hands closed around the gem, my head tingled, and I experienced a vision of Luxor in Egypt. Atlantean words that meant "pass tests, find the Blue Dragon in the Dark Continent, save them" kept repeating in my head.

I understood the strange language because Atlantean triplets had telepathically transferred all their knowledge of ancient Atlantis to me, the last queen, before they were killed. I created a translation program for the U.S. government so their experts could read all the scrolls recovered from the Hall of Records, but I kept the rest of my knowledge secret for self-preservation. I'd never admit my new ability to mentally control Earth's electromagnetic energy, and I prayed I'd never need to use it. That power had earned the triplets a death sentence, and I wasn't eager to join them.

I possessed some unusual abilities, and my body carried a rare frequency of electromagnetic energy passed down from my ancestors who had been worshipped as goddesses in ancient Atlantis. They were the only women qualified to serve as queens, and it turned out I was the last heir to the throne of a nation I had never known. Now that all the Atlanteans were dead, and their home rested on the bottom of the Atlantic Ocean, I didn't think the crown mattered. Queen of Atlantis was a title I didn't want or need.

Wondering what to think about the vision and its message, I tugged the sack up over the diamond, tied the drawstring, and locked the safe.

Maybe the message was meant to help me save Ross and Derek. Had to be. Being queen of a dead nation might have some perks after all.

In minutes, I was in my SUV heading for the general aviation side of Palm Beach International Airport.

TWO

Africa

Inside a noisy truck bed, Ross and Derek had few options as they lay with their wrists and ankles bound and their heads covered with black sacks.

Drifting in and out of consciousness, Ross wondered how long they'd been traveling. He had no idea how far they'd gone or if they were still in Somalia. And so far, Derek hadn't made a sound. Maybe his injuries were more severe. He prayed his best friend would survive.

The truck turned onto another road covered with deep potholes. Each jolt bounced his body, and pain knifed through his cracked ribs. The agony was so intense, Ross could barely catch his breath. The torturous ride brought about a wave of nausea, and he was close to vomiting when the truck stopped.

Slow, deep breaths helped him calm his stomach as he listened for clues. Muffled voices blended with the distant roar of a lion as rain pattered on the truck's canvas roof. Exhausted, Ross was almost asleep when the tailgate dropped open with a loud clang.

Someone gripped his ankles and yanked him out. He landed on his back in soft mud, and something thudded onto the ground beside him. The rain stopped moments later, and his soaked hood almost choked him.

A man with a deep voice said in Arabic, "Uncover their heads so I can see if they're the right men."

A soldier yanked off Ross's sack. Dizzy, his vision blurred when he squinted into a bright floodlight and glanced to his left. Derek lay unconscious beside him. He looked up at the man giving the orders and recognized him as an ISIS leader, Ismail Mustapha.

Nearby, men in black fatigues unloaded supplies from military trucks and stacked the boxes. A sea of dark tents housing hundreds of ISIS soldiers filled a narrow clearing beside a mountain.

"Wake that one," Ismail yelled in Arabic, pointing at Derek.

A soldier doused Derek's head with a bucket of water, and some of it splashed onto Ross's face. He ran his tongue over his wet lips, eager for any moisture.

"His eyes are open now. Cut their ankle ties." Ismail stared at his prisoners.

A guard reached for Ross and pulled him to his feet.

"Walk them inside before a spy satellite passes over. Hurry!" Dressed all in black, the local ISIS leader had a full beard and dark, emotionless eyes. A keffiyeh covered his head, and a gold lion medallion hung on a heavy gold chain around his neck.

Two men shoved Ross into a dark, musty cave and led him into a long passage. He glanced back in the dim lantern light and nodded at Derek stumbling behind him, his ankles also untethered. Using his fingers, Ross signaled him to attack their captors in ten seconds.

About twenty yards inside the cave and far enough away from the majority of soldiers, Ross and Derek summoned every ounce of strength left in them for one last chance to escape. They landed hard kicks into the groins of their forward guards. The surprised men dropped, writhing in agony, and the SAS soldiers kicked their heads at just the right angle to snap their necks. The attacks were accomplished in a few seconds.

The remaining two guards charged them from behind, and the elite British soldiers turned and headbutted their faces, crushing their noses. Blood spurted from their smashed nostrils as the guards spit up blood and bent over, trying to catch their breath. The duo rammed their knees under their captors' jaws while simultaneously headbutting them for maximum effect. The injured men crumpled to the ground, and Ross and Derek stomped their windpipes.

The sounds of their battle had echoed through the cave. Ross tried to get his fingers around a dead guard's sheathed knife, but he didn't have time. In seconds, he and Derek were surrounded by armed men. An angry soldier hit Ross hard on the back of his head with a rifle butt, and his world went black.

He woke with his wrists chained to brackets above his head and Derek chained beside him. He grimaced, every inch of his body throbbing in agony. On the opposite wall, two white men in dirty civilian clothing hung limply from similar chains. Their faces were swollen, and their eyes were closed.

Ross glanced at Derek, bruised and bloodied. He whispered, "You okay?"

"I'm worried I might live," he rasped. "You look as bad as I feel."

Ismail strode in and glared at his men. "Fools! You allowed these infidels to kill four of our comrades." He pointed. "Stretch the banner across the cave over there and get the video equipment and floodlights ready."

Ross looked at the ISIS banner. As long as he and Derek were alive, there was hope. He feared the worst had already happened to Chris and Ian. And now his new captors probably planned to tape a beheading video like the one Khalif had set up earlier. The thought of Sam seeing such a gory execution turned his stomach.

Despite the pain, Ross closed his eyes and tried to relax. He had several cracked ribs, lacerations on his head and arms, and severe bruising all over. One eye was swollen shut. Derek nudged him with his leg.

"Try to send a mental message to Sam." He licked blood off his split lip.

"And how do I do that?" Ross looked at him. "I'm not telepathic."

"Aye, but she is. Try shouting her name over and over in your head until she answers you." Derek paused, then said, "We'll both do it."

"It's worth a try," Ross whispered. "She may be our only chance."

"All right, mate, do it now."

Palm Beach

I rushed through the corporate hangar, pulling my roller suitcase and carrying a backpack. A Learjet waited outside on the ramp with its door open and the airstairs down.

Chief Pilot Bill Hiller rounded the airplane and trotted over. "Hi, Sam, let me get those for you." He grabbed my bags and walked beside me.

An airliner taking off roared in the distance at the busy international airport.

"Are you flying me to Jacksonville?"

Bill nodded. "I like to stay current on all our airplanes, and I haven't flown the Lear 35 in a while. I did the walkaround inspection to save time." He glanced over my shoulder. "Ah, there's my copilot."

A young woman hurried to meet us, her blond hair billowing in the wind. Out of breath, she said, "Sorry, boss, I got stuck waiting for the stupid draw-bridge on Southern." She glanced at me, and her jaw dropped. "Oh, geez, you're that famous airline pilot. I'm new here and was hoping I'd get a chance to meet you sometime."

I held out my hand and smiled.

Petite and pretty, she shook my hand and grinned. "I'm Laura Burke. It's an honor to meet you, Sir Lady Samantha."

"Just Sam, please."

A deep masculine voice with a Texas accent yelled, "Hey, wait for me!"

I turned and spotted my favorite copilot at Luxury International Airlines, Lance Bowie, trotting toward us with a duffel bag slung over his shoulder. He and I had been stranded in South America a month ago and shared some harrowing experiences. Tall, dark, and hand-some, he was way too good-looking with liquid-green eyes and a body that would be the envy of any male sports model. What was he doing here?

I stopped at the bottom of the airstairs while Bill and Laura climbed aboard.

"Sam, I'm sorry about Ross and his team. Mike told me all about it." Lance squeezed my hand.

"Thank you, but I can't waste time chatting. There's a C-17 waiting for me at NAS JAX."

"I know." He ushered me up the stairs. "Let's get going."

He stuffed his duffel between two seats as Laura retracted the boarding stairs.

"Wait," I said to Lance. "You can't come. I'm going on a covert military mission."

Lance waved at the copilot. "Close the door. We're good."

"No, we're not. Get off the airplane." I pointed at the door.

"Sam, calm down. Mike invited me to join the mission." He nodded to Laura.

She secured the door and entered the cockpit. Bill already had the starboard engine running.

I plopped onto a leather recliner and fastened my seatbelt. "Dammit, Lance, what do you think you're doing?"

He sat beside me. "I'm trying to redeem myself with Ross and keep your sexy ass safe."

"You have nothing to redeem. Our one kiss in Hong Kong was necessary to fool the Chinese Secret Service, and I never told anyone about it anyway, so you can stand down. I've got two Navy SEALs, an SAS lieutenant, and an MI6 agent to keep me safe in Africa."

"Uh, my thing with Ross has nothing to do with Hong Kong."

"This isn't about me climbing up you in South America when I was trying to get away from that giant spider, is it?"

He laughed. "That's the only time I've ever seen you lose your cool, and as you'll recall, I saved you from that nasty Goliath birdeater." He grinned. "Ross wouldn't have an issue with that."

"Well, what is it then? I thought I knew everything about you two."

"Not everything. You'll have to ask Ross." His face flushed, and he averted his eyes.

Was he red from guilt or embarrassment? He turned away and stared out the window as we rocketed down the runway. In seconds, we were airborne and turning toward Jacksonville.

Confused about Lance's comments, I tried to clear my head and figure it out. I leaned back and reclined my seat. Everything was happening too fast.

The instant I closed my eyes, *"Sam! Sam! Sam!"* repeated over and over in my head. It sounded like Ross and Derek calling me.

My mind filled with a vision of them chained to a rock wall inside a dark cave. Their faces were bloody and swollen. A man dressed in black, wearing a balaclava and an ISIS armband, came into view. Blood dripped from a scimitar hanging on his belt.

"No," I shouted and sat up.

The vision vanished.

Africa

Ten minutes after Ross and Derek started calling to Sam in their heads, an ISIS soldier entered carrying a bucket and towels. "Time to make you pretty for the beheading videos." He smirked. A long, curved blade hung from his belt.

Ismail walked over and thumbed at the prisoners on the opposite wall. "Do them first." He sneered at Ross and Derek. "Let these SAS cowards see what happens to infidels."

Ross watched a preview of his fate as the battered civilian men were shoved onto their knees, the banner above them in the background. Too weak to struggle, fear radiated from their eyes, and their bodies trembled as they braced for the blades.

Ismail stepped in front of them and made a long speech about ISIS and their holy war. Then he walked behind the camera and motioned for the executions to begin.

The executioners grasped the victims' hair, lifting their bowed heads up, and swung their gleaming blades. Still clutching the hair, they displayed the severed heads dripping blood and cheered, "*Allahu akbar!*"

Bile rose in Ross's throat. He swallowed hard, fighting the burgeoning nausea.

Guards dropped the severed heads into a big sack and tossed the bodies into a wheelbarrow.

The leader pointed at the Scotsmen and grinned. "You're next."

Their ankles had been zip-tied to prevent a repeat of their earlier attack. Four soldiers unchained them and dragged them in front of the ISIS banner.

Ross managed to headbutt one guard before two muscular men pinned him on his knees. He sucked in his breath, trying not to show the stabbing pain that shot through him with every movement. Derek's expression was stoic. It would all be over soon, and Ross resolved to face it without fear. He wouldn't give these thugs the satisfaction of seeing an SAS officer afraid.

The guards held them facing the camera while the leader made another long-winded speech. When Ismail finished, the masked executioners approached holding scimitars dripping fresh blood. They positioned themselves behind the kneeling Scotsmen and raised their blades high.

The guards stepped aside.

Ross and Derek shared winks and grins, their final acts of bravado.

The ISIS leader stood beside the camera operator. His satellite phone trilled, and he raised his hand, signaling his men to wait.

Ismail paced as he listened, then said, "Understood. It shall be so." He reached over and switched off the camera as he beckoned the executioners.

The leader whispered something to his men, and their faces flushed with anger.

Ross tried to understand what was being said in Arabic as adrenaline surged through him.

One man demanded, "Give us one good reason."

Ismail rubbed his fingers together. "We have ten million reasons. Do as I command."

The executioners turned and pulled head sacks from their back pockets. They strode to Ross and Derek, yanked the cloths over their heads, and waved for guards to help drag them back to the wall chains.

Ross couldn't believe they'd been spared again. Someone had bought them for ten million. No way to know what would happen next, but he had hope.

He had no idea how much time had passed when soldiers dragged him outside. Voices speaking Arabic confirmed their ride had arrived with a satchel of cash.

The open air was much warmer than the cave had been. By the time guards tossed Ross into the vehicle, he was soaked with sweat. Another body landed next to him. Unable to see with a sack covering his head, he hoped it was Derek.

Unknown circumstances had saved them from appearing in two separate beheading videos. Where were they going this time? The stress, pain, and heat he'd endured since his capture many hours ago had dehydrated him, and his body throbbed as he longed for a cool bottle of water.

Ross focused on counting the minutes so he could estimate how far they had gone when they arrived at the destination. Mentally keeping track of the elapsed time also helped distract him from the constant pain radiating from his cracked ribs and multiple contusions.

Eventually, the vehicle stopped for fuel. Gas fumes filtered into the back of the truck before it resumed traveling along crude, bumpy roads. Ross managed to tap Morse code for "Derek" onto the body beside him. Derek's foot tapped code against him, confirming he was his friend. Speaking would've earned them another beating. Ross signaled Derek that he'd try to contact Sam again.

He pictured her face as he mentally shouted her name. Every few minutes, he'd pause and listen, hoping to hear her voice in his head.

No answer.

Learjet En Route to NAS JAX

I bit my lip and tried not to cry. My eyes filled with tears as I took deep breaths and struggled to master my emotions. Lance turned and stared at me.

"I, uh, I saw Ross and Derek, badly beaten and chained inside a cave. The vision shifted to a masked ISIS soldier." I paused and sobbed. "He was holding a bloody scimitar."

"You're jumping to conclusions." He squeezed my hand. "Calm down so you can get more visions." Lance hugged me. "It'll be okay, Sam."

"I should call Mike." I pulled out my cell and hit his number on speed-dial.

Mike knew why I was calling—brother's intuition. "Take a breath, Sam. It wasn't Ross or Derek. ISIS posted the beheading video on Al Jazeera. The murdered men were corporate executives from England and America."

I sighed and blew my nose into a tissue. "It's terrible that two families lost loved ones. I hate those ISIS bastards."

"We all do. Now tell me what you saw." Mike's voice had a calming effect on me.

I described every detail I could remember about the cave and the people I saw inside it.

"Good work, sis. Our drones found an ISIS camp in a narrow valley sheltered by Mount Kenya. Alpha Team is going in with the Brits. I'll call as soon as I know something. In the meantime, keep the faith and stick with our plan."

"That reminds me, did you invite Lance to join our team?"

Mike sighed. "He was a last-minute addition."

"Okay, but why?"

"When he heard you were going, he asked to be included. Lance is ex-military, and he's been on almost all of your Danger Magnet adventures. Besides, it might come in handy to have two pilots on the mission. He's an asset. End of story."

"Whatever you say, brother dear. I'm just grateful to be included."

"I like the sound of that. Now, calm down and try to get more visions."

"Okay. I'll work on getting my emotions under control. See you soon."

I leaned back and closed my eyes, took slow, steady breaths, and felt the tension leave my body.

"Sam! Sam! Sam!" Ross's voice filled my head.

I concentrated hard. *"Ross, I hear you. Where are you?"*

"Sam! Sam! Sam!" he shouted telepathically.

I waited until he stopped and tried sending an answer.

No response.

He yelled my name again.

Hearing him but not being able to talk to him frustrated me.

A vision flashed into my head. He and Derek were lying in the back of a canvas-covered truck. I knew it was a truck because their bodies kept bouncing over bumps in the road, and I saw the tailgate near their feet.

The scene vanished.

I called Mike, put the phone on speaker, and described the vision.

"That explains why they weren't at the camp when our guys stormed the place. I wish we knew when they left. We'll have drones search for the truck, but as far as you're concerned, our mission is still on."

"We're about to land at the Jacksonville Naval Air Station. See you soon." I slipped my phone into my purse and glanced at Lance as I raised my seatback.

"I told you they're alive." He patted my hand. "We'll find them."

Africa

Except for fuel stops, the vehicle kept going for too many hours to mentally keep track of the time. Ross was so dehydrated it didn't matter that he hadn't been given any bathroom breaks during the long, unpleasant ride.

The noisy truck slowed and stopped, and so did the engine. It seemed they had finally reached their destination. For the first time since they had begun the journey, the tailgate was opened.

Someone grasped Ross's ankles and yanked him out of the truck. His head slammed against the rear bumper on the way out, and a pounding headache added to the throbbing pain torturing his battered body. Someone thudded to the ground beside him and groaned. Derek.

Moments later, guards jerked Ross up onto rubbery legs and severed his ankle ties. They dragged him up two steps into a building, across a wood-planked floor, and shoved him into a chair. Weak and almost delirious from dehydration, he struggled to catch his breath.

A guard cut the plastic tie binding his wrists and zip-tied them to the arms on the chair. After the guard ripped the sack off his head, it took a moment for Ross's eyes to focus in the dim interior. He blinked and spotted Derek seated beside him.

They were in a small wooden structure—more of a hut than a building. The planked floor hadn't been joined properly, leaving thin spaces between slats.

Ross caught a quick smile from Derek before a tall man with ebony skin appeared and held a bottle of water to his mouth. Another man did the same for Ross. They drank greedily until the bottles were empty, and then the men disappeared somewhere behind them.

Ross whispered, "Third time's the charm?"

"Better that than three strikes, you're out," Derek said, tugging at his wrist ties.

Ross looked around the room, searching for clues to their fate.

After a few minutes of silence, the floor creaked

as someone approached from behind. The new arrival stepped in front of them.

"I've waited a long time for this," he said with a lowborn English accent. "You two and that blond bitch have cost me a fortune and ruined major operations that were important to me. Now you're mine, and soon, she will be too."

Ross's jaw dropped. "You're supposed to be dead."

"Rumors of my death have been greatly exaggerated." The short, balding man held a *skean du* dagger with a jeweled hilt. "I thought you might appreciate this traditional weapon from your homeland."

Ross glared at him. "I'd prefer viewing it embedded in your chest."

Lord Edgar Sweetwater tossed the dagger back and forth in his hands as he watched his captives, the evil grin never leaving his face.

"Ah, revenge will be sweet."

C-17 Globemaster III

A courtesy vehicle drove us past the C-17's nosecone. The pilots were already in the cockpit, and the huge aft entry door stood open. We stopped and got out behind the massive aircraft. As Lance pulled my wheeled suitcase up the loading ramp, I heard a familiar voice behind me.

"Wait up, Your Majesty."

I paused and turned. A handsome SEAL towered over me. He looked like he could be actor Dwayne Johnson's younger brother.

"Good to see you again, Banger, but what's with the Your Majesty crap?" I grinned and hugged him, my face against his solar plexus. His body was as hard as granite.

He grinned. "Last time I checked, you're still Queen of Atlantis." He made a show of bowing.

I groaned. "Lucky me—queen of a dead city buried under two thousand feet of seawater. Now please, go back to calling me Sam." I nodded to my left. "You remember Lance, don't you?"

Banger grinned and shook Lance's hand. "How could I forget? We've shared some interesting adventures."

"Some, as in more than one?" I caught them sharing a meaningful look. "I thought you two met in South America?"

"Uh, did I say 'some'? Maybe because it felt like more than one. I'm not a fan of giant snakes." Banger checked his watch. "Time to go." He ushered us up the ramp.

What were they hiding? I didn't like them knowing something I didn't know and keeping it from me. Lance already had a secret about Ross. Now this. What the heck?

Military equipment enclosed in large wood pallets filled the wide interior of the cargo jet, and ten upright troop seats faced inward along the right and left sidewalls.

I stood by the starboard row of seats and nudged Lance. "This is a drastic change from what we're used to on Luxury International."

"Eighteen hours in one of these seats will make you long for our airline's leather recliners," Lance agreed, testing a thin seat cushion.

"Navy SEALs get special accommodations." Banger grinned and pulled a netted hammock out of a duffel. He hooked one end to a wall grommet and the other end to a binding strap on a pallet. "I knew you spoiled airline pilots would whine about the seats, so I brought extra hammocks." He pulled two more out of the duffel and handed them to us.

I kissed his cheek. "Thanks, Banger." I bit my lip and turned away, thinking about Ross and trying not to cry. If I showed my true emotions, they'd never let me go with them.

Lance slapped him on the back. "Thank you kindly, good buddy." He peeked into the duffel. "Where'd you pack the pillows and blankets?"

"Funny." Banger showed us attach points on the sidewall and on nearby pallets. "Hang your sleeper slings and then strap into a seat for takeoff."

I hooked my hammock next to Banger's, and Lance secured his next to mine. That put me in the perfect position to enjoy stereo snoring during the long flight to Somalia.

"Samantha Starr?" a crew member asked.

I nodded.

He handed me a satellite phone. "If you receive any intel that will aid your mission, hit the preset number on speed-dial and report to your team leader."

I smiled and nodded. "Understood. Thank you."

He said to us, "Smart move with the hammocks. The flight will take about eighteen hours, including inflight refueling. Buckle into the troop seats for takeoff and landing. If you get hungry or thirsty, we have food and beverages up front in the crew compartment. And the toilets are up there too." He pointed forward. "Any questions?"

We shook our heads.

"Good." He hit a switch and closed the aft loading door.

We took our seats and buckled up as the airplane began taxiing to the active runway. In minutes, we were airborne and turning toward Africa.

Sweetwater's Hideout

Sweetwater pulled up a chair and faced Ross and Derek. A soldier in dark green fatigues placed a tray filled with bottled water and sandwiches on a table beside the chubby little bald man.

"Gentlemen, if you want to prolong your lives, you'll answer my questions truthfully. Correct answers will earn you food and water." He reached over and snatched a water bottle from the table, opened it, and took a long gulp. "Wrong answers will give me an excuse to use this." He impaled a sandwich with the Scottish dagger.

"What do you want to know?" Ross tested the bindings on his wrists.

Sweetwater licked his lips. "Were you involved in anything that happened in Atlantis?"

Ross gave Derek an almost imperceptible nod. "We were there briefly."

"Good. Tell me about the obsidian pyramid." His eyes shifted between Derek and Ross.

Ross shrugged. "It was destroyed by an American submarine."

"Really?" Sweetwater twisted the dagger as he turned to Derek.

"It's true. The USS *Texas* fired several torpedoes into it. It's a big pile of rubble now."

"That was to destroy the Atlantean weapon known as Poseidon's Sword?"

Ross exchanged another quick glance with Derek and nodded. "It was the only way to ensure the weapon would never be fired."

Sweetwater pounded the table, and the metal tray clattered. "Months of work wasted!" He held off a moment, regaining his composure. "Legends say a giant diamond, about two feet long and in the shape of a rhombus, was part of the weapon. Was the diamond recovered?" His dark eyes filled with intense interest.

Ross shook his head. "Time was critical. America was more concerned about saving its eastern seaboard than preserving a giant gem. The jewel is buried under tons of obsidian rock." He gambled his captor didn't know that Sam had carried the diamond out of the pyramid before the submarine destroyed it. He'd risk everything to keep her safe.

Sweetwater held Ross's gaze, searching for a hint of deception. Then he looked at Derek, his tone tight with frustration. "Is the diamond buried under rubble two thousand feet down?"

Derek nodded. "I guess you could try to dig it out, but that would be expensive with no guarantee of success."

Sweetwater's face reddened, but he maintained control. "My researchers found scrolls in a submerged temple near Santorini that described Poseidon's Sword and three enormous diamonds capable of storing tremendous energy." He bit a small chunk of sandwich off the tip of the dagger and swallowed it. "One diamond was in the Atlantean enclave in the Himalayas. I know the U.S. military destroyed that entire village and everything in it. And they probably destroyed the giant diamond undersea in Atlantis. That leaves the third power diamond, known as the Blue Dragon, hidden somewhere in Africa."

Surprised, Ross shook his head. "I don't think either America or my country knows anything about another diamond." He paused. "Is it part of a weapon like the other two were?"

"It had better be." Sweetwater glared. "I'd hate to miss out again."

"Africa's a big place," Derek said.

"True, but I have a research team on it twenty-four seven." He scrutinized their faces. "You're certain you've heard nothing about the Blue Dragon Diamond?"

Ross nodded. "Positive."

"Not a whisper," Derek said.

"Good." Sweetwater smiled. "That means no one will be looking for it. Now you can eat."

THREE

Somalia, 10:00 p.m.

Mike greeted us as we exited the C-17 into hot, humid air. He drove us to a large building in Camp Baledogle where we followed him into an air-conditioned conference room.

"You all know MI6 agent Lisa Atwater, and this is SAS Lieutenant Bryce Manning." Mike thumbed at a slender redhead and a tall, broad-shouldered man.

I knew Lisa from our recent South American adventure where she and Derek had rekindled their romance. A few weeks before South America, Bryce and I had battled Lord Sweetwater's mercenaries in a dense forest near Duxford.

"Hello, Lisa." I gave her a quick hug and

turned to Bryce. "It's good to see you again. Thanks for joining our team."

"Anything for Ross and Derek." Bryce's sky-blue eyes blazed with intensity. "After Ross helped us survive the attack in the forest, I promised I'd help him nail Sweetwater if we ever got a chance. I never dreamed he and Derek would be kidnapped by ISIS."

Lisa's emerald eyes moistened. "I hope to God Derek and Ross are still alive."

I squeezed her shoulder. "They're alive. I saw them in a vision."

Lisa glanced at Mike. "I know, but that was hours ago."

"Let's get started." Mike motioned for everyone to be seated. "Any ideas, sis?"

I pointed near the top right side of the wall map of Africa. "I need to go to Luxor."

Mike's eyebrows shot up. "Why? Ross and Derek are nowhere near Egypt."

"True, but there's a hidden artifact in the Temple of Luxor that might help us find them."

Bryce crossed his arms. "How do you know that?"

I closed the door and lowered my voice. "Some of you know about a thing from Atlantis that I keep locked in my safe. Before I left, I put my hands on it and received a message."

Bryce and Lisa dropped their jaws and looked at me like I was from another planet.

Lance shook his head. "Considering all the things I've seen her do, I'm not surprised."

"What was the message?" Lisa leaned forward.

"I saw a vision of Luxor Temple and heard words in Atlantean that said, 'Pass tests, find the Blue Dragon in the Dark Continent, save them.' Then the image vanished, and there was silence."

"What do they mean by Dark Continent?" Lance asked.

"Explorers have always referred to Africa as the Dark Continent because so little is known about the diverse landmass, and it still holds many mysteries," I explained.

"What tests?" Banger arched a brow. "Not spears, I hope. I don't want to be ventilated like Crenshaw and Ace were in that underwater pyramid."

"Sorry, Banger, but I won't know until we get there. The tests are probably designed to ensure only the Queen of Atlantis finds the Blue Dragon." I shrugged. "That seems to be me."

Banger tapped his smartphone. "Google says the Luxor Temple is a huge complex. How will you find a hidden artifact, assuming it's still there?"

"It's there, and the dragon currents, you know —ley lines—will lead me right to it."

"Wait," Bryce interrupted. "What are ley lines?"

"They're rivers of concentrated electromagnetic energy that crisscross Earth." I scanned the team.

"Unless the military has solid intel on Ross and Derek's location, we need that artifact."

Lisa sat back. "What does it look like?"

"It's probably small, like the medallion key I found in the Taj Mahal." I pulled out the gold pendant, which was hanging on a long chain under my shirt, and cradled it in my palm.

"The Taj has been there for centuries," Bryce said, shaking his head. "How is it possible no one found that before you got it?"

"It was in a secret compartment that popped open when I touched a tiny gold trident that marked the spot." I fingered the pyramid-shaped diamond embedded in the medallion, and it lit up. "When I removed the key, the compartment closed and blended with the wall again. It was the first time I had ever found anything hidden like that."

"That's a key?" Banger leaned in for a closer look.

Lance nodded. "I saw her use it to open hidden doors in Petra. It mated with a mirror image of itself embedded in the rock."

"Interesting stuff, but what does it have to do with Ross and Derek?" Lisa looked at me.

"Atlantean technology is two hundred thousand years ahead of ours. That item in my safe must've been programmed thousands of years ago. I'm probably receiving help now because I'm the last Atlantean queen." I slipped the medallion under my shirt. "My gut tells me the artifact hidden in Luxor will help us save Ross and Derek."

"What if the Blue Dragon turns out to be something similar to what you found underwater in the obsidian pyramid?" Mike paused. "We could be on the trail of another WMD."

Banger frowned. "We need more info. Maybe the artifact in Luxor will provide the answers."

"It's worth a try." Bryce shrugged. "We don't have a clue where Ross and Derek are."

Lance looked into my eyes. "Just be careful you don't open another can of worms like you did on that charter flight last fall."

"The Atlanteans and the Black Sun cult are out of the picture." I looked at everyone. "We should be in the clear this time."

Mike arched a brow and murmured, "Unless Sweetwater surfaces and sticks his nose in."

"Sweetwater?" My gut tightened. "I thought he died in a helicopter crash last month."

"His body was never found, and our military has intel that he's hiding out somewhere."

I let out a big sigh. "Just when I thought I was finally rid of him."

"Back to our mission." Mike glanced at the wall map. "Any idea how long it will take to find the artifact?"

I checked my Africa guidebook and measured the flight distance on the map. "I estimate five hours en route to Luxor in a jet, ten minutes from the airport to the temple, and maybe thirty minutes or less on site."

Mike stood. "Then we'll plan twelve hours for the round trip. General Ryan is on base and knows Sam's history with Atlantean artifacts. Hang tight while I check if our team can borrow his jet." He strode from the room.

Banger looked at me. "Based on past experiences with Sam, we should be armed for this."

Everyone chuckled.

I glanced at my teammates. "He's right. Sweetwater hates me, and he must have moles in the U.S. military."

Lance frowned. "But how do we get the weapons into Luxor?"

"MI6 might be able to help us with that." Lisa pulled out her cell. "Maybe they can arrange a diplomatic mission." She stepped outside to make the call.

I paced the room while I waited for Mike and Lisa. Every minute mattered for Ross and Derek.

Sweetwater's Hideout

Sweetwater paced as he spoke into his satellite phone. "How's the search for the Blue Dragon coming?"

A voice on the other end said, "The ancient scrolls I found say it's in Africa in a cave bordered by water. We're researching caves along the African coasts, looking for ones that haven't been explored."

"That could take years," Sweetwater fumed. "You need better intel." He paused. "I've got a team headed to Atlantis in my new submarine. If they can find the Hall of Records, there might be a map there that leads to the blue power diamond."

"We're running the scrolls' info through a computer, searching for keywords that might help us locate the artifact."

"If it's in a cave on a coast, find out which coast." Sweetwater clenched his fist. "The Atlanteans wouldn't have hidden it with no way to find it thousands of years later. There must be clues that mention nearby landmarks. Keep looking."

"We're doing the best we can, but this could take a while." He was silent a moment. "Don't forget I'm an archaeologist. There could be a reason it hasn't been found in millennia."

Sweetwater stopped pacing. "You made your point. I know someone who has a knack for finding ancient artifacts. Keep searching while I arrange to add her to our team."

He hung up and dialed again. When a man answered, Sweetwater said, "Where is she?"

The man replied, "Camp Baledogle in Somalia. She probably flew in to help search for her boyfriend."

"Perfect." Sweetwater smiled. "Grab her when she leaves."

Camp Baledogle, Somalia

Lisa returned with a smile. "We're good to go. A courier from our embassy in Mogadishu will deliver diplomatic passports for us. First I have to email them our photos." She led Lance to a blank wall. "Stand here while I get your headshot."

"Good, now take one of me." Lisa handed Lance her cell.

He took her picture and handed back the phone. She motioned for Banger and Bryce.

Mike returned just as Lisa snapped my picture. "You're next, Mike. Stand right there."

He paused while she took his photo. "What's this for?"

"Diplomatic passports from the UK for the Luxor mission, so we can carry concealed weapons." Lisa checked his photo. "Did you find us a ride?"

Mike glanced at his watch. "We can borrow the general's Gulfstream jet tomorrow morning as long as we have it back by 8:00 p.m. local time. Luxor is one hour earlier. If we leave here at zero-four-hundred hours, we'll arrive around zero-eight-hundred. The temple opens then, so we'll have plenty of time to grab the artifact and fly back. How soon can we get the diplomatic passports?"

Lisa checked a text message. "A courier will be here in two hours."

"Good," Mike said, "because we'll definitely

need weapons. General Ryan just told me Sweetwater is alive and has informants in our military and in the UK's. And he has a small army of mercenaries working for him. Let's go grab some firepower." He led us to the armory.

We chose Sig Sauer P365 9mm pistols and included extra ammo magazines. They'd be easy to conceal and give us ten rounds in the mag plus one in the chamber. I hoped we wouldn't need them, but it was better to be prepared.

A courier arrived early and handed Lisa a pouch with our diplomatic passports under fake names. She handed them out, and we checked them to ensure everything was in order.

"All right, let's grab some chow." Mike took us to the mess hall. "Eat up. We take off in four hours."

Sweetwater's Hideout

Sweetwater received a call on his encrypted satellite phone. "What? She's going where?"

"Luxor, early tomorrow morning in a military Gulfstream jet."

"Makes no sense. The U.S. military knows her boyfriend isn't in Egypt. Wait a second—she might be in Africa for a different reason." Sweetwater thought a moment. "Luxor is on the Nile. It could be the water mentioned in the scrolls. She might beat me to the Blue Dragon. Follow her, but don't grab her until she's on her way back to the airport. I want whatever she finds in Luxor."

"I'll take the team there now. We'll be ready when she arrives."

"Good. I'm counting on you." Sweetwater paused, then added, "Don't hurt her. I might need her help with the artifact."

Camp Baledogle

At 4:05 a.m., our team buckled their seatbelts and settled in for a five-hour flight to Luxor on the general's jet.

When we reached cruise altitude, Mike stood and briefed us. "Expect an ambush in Luxor. Informants in Egypt reported that a small mercenary team arrived there last night. They bribed local officials to let them enter with weapons. Sam's the obvious target, so stay tight around her. Questions?"

"Rules of engagement?" Banger looked at Mike.

"If we're attacked, shoot to kill and get the team back to the airplane." Mike glanced around. "No one gets left behind."

"Understood." Lance, a former USAF fighter pilot, rechecked his Sig.

"Our diplomatic passports mean they can't search us. Just keep your weapons out of sight and let our two Brits do the talking. Let's make this quick and clean." Mike sat down and closed his eyes.

―――――――

Five hours later, we arrived at Luxor International Airport.

An Egyptian official boarded and checked our passports. I tried to look calm as he spent way too much time studying our photos and info. Finally, he handed back our documents and headed for the open door. He glanced over his shoulder. "You may disembark now. Enjoy your visit to our beautiful city."

I slung my purse's shoulder strap diagonally across my chest and followed the team to the rental counter inside the terminal. In line, I glanced around, looking for possible attackers, even though I doubted anything bad would happen at the airport.

In keeping with Egypt's male-dominated culture, Bryce took the lead. "We need a vehicle big enough to seat six people," he said in his crisp British accent.

"Sorry, sir, we only rent small cars. You'll need to hire a van driver." He pointed. "Over there."

As we approached the taxi stand, Mike said, "Grab the guy with the minivan."

Bryce beckoned the van driver. "We'd like to hire your vehicle for the next hour or two."

"Where would you like to go?" The middle-aged guy slid open the side door.

"Luxor Temple." Bryce scrutinized the driver. "And we'd like you to wait for us."

"The temple is only six miles from here." He rubbed his thumb against his forefingers. "You'd save a lot of money if you just hire a couple of taxis when you're ready to return."

"I know, but we don't plan to stay long, and we prefer to ride together." Bryce climbed into the front passenger seat and negotiated a price with the driver as we slid into the van.

I scanned the area, looking for people who might be watching our group, but everyone seemed to be concentrating on their cell phones. No mercenaries lurking around.

We pulled into the temple parking lot ten minutes later. Bryce gave the driver a deposit as we exited the van.

The scent of the Nile River dominated the calm, early morning air as I glanced around at the awe-inspiring site that was once ancient Thebes.

After Bryce purchased the expensive tickets for our group, we headed for the entrance to Luxor Temple. Built from Nubian sandstone around 1400 BC, the temple complex stood on the east bank of the Nile. My guidebook explained the east side of the river had been dedicated to the living and was where many Egyptian kings had been crowned.

Mike nudged me as he looked across the river. "Are you sure it's not somewhere over there?"

I paused and turned. "Yep, that's the Valley of the Kings, and it's dedicated to the dead. According to my handy guidebook, the west side of the river was once called the Great Necropolis of Millions of Years of Pharaohs and has sixty-three magnificent royal tombs."

"*Millions of Years* seems like quite an exaggeration," Lance said as he gazed across the water.

"Or maybe they knew something we don't." Lisa looked at both sides of the river. "Too bad there isn't time to see it all."

I glanced around as we walked toward the temple complex. What secrets did this ancient site hold? One of my inherited abilities allowed me to sense energy contained in objects and also the presence of strong electromagnetic energy, like the concentrated power that flowed through ley lines, also called dragon currents. I felt it here.

"The EME is increasing as we get closer to the temple entrance." My head tingled as I scanned the temple's front walls, statues, and the obelisk to the left of the entrance. Too bad the obelisk that had been on the right side was now in Paris. "We might not need to go very far inside. Stay close."

Banger eased up to me and leaned in. "I spotted some men in the crowd who look out of place—hard cases."

"Maybe they're waiting to see if we find anything." Lance stood close to me and searched the crowd.

A German tour group exited a huge bus and jockeyed with an equal number of Asian tourists from another bus, all rushing toward us and the temple entrance.

Mike frowned. "Maintain a tight perimeter around Sam when we enter the temple."

Too late.

The crowd swept us inside, pushing and shoving like they thought entering the temple was a competition. The Germans seemed determined to beat the Asians to the front of the line, and they had the size advantage. My blond hair must've fooled the Germans into thinking I was with them. They grabbed my arms, separating me from my team, and pulled me down a main walkway lined with giant columns.

The strength of the electromagnetic energy field decreased the farther I moved from the entrance. I tried to break free and turn around, but the crowd hemmed me in and swept me forward. I'd have to wait until they stopped to look at something. In the meantime, I caught glimpses of men with hard eyes and crew cuts on the crowd's perimeter.

Someone behind me grabbed my waist and lifted me up. Banger's deep voice said, "Relax, I'll get you away from this Nordic mob."

He forced his way out the left side of the tour group and set me down in a stone alcove.

"Thanks for the save," I said with a grin. At five-nine, I still had to stand on my tiptoes to kiss his cheek.

He studied the people around us. "Mercenaries are lurking nearby."

"Any idea how we can lose them and get back to the entrance?" I tugged my shirt down over my hips, readjusting it after my jostling.

Banger raised a brow. "Having doubts about finding the artifact?"

I glanced around and lowered my voice. "We already passed it. What we want is near the entrance."

His eyes widened. "You saw it?"

"No, but the dragon current is strongest back where we entered. The crowd swept me away so fast I didn't get a chance to look for it."

"Call Mike on your SAT phone and tell him to gather the team and run interference for us." He positioned himself so that he blocked me from being seen by Sweetwater's goons.

Mike answered on the first ring. "Where are you?"

"With Banger, about a hundred yards from the entrance in a stone alcove to the left of the main walkway. Mercs are circling like sharks."

"Hang tight. The rest of the team is with me. We'll be right there."

I nudged Banger. "Expect the team any minute."

It wasn't long before he waved, and our friends crowded in around us.

Lance hugged me, relief in his eyes.

"According to Sam, the item is close to the entrance." Banger thumbed in that direction. "We need you to keep the mercs away while we retrieve it."

Mike glanced around. "All right, Banger will stick with Sam while we fan out and block the enemy soldiers." He checked his watch. "Meet at the van in fifteen."

"Wait." Lisa grabbed Mike's arm. "They're watching us, so let's pretend to search the temple. Then we'll act frustrated, argue, and behave like we're angry that we didn't find anything."

Bryce nodded. "Good idea. We can end by yelling that we should've gone to Giza first."

"Right." I looked at Mike. "They'll think we haven't found it, and they won't attack us."

Mike paused. "It's a solid plan. Meet at the refreshment stand near the parking lot, order drinks, and act like we're arguing about where to go next."

Our team fanned out and began their ruse, while Banger and I strolled down a side corridor and pretended to study the stones. As we backtracked, we passed more guys who looked like mercenaries—buff, tattooed, buzz cuts, hard eyes.

"Keep moving, nice and easy." Banger placed his hand on the small of my back.

A steady stream of people poured in as we

neared the entrance. The exit was in a different part of the temple along the side. We had to go against the flow to leave through the entry.

Banger eased me in front of him as he planted himself in one side of the entrance, forcing the crowd to go around him. In seconds, we were outside the temple.

We glanced back. The crowd had closed our exit hole, and no one had followed us.

I felt tingling and a pull to my right.

The obelisk hummed with energy.

I examined the back side. Approximately six feet above the ground, faint carvings of tridents, partially eroded by time, surrounded a large eye carved into the surface.

I elbowed the big guy. "Cover me so no one will see what I'm doing."

He turned around and backed against me, watching for anyone sneaking toward us.

I reached up and placed my right palm over the eye, my fingertips tingling as they touched several of the tridents.

A small block of stone slid outward, and I reached inside it.

The block was hollow and open at the top, like a tiny stone box. A leather pouch lay inside. I grabbed it, and the stone box slid back flush with the obelisk.

Gold writing in Atlantean adorned the leather. Thanks to the triplets, I knew what it said and slipped the pouch down the front of my pants. The item in the sack felt solid and about four inches long, three inches wide, and two inches deep. I tied the ends of the drawstring to a belt loop and pulled my shirt down so it would cover the slight bulge.

"Mission accomplished." I gave Banger a nudge. "Time to go."

Sweetwater's Hideout

After Ross and Derek had finished their meager meal of stale sandwiches, guards tossed them into a tall, eight-foot-square cage surrounded by penned-in lions. They reclined on the dirt floor. A high metal fence topped by barbed wire confined the beasts, and a narrow fenced-in pathway with electronic gates connected the men's enclosure to the area outside the pen.

Sweetwater's voice blared over a speaker blasting from a high corner in their tiny prison. "I'd hate for you to get lonely here, gentlemen. Enjoy the view. As you can see, your neighbors are rather thin and eager for fresh meat." His cruel laugh filtered through the open air.

Weak from dehydration and brutal beatings, Ross and Derek were left with their hands and feet free.

A large male lion rubbed against the cage and sniffed at them.

"Nice kitty." Derek lifted his head from a prone position.

Ross groaned and sat up. "I hope Sweetwater isn't using us as bait to lure Sam here."

Derek struggled into a sitting position. "Maybe she'll sneak in with an SAS regiment—teach that slimy bastard a thing or two."

Ross watched the pride of lions circling their cage. They growled and pawed at the bars. "He wants that power diamond, and he might need Sam to find it."

"Those big cats are looking for a way in." Derek tugged on a vertical bar. "I hope this cage is sturdier than it looks."

The speaker blasted Sweetwater's voice again. "Some entertainment for you. Watch what happens to those who fail me."

One end of a double gate in the lion enclosure opened, and two guards dragged a terrified white man with shackled feet through the outer gate. The prisoner jerked back and forth against his captors, struggling to break free. Naked, so the lions wouldn't choke on his clothes, tattoos covered his arms and torso, and his biceps bulged against the strain of having his wrists bound behind him. Red rivulets ran down his chest and abdomen where shallow wounds had been carved into his flesh. In his mid-thirties with a buzz cut, he had the hard look of a mercenary. The guards shoved him inside and exited.

The first gate closed, and the second gate opened automatically. The prisoner backed against the outer gate and struggled to open it with his fingers, but it was locked.

The rattling metal attracted the lions' attention. Growling and baring their teeth as they eased closer, the hungry pride crept up to the open inner gate. The male shook his shaggy mane and roared, waiting for the alpha lioness to bring him the prize. She leaped at the trapped man. His screams ended when she closed her jaws over his head and dragged him to her mate.

Ross and Derek stood, backed up a few feet, and gasped, their eyes wide and their skin prickled with goosebumps.

The huge male sank his teeth into the helpless man, shook him like a rag doll, ripped a large chunk out of his torso, and left the rest for the four females. Snarling, the lionesses tore into the body, tugging in opposite directions, each retreating with a shredded portion of flesh. Blood from the grisly attack splattered onto the nearby Scotsmen.

Nothing remained of the man but a mess of blood, bones, and guts. Birds dived in to snatch bits of flesh while the lions gnawed on pieces of his skeleton. In minutes, most of him was gone.

Ross wiped blood off his arms and looked at Derek. "Sweetwater is one sick sonofabitch."

FOUR

Luxor

We strolled to the refreshment stand and bought cold bottles of water for the team. Banger and I sat at a table for six, and our comrades trickled in one at a time. We sipped water and gazed around at the grounds.

"The mercs are circling," I whispered. "Now would be a good time to have a loud argument about where to search next."

Mike jumped right in. "What the hell, Sam? *You* said we'd find it here."

Lance pounded the table. "What are we supposed to do now?"

Lisa glared at me. "I *told* you we should've gone to Giza first!"

"I'm sorry, okay? I really thought it was here." I

hung my head like I was sulking.

Bryce glanced at his watch. "It's only nine in the morning. We have plenty of time to fly to Cairo and keep searching."

Banger stood. "Let's go."

We followed him to the parking lot, all of us grumbling as we walked.

The van driver seemed surprised to see us back so soon. He dropped the paper he'd been reading, jumped out, and opened the doors for us.

I didn't see any suspicious-looking guys nearby when Lance slid in beside me in the back seat, and Lisa followed him. Mike and Banger settled in the middle seat, and Bryce sat in the front.

Bryce turned to the driver. "Take us back to the airport."

Mike pulled out his satellite phone and called our pilots. "We're coming. Wheels up in fifteen."

The driver pulled into the morning traffic where cars and trucks jostled for position on the busy road.

I looked out a left side window, searching for the men we'd seen earlier as horns honked, noisy engines rumbled, and loads rattled and clanked on nearby trucks.

Banger scanned the area ahead and on the right. "If they attack, it'll be soon."

"They won't wait until we're at the airport." Lisa looked out the back window. "Too risky."

The driver braked. "Traffic jam ahead. Probably an accident."

"Take a different route," Bryce instructed, looking around for possible attackers.

The driver checked traffic. "No opening to turn off."

Bryce pulled out his pistol and racked the slide. "Make one."

Too late.

The windshield cracked into a spider-web pattern on the driver's side a nanosecond before the cabbie slumped onto the steering wheel, a bullet in his head.

Everyone ducked.

Bryce reached over the dead man, opened the door, and shoved him out. He slid into the driver's seat and threw the van into reverse. Stomping on the accelerator, he rammed into the car behind us, forcing it back.

Bullets shattered windows on the left side, covering Mike and me with broken glass. Bryce shifted gears and turned onto the sidewalk, scattering pedestrians. He zoomed down the block and turned right on a side street.

We sped off and turned left, trying to get back on course for the airport. An SUV screeched around a corner and accelerated toward us. Seconds later, our back window shattered, showering Lisa, Lance, and me with tiny shards.

We racked our Sigs and blasted the approaching vehicle with a barrage of bullets while ducking return fire. When Bryce zigzagged through traffic, we stopped firing. Too many pedestrians nearby. I expected local police to show up any minute, but so far, we were on our own.

A flatbed truck entered the road from a side street and pulled between us and the shooters. Someone in the SUV shot the truck driver.

Big mistake.

In seconds, the long vehicle swerved and flipped onto its side, blocking their path.

Bryce took advantage of their delay, made the first turn back onto the road to the airport, and sped away.

In minutes, our van slid to a stop in the parking lot, and we rushed into the terminal to clear security and get to our airplane.

Banger stopped us. "Take a few seconds and brush off the broken glass."

We helped each other tidy up and then strolled through the checkpoint. I didn't breathe easy until we were airborne.

"I feel terrible about our driver getting killed." I looked down at the receding city on the Nile. "And I don't know if we'll ever be able to come back to Egypt."

"Our diplomatic passports had fake names, which we'll never use here again, and MI6 will compensate the driver's family." Lisa shook her head. "I know money is no substitute for losing a family member, but it's better than nothing."

As soon as we leveled off, the team gathered around me.

Mike arched his brows. "Well? Show us what you found."

I reached under my shirt and pulled out the leather pouch. After untying the drawstrings from my belt loop, I loosened them and peeked inside.

"Uh oh, I'm not touching this while we're in the air."

"Why not?" Lisa stared at the pouch. "What is it?"

"It might be a weapon, and my touch could activate it." I pulled the drawstring tight.

"Seems kind of small to be a weapon." Bryce peered over the seat back.

Banger tilted his head, looking at the gold lettering. "Can you translate that for us, Sam?"

I nodded. "It means Eye of Atlantis."

Banger's eyes widened. "If that's anything like the eye I found in the upper chamber of the obsidian pyramid, don't mess with it here. Wait until we're on the ground back at the base. We'll put you in a windowless room and evacuate the building while you figure out what it does."

"Lucky me." I bit my lip.

Lance squeezed my shoulder. "Babe, trust your instincts. Remember, you're the one who insisted we go to Luxor and find that thing."

"Yes, I did, and now I'm reminded of that old saying, 'Be careful what you wish for.'"

Camp Baledogle

Mike led me into a windowless room. "Be careful, sis. We'll wait for you in the conference room."

When the door closed behind him, I loosened the pull-tie on the pouch and let the Eye of Atlantis slip out onto the metal table without touching it. Finding it had been the first test. It was beautiful, sparkling under the fluorescent lights. The clear crystal eye had an aquamarine iris flecked with deep blue and emerald green, like my eyes, and the pupil looked like a black diamond.

I took a deep breath and exhaled, steeling myself for what might happen when I touched it. The instant I held the Eye in my hand, it filled with bright light and beamed a hologram into the room. The image spanned several rock-hewn buildings whose roofs were even with ground level. Each of the spacious structures had been carved downward into solid bedrock. The symbols chiseled into the roofs looked medieval, and I had a vague memory of reading about a place like that in Ethiopia.

Using my other hand on my cell phone, I described the place in a Google search. An image of Lalibela, a village in the mountainous Amhara Region of Ethiopia, filled the screen. It matched the hologram. The rock-hewn buildings were monolithic Christian churches, and their multistory subterranean construction was described by experts as scientifically inexplicable. Legends claimed that in approximately AD 1200, angels carved the structures at night while the villagers slept.

A strange voice whispered in my head, *"Pass tests in Lalibela."*

As I stood in silence, the hologram vanished, and I wondered what the tests would entail.

I dropped the Eye into the leather pouch, and its inner light extinguished.

Time to meet with the team and decide our next move.

Lisa spoke the moment I closed the door. "What happened with the Eye?"

"When I held it, it projected a hologram of the rock-hewn churches in Lalibela, Ethiopia."

"How many are there?" Lance picked up an atlas of Africa that was on the table.

I pulled out my cell and Googled Lalibela. "Eleven churches carved downward into solid rock. Their roofs are at ground level, and tunnels or trenches connect most of them."

Lance grinned. "Sounds promising. Sam's good at opening doors hidden in rock walls."

"So, we search the churches, find the Blue Dragon, and then it will somehow show us Ross and Derek's location." Banger spread his hands. "Easy peasy."

"Maybe not." Lisa looked at her cell. "Lalibela

is a protected UNESCO World Heritage holy site with lots of rules and regulations. Many areas prohibit women."

Everyone turned to me.

"Lisa and I will disguise ourselves as men." I shrugged and glanced at the team. "Google says the majority of visitors are Christian pilgrims. We'll pose as a religious contingent from America."

Lance smirked. "Good luck hiding those." He nodded pointedly at my chest. "And what about your long blond hair and Lisa's red mane?"

I crossed my arms. "Thanks for your concern, Lance, but my shape won't be a problem. I'll wear padding over my torso for a fireplug physique, and Lisa and I will wear shoulder pads under our clothes and the male version of head scarves to hide our hair."

"It's hot as hell here. That padding will make you overheat." Bryce frowned, looking concerned.

"Not in Lalibela. It'll be chilly at eight thousand feet, and the padding will give me extra warmth." I looked at Banger. "You should pose as our leader. We'll wear traditional white robes, like the religious pilgrims in these pictures." I held out my phone. "You're good with that, right?"

Banger grinned. "Only if I get to play the big cheese."

Mike arched a brow. "Uh, sister dear, have you forgotten I'm the team leader?"

I patted his back. "You're the real boss, but we

should act like Banger is our leader. The locals will respond more favorably to a man who looks like an African king than to a blond white guy."

Lance laughed. "Especially since he'll be surrounded by white guys catering to him."

"Sweet." Banger leaned back.

I nudged Mike. "Is there an intelligence officer here who can gather all the info we'll need for this op?"

"Sit tight while I check with the base commander." Mike turned and strode out the door.

"Sam, what if Lalibela turns out to be like your last quest?" Lance crossed his arms.

Lisa glanced from Lance to me. "What does he mean?"

I pulled the medallion out of my shirt. "This key opened hidden doors in Petra where we found secret chambers with info about Atlantis and a WMD called Poseidon's Sword."

"Yeah, but she didn't find the weapon until much later." Lance tapped his watch. "What if it takes a long time to find the Blue Dragon?"

Lisa frowned. "And if it's a powerful weapon, how will it help us find our men?"

Bryce took a long swig from his water bottle. "Good point. What do you think, Sam?"

"I think if we go to Lalibela, we'll either find the Blue Dragon, and it'll help us, or the Eye will show me something else that will help."

"Ethiopia is right next door." Banger pointed

at the map on the wall. "If General Ryan will loan us his jet again, we can fly to Lalibela Airport and rent a car." He held a measuring device against the map. "Looks like about eight hundred miles."

Lisa studied the map. "You're right about the distance, but it's easier to travel in and out of foreign countries on a private jet." She looked at me. "Any chance you can arrange for one of the Starr Corporation's jets to fly us around?"

"Good idea, Lisa. A private jet won't attract as much attention as a military one." I pulled out my cell. "I'll call the chief pilot."

Captain Bill Hiller answered on the first ring. "Hello, Sam, did you find Ross?"

"Not yet, and it looks like we may need to travel to several countries in Africa. Can you send one of our Gulfstream G650s to Camp Baledogle in Somalia as soon as possible?"

"Why the G650? Didn't you say you only have six people on the team?"

"Yes, but we might carry a lot of gear, and the G650 is the only jet we can safely parachute from if the need arises." I hesitated. "We'll need it and a crew for one to two weeks."

Bill hesitated. "Let me make a few calls and I'll get right back to you."

I hung up as Mike strode in with Navy Intelligence Officer Robert Metz.

Mike glanced at me. "Sam and Lance, you remember Commander Metz from your escapade on the aircraft carrier."

The man in blue fatigues with a dark blond buzz cut offered me his hand.

"Good to see you again, Bob." I squeezed his hand.

Lance grinned. "Small world, isn't it?"

Mike introduced the rest of the team, and we settled at the table for Bob's briefing.

He began, "I've got people in town procuring your clothing and disguises. Lalibela is a medieval Christian site of great significance, so your cover will be a religious pilgrimage."

I nodded. "That's what we planned."

Bryce looked at Bob. "Will it fit our cover to arrive in a jet?"

"Pastors of American megachurches have private jets. Plan to depart tomorrow morning at oh-four-thirty." Bob glanced at his watch. "It's too late to go today. You wouldn't arrive before the site closes. They'll reopen at oh-eight-hundred."

"What's the plan?" Mike checked a site map for Lalibela.

Bob glanced at the big SEAL. "Banger will pose as a wealthy Christian leader from America. Lalibela is in the far north of Ethiopia, so you'll borrow General Ryan's G650 again. He'll be back in a few hours. Questions?"

I raised a hand. "I'm waiting for a call back from the chief pilot at the Starr Corporation. We're hoping to use one of their Gulfstream jets for the rest of our flights."

"That's great, but if they're coming from Florida, they won't get here in time for the early departure tomorrow morning." Bob glanced at his watch. "Plan on using their jet after Lalibela."

"All right, I'm expecting his call any minute." I checked my cell phone.

"My knowledge of the Bible is fairly extensive." Banger arched his brows. "Will that suffice?"

Bob nodded. "Use your stature to intimidate troublemakers. Tell them the Lord sent you."

Banger grinned. "That sounds good. Who can argue with what the Lord wants?"

"What's the exit plan?" Mike asked as he studied the terrain on the map.

"That depends on what you find." Bob glanced at me. "If Sam discovers a hidden passage that leads to wherever, you may need to change your travel plans. And no explosives on the sacred site. We'll wait for your call." He handed me a SATCOM and handed another one to Mike. "Use these for team communications to home base. Don't forget Sweetwater has informants inside our military, so there's a chance you may pick up a tail."

A soldier entered and placed a large tray of sandwiches on the table. Another serviceman handed out cold bottles of water.

Lisa took a ham and cheese sandwich. "What about the rest of us? What roles are we playing?"

"Pilgrims serving your leader, so be submissive around Banger and let him do the talking." Bob studied the team. "And remember, you're all men in this case, so don't treat Sam and Lisa differently." He looked at Lisa and me. "No makeup, perfume, or nail polish, ladies, and trim your nails short."

I glanced at my fingernails, which had been painted for my expected date with Ross, and checked my watch. "When do we get our clothes and stuff?"

"Your robes will be delivered by a sergeant who's good with disguises. He'll help Sam and Lisa suit up. And he'll advise everyone on the best places to hide your weapons. Carry as much as possible under your robes in case you find a secret passage and end up somewhere else, like Sam and Lance did in Petra. Once Sam and Lisa are wearing their disguises, you'll need to send new pictures to the embassy to update your fake diplomatic passports for Ethiopia."

My cell rang. I answered, "Hi, Bill, were you able to get me a G650?"

"I'll bring it to you myself. Laura Burke and I will be your pilots for as long as you need us, and we'll land in Somalia tomorrow evening around six local time."

"Thanks, Bill. My team won't be there when you arrive, so relax and rest up for the next flight when we return." I hung up and told Bob and my team the news.

Bob smiled at us before he left. "I'll ensure the corporate pilots are taken care of. Good luck."

———

Two hours later, a guy named Sergeant Beaumont showed up. He set two large duffel bags on the conference table. "I'll get you set up with everything you'll need for your mission."

He pulled reversible robes out of a duffel, checked the sizes, and handed them to the men. "Wear these over your clothes with the white side showing. The black side could be useful later if you find yourselves in a stealth situation in the dark." He handed them several full ammo magazines.

"What about us?" Lisa peeked into one of the bags.

"I have reversible robes with shoulder pads for both ladies, and this torso padding for the blonde." He handed us the garments and passed me the padding.

"What are these for?" I stuck my hands inside pockets hidden in the padding.

"The big one on the right is for your pistol, the two on the left are for your item in the leather pouch and rations of beef jerky, and the compartments along the front are for extra ammo. There's also a large folded canvas satchel attached along the bottom edge." He handed me four full mags.

The sergeant handed Lisa a padded vest with

an inner holster and inner compartments. "Load this with your weapon and ammo and wear it under the robe."

"What about their long hair?" Lance glanced at us.

Beaumont pulled out six reversible turbans and handed them to everyone. "The women will hide their hair inside the turbans, white side out. Everyone will be dressed the same." He grabbed a bag full of mini magnesium flashlights and handed them out. "Put these in your robe pockets." Then he reached inside and pulled out six combat knives in sheaths and several packages of beef jerky. "Hide these wherever they fit best."

I loaded the padding and wrapped it around my torso, fastening it with Velcro straps. Then I slipped on the robe, twisted my hair, and stuffed it inside the turban.

Beaumont handed me a jar full of clear liquid and a rag. "Clean off the nail polish." He nodded at Lisa. "You too."

Banger circled Lisa and me and then stared at our faces. "No good. They're too pretty to pass for guys."

"I'm not finished." The sergeant opened a small case and pulled out our disguises. He lifted my chin. "Hold still and don't speak until the glue dries." He brushed glue above my upper lip and on the back of a fake mustache and then pressed it onto my skin. Next came a matching goatee.

Mike busted out laughing, and everyone else snickered.

"Let me see." I pulled out a small makeup mirror. "I think I look distinguished."

I glanced at Lisa with her newly applied facial hair and grinned.

She grabbed my mirror. "Not bad. How long will the glue last?"

Beaumont handed us small tubes. "The disguises won't come off until you massage that glue remover into the hair. You can shower, eat, wash your faces, whatever—they're not coming off."

I glanced at the men. "Do we look masculine *now*?"

Bryce crossed his arms. "If you don't speak. Your voices are too high."

Banger grinned. "I'll do the talking." He pulled out his cell and took pictures. "These will make amusing memories. I can't wait to show Tiesha."

I nudged him. "Are you two still on a fast track to marriage?"

"We already have a venue booked." Banger chuckled. "I hope you'll have that facial hair off by then."

"It had better be off by tomorrow night." I glanced at the sergeant. "Are we done?"

"Yes, ma'am." He gathered the duffels, saluted, and left.

Lisa handed Mike her cell phone. "Take headshots of Sam and me for our new passports."

FIVE

Lalibela

The next morning, we landed at Lalibela Airport, which was about sixty-five hundred feet above sea level. By 7:00 a.m., Mike had rented a minivan for the fourteen-mile drive to the city. We watched General Ryan's jet fly away as we drove up a winding road that led almost two thousand feet higher into the mountains.

The primitive village of Lalibela looked like a place time had forgotten. Some of the homes were round two-story tukul huts built of stone, and others were round one-story chika huts built of earth and wattle.

The buildings in Atlantis had been circular. *Hmmn.*

We pulled into the World Heritage site's parking

lot and looked around. All the monolithic churches were below ground level. UNESCO had built protective roofs over many of the churches, and those roofs were the only things visible above ground in the bright sunlight. The air at over eight thousand feet was a chilly forty degrees, but our robes and the clothes beneath them kept us warm.

Mike waited until we gathered around him. "Check that your weapons are well hidden."

We gave each other the once over. Everyone looked like typical white-robed pilgrim men.

Banger leaned close to me. "Which church should we search first?"

"The first one, the House of the Savior of the World, is the largest—almost a hundred feet long, seventy feet wide, and three and a half stories." I glanced at my guidebook. "It's one of the five churches in the Northern Group on this side of the river Jordan. May as well start there since it'll take a while to cover it."

"Isn't there a better way to choose the right church?" Mike looked at my guidebook.

"The Atlanteans used Earth's electromagnetic energy as their main power source. If one of the churches sits on an intersection of ley lines, that will be the likely choice. We just have to find it." I headed toward the site's steps.

Bryce frowned. "How are we supposed to know where the ley lines intersect?"

"Like I explained in Luxor, I've developed a

sensitivity to the energy fields." I tapped my fore-head. "When I get close, the intersection will make my head buzz."

"Okay, so once we figure out which church, then what?" Banger glanced around at the site.

"Look for gold tridents on the walls, floor, or ceiling—or anything that doesn't belong." I nudged Banger. "Lead on, my liege."

The men on our team were all over six feet, but Banger was a few inches taller and a lot broader than the next-tallest guy. He strode down the path to the House of the Savior of the World with a con-fident swagger, as if all eleven churches had been built for him. The crowd parted when he ap-proached the entrance.

I followed him down the rock-hewn steps, and Lance stuck to my six o'clock like glue. The rest of the team trailed behind us as we descended about forty feet to the base of the magnificent structure.

When we stepped inside the enormous church with its five aisles, I tugged at Banger's robe and whispered, "Lead us down the center aisle."

He nodded.

Halfway down the long aisle, I tugged his robe again.

He stopped and leaned in. "What?"

"No ley lines under this church," I whispered. "Lead us to the next one."

Banger continued out the back door and into the connecting trench to the next church—the oldest and most popular, the House of Mary. A long line of pilgrims waited to enter, probably because it contained replicas of the tombs of Adam and Christ.

I nudged our leader. "Forget the line. If we walk around the outside of the church, I'll sense whether this is the right place or not."

He beckoned us forward. When he reached the far side of the monolithic church, he paused and turned to me. "Anything?"

I shook my head. "Next on the list is the House of Golgotha Mikael, believed to contain the hidden tomb of King Lalibela. Maybe that's it."

Banger turned and led us through a tunnel trench that connected to the next site. It was dark and narrow and barely wide enough for one person. In some parts, the sky could be seen high above, but only by looking straight up. At least it wasn't confined enough for my claustrophobia to fully kick in. Just a little extra sweating and chest-tightening.

A wave of relief swept over me when I stepped into the open area around the church. Beautiful artistic stone carvings set this one apart from the others, and the entry line was shorter. In minutes, we entered the dark structure and stood admiring the intricate interior.

"Spread out and search the building," Banger whispered.

My head tingled, but not like it would if we

were over an intersection of ley lines. An invisible force beckoned me deeper inside.

Lisa sidled up to me. "I found something."

"Show me."

She led me to a small alcove carved into a thick wall near the center of the church. Goosebumps prickled my skin as she pointed at a dark corner inside. I crept closer and spotted a Coptic cross carved into the stone. A gold trident pierced it diagonally. The alcove was too small for more than one person to stand inside.

I glanced around. No one except Lisa watched, so I slipped inside. A powerful force drew me to the trident. Soft whispers sent chills down my spine.

I spun around. "Did you say something?"

Lisa shook her head. "No, why?"

"Uh, nothing. Stand watch in case something weird happens."

Raising a brow, Lisa took a step back and glanced behind her.

I hesitated, reached out, and placed my hand over the gold trident. My fingers tingled as a deep grinding sound reverberated in the stone church, and a small section of the alcove's wall opened inward. A puff of stone dust swirled around me as cool air escaped through the opening. I pulled a small mag light from my pocket and peered inside. Spiral steps led downward into darkness.

Oh no.

Loud shouting accompanied running footsteps approaching from behind me.

Now or never.

Leaving Lisa, I ducked through the door and entered the stairwell. The door thudded shut behind me, leaving me alone on the dank stone steps. No light, except from my tiny flashlight.

Claustrophobic alarm bells rang in my head, keeping time with my pounding heart, as I descended to a dark room about twenty feet below the church.

Inside the room, I swung my light around, revealing a lavishly carved burial chamber about fifteen-feet square with an ornate stone sarcophagus in the center—probably King Lalibela's tomb. Was the Blue Dragon hidden inside the stone coffin?

As I crept closer to the sarcophagus, darkness seemed to close in around me, the tiny beam of my mag light not providing enough illumination.

My heart raced and my breath came in spurts.

Calm down or you'll hyperventilate and pass out.

I closed my eyes, filled my lungs with stale, musty air, and let it out slowly. When I opened my eyes, I focused on the beam of light illuminating the coffin's lid and searched for an Atlantean symbol. An engraved Coptic cross with a gold trident piercing it at an angle, like the symbol in the alcove, adorned the center.

One more glance around the room reassured me that I was alone.

Claustrophobia sucks.

I reached out and touched the trident.

The stone lid vibrated, and I jumped back. It scraped against the sarcophagus as it slid slowly to one side. Worried something might leap out at me, I backed farther into the shadows and held my breath. Was that a whisper coming from the coffin?

Silly girl. Probably just an old skeleton in there. Still, better safe than sorry.

I waited, barely breathing.

No sound, except my pounding heart.

Nothing moved.

Sweetwater's Hideout

Sweetwater held a phone to his ear and paced inside his air-conditioned hut, barely controlling his rage. "Did you catch up with the team that failed me?"

A deep voice on the satellite phone said, "We found them hiding in Libya."

"Good." Sweetwater stopped pacing. "Did you take them alive?"

"Yes, sir, with just a few minor wounds."

He glanced out the window at the lions in the pen and grinned. "Bring me those incompetent bastards." He disconnected and punched in another number. "Did she find the Blue Dragon?"

"She found something, but it was much too small to be a two-foot-long diamond."

Sweetwater clenched his fist. "Well, dammit, what was it?"

"Don't know exactly. It's about four inches long, and she carries it in a leather pouch."

He rubbed his balding head. "Where is she and what's she doing with it?"

"Their jet left for Lalibela before dawn this morning."

Sweetwater pounded his fist on a table. "Isn't that in Ethiopia? Bloody hell! Why didn't you warn me yesterday?"

"The U.S. military knows you have people on the inside. They're being very secretive. I just found out about Lalibela this morning."

He paused and took a deep breath. "Do we have a way to track her?"

"I bugged their satellite phones. They're touring the monolithic churches."

Sweetwater gripped the phone so hard his knuckles turned white. "Keep a close watch on their whereabouts. I'm sending a team." He ended the call and dialed the commander of his mercenary army.

Lalibela

Edging close to the open coffin, I peeked inside.

I gasped as King Lalibela's skeleton stared back at me, his gold-capped teeth forming a creepy grin. A royal crown, inset with jewels, gleamed on his skull, and he wore a ruby ring on his right hand.

My body shaking, I inched closer and examined the coffin with my light, avoiding another look at the scary skull. There was nothing resembling a Blue Dragon inside the stone burial box.

I knew it wouldn't be this easy.

I pulled out my cell and took pictures of the creepy king and the contents of his resting place.

A distant noise made me jump. I froze and listened.

Faint sounds of pounding on stone filtered down from above. What if the locals broke through the stone door and found me down here in their beloved king's crypt?

I wiped sweat from my brow, even though the burial chamber was cool. The king's skeleton had really freaked me out. I didn't have the right stuff to be a tomb raider. I jerked my head toward the coffin. Did something move in there?

Better try to close the sarcophagus before somebody comes down here. Wouldn't want anyone to know I disturbed their sacred king.

I reached out with a shaky hand and touched the trident symbol again. The lid slid into the closed position.

Thank God.

The pounding grew louder.

Worried about how much time I had before they broke through above, I backed away from the coffin and bumped against the back of a niche recessed into the wall.

I jumped forward, fearing the crypt was trying to trap me inside a wall.

I took a deep breath. No more horror movies for this girl.

Withdrawing the leather pouch, I slid the Eye of Atlantis into my right hand. It filled with light and projected an image of the only monolithic church in Lalibela that stood apart from all the others—the Church of Saint George. The entire edifice had been built in the shape of a Coptic cross.

A voice in my head whispered, *"Pass next test here."*

Had finding King Lalibela been a test too?

I replaced the Eye, tied the pouch shut, and secreted it in the padding under my robe. *Too bad the first hologram hadn't been more specific. Could've saved me a lot of time.*

Loud pounding from above interrupted my thoughts. I sighed. It was time to return and feign stupidity around the church officials.

I climbed the stairs to the landing and found another engraving of a Coptic cross pierced by a trident. My touch opened the stone door.

A group of anxious Ethiopians stood outside the alcove. The instant I exited the stairwell, the door closed behind me. Church officials pulled me out and rushed to reopen it.

Good luck with that.

It didn't take long for them to realize they had no idea how to make it open.

One of them pointed at me. "You! Open the door."

I grabbed Banger, who had rushed over to me, and whispered, "Tell them I have a weak voice, but I told you they need something to hold it open."

He nodded and relayed my message.

A few minutes later, two guys carried in a big, rectangular stone and set it on the alcove's floor.

The apparent leader waved me forward.

I stepped inside and ran my hands all over the wall, like I didn't know what I was doing. When my fingers slid over the trident symbol, the door opened, and I backed out.

Men shoved the block into the doorway, preventing the stone door from closing. Excited, they forgot about me and rushed down the spiral steps.

Lisa had summoned the team while I was in the crypt.

I elbowed Banger. "Time to go."

Banger led us out and away from the church. "Now what?" he asked.

"We need to go to the Church of Saint George, which is in a separate location. First, we'll have to follow the trail past the last two churches down here to reach the steps topside." I pointed at a spot on the guide map.

"We'd better get moving before they come looking for us," Mike said, waving us forward.

We bypassed the last two buildings and rushed up the steps to ground level.

I consulted the site map. "The Church of Saint George is that way." I showed Banger the spot on the map, and he set off at a brisk walk. For me, the view of the mountains and valleys was a welcome change from the dark interior of the king's tomb.

As we approached the church, Banger slowed and leaned in toward me. "What did you find back there?"

The team crowded around us to listen.

"It was King Lalibela's tomb," I said. "His skeleton was in the coffin, but no Blue Dragon, so I activated the Eye. It showed me a hologram of St. George's Church. I hope that one is built over inter-secting ley lines."

Banger pulled me forward. "Let's find out."

He led me down thirty-five rock-hewn steps that ended in a narrow open area outside the church. My head tingled with electromagnetic energy, the intensity increasing as I neared the entrance.

I stopped for a moment, my head buzzing. "Guys, this is definitely the place. I feel the ley lines."

Banger signaled a halt before we entered. "This time, if you open a secret door, we're all going."

"Look for a trident symbol," I said as I climbed the four steps into the ancient church.

We spread out and searched the walls and floor. The ceiling was almost four stories high, and it was too dark inside to see what might be up there.

The entire building was carved into the shape of a giant Coptic cross, and artisans had spent many hours creating beautiful images on the stone interior.

Following the energy intensity, I discovered the strongest concentration where the building's four cross sections came together in the middle.

I found a Coptic cross about three feet wide engraved in the center of the stone floor. A gold trident pierced it at a forty-five-degree angle, just like the symbols I'd found in the alcove and tomb in the previous church. I called my team.

When we were gathered around the cross, I bent down. "Ready?"

They nodded.

I reached down and touched the trident.

The three-foot-square stone with the engraved cross dropped a foot and slid under the floor.

My breath caught, and I jumped back as stale cool air rose from the black hole.

I crept forward and peeked inside. Spiral stone steps descended into a dark void.

Not again.

Lance eased up beside me and shined his light into the stairwell. "Looks deep."

Lisa nudged me. "I don't know about this— could be a death trap."

SIX

B anger aimed his mag light in. "Or maybe this leads to where the Blue Dragon is hidden."

"Well, if it's like the other places I've opened, everyone has to go in ahead of me," I said. "The stone slab will close as soon as I enter."

Mike glanced at me. "Are you sure we should go down there?"

I hesitated, my gut twisting into a knot. "The Eye directed me here, so I guess I'm supposed to go." I peered into the depths. "Maybe the rest of you should stay behind and wait for me."

Lance patted my back. "Two is better than one. I'll go with you."

"Wait." Lisa took a few steps down the stairwell and tried to see how far it descended. Her voice tightened. "Too dark. Can't see past the short beam of my mag light." She climbed out and dropped a fifty-pence coin down the stairs. It pinged off each step and faded into a distant echo. "Sounds like it goes down a lot deeper than the steps to the king's tomb at the other church."

"Don't forget all the churches are over eight thousand feet above sea level." Bryce peered into the blackness. "Plenty of room for a deep staircase."

Mike said, "Yeah, but how could they have carved so many steps downward into solid rock?"

"The same way 'they' carved the huge, three-story monolithic churches. Right?" I tapped my guidebook.

Mike crossed his arms. "You said all the experts agree that these stone churches are scientifically in-explicable."

"Scientists, engineers, and architects have studied the site." I shrugged. "Nobody can figure out how the churches were carved. I think those experts would reach the same conclusion for these steps."

Mike peered down the stairwell and frowned. "Well, I suppose it's possible this will lead to what we came for. Do you think the Atlanteans made this?"

"I know Atlantis ruled the world thousands of years ago and left their unusual creations on every continent. Don't forget I found this Atlantean medallion key in India." I held it out. "And I found secret chambers and other Atlantean artifacts in Scotland, Petra, and on a remote mesa in South

America, not to mention their sunken city near Cuba."

"But Lalibela's churches weren't carved until the Middle Ages," Lisa countered, scanning the building.

"True, but until they were wiped out earlier this year, Atlanteans sent trained workers all over the world for many centuries, and they had the benefit of two hundred thousand years of scientific knowledge." I glanced around. "It's possible they made this. I mean, these trident symbols activate when I touch them, just like they did in Petra and other places."

"I was with Sam in India, Petra, and South America." Lance patted my back. "She'll get us to where we're supposed to go."

Lisa turned to Bryce. "I saw her activate Atlantean crystals in South America. Let's find what's down there."

Bryce nodded. "I'm in."

Banger glanced around. "Seems like all the pilgrims are still at King Lalibela's tomb. Let's go in before anyone sees what we're doing." He started down the steps, and the team followed.

I sucked in a deep breath and lifted my medallion key. When I stroked the pyramid-shaped diamond embedded in the gold, it filled with brilliant light and illuminated a small portion of the steep staircase.

The moment I passed below the opening in the floor, the slab slid closed above me.

My heart hammered my chest.

Darn my claustrophobia!

I continued down the seemingly endless spiral steps.

As I slowly descended, I distracted myself from my fear by counting each step.

After what felt like a long time, I checked my watch—forty minutes had passed.

So far, I'd counted five hundred steps, and there was no end in sight.

How could there be so many?

My mind wandered. *Could these steps have been here long before the churches were carved?*

The dark void made my heart race, and my breath came in short spurts.

"Anybody see anything down there?" My voice sounded squeaky.

"Nothing so far," Banger's deep voice echoed up the stairwell.

Nothing? What have I gotten us into this time?

The steps wound down almost eight hundred feet. Finally, I rounded the last turn and entered a long, empty corridor. My teammates, who weren't hindered by claustrophobia, must've descended a lot faster. Distant voices filtered down the rock-hewn hallway.

The dark passage looked level. Eager to rejoin my team, I followed it sixty paces to where it dead-ended beside an open door. Inside, I found a circular chamber about twenty feet in diameter. It had a high ceiling which helped relieve my exacerbated claus-trophobia. The five flashlights held by my comrades revealed hundreds of ancient symbols covering the curved rock walls. When I walked in, they aimed their lights at an object in the center of the room.

"Check this out, Sam." Mike stood beside a tall, narrow pedestal table.

The round, four-foot-high table held a silvery-blue globe resting on four tiny legs that extended from inside it. An opening in the metal sphere's top revealed the pointed tip of a long marquise-shaped blue diamond mounted vertically.

I took a closer look. In an effort to ease the ten-sion, I said, "It looks like it might be made of blue anodized titanium, or what my aircraft builder friends refer to as unobtainium."

Nobody laughed.

I sized it up visually. "Maybe this soccer-ball sized device with the large blue diamond is the Blue Dragon."

"Don't you know what it looks like?" Bryce took a step closer.

"I wasn't given a description—just the name. I

think it's reasonable to assume what we're looking for is blue, that it might even be a blue diamond, or it might be made of something blue that looks like a dragon." I spread my hands. "Sorry. That's all I know."

"Well, this thing is silvery-blue with a blue diamond." Banger stood next to me with his arms crossed. "You've had plenty of experience with Atlantean artifacts. What's it supposed to do?"

"I don't know." I eased closer to it. "Should I try to activate it?"

"Wait." Mike held his hands near each side of it and then eased them against it. He yanked his hands back. "Whoa! It shocked me."

"Maybe that was static electricity." I tentatively touched the gem with my right index finger.

It instantly filled with brilliant light.

I yanked my hand away and jumped back, shading my eyes.

The entire chamber became as bright as midday, and a low hum resonated from the sphere.

I stepped back farther. "Everyone against a wall until we see what this thing does."

The round device vibrated, and the humming intensified, echoing off the rock walls. In seconds, the entire chamber resonated with the strange sound.

Mike glanced at me. "Sam, what the—"

A powerful laser, its light so bright I had to

shield my eyes, shot from the diamond's tip straight up to a round hatch in the stone ceiling.

The beam hit the center of crossed gold tridents engraved on the metal hatch, activating a mechanism that disengaged the lock. In an instant, the laser shut off, and the hatch swung open.

I took a few steps forward and looked up through the opening.

A tubular vertical tunnel ascended into darkness. The strange humming started again, and I almost tripped, rushing backward to the wall.

The laser switched back on and fired straight up the tunnel, apparently opening a hatch at the surface. The beam extinguished, and I heard a faint echo when the surface hatch clanked open.

Seconds later, small clumps of dirt dropped from above and slid off the globe onto the floor.

"Bloody hell!" Bryce stared at the sphere.

Lisa elbowed me. "Now what?"

"I wish I knew." I edged closer to the device.

A tiny metal panel closed over the diamond, and the legs retracted, sealing the sphere.

The room became silent.

Instantly, and without making a sound, the strange globe zoomed up through the narrow tunnel and disappeared into the sky.

"Whoa." Lance stared at the open hatch.

"What did you do, sis?" Mike rushed to the pedestal.

I looked up at the pinpoint of light from the

open hatch eight hundred feet above us. "Well, I never expected *that* to happen. I hope that thing wasn't the Blue Dragon."

Tension permeated the team. Everyone glared at me, and no one spoke.

Lisa finally broke the silence. "You said the Eye led us here. If you activate it again, maybe it'll show us something useful."

I pulled out the leather pouch. When I slid the Eye into my hand, it filled with light and projected a hologram of the sphere flying low over an ocean at dizzying speed.

The image faded.

"That was wild." Lance stared at the fading image.

Banger nodded. "I bet it's returning to Atlantis."

"Maybe, but it doesn't know Atlantis is deep underwater now." I slipped the Eye into its pouch and pocketed it.

"A more pressing question is whether anyone near the church saw the sphere." Bryce pointed at the vertical tunnel. "We may get an angry reception if we have to return the way we came."

"I don't see another exit." Mike scanned the curved wall with his light.

"Climbing up eight hundred steps isn't my idea of a good time," Banger said, as he ran his hands over the wall opposite the door.

Lance glanced around. "Sam and I encountered

places like this in Petra, and she always found another way out."

I surveyed the room and studied the symbols engraved on the walls. My light lingered on a familiar one.

"Here. This is like the ones I used in Petra." I pressed my medallion against a mirror image of it recessed into the wall.

The floor vibrated as a stone door ground open on the opposite side of the room from where we had entered. Tiny stone particles reflected in our flashlight beams as a cool breeze rushed into the chamber.

Goosebumps erupted under my sleeves. "I hope this leads to a nearby exit to the outside world." I shined my light through the open door. "No light at the other end—too dark to see where it goes."

Mike moved me aside. "Stay here while I take a look." He took a few steps inside, waving his light around. "Another dark, narrow passage. Looks like it slants downward at a thirty-degree angle." He walked back to us.

"Should we follow it or climb back up the steps?" Bryce stuck his head through the door.

Banger shook his head. "Eight hundred steps? I vote we go that way." He waved at the dark passage.

Lance turned to me. "We can always return this way if it doesn't pan out. Right, Sam?"

Lisa grabbed my shoulders and spun me

around, her voice tight with tension. "That thing is back."

I faced the silent sphere. "Holy crap! I didn't hear a thing." Glancing up, I noticed the overhead hatch in the ceiling had closed. "What the heck?"

Everyone gathered around the pedestal table and stared at the sphere.

Bryce nudged Mike. "Is this situation normal for your sister, or should I be worried?"

Mike hesitated and glanced at Lance and Banger. "There's a reason my brother and I nick-named her Danger Magnet."

Nervous chuckles filled the chamber.

Lisa squeezed Bryce's shoulder. "Expect the un-expected when Sam's around."

Bryce glanced my way. "That shitstorm at Dux-ford was certainly unexpected, but it was nothing like *this*." He waved his flashlight around the room and paused it on the silvery-blue sphere.

"If the Blue Dragon is a weapon like Poseidon's Sword," I said, "then this little sphere might be an important component, like that artifact I found in Hong Kong. We should take it with us." I pulled out the canvas satchel attached to my padding and handed it to Lisa. "Hold this open."

"Are you *sure* about this?" She opened the satchel and glanced at the sphere like it was a live cobra.

"If it doesn't like it in there, it'll laser its way

out. So, don't lean over the bag." I grabbed the sphere and dropped it in.

No electric shock for me.

Lisa yanked the zipper closed and thrust it into my hands. "It's all yours."

I held it with outstretched arms and waited.

Nothing happened.

I exhaled and grinned at the team. "Alrighty, let's go." I followed them into the dark, slanted passage carved into the bedrock.

The door closed behind me with a loud thud.

Claustrophobic alarm bells clanged inside my head again as I concentrated on controlling my breathing.

We had to walk single-file, the pathway was so narrow. My medallion's light reflected off the stone walls and ceiling, illuminating a tiny area in the endless blackness.

Must stay calm. The team is counting on me.

"Banger, any sign of an end up ahead?" I tried not to sound anxious.

"Hard to tell," he said. "My mag light only reaches maybe ten feet."

Slow, deep breaths. Good thing they can't see the panic in my eyes.

SEVEN

We trudged downward for over an hour, seeing nothing but dark stone walls. Then the passage opened into a wide cavern where roaring water echoed off the granite. Our path ended beside an underground river that flowed swiftly into the darkness.

"I hope we're close to getting out of here," I muttered, unable to hide the tension in my voice.

Mike sat on the bank. "Let's take a break and consider our options."

"Options?" Lance peered at the water. "You mean swim or return the way we came?"

We sat beside the river, and I dipped my hand into the water. It looked clear and fresh, probably filtered through the rocks.

Banger stuck his hand in. "Cold—wouldn't

want to swim in this for more than a minute or two."

Lisa tested it and jerked her hand out. "I wouldn't want to swim in it for two seconds."

"Neither would I." I shined my flashlight along the riverbank. "Hey, what's that?"

A large, dark object loomed beside the water about thirty feet away. It wasn't moving.

Banger led us to what looked like a tubular metal watercraft mounted on a lift rack. The strange boat had a pointed bow, a curved keel, and a rudder protruding beneath the aft end. A curved clear section covering the roof appeared to be a long canopy hatch. Three large metal cylinders were mounted side-by-side on the outside of the flat stern, the outer two connecting to the central one. On the port side, I spotted a mirror-image symbol of my medallion recessed into the metal near the canopy's forward rim.

I pressed my medallion into it, and the canopy lifted open.

A small instrument panel with gauges I didn't recognize was mounted in front of a nose-cone seat with two rows of double seats behind it in the cabin.

Our team had six people, so we were short one seat.

Mike examined the interior. "If we decide to take this, Sam should sit in the control seat, the men will sit in passenger seats, and Lisa can sit on my lap."

"Wait." Bryce studied the small cabin. "We don't know how much time we'll be underground in this thing or how long the cabin air can sustain six people."

I checked out the mechanism mounted on the stern. "This one is more exotic, but it looks a lot like the oxygen generators I've seen mounted in the seatbacks of old DC-9s. The chemicals in the outer cylinders combine to create oxygen, but the process produces heat. These are probably mounted on the outside so water will cool the cylinders."

Lance studied the device. "She could be right—see the air vents where the hoses from the center cylinder connect to the cabin?"

"Any chance this is an execution chamber and those tanks are filled with poison gas?" Lisa asked, her voice a higher pitch.

Banger studied the lift rack. "Considering where this craft is located, the logical assumption is that it's an escape boat."

"Yeah, but this river is rushing downhill, and we don't know when this boat was built, how strong it is, or how long it's been sitting here." Lisa ran her hands over the metal body. "This seems … different. Anybody know what type of metal this is?"

Always the smartass, especially in tense situations, Banger said, "Looks like unobtainium."

"*Funny*." Mike arched a brow. "I don't know—it

looks sturdy, and I don't see any corrosion. Do we want to chance it? I can't see another way out of here other than the way we came."

Lance nudged me. "Uh, Sam, are there any more hidden doors?"

"I'll look." I checked the rock wall from the corridor exit to where it ended in the water. "Sorry, no door."

Mike gathered us. "I think this calls for a vote—take this boat or go back up the steps?"

Everyone hesitated and took another long look at the weird watercraft.

"Well?" Mike asked.

"Boat," we replied as one.

Mike nodded. "Okay, climb aboard."

"Good." I shivered, rubbing my arms. "I've had my fill of dark, closed-in places."

"Sorry, sis, I forgot about your claustrophobia. You hide it well." Mike patted my back.

Lance grabbed my arm. "Assuming this boat is like everything else your touch activates, you'd better climb in last."

I took a step back. "He's right. Everyone else in first."

Lance and Mike sat in the front row, with Banger and Bryce in the back. Then Lisa climbed in and sat sideways on Mike's lap with her legs over Lance's knees.

"Ready?" I sucked in a breath and tentatively swung a leg over the rail.

So far, so good.

I stepped in and sat in the control seat, being careful to hold the sack with the sphere between my knees.

"Give us a good ride, Captain." Lance reached forward and patted my left shoulder.

A moment later, the hatch closed automatically, and the lift rack tilted to one side. We slid into the river, and the swift current carried us downstream in the dark, turbulent water.

"This baby is fast," Banger, a typical fearless Navy SEAL, said as we zoomed through the whitewater.

Not feeling quite so brave, I kept my medallion lit in the cramped metal coffin. The river was ensconced in total darkness, rendering our clear canopy useless.

"Ow!" Lisa yelped when her head banged against the glass after a collision with a rocky curve.

"Sorry, Lisa." Mike squeezed her. "I'll hold you tighter."

Foaming water splashed over the boat as we ricocheted off rocks along the turns in the winding river.

I couldn't see anything outside as I braced my feet and held a white-knuckled grip on the panel.

Lisa clutched my seatback. "I hope this old bucket holds together."

Mike ran his hand over the starboard side wall. "It must be stronger than it looks. I don't see any indentations where we smashed up against rocks."

Lance checked the port rail. "Nothing on my side either."

"We're good back here too," Bryce chimed in.

Lance tapped my shoulder. "How's it looking up front?"

Trying to sound calm, I said, "Dark and foamy outside—no leaks up here." I had a death grip on the front panel as the boat rocked, rolled, and pitched like an amusement-park ride from Hell.

I stole a glance at my DARPA dive watch. The luminous dial indicated we'd been traveling five minutes.

It seemed a lot longer to me.

Why do all my Atlantis-related adventures involve deep dives and scary underground passages?

I longed for wide-open views and fresh outside air as our strange watercraft rushed down the Stygian path to Hades and slammed up against stone walls at every curve.

We'd been flailing around inside the craft for about twenty minutes when something made a hissing noise.

"Bugger! What was that?" Bryce looked around.

"Sounds like the oxygen generator just kicked in," Lance said in his Texas twang. "That'd be a good thing."

Lisa's voice tightened. "God, I hope you're right."

I took a tentative breath. "Smell that air coming in? Definitely oxygen."

Hurray for Atlantean technology.

"I hope it's enough to last us until we get out of here." Bryce's tone radiated concern.

"Depends on how far the cave goes—not that we have a choice." Mike tried shining his flashlight through the canopy. "Can't see a thing except foam and blackness."

As the long minutes passed, the river became more turbulent, and my heart rate bumped up another notch. I hated being shut inside a dark little boat on an even darker river.

Lance peered over my left shoulder. "Anything on the panel that indicates when we might be done with this whitewater adventure?"

"It's hard to say." I pointed a shaky finger. "That gauge looks like it might be measuring the cabin oxygen level—so far, so good." I took a breath. "It's in the green."

Lance reached over my shoulder and tapped an instrument that read twenty-two. "What about this other one?"

"I think that might be our forward speed—twenty-two knots." I shrugged. "But that's just a guess. The gauges aren't labeled."

"What about directional controls?" Mike tapped my right shoulder.

"Just rudder pedals." I zigzagged with short right and left turns to demonstrate.

We slammed into something hard and ricocheted back into the fast-moving river.

"Sonofabitch!" Mike swore. "How about missing some of those friggin' rocks, sis?"

"How do you suggest I do that? I can't see anything outside, *brother dear*."

Banger cut in, trying to calm us down. "No sibling rivalry allowed on the mission, you two."

"As you command, my liege." I glanced back, saluted Banger, and glared at Mike.

We banged into another rock, and a foamy wave rolled over the canopy.

Banger chuckled. "If we survive, I could get used to this 'my liege' stuff."

About half an hour later, the current spit us out of the river partway down a big waterfall.

"Hold on, we're falling!" I white-knuckled my seat.

We plunged into the churning water at the bottom of the falls and bobbed to the surface. I closed my eyes a moment to clear my dizziness as we spun around under the thundering water. After a few nauseating minutes, the current carried us past the cascading water that had been pounding the canopy. We drifted beyond the falls, and I looked up at a full moon shining over us.

Thank God.

"Everybody okay back there?" I glanced over my shoulder.

"Lucky I'm not prone to seasickness or this would've been the vomit express." Lance took a swig from his water bottle.

"Mike had to hold me so tight I might have some bruised ribs, but at least he kept me from slamming into the canopy." Lisa rubbed her head.

"Hey, don't I get credit for holding your ankles?" Lance gave her legs a gentle squeeze.

"Uh, we're good back here too, not that anybody cares," Banger grumbled.

"Your boat captain cares." I turned and saluted them.

"That's better."

I steered us down the center of the river, and the current slowed to five knots, according to the gauge on the panel.

"Where do you think we are, Sam?" Mike scanned the riverbanks.

"The only waterfall near Lalibela is the Blue Nile Falls, which means our underground journey took us several thousand feet down to the Blue Nile River. All the *blue* names are encouraging. Maybe this river will take us to the Blue Dragon—if it's not the little sphere already in my bag."

"Hope springs eternal," Banger said with his usual sarcastic tone.

Sweetwater's Hideout

Deep rumblings dominated the night sounds around their cage.

"Well, now we know lions snore after a heavy meal." Ross lay on his back and looked up at a brilliant, star-filled sky.

"What do you think Sweetwater will do if Sam comes here?" Derek rolled onto his side and glanced at the remains of the earlier carnage. Small chunks of torn limbs were strewn around the lion pen—all that remained of the mercenaries who'd been tossed in a few hours before sunset.

"He'll probably make her watch while lions tear us apart. Then he'll kill her slowly and painfully."

Derek nudged him. "Bugger, don't sugarcoat it, mate."

Ross whispered, "Wouldn't it be great if Sam could control the lions the way she controlled the kraken?"

Derek shook his head. "That giant squid was scary as hell."

"Aye, but it obeyed Sam's commands." Ross yawned. "Maybe she can do the same with other animals."

"So, ask her to send a hundred lions to eat Sweetwater. I'd love to watch that." Derek rubbed dried blood spatter off his arm.

"Should I try to contact her again?" Ross glanced at him.

"May as well have a go. Might trigger a vision of where we are."

"All right, here goes nothing." Ross concentrated on mentally shouting Sam's name over and over.

EIGHT

Blue Nile River

"*S*am! Sam! Sam!*" Ross shouted telepathically.

"*Ross, I hear you. Where are you?*" I concentrated hard on sending a mental message.

A pause, then "*Sam! Sam! Sam!*" again.

Frustrated, I hated not being able to reach him.

A vision of Ross and Derek flashed into my head. They were trapped in a cage inside a lion pen. A pride of lions slept nearby amidst what looked like torn and chewed human body parts. The big cats were covered with blood. So were the men.

"Oh, god!"

Lisa reached forward and squeezed my shoulder. "What's wrong?"

"Ross contacted me telepathically, but he

couldn't hear my answer. Then I had a vision of him with Derek." I told her what I'd seen.

Mike leaned forward. "Where's the camp?"

"It was bordered by dense foliage." I bit my lip. "Could be almost anywhere in the jungle regions of Africa."

Something big bumped the underside of our craft, lifting us up a few feet and then sending us splashing down.

"What was that?" Banger strained to see over the side through the glass canopy.

"Did we hit a rock?" Lisa glanced around.

Another bump from underneath lifted the aft end of our boat and buried the bow in the water.

"That definitely wasn't a rock." Mike searched the water. "If we were on the ocean, I'd think it was a big shark."

"Oh geez, I just remembered the guidebook mentioned large colonies of hippos in this river." I peered into the dark water. "They're the most dangerous animals in Africa."

I looked up when a massive head rose in front of us. Its enormous mouth, at least two-feet wide, had a jaw-span of almost five feet when it was fully opened. Pointed tusks, some as long as sixteen inches, protruded from its menacing jaws and clamped down on the bow.

"Bugger! That hippo is trying to eat the boat," Lisa yelled.

"I read they can chomp down with a force of

two thousand pounds per square inch." Lance gripped the sidewall.

"Screw that!" Mike poked me. "Open the hatch so I can shoot it."

Before I could react, our boat rolled, lifted, and fell again as a pod of hippos repeatedly rammed our metal craft.

"A fifty-cal. would come in handy right about now." Bryce pounded the glass beside a hippo.

"We need a bigger boat,'" Banger said.

Another hard blow slammed me sideways. "It's like we're in a demolition derby, and we're losing."

Lisa squeezed my arm. "Open the hatch and shoot the buggers."

I looked around at the angry pod of hippos. "If I open the canopy, we might sink before we can shoot them all. Our nine-mil Sigs might not kill them, but their tusks can definitely kill us."

A bullet glanced off our canopy.

Banger yelled, "Heads up, people. There's an inflatable boat full of mercenaries on our six."

Mike glanced behind. "Dammit, Sam, open the canopy so we can return fire!"

Water sloshed over the clear canopy as we rocked and rolled under the fierce assault from the beasts in the water.

"Opening it could be disastrous." Another beast knocked me sideways.

"Sis, if you've got a better idea, let's hear it."

Mike jabbed my shoulder when another bullet pinged off the starboard side. "And make it fast!"

"Duck down while I try to command the hippos like I controlled the kraken."

"Hurry, this boat probably isn't bulletproof." Mike slid down in his seat, and Lisa leaned forward with her head down beside my seat.

I slouched down, closed my eyes, and concentrated on making a telepathic connection with the ferocious beasts ramming us. Meanwhile, more bullets pinged off our metal craft.

In moments, the pounding stopped. Two hippos began pushing our boat, and our speed tripled.

I glanced back and spotted the rest of the pod attacking the inflatable boat. Their violent assault sent men flying into the water. Jaws full of deadly tusks opened wide and crushed the swimmers as their boat foundered. Meanwhile, our boat pulled away, thanks to our animal-powered propulsion.

"Well done, sis." Mike checked behind us. "Looks like the hippos are taking out the mercs for us."

"Nice to have the big fellas on our side now." Lance high-fived me.

I waited until we rounded a curve in the river. No one pursued us on the water, so I sent our helpers away and used my key to open the canopy. A cool breeze caressed my sweaty face.

"Whew, that was exciting." Bryce turned and

looked behind us. "Nobody there. Our giant friends must've sunk them."

I pulled out my military satellite phone and held it up. "It wasn't a coincidence those soldiers found us. My guess is somebody on Sweetwater's payroll bugged our SATCOMs."

My teammates stared at the phone.

Lisa reached over my shoulder. "Give it to me. I'll check." She took it apart and found the bug.

"Aha!" She held up the tiny device and dropped it in the river. Moments later, my phone was back together. "Here." Lisa handed it to me.

"Better check mine too." Mike handed her his SATCOM.

It wasn't long before Lisa dropped another bug overboard and reassembled his phone.

"Well, that solves one mystery." Mike pocketed his SATCOM. "But I wish we knew who bugged our phones."

Banger pounded the sidewall. "I don't like this. We need to know who we can trust."

"Sweetwater's billions open a lot of doors." Bryce shook his head. "No telling how many military people he bribed."

I looked back at my friends. "I know one thing —I trust my teammates. Everyone else is suspect."

"Right, so we'll keep a tight lid on our plans going forward." Mike glanced at the team.

I was so distracted by our conversation that I failed to pay attention to our forward progress on the river. Our strange watercraft jolted us when it bumped against an embankment at the end of a short, narrow side channel. We had landed inside a natural boat dock.

I checked the area. "Ride's over. Everybody out." I waited while my team exited.

Bryce and Banger climbed out and then reached in for Lisa. Mike and Lance followed. After I stepped out, the hatch closed. A loud hiss and bubbling water in front of the bow pushed the escape boat back into the river. In seconds, it submerged, disappearing under the dark water.

"Whoa—where did it go?" Mike scanned the water.

"Heck if I know." I checked our surroundings one more time. "Let's figure out where *we* are."

I pulled out the Eye of Atlantis and held it in my right hand. It projected a hologram of a huge stone statue of the goddess Isis with green emeralds embedded in her eyes and a large gold medallion mounted on the center of her headband. She appeared to be underwater.

"Nice statue." Lisa pointed at the water surrounding Isis. "It had better not be in *this* river."

"If it is, the hippos can have it." I glanced up the rocky bank as I stowed the Eye. "Let's look for a ride back to the base."

"Yeah, if we call for evac, the wrong people might show up." Banger climbed a few feet up the rocks and surveyed the river.

Sweetwater's Hideout

Sweetwater exhaled a cloud of blue-gray smoke from his Cohiba cigar and reached for a bottle of vintage brandy. A gas-powered generator kept his air-conditioned office and living quarters cool in the hot, humid jungle. He poured Armagnac Fauchon into two snifters and handed one to the man in command of his mercenary army. "Arkady, what brings you to my camp so late at night?" Sweetwater swirled his brandy in the crystal goblet.

Sweat beaded on the Russian's forehead as he the downed the drink and wiped his mouth with the back of his hand.

"General, you're behaving like a cretin. Fine brandy is meant to be savored. What's bothering you?"

"We lost boat team on Blue Nile River."

Sweetwater paused mid-sip. "What happened?"

Even though the room was cool, Arkady dabbed sweat from his face with a cotton kerchief. "My men tracked team on river. They were in strange metal boat under attack by hippos."

"What did your men do?"

"Fired at hippos—tried to scare them off, but entire pod attacked inflatable boat." He wiped his sweaty hands on his camouflage fatigues. "Soldiers sent Mayday text before boat sank. Since then, no contact."

Sweetwater drained his glass and slammed it on the table. "What about the woman and her team?"

The Russian recoiled. "GPS trackers in their satellite phones went dead ten minutes after Mayday text. Two helicopters with floodlights will arrive on site in three hours and search river."

Sweetwater bit his cigar in half, and the lit end fell onto the floor. He spit out the end stuck in his mouth and stomped on the lighted stub. "Are you saying there were no survivors in either boat?"

"Choppers will search for survivors." The general glanced at his watch. "Will be easier to search in daylight, but sunrise is eight hours from now."

"I can't believe your team of heavily armed commandos was bested by a pod of hippos. You'd better pray Samantha Starr survived. She's essential to my plan for revenge, and you *know* how I feel about vengeance. Do whatever it takes to capture her unharmed. Understand?"

The general wiped his sweaty hands on his pants again and stood. "*Da*, my men will find her." He hurried to the door.

"And bring me whatever's in that little leather pouch she carries," Sweetwater yelled.

The vindictive little man watched the commander of his private army climb the stairs to the treetop helipad.

If you fail me, you're a dead man.

Blue Nile River

Crickets and frogs made their nightly calls as I scanned the water. "I don't see anybody."

"That's because sane people don't take boats through hippo territory, especially at night," Banger said with his usual sarcastic tone.

"You can bet Sweetwater will send helicopters to look for his team—and us." Mike searched the sky.

"Yeah, we'd better head inland before search teams scour the river." Banger climbed up the bank and waited for us.

Lance glanced down. "Time to reverse these white robes. Black is better, especially under a full moon in a clear sky."

Everyone agreed.

A light breeze stirred up the cold night air and carried the scent of the river.

Lisa rubbed her arms. "We'd better find shelter soon."

"Right." Bryce reversed his robe to black. "Let's get cracking."

"Don't forget to flip the turbans too." Lisa turned her turban inside out and stuffed her long red hair into the black cloth.

I made the color switch, slung the satchel carrying the silver-blue sphere over my right shoulder, and climbed up through the rocks. After reaching higher ground, I spotted a village in the distance along the riverbank. "Let's see if we can find transportation." I pointed. "That looks like a road."

"Good idea. We'll grab a ride and get the hell out of Dodge before more mercs show up." Mike led us toward the village.

Banger glanced at his watch. "It's after eleven. Most of the villagers should be asleep."

"We'll steal a vehicle and pay for it later." Lance patted my back. "Sam did that when she was on the run in Scotland, and it worked out okay."

"She saved nine noble bloodlines and prevented a war in Northern Ireland." Lisa high-fived me. "The authorities tend to be forgiving in situations like that."

Bryce checked his weapon. "Understood. Don't get caught, and put things right later."

"Sounds like a plan." I moved up beside Mike. "Somebody's bound to have a truck or van."

Twenty minutes later, we reached the dark village and listened.

Silence, except for the crickets.

Mike whispered, "Spread out and search for a vehicle."

A faint odor of horse manure hung in the air as I slipped into a barn on the outskirts of town. A big draft horse stuck his nose out of a stall and looked at me. A covered horse cart was parked nearby. It looked large enough to carry our team.

A low growl drew my attention to a dark corner. A medium-sized mongrel dog bared his teeth and crept closer. I reached under my robe and pulled a packet of beef jerky rations out of my padding.

"Here, boy, have some beef."

He snarled and bared his teeth as I tossed the dried meat in front of him.

The skinny dog kept growling as he sniffed my gift. Then he gulped it down, barely chewing it. I tossed him several strips of the cured meat.

While the dog was busy eating, I petted the huge black horse. Tall and muscular, he was bred for heavy work. I checked his water trough and feed bin. Plenty of water, but no food. Bales of hay were stacked nearby. I tore off a generous portion and dropped hay in his feed bin so he'd have plenty of energy in case we couldn't find motorized trans-portation.

Just when I was about to turn away from the horse, a strong arm wrapped around me, and the sharp edge of a machete pressed against my neck.

A deep voice said, "Move and you die."

I couldn't see the guy behind me, but his arms were massive, and his voice sounded like his mouth was a foot above my head.

NINE

Mike met up with the team. "Looks like this village is just a few small homes and barns. Anybody find a vehicle?"

"One horse, a bit on the skinny side." Lisa pointed. "Over there in that little barn."

"I found an old motorcycle, but the front tire's flat." Lance thumbed toward a small house with a shed alongside it.

Dogs barked from somewhere nearby.

Mike glanced from Banger to Bryce. "What about you guys? Find anything?"

Banger shook his head. "Nada."

Bryce spread his hands. "Sorry, nothing."

Lisa looked in every direction. "Where's Sam?"

Mike turned. "She went into a big barn when we spread out. It's back at the other end of the neighborhood."

"We'd better look for her." Banger searched the street. "She might be in trouble."

"*My* sister in trouble?" Mike said in a sarcastic tone.

"*Always*," Banger replied with even more sarcasm.

"We'd better hurry before those dogs wake everyone." Lance looked around.

"Too late." Bryce nodded at several male villagers approaching from all sides, clutching hoes and sickles.

"Keep your weapons hidden." Mike stood in the center of his team. "I'll do the talking."

An elderly man in tattered clothes stepped forward. He spoke in the local Oromo dialect and asked a question.

Mike shook his head. "English?"

The man gave a slight nod and turned to a younger man from the village. The man, who appeared to be in his early twenties, stood beside the elder. "I am John. Who you?"

"I'm Michael. We're religious tourists." He spread his arms toward his teammates, and they smiled and nodded. "We visited Lalibela and then took a boat trip on the Blue Nile. Our boat was attacked by hippos. We barely made it to shore before the boat sank."

"Why you look here?" John wore torn jeans and a thick cotton jacket.

"My brother is missing. We're trying to find

him. He's about this tall." Mike held his hand at chin level. "He loves horses. That's why we searched the barns. We need to check that one." Mike pointed at the big barn at the other end of the village.

The small group of locals conferred in their native language, sounding anxious.

John turned back to Mike. "Big barn is Nathaniel's. He no like strangers. We go with you."

The group hurried down the dirt lane. The elder took the lead when they approached the barn. He stepped inside first and shouted.

Everyone rushed in. A man almost as big as Banger held a machete to Sam's throat. Still in disguise with the beard and mustache, she looked like a frightened young man, her eyes wide.

"Stop!" Nathaniel tightened his arm around his victim.

Mike and the team froze, looking harmless with their weapons hidden under their robes.

Mike eased up beside John and the elder. "We mean no harm."

"Why he here?" The man with the machete directed the question to John.

John gestured at Sam. "He loves horses. Let him go, Nathaniel." John's voice wavered, obviously afraid of the much larger man holding the blade.

Mike carried our emergency funds and pulled out a wad of cash. "How much to rent your horse and cart for a few hours with you driving?"

Nathaniel hesitated, his eyes focusing on the money. "Now? Where you go?"

"Away from the river." Mike held out $2,000 in twenties. "Is there an airport nearby?"

The man pointed his machete in the direction of the ridge. "Grass airport six kilometers east." He released Sam and took the cash.

A thin line of blood traced across her neck where the blade had been. She kept silent.

"Any airplanes there?" Mike glanced at the machete.

"Old plane takes passengers and cargo. Pilot keeps it beside runway." He slipped the machete into a sheath hooked to his belt.

"Take us to the airport?" Mike pulled out more cash. "For the late hour."

"I take you, but pilot won't be there."

"We'll go and wait for the pilot. I'm Mike, and this is Banger." Banger stepped forward. "He'll ride up front with you, and I'll ride in your cart with my friends."

He nodded. "I am Nathaniel. Help push cart out."

The men shoved the cart out of the barn, and Nathaniel harnessed the horse to it. He climbed onto the wood seat.

Banger sat beside him and said, "All aboard."

Mike waved at the villagers. "Thank you." He joined the team in the covered cart.

I waited until we were inside the cart before I wiped the blood from the hairline cut on my neck. "That was close," I whispered.

Mike leaned in. "You okay?"

"Just a razor-thin cut. Thanks for handling things." I dabbed my neck with a tissue.

Curved roof ribs allowed us to sit comfortably beneath the canvas cover. I held the satchel on my lap. So far, the sphere hadn't moved, not even when I'd been attacked. Apparently, it wasn't meant to defend the bearer.

Nathaniel's dog jumped into the cart and snuggled between Lisa and Mike. He must've smelled meat on them. Lisa gave him a strip of beef jerky.

The huge horse pulled us at a steady but slow pace on a dirt road that wound through the valley away from the river.

Mike lifted the cover and peeked out the left side. "At least the full moon provides enough light to follow the road."

"And we don't have lights on the cart that would attract attention." Lisa looked outside.

I pulled out a map of Ethiopia and opened it to the Blue Nile region. "No harm in trying to find the airport."

"Good idea." Lance leaned in as I shined my mag light on the map.

"Hey, that looks like an airplane symbol." I tapped it. "What do you think?"

Lance studied the spot. "Looks like it's along that ridgeline on the eastern edge of this valley." He showed it to Mike. "I guess Nathaniel told the truth."

"Good, we don't want to be in the valley when the sun comes up." Mike lifted the front cover and checked on Banger. He and the driver seemed to be comfortable with each other.

"Don't worry, Buster will get us there." I patted Mike's arm.

Mike arched a brow. "Buster?"

"The horse—his name is carved on the stall door."

Bryce glanced out at the sky. "No helicopters."

We sat quietly as the cart rattled down the lane. I was half asleep when thundering rotor blades jolted me wide awake.

"Sweetwater's mercenaries are back." I peeked out the side. "Looks like they're coming from the northeast and heading for the river."

"Maybe they won't spot us." Bryce lifted the side cover a few inches. "Two choppers flying at top speed."

Mike peeked out the front. "Hey, Banger, how close are we to the ridgeline?"

"We're almost there. Maybe another mile."

One of the choppers peeled off and headed

straight for us. We pulled the cover down and hunkered inside the cart.

Banger said to Nathaniel, "Smile and wave when that helicopter gets closer."

The pilot circled as his spotlight bathed the horse cart in bright light. Buster whinnied and broke into a run.

Nathaniel yelled, "Whoa!" and hauled back on the reins as we peeked out at the departing chopper. Buster ignored his master and bolted, the cart rocking violently from side to side.

The helicopters descended on the river, their floodlights blazing.

"Good thing they don't have infrared scopes." Lisa gripped the sidewall. "I hope they take a long time searching the river."

My head hit a cover arch when Buster ran over a deep pothole. "That horse had better slow down before the cart breaks."

Nathaniel finally gained control of his frightened horse. Buster slowed to a trot and then a fast walk.

A few minutes later, Banger lifted the front cover. "Ride's over. Everybody out."

I jumped out and spotted a big cabin biplane tied down beside a grass-strip runway.

Banger shook Nathaniel's hand. "Thanks for the ride."

Mike reached up and handed Nathaniel another $500. "Forget you saw us and steer clear of those helicopters. We'll rest and wait for the pilot."

Nathaniel nodded and turned the horse back toward the village. His dog stayed in the cart.

I thumbed at the airplane. "That's an old twelve-passenger Russian Antonov AN-2. It lands at thirty mph."

"I saw one at an airshow." Lance patted the engine. "This thousand-hp radial engine and the bi-wings produce enough lift for short takeoff rolls, but there's no telling how old the engine is or if it's been properly maintained."

Mike stood, hands on hips, surveying the airplane. "The puddle of oil under the cowling might be a clue. Either of you ever flown one of these?"

"Radial engines always drip oil when they're parked. A friend of mine brought his AN-2 to an EAA airshow in Oshkosh." I checked the left main wheel. "He let me fly it."

"How does it handle?" Lance gripped the upper wing on the left side and gave it a tug.

"Slow and sluggish, like driving a heavy truck, but it takes off and lands in under a thousand feet." I grinned. "It's a hoot to fly."

"Check if it has enough fuel, and let's get airborne before those mercs come looking for us." Mike glanced toward the river. "Bryce and I will do a quick runway inspection."

I opened the cabin entry door on the port side just aft of the left wings and pulled down the folding steps. After walking up to the cockpit, I checked that all the switches were off and set the brakes before I joined Lance outside.

The airplane sat nose high with two balloon tires on the main wheels and a much smaller tailwheel in the back. Not willing to trust the fuel gauges, Lance hoisted me up to the top wings to shine a light into the fuel tanks. Airplane tanks were usually kept full, a common practice to avoid condensation.

"Tanks are full. Check the oil and then pull the prop through ten or fifteen times to distribute the oil in all nine cylinders before we start the engine." I picked up the sphere satchel, spun around, and headed for the entry door.

Lance turned. "You check the cockpit, and I'll do the walkaround."

Banger untied the airplane and pulled the wooden chocks away from the main wheels, while Lisa inspected the cabin.

I walked uphill again through the narrow aisle toward the cockpit. Rows of single wicker seats on the left and double seats on the right accommodated twelve passengers, and a large outdated radio bay filled the starboard side behind the cockpit bulkhead. Two steps in the front of the cabin led up to the open entry into the cockpit. I climbed into the pilot seat on the left side and hooked the satchel's straps over the left armrest.

Before I began the preflight checks, Lance

yelled up to me, "Engine needs oil. Keep the switches off while I check if there's a can in the baggage compartment."

I shined my light around the cockpit while I waited. Everything was labeled in Russian.

Lance rapped on the left side of the cockpit. "I found a gallon of oil and an aluminum stepladder. Give me a few minutes to add oil and pull the prop through."

I opened the side window. "I'll wait until you join me inside."

It took ten minutes for Lance to pull the prop through several times and put away the oil can and ladder.

He slid into the right seat. "Whoa, this cockpit looks ancient."

"Let's hope the engine is newer than it looks." I flipped some switches and ran through the usual cockpit preflight checks.

Mike and Bryce finished the runway inspection and entered the cabin.

"Runway looks good." Mike settled in a single seat in the front row.

Banger sat on a double seat near the front. "Cabin is secure."

"Everyone's on board, the airplane is buttoned up, and we're ready to roll," Lance said.

I yelled, "Clear!" and hit the starter. After a few coughs and sputters, the big radial engine rumbled to life. An exhaust pipe belched smoke on the starboard side until the engine settled into a smooth idle.

When I pushed the throttle forward and pulled onto the runway, the powerful Shvetsov engine and four-bladed prop sent vibrations into the cockpit, shaking my seat and rattling the controls.

The old biplane felt alive.

I did the usual pre-takeoff checks and taxied to the end of the grass runway. When I turned the airplane into the wind, I spotted the helicopters flying low over the river.

"Everyone ready?" I yelled over my shoulder and heard five affirmatives. "This'll be a low flight over the mountains to avoid detection. The choppers are only about five miles southwest of us."

I eased the throttle up to takeoff power and used the rudder pedals to keep us rolling straight ahead. The radial engine gave a deep, throaty roar as we bumped and bounced along the runway. I eased the yoke forward a little to lift the tailwheel off the ground. Seconds after that, I pulled the yoke back, and we were airborne.

Keeping the airplane in a shallow climb, I waited as the airspeed slowly increased. The noisy cockpit vibrated. Once we were at optimum climb speed, I pulled back on the yoke and climbed higher than the ridgeline. Then I added full right aileron and right rudder and waited. A second or two later, the airplane began a slow right turn over the ridge.

"See what I mean about the sluggish controls?" I glanced at Lance, who was on my right in the copilot seat.

"Yeah, but she was off the ground in no time." He studied the Russian instruments. "Look at this weird artificial horizon." He tapped a round gauge. "The sky is black, and the ground is white."

"Maybe it was meant for use in Siberia, where the ground is covered with snow, and the sky is dark a lot." I tapped another gauge. "This altimeter measures altitude in meters."

"I guess now would be a good time to discuss where we're going." Lance pulled out an aviation chart from a flight bag stored next to the copilot's seat. "At least this chart is in English."

"Thank god for international aviation rules requiring a standard language." I tapped the airspeed indicator. "Normal cruise speed is a hundred knots, but I'm pushing one-twenty to put some distance between us and those choppers."

"That'll affect our fuel consumption." Lance glanced at the fuel gauges.

"Find an uncontrolled airport about halfway to Camp Baledogle that has 100-octane avgas. We should maintain radio silence until we're close to home base."

Mike entered the cockpit. "Better do a three-sixty and see if the choppers are on our six."

"Okay, but that'll take a while." I looked out the port side window and turned the yoke to full left aileron as I added left rudder. Nothing happened at first, and then the airplane slowly banked left.

Lance pointed. "Dang! They're headed this way."

"Maybe they decided to take a closer look at the horse cart." Mike stared at the choppers. "If they spot Nathaniel alone, they might guess he transported us."

"And if they realize we took an airplane—" Lance craned his neck as I continued the 360-degree turn.

"I'll duck below the eastern side of the ridge and keep us out of sight until we have to climb over that mountain in the distance." I shoved the yoke forward to dive and waited as we hung in the air.

"Mike, get everyone in the cabin looking out the windows for those choppers. If they spot us, we're dead meat." I breathed easier when the airplane finally began a dive behind the ridgeline.

"Yeah, the helos can run circles around this old biplane, but don't get too low. Might be unlighted hazards out there." Lance surveyed the dark ridge.

"Microwave tower! The obstruction lights must be inop." I turned a hard right and prayed.

As usual, the airplane was slow to respond to my control inputs. Our left wingtips brushed past it, barely missing the metal structure.

"Dang, that was close." Lance glanced over his shoulder. "Anybody see a helicopter?"

"Yeah, they're searching the other side of the

ridge." Mike pointed. "I can see their floodlights on the trees."

I pushed the throttle to the stops. "I'll run at full throttle awhile and hope the engine holds together."

The vibrations in the cockpit increased along with the engine noise.

Lance patted the center console. "Hang in there, old girl." He studied the flight chart with his mag light. "I found a field with fuel a little over halfway to Baledogle." He tapped the compass. "Hold this heading, and we'll get there in about four hours."

"Sounds good." I scanned the dark horizon. "Keep your eyes peeled for obstructions."

TEN

Sweetwater's Hideout

Sweetwater held a satellite phone to his ear. "My new submarine vanished in Atlantis? Are you certain?"

A nervous voice on the other end said, "Yes, sir. There's been no communication in twenty-four hours, and the sonar on your yacht can't find it."

Sweetwater clenched his fist. "Tell them to send down the minisub."

"Uh, that might not be safe, sir. They've heard rumors of a sea monster that guards the city."

"*Sea monster*?" Sweetwater's voice hardened. "You fool. That rumor was spread to keep subs and Hardsuit divers away. Now launch that minisub and find my submarine."

"Yes, sir. Right away, sir. I'll call as soon as they find something."

———

Four hours later, Sweetwater received a call from *Invincible*, his two-hundred-foot yacht, anchored over Atlantis. "Yes, what did they find?"

"The minisub found *Pelagic Predator II* wedged between marble buildings. The hull is crushed and covered with cracks along its length. No survivors. The crew would be mush at that depth."

"Bloody hell! The Americans must have a new underwater weapon. Have the minisub search for Atlantis's Hall of Records."

"Uh, about that—more bad news." The tense voice hesitated. "We lost contact with the minisub a few minutes after they reported finding your submarine."

"Can you see them on sonar?" Sweetwater poured a generous portion of Glenglassaugh whisky and drank half of it.

"No ... nothing." He hesitated. "Wait, there's something huge on the sonar, and it's headed straight for us."

"A boomer? Russian or American?" Sweetwater asked, referring to the big nuclear subs that carried long-range missiles.

"No, it's ... it's ... aahhhh, noooo!" One final scream came through before the call cut off.

Sweetwater wouldn't accept that the line was dead. "Hello? Are you there?"

He paced a few minutes, thinking. *Bloody hell. Can't believe I lost my yacht and my new submarine.* He gulped his whisky. *Insurance will take care of my losses. A bigger problem is missing out on critical information in the Hall of Records that might lead me to the Blue Dragon. I need that power diamond, and there's only one option now.*

He called his contact at Camp Baledogle on the encrypted satellite phone. "Everything's changed. Have you heard from Samantha Starr?"

"Not yet. They disappeared inside a church in Lalibela and somehow ended up on the Blue Nile River."

"I know. My team followed them downriver where they were attacked by a pod of hippos—sank the RHIB and probably killed my men. I'm hoping Miss Starr escaped."

"I'll call as soon as I know something."

"If she survived, don't grab her. Instead, type these instructions and explain they were delivered by a stranger." Sweetwater dictated the message.

"Understood. I'll relay your ultimatum after her team checks in."

Antonov AN-2

Once we had plenty of distance between us and the choppers, I throttled back to normal cruise power. Four hours after takeoff, I landed the airplane at a small, uncontrolled airport a little over halfway to Camp Baledogle. It was 4:20 a.m., and we had to wait until 6:00 a.m. for the fueler to open for business. It was unlikely the airplane's owner would notice it missing in the middle of the night and notify all the airports, so we relaxed and enjoyed a nap.

After refueling and adding a gallon of oil, we were airborne again. This time, it was Lance's turn at the dual controls.

I checked the chart and glanced at him. "Hold this heading and one hundred and ten knots, and we'll be there in another four hours with this light tailwind."

Lance grinned. "I like flying this antique airliner —makes me feel like I went through a time warp."

The sun hovered over the eastern horizon as Mike stuck his head in the cockpit and grinned like a mischievous kid. "Are we there yet?"

"I wish." I glanced over my right shoulder at him. "Take a long nap and see if Lance can land without waking you."

Three hours later, the engine overheated and spit oil all over the windshield.

"Dang it!" Lance eased the throttle back to below normal cruise power.

"Try to nurse it back to Baledogle." I consulted

the chart. "The tailwind helped. We have less than an hour to go."

Thirty tense minutes passed before the engine began clanking and smoking. My seat vibrated so much it made my teeth chatter.

"Hang on a little longer, old girl." Lance patted the airplane.

Twenty miles from our destination, the engine belched huge clouds of black smoke and vibrated like a runaway coal-fired locomotive.

I turned and yelled back, "Strap in tight. We might not land on the runway."

"Come on baby, you can make it." Lance tried to coax the engine into lasting a few more minutes. He glanced at me. "I'll hold this altitude in case the engine fails."

"Good idea. You can always slip it down for the landing." I squinted through the oil-splattered windshield. "I think I see the runway a little to your left. Line up for a straight-in approach."

He leaned forward and peered through the oil. "Got it."

I called the tower at Camp Baledogle and gave them our team code. "We're in an old Russian biplane, an Antonov AN-2, so don't shoot us down. We're ten miles west on a straight-in for Runway Niner. Expect landing in five minutes." I glanced at Lance, and he nodded.

The controller said, "Are you the biplane trailing black smoke?"

"Affirmative. Notify the fire trucks."

"Understood. Antonov is cleared to land on Runway Niner."

Two minutes later, the engine clanked louder, then seized. Flames burst from the right side, and smoke seeped into the cockpit.

I coughed and called the tower. "Antonov is on fire and landing dead-stick."

"Understand engine failed. Fire trucks are standing by. Antonov is cleared to land on Runway Niner."

Lance put the airplane in a shallow glide until he was certain we could reach the runway.

"Time for a steep slip." He selected cross controls and slipped the airplane in a left-wings-down sideways descent toward the runway. The sideslip temporarily kept the flames and smoke away from the cockpit and allowed him a better view out the left side window.

Close to the pavement, Lance straightened the airplane, made a smooth touchdown, and rolled to a stop. He set the brake. "Everybody out!"

I had already turned off all the appropriate switches. The airplane was still and silent, but my body kept vibrating as I grabbed the satchel holding the sphere and bolted from the cockpit.

Lance ran close behind me as the fire trucks doused the flames.

I stopped fifty feet from the Antonov and turned

to him. "Well, that was quite an experience." I hugged him. "Great landing."

The late-morning heat and humidity enveloped us. Sweat covered my body under my clothes, padding, and heavy robe. The fire-heated cockpit hadn't helped.

He leaned in and coughed. "I could really use a good long sleep. How about you?"

"I can barely keep my eyes open, but I'd like to have breakfast first so my stomach doesn't wake me later." My belly rumbled. "Let's hurry into that air-conditioned conference room."

"The base commander will want an after-action report. Keep it short and simple. My gut's howlin' for some chow."

I poked Lance. "Hey, that's the Starr Corporation's G650 parked over there."

Lance smiled. "I knew we could count on them. They'll do anything for your family."

We straggled into the briefing room and settled around the conference table with our teammates. The satchel holding the sphere lay motionless on my lap.

The base commander sat at one end of the table, and our friend, Commander Robert Metz from Navy Intelligence, sat at the other end. He didn't look happy. Bob waved a printed paper at me. "I was told a soldier got this from a civilian who was paid to deliver it here to Samantha Starr."

"Me? What does it say?" I had a feeling it wasn't good news.

"The message is from Lord Edgar Sweetwater. It reads: 'Samantha, I have Captain Ross Sinclair and Lieutenant Derek Dunbar. Deliver the Blue Dragon to me within seven days from now or I'll feed your boyfriend and his buddy to my hungry lions. You'll receive delivery instructions later.'"

I glanced at my alarmed teammates.

The base commander leaned forward. "Blue Dragon? Is that some sort of weapon?"

Probably worried about her boyfriend Derek, Lisa bit her lip. "We might have it. Sam, show the commanders what we found in that underground chamber."

My team slid their chairs back when I unzipped the canvas satchel.

Noting my teammates' apprehension, Bob asked, "Is that thing safe?"

"I'll keep it pointed at the ceiling just in case." I pulled out the silver-blue sphere. "There's a long, blue marquise diamond inside mounted vertically, and it fires a laser."

Bob looked at me. "Is it a weapon, like that pyramid sculpture you found in Hong Kong?"

I nodded. "Both artifacts have powerful laser beams."

The base commander focused on it. "Is the round casing made of anodized aluminum?"

Banger couldn't resist saying, "Sam said it might be a rare metal she calls unobtainium."

I glared at the big guy. "He's joking, but the device could be the Blue Dragon. Let me call Harvard Professor Ben Armitage and verify it. He's an expert on ancient artifacts."

Bob and the base commander nodded.

I dialed Ben's number on my satellite phone and put it on speaker. When he answered, I said, "Hi, Ben, it's Sam. No time for chit-chat. I need your expertise on a life-or-death matter concerning an ancient artifact. Do you know anything about something called the Blue Dragon hidden somewhere in Africa?"

"Well, hello to you too, Sam. I've been consulting with the Pentagon on those Atlantean archives you recovered. The translation program you helped them set up has proved invaluable. The government asked me to help them search the archives for mention of more weapons of mass destruction that Atlanteans may have hidden around the world." He hesitated. "I recall reading about something called the Blue Dragon. Hold on while I consult my notes."

We waited a few minutes.

"Ah, here it is: a fail-safe project the Atlanteans called the Blue Dragon, which was intended to ensure their future. The description is vague except for a blue, two-foot-long, marquise-shaped power diamond, similar in size to the power diamonds in the two halves of the Poseidon's Sword WMD."

"Could it need an unusual key to operate it, like the artifact I found in Hong Kong for Poseidon's Sword?" I stroked the shiny, silver-blue sphere.

"It's possible, Sam. Did you find something like that?"

"We found a sphere in a circular chamber eight hundred feet beneath a church in Lalibela, Ethiopia. It's ten inches in diameter and made of an unknown silver-blue metal. And it has a portal that opens above a long, blue marquise diamond that shoots a powerful laser beam. Oh, and it flies on its own at great speed without making a sound."

I glanced at Bob. His jaw dropped.

"How do you know that?" Ben asked, his tone incredulous.

"I saw it do those things. The laser activated shortly after I touched the tip of the diamond." I explained everything I'd seen. "It seems I'm the only one who can touch the sphere without getting shocked." I glanced at both commanders, who stared at me, mouths agape. Was it my fake facial hair or the silver-blue ball?

"Sounds like it may be an important component of the Blue Dragon device. Better keep it with you when you search." Ben paused. "I flagged every reference to any Queen of Atlantis. There's something that might help you find that weapon. I don't know precisely where it's hidden, but the scrolls say there's a gold cylinder in Thonis-Heracleion that will guide the Queen of Atlantis to the location of the Blue Dragon."

"And where is Thonis-Heracleion?"

"Ah, it was an ancient city built around the twelfth century BC near the Canopic mouth of the Nile, thirty-two kilometers northeast of Alexandria."

"Are you saying I can drive there?"

"Not now. After a combination of earthquakes, tsunamis, rising sea levels, and a severe flood, the clay ground rapidly liquefied, causing the buildings to submerge." He paused. "The city sank beneath the Mediterranean Sea at the mouth of the Nile. Its ruins are currently located in Abu Qir Bay, thirty feet underwater approximately two and a half kilometers off the coast. Frank Goddio's team found it twenty years ago and is slowly excavating the site, bringing up huge statues intact, gold coins, and artifacts."

"Have they recovered the item I need?"

"Not yet. I've been keeping abreast of their discoveries—lots of exciting finds. I doubt they know about the cylinder." He paused. "I visited the site last year, and it's well guarded, so I suggest you sneak in underwater late at night. Chances are the artifact will be where powerful ley lines intersect."

"Thanks for your help, Ben. I hope this works out."

"My pleasure, Sam. Call me if there's anything else I can do." He disconnected.

I placed the sphere back inside the satchel. "We'll need breakfast and sleep before we go scuba diving in Egypt. I saw the corporate Gulfstream parked at the airfield. Is the crew rested?"

"They arrived yesterday evening, and the jet is fueled and ready." Bob glanced at the base commander. "Now that there's a possible WMD involved, your team will get priority—whatever you need to find the Blue Dragon. Obviously, you won't hand it over to Lord Sweetwater."

"No, but we'll need a plan to make it seem like I'm delivering it to him. We have to save Ross and Derek."

"If you find it within the allotted time, we'll figure something out. I suggest you bring along whatever equipment you may need to explore other locations in addition to the dive site." Bob hesitated. "I can see you're exhausted. You and Lisa might want to remove your beards and mustaches before breakfast. Shower and change clothes while I handle the details. You can sleep in the reclining seats on your jet. That way you'll get to Alexandria in time for a night dive."

Mike jotted down several items. "Here's our necessary equipment list. Any chance DARPA has underwater night-vision goggles?"

Bob nodded. "I'll have them send three on a

fast-mover for you, Banger, and Sam. The rest of your team should remain topside and keep watch."

"Thank you." Mike turned to the base commander. "Sir, will you make arrangements to compensate the AN-2's owner and help him get his airplane repaired?"

"I'll take care of it." He glanced at Lisa. "Can you get new diplomatic passports for the team and the corporate pilots?"

"No problem. The embassy in Mogadishu can make new ones easily now that we're in their database. I'll send them photos of the pilots. I'd better use their real names so the passports match their pilot licenses."

"Their names are Captain Bill Hiller and First Officer Laura Burke. You'll find them in the mess hall." The base commander stood. "Team dismissed."

ELEVEN

Sweetwater's Hideout

Sweetwater's voice blared on the loudspeaker in Ross and Derek's cage. "I'd hate for you to get bored, so I've arranged a show for you—another man who failed me. Consider this a preview of coming attractions, starring you."

Ross stood and whispered to Derek, "Not again."

"Looks that way," Derek whispered. "Sweetwater's a sick bastard."

"True, but I don't think he's keeping us alive just to prolong our angst about becoming dinner." Ross paused when guards shoved a naked man through the entry gate for the lion pen.

His hands were tied behind his back, and his

chest and belly bled from numerous shallow wounds.

"Hey, I recognize him." Ross squinted in the afternoon sun. "Aye, that's Arkady Baranov, Sweetwater's general."

"Looks like he's about to be permanently demoted." Derek moved closer to the bars.

"Why haven't his soldiers killed Sweetwater?" Ross shook his head. "There can't be any loyalty to a man like that."

Derek rubbed his thumb against his fingers. "It's all about the money. As long as he pays top dollar, they'll stay and roll the dice."

Lions closed in on the bleeding Russian, and he made a run for the cage in the center of the pen. He'd almost reached the bars when a lioness pounced on his back and shredded his flesh with her claws. His shrill screams were short-lived.

Goosebumps covered the Scotsmen. They turned away as blood from Arkady's severed artery sprayed the cage.

Ross clenched his fists. "I hope a lion tears Sweetwater to shreds."

Thonis-Heracleion

Running lights on guard boats patrolling the archaeological site, combined with reflections from a starry sky and a bright full moon, shimmered on the calm water of Abu Qir Bay.

Warm air swirled around me as I zipped up my neoprene wetsuit and studied the full facemask newly developed by DARPA. "Guys, I love this mask—night vision combined with a voice-activated microphone."

Mike nodded. "The underwater dig is only a mile and a half from shore, but it's spread out over a wide area." He checked the dive gear and loaded the special vest-mounted rebreather air tanks into the boat. "Good thing we have the GPS coordinates for that intersection of ley lines."

"With any luck, we won't need these lights with the night-vision masks." Banger clipped dive lights on the buoyancy-compensator vests. "And our rebreather units won't leave bubbles for the guards to spot."

"I just hope we won't need to dig." Mike fingered his mask. "The water is clear now, but the instant we disturb the silt, visibility will go to zero."

I glanced out over the dark water as I pulled on my dive gloves. "The cylinder was meant to be found by an Atlantean queen, so it has to radiate energy that can be felt. Otherwise, I may never find it." I zipped the Eye into a side pocket on my BC vest.

Mike handed me some unusual-looking bags. "These are tactical lift bags. You shove the U-shaped cuff around an enemy's ankle and squeeze it together to lock it. The lock triggers a CO_2 cartridge that instantly inflates the bag and yanks the bad guy feet-first to the surface." He grinned. "The Navy uses these to interdict enemy divers trying to sneak into our submarine bases."

"It's always fun to have a new toy." I clipped a lift bag to my vest.

Lance patted one of the two 400-hp Mercury outboard motors mounted on the stern. "These babies will outrun those guard boats—probably make seventy knots or more."

"We'd better anchor about a half mile outside the restricted area so guards don't spot the dive gear." Lisa pointed off to the side of a lighted buoy.

Mike stepped aboard and slipped into his BC vest, then glanced at Banger and me. "I want us ready to go over the side the moment the boat stops. Bryce will monitor our comms, and Lisa and Lance will keep watch." He turned to Bryce. "If you have to leave us to maintain your fishing cover, do it. We can always swim a mile and a half to shore."

I climbed aboard, donned my dive gear, and clipped a waterproof pouch holding the sphere to the front of my BC vest. Then I sat along the side rail and pulled on my fins. "Lovely night for a dive. Should be fun."

"Why are you taking that thing on the dive?" Mike edged away from me on the seat.

"We don't want to risk losing it." I set the bagged device on my lap and stared at it. "It's been dormant since I started carrying it. I'm worried if I leave it behind, it might decide to fly away."

"Then don't swim directly behind me in case it decides to turn on the laser again." Mike gave the bag a sideways glance and checked his weapons.

Something big disturbed the water nearby, leaving a trail of ripples.

Banger sat across from me. "This'll be a lot easier than diving in Atlantis. No megalodons or krakens in these shallow waters." He scanned the Mediterranean Sea on the dark horizon. "Could be sharks." He handed me a ballistic speargun.

Lisa cracked open the breach on her rifle as Lance shoved us away from the pier. Bryce shifted into forward gear and eased the throttles up to the stops, the marine engines roaring as we raced into the bay. I grabbed the side rail as we skimmed over the calm water. The wind helped cool my wet-suited body in the warm Egyptian air.

When we neared our chosen drop point, Mike signaled for us divers to do a communications check with each other and with Bryce on the surface radio.

I twisted the knob that opened my rebreather tank's air valve and donned the full facemask.

"Testing, one, two, three," Bryce said, followed by Mike, Banger, and me responding.

The dive team agreed everyone came through loud and clear.

I pulled off my mask, turned off the air, and waited as sweat trickled down my back under the hot wetsuit.

"After we enter the water, the boat will ease up as close as possible to the restricted area, and the surface team will pretend to fish." Mike tapped his mask. "Our DARPA comm system has a thousand-foot range, which is farther than civilian comms, but even at a shallow depth, we'll be out of range with the dive boat for most of our dive."

A few minutes later, Mike looked at Banger and me. "Dive in ten seconds."

We turned on our air and fitted our masks as the boat coasted to a stop. I sat on the rail, clipped a speargun to my vest, and rolled backward into the bay. Cool water invaded my wetsuit, giving me instant relief from the heat as I descended and paused a few seconds to clear my ears.

In moments, Mike and Banger were at my side.

"The bottom is at thirty feet, and we don't want to stir up the silt, so maintain fifteen feet on the way there. I'll lead." Mike checked us over before he swam ahead.

"Copy that, brother dear." I liked that we were able to talk to each other via the comm units inside our full facemasks.

We set out in a V-formation with me on Mike's left and Banger on his right.

We'd covered about a thousand yards when the sphere seemed to come alive. The bag holding it jerked in front of me, straining against the two-foot tether. I grabbed the line as the device pulled me forward and accelerated. My body twisted from side to side as the speed increased.

When I zoomed past him, Mike yelled, "Sam, what's happening?"

"The sphere is pulling me really fast, but I don't know where or why."

"Hang on and we'll try to track you." Mike's voice was fading.

"I hope it's pulling me to the ley-line intersection we plotted."

"Try to stay low and out of view from surface boats." Mike's voice sounded fainter.

"Maybe I'll meet you with cylinder in hand." Despite my best efforts, my tone radiated fear.

"Right, because everything's always easy when you're involved," Banger said, his sarcastic voice fading too.

"Hey, I'm doing my best." I gripped the tether tightly as the globe increased speed, the water blurring around me. In seconds, I was out of comm range.

Nearby outboard motors made deep rumbling noises as I entered the guarded area. *Wish I knew where this thing was going.*

Huge statues of pharaohs, gods, and goddesses rose up out of the bottom silt in a macabre reminder of an ancient disaster. Most of the sculptures seemed intact, all trapped in the port city that had sunk into the sea thousands of years ago. Columns covered in Egyptian hieroglyphics marked the remains of government buildings and temples.

Even though my team probably couldn't hear me, I said, "Almost there—I hear guard boats." I winced when the artifact pulling me made a sharp zigzag to miss a big statue, and my body glanced off the side of the stone sculpture.

I had barely recovered from my painful collision when the round device stopped in front of an enormous stone head and torso depicting the goddess Isis. My momentum caused me to slam into the statue. I recognized her from the image the Eye had shown me on the bank of the Blue Nile River. Her lower half was still buried in silt. Judging by the proportions, she had to be at least twenty feet tall.

The satchel holding the silver-blue globe floated in front of me, and the tether was still secured to my vest. *Am I safe now? Is it dormant again?*

The huge face in front of me looked serene. Isis wore a headband embedded in the stone with a four-inch-diameter gold medallion in its center. Giant emeralds formed her eyes.

My head tingled, sensing the electromagnetic energy emanating from her. I was about to touch her face when the sphere switched on its laser and fired through the waterproof bag, zapping the center of the gold medallion.

Just one quick blast of energy, then the laser extinguished.

I shut my eyes the instant the laser flashed on, but stars blazed across my vision for a few minutes because the night-vision facemask magnified the light. When my sight had recovered, I stared into an opening in Isis's forehead. The medallion had been a hatch, opened by the laser.

I took a breath. Gold gleamed inside, bathed in a faint glow from an unseen light source.

Geez, I hope I didn't activate a timer on an explosive device. Why is it glowing inside?

I sucked in a breath and eased my mask close to the hole. A two-inch-diameter gold cylinder six inches long lay inside—possibly the very object Ben had sent me to retrieve.

I prayed it wouldn't hurt me when I reached in and grabbed it. My hands tingled through the dive gloves as I pulled it out. Worried about dropping it in the silt, I zipped it inside my wetsuit between my breasts.

Hope the bright laser didn't alert anyone to my presence.

Satisfied I'd found what I came for, I turned to swim away.

A diver swam straight at me with a speargun aimed at my heart. Good thing the air in rebreather units lasted longer than regular air tanks because I inhaled at least ten minutes of air in one gasp. Frozen with my hands up, I tried to look harmless. The man with the speargun eased closer, and I did my best not to gulp air.

I needed a distraction, so I half-turned and pointed at the dimly lit opening in the statue's head. The diver spotted the hole, surprise registering on his face. When he focused his attention on the golden glow inside, I dropped down, clamped a lift-bag on his left ankle, and locked it. Instantly, the bag inflated and yanked him upside down to the surface. At this shallow depth, he'd be okay as long as he didn't hold his breath. I had to save myself, but I didn't want to hurt him for just doing his job.

He tried to shoot me, but he was dragged away before he had time to aim, and his spear zipped past me. He wouldn't be able to remove the cuff, but he could deflate the bag with his dive knife once he reached the surface. It wouldn't take long for him to return, so I swam away as fast as I could. Too bad the sphere didn't activate again and propel me back the way I'd come.

Chances were the diver would return with a few buddies. I didn't want to end up dead or locked in an Egyptian prison.

I swam faster.

After a few minutes of hard kicking, I heard Mike's frantic voice, faint in the distance. "Sam, don't come back this way. We're under attack by a giant crocodile!"

Oh, crap! I continued swimming in their direction. *Maybe I can gain control of it.*

"Gotta be a twenty-footer," Banger yelled, sounding a little louder now.

"Hang on while I try to take control of the croc." I searched ahead, trying to spot them. "We might need it. Enemy divers will be here any second."

"We'll head toward you in the boat." Bryce's voice sounded faint in the distance.

"No, you'll get in a shootout with the guards," I yelled. "Meet us at the dock."

A spear brushed past me, and I swam faster. It was difficult concentrating on an unseen crocodile with so much going on. Nile crocs were known for being aggressive, and they could live up to a hundred years. Plenty of time to grow huge and nasty.

Up ahead, the water churned as I came in range of the underwater battle. Mike and Banger clung to the monster's back, their arms and legs wrapped around it, avoiding its sharp teeth and claws and its powerful tail. Blood trailed from several places on the men where the croc's sharp, rough hide had torn their wetsuits and scraped their skin.

The beast rolled its huge body and thrashed its massive tail, trying to dislodge them.

Water currents created by the crocodile's violent movements buffeted me as I eased closer and struggled to telepathically contact the huge reptile.

A quick glance behind me revealed four armed divers closing in. They were so focused on catching me, they didn't seem to notice the giant predator.

Ahead, the croc moved with such force, Mike

and Banger were unable to stab or shoot it. They had to hang on with all their strength.

The monster turned and headed straight for me, its giant jaws snapping.

TWELVE

Still focused on gaining control of the beast, I held my position, my breath coming in short spurts. A quick glance behind me revealed that the divers on my six had frozen.

I clutched the bag with the sphere against my pounding chest and concentrated as hard as I could. The vicious reptile was two feet away when it turned and swept past me, sharp teeth lining its bone-crushing jaws. Mike and Banger were still clinging to its back.

My new buddy closed in on the enemy divers, made a sudden turn, and swatted them with a quick snap of its powerful tail. The impact sent them tumbling backward.

The croc glided next to me and paused.

Oh boy, am I really getting on this beast?

I hesitated, then straddled it behind its neck. "Hang on, guys."

"Like we have a choice." Banger sounded breathless.

Our ride zoomed through the water toward shore, blurring my view. No way the other divers could catch us now. My guess was they weren't getting paid enough to tangle with the legendary denizen of the Nile.

We reached the marina in a few minutes and climbed off our reptile taxi a few feet from where our team waited on the bank. They stepped back and drew their weapons.

"That bloody croc is huge." Bryce took aim at its head.

"Stand down. He's on our side." I stepped in front of the reptile.

Bryce held his ground. "That's not what Mike and Banger said."

"That was before Sam got control of it." Mike glanced back at the open water. "We had four divers after us, and they're bound to contact the authorities soon."

I sent the beast back in the direction of the divers to buy us time for a getaway. Its instructions were to scare them away.

Sirens blared in the distance.

"Hurry, we have to get out of here before cops close off the marina." I unzipped the Eye from my BC and shoved it into my wetsuit where I'd put the canister, unclipped the bag holding the sphere, then slipped out of my dive vest and handed the scuba gear to Lance.

Lisa pulled the Range Rover close by while Bryce and Lance helped load the dive gear. We tossed everything in the back and piled into the SUV.

"Step on it." Mike scanned the marina.

Lisa burned rubber out of the parking lot. I didn't breathe easy until we pulled onto the highway, headed for the airport.

I pulled a first aid kit out of a duffel bag and handed it to Mike. "You and Banger should bandage the cuts on your arms and legs before we get to the airport."

"Well? Did you get it?" Lance looked at me.

I unzipped my wetsuit and handed him the gold cylinder. "Hold this while I wiggle out of this hot neoprene." I set the Eye on my seat and pulled off my dive gloves.

"Whoa." Lance juggled the cylinder like a live grenade. "Is it safe?"

"Did it zap you?" Banger checked Lance's hands.

"No, but I never know what to expect from the stuff Sam finds." He held it at arm's length.

I struggled out of the wetsuit and pulled on a T-shirt and shorts over my bikini. "Maybe I shouldn't handle it until we get to a secure location."

"Why? What's it going to do?" Lance looked at me, his tone tense.

"I'm afraid if I hold it in my bare hands, it'll pop open and blast somebody with a laser or do something equally unpleasant." I checked the bag with the silvery globe inside. "The sphere's laser shot a hole through the waterproof bag and unlocked a hatch hiding the cylinder."

I opened the bag and peered at the silvery-blue ball. "It seems fine. I guess it's waterproof." Covering my right hand with part of my T-shirt, I slipped the Eye back into its leather pouch, which was tied to a belt loop on my shorts. "I don't know how many more of these weird artifacts I can carry." The gold medallion on its chain was still hanging around my neck.

Lance glanced at Mike, Banger, and me. "Care to explain the twenty-foot crocodile you guys rode to shore? Nile crocs aren't supposed to be this far north."

"Just goes to show you can't always believe what you read." Banger looked at me and grinned. "I just found a story on my smartphone about crocodiles invading Cairo."

"All I know is Sam's telepathic ability with animals really came in handy." Mike patted my back.

Lisa turned onto a remote two-lane dirt road, then pulled over and stopped the SUV about a mile from the highway. "Sam, you'd better find out what that thing does before we take it on an airplane."

Mike nodded. "Give it to her, Lance."

"Wait." I stepped outside, and a warm breeze ruffled my wet hair as crickets chirped nearby.

Lance thrust the gold artifact at me through an open window.

I hesitated, not certain what would happen. The instant my bare hands held the device, it made a strange humming sound, and the end popped open. I jumped back and turned away from the car, worried it might zap something.

Nothing happened.

"Hand me a flashlight."

I grabbed a mag light with my left hand and shined it into the opening. A thin strip of gold, an inch wide and almost the length of its container, lay inside. I held the light in my mouth as I tilted the cylinder and slid the metal strip into my open hand. Atlantean words were engraved on it.

I memorized the message and replaced the strip.

"It's not a weapon." I climbed into the SUV. "Let's hurry to the airport and get the heck out of Egypt."

"What was inside?" Mike glanced at the artifact.

"A metal strip with a message on it." I shoved the container inside my backpack.

"Did it say where to find the Blue Dragon?" Lisa looked over her shoulder at me.

"Yeah, but we need to figure it out first." I sighed. "Translated, it says, 'The Blue Dragon lies in the Dark Continent, ensconced in an arid enigma and a primordial paradox, cloaked in eternal darkness. Save them.'"

"What does that mean?" Bryce looked at me. "And save who?"

"Beats me. The first message I received before I left my condo also ended with the command, 'Save them.' I thought it meant save Ross and Derek, but maybe I misunderstood it."

"It's in eternal darkness?" Banger arched a brow. "Maybe it's in Hell or whatever the Atlantean equivalent of that might be."

"Geez, I hope not." Mike glanced at me. "I bet it's in a cave."

"And we know how much Sam likes caves." Banger grinned in my direction.

I gave him an exaggerated eye roll.

"Run it past Professor Armitage." Lance patted my knee. "He might know what this mumbo jumbo means."

"Good idea." I gazed out the window as we pulled onto the highway. "I'll wait until we're airborne and call Ben on the satellite phone."

"Better call him now." Bryce shrugged. "We don't want to fly away only to discover it's in Egypt."

I pulled out the SATCOM and dialed. When Ben answered, I dived right into our problem and recited the message, then waited a few seconds for him to process it. "Any ideas on the location?"

"Hello again, Sam, and yes, several ideas come to mind. Arid enigma must refer to something puzzling in a desert—could be the Great Sphinx or the Great Pyramid of Giza. There are spaces inside both that are always in darkness, and my study of the Atlantean records you recovered indicate both sites are over ten thousand years old, not the forty-five hundred years claimed by Egypt."

"That would mean they weren't built by the Egyptians. Are the Atlanteans claiming they built them?" My mind raced.

"Yes, and they also claim they stored copies of many of the documents from their primary Hall of Records in a chamber under the right front paw of the Great Sphinx."

"But what about the primordial paradox? Neither site dates back that far."

"True, but info about that might be hidden inside the Great Pyramid or in a chamber under one of the front paws of the Sphinx." Ben paused. "Or … perhaps it's referring to the Lost Sahara Civilization … or possibly the Cradle of Humankind."

My voice rose an octave. "I hope it's not in the Sahara. That desert is as big as the entire continental USA, and the lost civilization must cover a vast area buried beneath tons of sand."

"Relax, Sam, maybe the Blue Dragon is in a desert cave that never sees the sun." Ben's voice conveyed a soothing tone.

"What about the Cradle of Humankind?" I tried not to sound frustrated. "Where's that?"

"Actually, there are two possible locations. Ethiopia claims it's in the vicinity of Hadar, a village in the northeastern part of the country on the southern edge of the Afar Triangle, which is part of Africa's Great Rift Valley. That's where the well-known 3.2-million-year-old hominin fossil, Lucy, was found."

"And the other site?"

"It's in a complex of limestone caves in South Africa, thirty-one miles northwest of Johannesburg. The primary area is known as the Sterkfontein Caves. A 2.3-million-year-old hominid fossil named Mrs. Ples was found there."

"I'm worried, Ben. Day one of our seven-day ultimatum is over. That leaves six days to find a needle in a million haystacks, and if we fail, the man I love dies along with the man Lisa loves." My voice cracked.

"Look, I know how much Ross means to you. I suggest you check the Great Sphinx and the Great Pyramid before you try the more widespread sites." Ben paused. "Sorry I couldn't pinpoint the exact location."

"Do you know anyone in Egypt's archaeological hierarchy who can get me inside the Sphinx and the Pyramid?"

"Sorry, Sam, they haven't let anyone inside the Great Sphinx since 1993, when an American Egyptologist discovered that the erosions on it made it at least ten thousand years old. He also used a seismograph to discover two rectangular chambers at least twenty-five feet beneath the front paws, and claimed one was the location of the famed Atlantean Hall of Records that Plato spoke of."

"So why didn't they explore those chambers?" My frustration grew.

"Egypt doesn't want anyone to find more evidence that proves they didn't build the Great Sphinx or the Great Pyramid. If they refuse further investigations, they can cling to the claim that Egyptians built all of it. Can't blame them for not wanting to destroy their heritage."

"Makes sense, but they have plenty of ancient sites to show the world their great heritage."

"Maybe not. Everything could be thrown into question—a proverbial giant can of worms opened, never to be closed again." Ben hesitated. "Considering your ability to open what appear to be solid rock walls, I suggest you go to the Sphinx first and sneak inside late at night. Maybe have your team create a diversion. My guess is the Blue Dragon will be in one of those chambers under the front paws, and there's bound to be a passage to it from somewhere inside the main body or the head."

"And if the Blue Dragon isn't there?" I tried to conceal the anxiety in my voice.

"Call me and I'll arrange a private tour of the Great Pyramid, or you could just sneak inside like you're going to do in the Sphinx. I hope you find it fast, Sam."

"Thanks, Ben." I ended the call, feeling like I had more questions than answers.

Mike raised his eyebrows. "Well?"

"We're going to Cairo for a late-night visit to the Great Sphinx. And if we don't find it there, our next stop is the Great Pyramid." I shoved my satellite phone into my shoulder bag. "Should be loads of fun."

"Do I detect a tone of sarcasm?" Banger arched one eyebrow. "That's my job."

"Sorry, I guess the frustration is getting to me. I wish the Atlanteans had left simpler directions."

"Where's the fun in that?" Banger squeezed my hand. "Relax, we'll find the Blue Dragon, probably later tonight."

THIRTEEN

Cairo, Egypt

Before departure, Mike, Banger, and I took turns in the Gulfstream's lavatory, taking what the men called Navy showers, meaning no more than three minutes. It felt good to be clean, but that would change on the desert plain of Giza.

I studied the guidebook and then addressed the team. "There's probably a hidden entrance behind the Great Sphinx's head, so Banger and I should paraglide down from the jet and land on its back in the dark." I paused. "Could be difficult. Its head is close to seven stories high, and its back is only a hundred and thirty feet long and sixty-two feet wide."

"Why Banger?" Mike's eyebrows arched.

"He's the tallest and strongest person on the

team. He might need to move something heavy or lift me up to reach something." I smiled at my big friend.

"What about the rest of us?" Mike asked, his arms crossed.

"Drive out there in a rental SUV and pick us up." I hesitated. "If we're spotted on the Sphinx, you may need to create a diversion. Just don't get caught. Ben said we might need to search the Great Pyramid if we don't find the Blue Dragon inside the Sphinx." I sighed. "And there's a list of other potential sites if it's not in Egypt, so we'll need a clean getaway."

Banger leaned back in his seat and looked up at me. "Are you an experienced jumper?"

"I've done some skydiving with my brothers, and I'm also a paraglider instructor."

Mike joined in. "Don't worry, Sam will be fine."

"Good thing we packed those black chutes." Banger stood. "Ready to suit up, Sam?"

"Sure, I just love jumping out of perfectly good airplanes."

Banger raised a brow. "Hey, there you go again. I'm supposed to deliver the sarcastic lines."

"Sorry, I'm trying not to worry about Ross and Derek, but Sweetwater hates them, and it might take too long to find the Blue Dragon."

Banger pulled me close and looked into my eyes. "We'll save them. Count on it."

"Thanks, Banger." I sighed and glanced down

at the large belly bag holding the sphere. "Better help me secure this under my harness. I'll zip the Eye in one of my pockets, but I think we can leave the gold cylinder on the airplane." I glanced at the team. "Right?"

Mike frowned. "Only if there's a good place on board to hide it."

I thought a moment, remembering all the specs for the Starr Corporation's G650s. "I'll need a Phillips screwdriver."

Everyone, including Lisa, reached inside their pockets and pulled out the equivalents of Swiss Army knives with all the attached tools.

"I usually carry my Leatherman, but in the rush to pack for Africa, I forgot it." I accepted the tool Mike carried on all his SEAL missions. "Thanks, brother dear."

"I want everyone on the team to know where you hide it, just in case, sis." Mike followed me.

I grabbed a small aircraft pillow, wrapped it around the cylinder, and held it tight. "There's a small space in the lavatory that's perfect." With the pillow under my arm, I unscrewed a wall panel in the bathroom.

"See? It fits in here." I crammed the rolled-up pillow into the empty space and replaced the panel. "Problem solved." I kept the tool.

As each team member looked into the bathroom, I tapped the panel where the cylinder was hidden. "Okay, I'd better go forward and discuss our mission with the pilots."

I stuck my head in the cockpit. "Hey, Bill and Laura, change of plans. Request a cruise altitude of six thousand feet for a short flight to Cairo International Airport after you secretly drop two jumpers over the Great Sphinx."

Bill turned and looked at me. "How do we explain the deviation to ATC?"

"Tell them your passengers wanted a brief aerial view of the ancient site under the full moon before landing. It shouldn't be an issue this late at night."

"All right, but the only safe exit for a parachute jump is through the baggage door. That compartment is pressurized and has a door that connects it to the cabin." He pulled out a diagram of the aircraft. "The baggage door is aft of the left wing and below the left engine intake, so you can make a clean exit from there without hitting the airplane or getting sucked into the engine."

"I know, Bill. Have you forgotten I'm checked out in all the Starr Corporation's jets?"

His eyes widened. "Of course, Sam. What was I thinking?"

"You were doing your job, but no worries, I've got this."

He smiled. "I'll depressurize the airplane before you jump and give you a five-minute and also a thirty-second warning before I announce when to jump."

"Perfect." I grinned. "Can you arrange for an SUV rental to be ready for the team?"

He nodded at the copilot. "Laura will take care of it. No one ever says no to her."

"Give us five minutes before you crank up the engines." I left the cockpit. *Are we doing the right thing? What if I miss the beast's back and land in the sand?*

Mike glanced at me when I returned. "All right, let's help Sam and Banger get geared up for the jump." He opened the door that connected the cabin to the pressurized baggage compartment.

At two in the morning, my ears popped as the airplane depressurized.

Bill announced, "Five minutes to jump."

The jet cruised at six thousand feet with the cabin and baggage compartment unpressurized to facilitate our jump. Banger and I moved to the outer baggage door, and he opened it. The noise level shot up several decibels as rushing air hissed past the opening.

Adrenaline surged through me as I rechecked my harness and the belly pack underneath that held the sphere inside the canvas satchel. Jumps like this were routine for Banger, but I'd never jumped from a jet—and never at night.

Rushing air distorted the pilot's voice. "Thirty seconds to green light. Wind is from the east at fifteen knots."

My jump partner's sarcastic quip filled my earpiece, "Oh good, a crosswind for the landing."

Banger and I pulled on our jump goggles and stood at the open door. I gave him a thumbs-up, and he returned the gesture. *Can he see me shaking?*

"Jump, jump, jump," Bill announced.

We dived into a bright night sky illuminated by a full moon and aimed for the Great Sphinx lying six thousand feet below us. Cool air buffeted my body. My plan was to land on the statue's back in the shadow behind the head, but I'd be happy to land anywhere on top of him.

Banger's deep voice came through my earbud, "Check your altimeter. Pull at two thousand feet."

"Copy, pull at two thousand." Shadowy ground covered in golden sand seemed to rush up at me, and my pulse quickened. "Try to land close behind the head."

"Wherever you land, I'll land behind you." His confidence reassured me.

I searched the ground and could barely make out two distant figures strolling side-by-side down the length of the mighty beast. Had to be guards this late at night. They didn't look up—at least, not so far.

We maneuvered toward the target and opened our chutes at the designated altitude.

My breath caught when a sharp jerk momentarily arrested my fall after my black rectangular chute deployed. Silence surrounded me as I floated downward, turning into the wind. We didn't need night-vision goggles with the bright moon lighting our path.

"Two good chutes," I reported to Laura on the jet's secondary comm frequency.

"Understand two good chutes. Your team will be on the ground in a few minutes and will drive to the site ASAP. Gulfstream out."

We circled the Great Sphinx, slowly descending as the pyramids of Giza gleamed in the moonlight. The brisk crosswind made our approach more challenging. We'd have to favor the windward side and allow for side drift over the narrow back before turning into the wind right before touchdown. Timing would be critical.

"Looking good for a landing on target." I peered at the giant statue beneath me, judging my rate of descent. "One more turn over the big guy."

"Copy that. I'm right behind you." Banger's voice radiated calm.

My final turn lined me up on the beast's "runway," which was about thirty-six feet longer and twelve feet wider than a basketball court. The head and front legs made up the rest of its two-hundred-forty-foot overall length. Its back didn't look any bigger as I glided closer, favoring the windward edge. Near my touchdown point, the head loomed in front of me. I had to time it just right or I'd smash into solid rock.

My heart pounded as I turned into the wind at the last second and yanked hard on the control risers, landing ten feet behind the massive head. The chute fell onto the Sphinx's back, and before I had a chance to gather it, the wind dragged the billowing canopy over the side, pulling me behind it.

Banger's strong hands grabbed my harness and snatched me away from the edge. "Don't unhook the chute," he whispered through my earbud. "We don't want it falling on the ground." He helped me pull it up and fold it.

His chute had already been secured. SEALs were so skilled they made everything look easy, and my big teammate was no exception.

"Alrighty, my queen, lead us into the darkness." His whispered words penetrated my earpiece as he grabbed the rolled-up chutes. "We'll stow these inside the beast. Where's the door?"

"I'm hoping there's one on the back of its head." I ran my hands over the stone up as high as I could reach. "I'm checking for an area of strong electromagnetic energy."

He studied the statue's head. "Well? Anything?"

"You're not going to like this, but the energy seems much stronger up there." I pointed straight up.

"Keep your legs stiff and I'll lift you." He bent down, grasped my ankles, and lifted me like I was weightless. He held my feet over his head. "How's this?"

I ran my hands over the stone. "A little to the left."

Banger sidestepped left, and my fingers tingled when they brushed a small area about the size of my medallion. I pulled out Mike's multi-tool and scraped off ten thousand years of accumulated dirt. Gold gleamed underneath. A little more scraping revealed a mirror-image of my medallion.

I whispered, "I found it," as my throat mike transmitted my words into Banger's earpiece.

"Good job." He hesitated. "I hope the guards didn't hear you scraping the stone."

After putting Mike's tool away, I pulled the medallion out from under my shirt, fitted it over the reverse image, face-to-face, and waited.

Nothing happened.

Crap. I used the cuff on my long sleeve and wiped dust off the gold lock, then reinserted my medallion.

No reaction.

I blew into the mechanism to remove fine dirt. Dust filled my nostrils, and I sneezed, causing me to lose my balance and fall.

"Ahhhhh!"

A heart-pounding second later, Banger caught me.

"That was scary." I kissed his cheek. "Thanks for the save."

"What happened, Sam?"

"I was trying to clean out the lock and lost my balance." I sighed. "Sorry, Banger. Can you lift me again?"

"No problem." He bent down and grabbed my ankles. "Better hurry in case the guards heard you yell."

When I reached the gold lock, I tried my medallion key again. Deep vibrations erupted, followed by grinding and a dirt cloud where a stone had moved up into a slot on my left. Had that been as loud as it seemed?

"Better hurry, Sam," Banger whispered into my radio earpiece. "Guards must've heard that."

The door was two feet wide and five feet tall. Assuming he could get up here, Banger would have to turn sideways and crawl through it. Peering inside the dark interior, I could barely make out a six-foot-square landing that led to stone stairs. Was this a passage to the underground chambers?

I pulled out the medallion, slipped the chain around my neck, and crawled partway inside, careful not to enter fully. Based on past experiences, entering all the way might cause the door to close. It wasn't easy turning around with one foot sticking out, but I managed it and prayed the door wouldn't slam down and crush me.

Kneeling on the stone, I stuck my head out and looked at Banger, fifteen feet below me. "Toss one of the chutes up to me, and I'll hook it to something so you can climb up."

He wadded one into a tight ball, secured by risers tied around it, and lobbed it up.

I wasn't at the best angle and missed it. "Oops, sorry."

"Here it comes again." Banger threw it directly into my outstretched hands.

"Give me a minute, and I'll rig it for you." I untied the lines.

"It's not like I have someplace else to be," he said with his usual dry humor.

My mini flashlight revealed another mirror image of my gold medallion above the door on the inside, meaning I should be able to open it if it closed.

"Don't worry, I think I can open the door from inside," I whispered into my comm. "I just need to step away and secure the chute."

The door closed with a thud the instant I moved away from the opening. Sconces carved from the stone walls held ancient oil lamps. With my flashlight in my mouth, I tied the chute to a stone sconce and placed my medallion in the gold slot above the door. Nothing happened.

Uh oh.

I pulled my medallion out, brushed dust away from the slot, re-inserted it, and pressed hard.

Loud rumbling heralded the door opening.

Good, but I hope the guards didn't hear that.

"The chute is secure." I dropped it out the door, then reached inside and pulled out my medallion. I hung the unusual key around my neck while being careful to remain in the doorway.

Banger reached up and grabbed the silk chute and climbed hand-over-hand to the opening.

"Now for the tricky part." I looked into his face. "There isn't room for both of us in the doorway, but if I move completely away from it, the door will close."

He held onto the chute just outside the door, cloaked in the moon's shadow. "What do you suggest?" He wasn't even out of breath from the climb.

"Well, if I can keep my hands inside the door while I hang outside, then you'll have room to get past me and enter." I turned around, dropped to my knees, and backed out.

He pushed himself to one side so I'd have room to lower myself next to him. I grasped a few parasail lines and kept my hands a foot inside the door opening as I eased down beside him. Good thing we were in a shadow cast by the moon.

"Hold tight while I squeeze inside." Banger pulled himself up and turned on his side to fit through the narrow door.

Everything went as planned until his foot smashed my hands when he pressed down to turn around.

"Ow, my fingers!" My right hand lost its grip, and my left hand slid several inches. I managed to clamp down an inch or two inside the door. Just when I thought I couldn't hold on another second, he reached out and yanked me through the door.

The instant my feet cleared the opening, the door slammed shut. Out of breath, I landed on his granite chest.

"This place wasn't built for big guys like me. You okay, Sam?"

"It might take a minute or two for my heart rate to return to normal, but yeah, I'm good. Thanks for another save."

"No problem. Let's go find that Blue Dragon."

"I'd better reopen the door first and pull in the chute before a guard sees it." I inserted my medallion in the key slot again, and the door opened. "And I want to keep the harness in case I need it for something later."

Dropping to my knees, I grabbed the edge of the torn chute an instant before it would've dropped from the open door. "Whew, that was close."

A spotlight panned the head just below the chute as Banger kneeled behind me and helped me pull it inside. "Dodged that bullet."

We backed onto the landing at the head of the stairs, and the door closed once again. I pulled my medallion out of the slot and hung it around my neck, then stuffed the paraglider harness into my backpack and left the ruined chute by the door.

He switched on his flashlight. "Looks like there's oil in the sconces. Should we light them?"

I nodded, pulled out my butane lighter, and flicked it on.

When I held the flame to the oil lamp, an interesting thing happened. A narrow line carved into the wall filled with flaming oil and lit sconces down the length of the steep staircase on the left side. "Whoa, I wasn't expecting that."

"Sweet. I'll try the other side." He lit the lamp on the right, and another oil river illuminated the staircase.

I switched off my flashlight. "May as well save the battery."

"Right, because that lithium battery will only last about a hundred thousand hours." More sarcasm from my huge buddy.

I punched his left arm, which only hurt my hand. "Ow! I'd be really annoyed if you weren't so good looking."

He grinned. "That's what all the girls tell me."

FOURTEEN

S am kicked hard underwater beneath a full moon. A spear flashed past her, and an enormous crocodile rushed at her, snapping jaws full of sharp teeth.

Ross choked as if he'd breathed in water. The last thing he saw was Sam, riding on the crocodile with Banger and Mike hanging on behind her.

Derek squeezed his shoulder. "Ross, wake up, mate. You're having a bad dream."

He sat up and coughed. "It seemed too real to be a dream—more like a vision." He explained what he'd seen, whispering so Sweetwater wouldn't hear it on surveillance recordings.

"Ever had a dream like that before tonight?" Derek stretched and glanced up at the stars.

"No, but maybe I'm becoming more psychically connected to Sam."

"Good. You might be able to contact her, and then she'll somehow figure out where we are."

Ross rubbed his eyes. "I don't want her coming here. Sweetwater will feed us to the lions and enjoy watching how long I can protect her before the beasts devour us."

"Ah, but you're forgetting we know something he doesn't about Sam and dangerous beasts." Derek smiled. "Call her."

The Great Sphinx

I descended steep stone stairs, the clunking of my boots echoing off the rock walls. "Good thing we're going down instead of up. It may be as much as a hundred feet."

"I'm counting on you finding another way out of here so we don't have to climb back up." Banger tightened the straps on his backpack. "But just in case we have to return this way, I have the good paraglider with me so we can fly down to the ground."

"It's a long drop from the back of the Sphinx. I hope your paraglider can carry both of us."

"And I hope we never have to test it because the wind would have to be just right to inflate the chute before we jump. There's bound to be another exit, like you've found everywhere else we've gone so far."

"I've got my medallion key, the Eye, and the

sphere to help us with that, but first we have to find the Blue Dragon." I stopped and turned around.

"What?" He looked at me.

"I just had a scary thought. If the Atlanteans built this, it might have defensive mechanisms like some of the ones we found in buildings in Atlantis."

"Like the trident spears in the obsidian pyramid?" Banger frowned. "I lost a teammate down there and almost got ventilated myself."

"If the Great Sphinx is like the other places they built, the defense system will recognize my body's unique electromagnetic frequency and allow me to proceed safely. Stick close to my six."

He glanced around. "Count on it."

I started down again, then paused. "Thought I heard someone."

"*Sam! Sam! Sam!*" Ross yelled inside my head.

I grabbed Banger's arm. "Wait, Ross is calling." I closed my eyes. "*I hear you, Ross. Where are you?*"

"*Sam? Is it really you?*"

"*Yes, are you okay? Is Derek with you?*"

"*Derek and I are in a cage inside a lion pen. We're all right. Sweetwater is holding us somewhere in the jungle in one of his secret camps.*"

"*He gave me an ultimatum to find the Blue Dragon Diamond in seven days and deliver it to him or he'll feed you and Derek to the lions. I only have six days left, but I have some good leads.*"

"*Don't come here. He wants to kill you.*"

"*Don't worry, turns out I can control dangerous animals*"

telepathically, like I did with the kraken. If those lions eat someone while I'm there, I guarantee you it won't be us."

"I miss you, sweetheart. Please don't do anything dangerous trying to save me."

"I miss you too. And don't worry. Mike and our friends are helping me."

"If I find out where we are, I'll contact you. At least, I hope I'll be able to reach you again. I love you, Sam."

"I love you too, Ross. Do whatever it takes to survive until we can rescue you. I promise we'll find you."

"Goodbye, Sam."

His voice faded from my mind.

Banger nudged me. "Sam?"

I grinned. "I just had a telepathic conversation with Ross." I told him everything Ross had said.

"Too bad he doesn't know where they are. We could send a few teams in and kick ass. Maybe even feed Sweetwater to those hungry lions. I hate to see animals suffer."

"Yeah, we wouldn't want those kitties to starve when there's a bald, chubby meal available."

"In the meantime, let's get our butts downstairs and grab the prize." Banger nudged me downward, our boots thudding against the stone.

The air in the stairwell was cool but stale and musty. What if no one had been in this part for the past ten thousand years? We rounded a turn in the Z-patterned stairwell, and I almost tripped over a skeleton skewered by two spears.

"Stop!" I reached back to protect Banger. "Stick

to my back like glue."

He peered over my shoulder. "Look at the red symmetrical cross on the tunic—he's a Knight Templar from medieval times." He reached down beside the fallen soldier and picked up his heavy wooden shield covered with metal. "I guess he didn't hold this in front of him. Too bad."

"How did he get in here? The lock on the Sphinx's head was hidden by an inch of sandstone, and he didn't have the key."

"We've descended well below the head. He must've entered from somewhere in the body."

I glanced around. "Could be more surprises waiting for us. We'd better go slower and watch for booby traps in case the ten-thousand-year-old defense system fails to recognize me." I stepped over the skeleton.

"The one in the obsidian pyramid recognized the triplets, but that's no guarantee this one will do the same for you. Proceed carefully, Sam." He squeezed my shoulders.

We crossed a landing and continued down the stairs as he held the shield in front of me.

A whooshing noise made me duck, and he crouched down with me as a spear shot past where his head would've been.

"Holy crap, that could've killed you," I said, my voice shaky.

"You think?"

I turned to him. "Sticking close isn't working

because you're a lot taller than me, and being on a stair behind me makes you even taller. We might not hear the next one coming."

He looked down at me. "No problem—wrap your legs around my waist, and I'll carry you so your head will be on the same level as mine." He slung the shield across my back and lifted me up.

"This had better work." I wrapped my arms around his neck as he eased us down the steps.

No spears.

About twenty minutes later, I said, "Geez, these stairs seem endless."

"Listen, little missy, you're on my team, and SEALs never whine. Got it?" He arched an eyebrow and looked into my eyes.

"I don't whine, I *comment*. We should be there by now, and you must be tired of carrying me."

He rounded the switchback on the umpteenth landing. "Ask and you shall receive."

The stairs ended in a dim circular chamber about twenty feet in diameter.

"Doesn't look like there are any doors, but we know better, don't we?" I grinned.

Banger pivoted, checking every inch of the walls. "Dare I set you down?"

"Okay, but stay sharp." I examined the walls and spotted two dust-covered gold-medallion door locks twenty feet apart and six feet above the floor. "Hmmn, shall we take door number one or door number two?"

"Let's try the one on the right." He gestured in its direction.

I pulled out my medallion key, brushed away the dust in the lock, and pressed the key against it. The sound of stone scraping against stone echoed in the chamber as a small section opened inward, sending swirls of fine sand into the air.

"You have to enter first, but be careful." I switched on my flashlight and peeked in. The room was large, about fifteen feet wide by thirty feet long.

He held the shield in front of him, ducked through the door, and shined his light around the rectangular room. "Looks like another Hall of Records, like Plato predicted."

A second later, spears shot out from the walls and bounced off his shield. "Sam, get your ass in here!"

I rushed in, and the door shut with a loud thud. In Atlantean, I shouted, "Cease fire." The spears stopped. "Thank god. I didn't really expect that command to work."

"Well done, my queen." He bowed but kept the shield in front of him.

Wall sconces held oil lamps, so I lit them as I circled the room. It was indeed another Atlantean Hall of Records. Floor-to-ceiling shelves on every wall held gold canisters filled with scrolls. Unlike the gold vaults in underwater Atlantis, there was no need for waterproof safes in a desert.

I glanced at Banger, who waited near the door.

"The spears stopped on my command. I think it's safe for you to walk around."

He nodded and pulled off his backpack.

A pedestal table in the center of the chamber held an ornate gold chest that measured about a foot square. I touched the chest, and the lid sprang open. A two-inch marquise-shaped blue diamond dominated the center of a beautiful gold bracelet engraved with Atlantean symbols. I tried it on my right wrist, and the gold instantly molded to my arm. I couldn't get it off.

"Uh oh. This might be a problem." I held up my wrist. "It's stuck."

Banger had been busy pulling things out of his backpack. He glanced at me. "It's too small to be the Blue Dragon, but keep it if you want. Nobody knows what's in here."

I stared at the items from his backpack and picked up what looked like a detonator. "What are you doing with this?"

"Separate mission." He connected wires to explosives planted between the canisters. "If we found another Hall of Records, which we just did, my orders were to destroy it."

"Why?" I hated to see ancient wisdom destroyed but suspected the reason.

He met my eyes. "America prefers to have the only set of scrolls."

I clutched the detonator. "I understand, but wait until we see what's in the other room."

He crossed his arms. "Why?"

"Because the Atlanteans have all sorts of mechanisms built into their chambers. Could be that if we blow this one, we won't be allowed into the other one. We might even get trapped. I'd like to look for the Blue Dragon before we do anything drastic."

He hesitated. "All right. Makes sense. I'll finish placing the charges and set the timer for one hour. That should give us plenty of time to search the other room. We won't need to come back here, right?"

"Let's hope not. I'll check the other chamber while you finish this."

He held up a hand. "No, we should stick together. This'll only take a few minutes." He ran wires between the charges and connected them to the detonator.

I was about to protest, but within seconds red LED lights counted down from sixty minutes. "Are you positive we won't destroy the Great Sphinx when you set these off? It looks like a lot of C-4."

"Relax, Sam, this isn't my first rodeo." He tapped his chest. "Navy SEAL."

"*Really*? I had no idea."

"There you go, stealing my lines again." He grinned.

"Let's see what's behind that other door." I inserted my medallion key and opened the exit for the

Hall of Records. It closed behind us as we crossed the circular room.

When I opened the door for the chamber under the left paw, Banger entered first with his shield up and lit the oil sconces. As usual, the door closed the instant I stepped inside, but there weren't any flying spears this time. Had my command carried into this room?

The left chamber was the same size but quite different from the right one. Huge diagrams covered the upper walls, and shelves beneath them held crystal pyramids and odd-looking copper devices. I searched every shelf.

"Well, the bad news is there's no Blue Dragon." I glanced around, looking for a symbol marking a hidden compartment. I ran my hands over the walls, but nothing popped open. "The good news is there's a subterranean tunnel that runs from here to the Great Pyramid." I grinned.

His eyebrows shot up. "How do you know that?"

I pointed at a diagram. "See this? It indicates the Great Pyramid is a power plant, and these are the specs for how it works." I tapped a spot on the diagram. "This valve allows water from the Nile to enter the pumphouse beneath the pyramid. Hydrodynamic pressure vibrates the stone blocks in the pyramid, activating the crystals, which in turn produce electricity. Amazing, huh?"

He studied the diagram. "Wow, Sam, I think

you're right." He tapped one of the crystal pyramids on a nearby shelf. "These must be spare parts, and I'm guessing some idiots who didn't understand their purpose took the originals a long time ago." He shook his head. "Awesome discovery."

I checked the drawings and glanced at Banger. "Maybe if we fire it up again, a secret chamber will open and reveal the Blue Dragon. How many of these crystals can you carry?" I pulled off my backpack.

"I've got room for six in my backpack if you can carry the chute and the other three." He unzipped his pack, handed me the paraglider, and began loading the crystals.

"They look heavy, but I can manage three and the chute." I pulled on gloves before touching them, in case my bare hands might activate them. It was the rare frequency of electromagnetic energy flowing through my body that had made me the default heir to the throne of a dead civilization buried two thousand feet beneath the sea.

I shoved the heavy pyramids into my backpack. They fit with a little room to spare, so I grabbed what looked like copper electrical devices and crammed them in before zipping it closed.

"Uh, just one problem." He glanced around. "Where's the entrance to the tunnel?"

Standing in the center of the rectangular room, I shined my flashlight on each wall.

"There." I pointed at the wall farthest from the

entry door. "It's in the middle of that diagram."

I strode across the room and stood in front of the wall. The number seventy-nine in Atlantean was engraved on an electrical diagram carved onto the wall. "That's the atomic number for gold."

My brother's tool helped me scrape off a thin layer of limestone covering a gold medallion lock hidden behind the number.

Turning to Banger, I grinned. "Voila." I inserted my gold key.

The floor vibrated as a door-sized section of stone dropped into a slot under the wall, sending musty air into the chamber.

He glanced at his watch and slipped on his backpack. "We've got twenty-six minutes before the charges detonate next door. I suggest we put as much distance as possible between us and this room."

I pulled on my backpack. "You're right. I'd better lead so we don't set off booby traps, but you'll have to exit first."

He switched on his flashlight. "Let's go." He held the ancient shield in front of him and waited outside the door so I could take the lead.

Keeping ahead of Banger was easier said than done. That man had a long stride and never seemed to get winded. I trotted ahead of him, weighed down by the crystals. He carried twice as many in his pack, so I could hardly complain. We were in a dark, narrow tunnel that seemed endless.

My claustrophobia reared its ugly head again, and the explosives under the Great Sphinx worried me. The possibility of being trapped in a tunnel no one knew existed made my heart race. So did the heavy load in my backpack. I continued on until I could barely catch my breath.

"Hey, big guy, need a break?" My voice was breathless and squeaky.

He turned me around. "Claustrophobia kicking in again, Sam?"

I sucked in a deep breath. "Maybe a little. Sorry."

He pulled me into his arms and gave me a bear hug. "You'll be okay. I guarantee it."

"Thanks, Banger. I guess we'd better get going. Your charges will be exploding any second."

It wasn't long before a loud boom echoed down the tunnel, followed by a swirling dirt cloud. Deep rumbling preceded a section of rock dropping into the tunnel behind us, sealing off the passage to the Great Sphinx and blanketing us in stone particles and sand.

He coughed and blinked his eyes. "Sorry, Sam, I thought the charges were safe."

I choked out dust. "They were probably fine, but this tunnel is thousands of years old and deep underground. Vibrations from the explosion must've caused the collapse. We'd better keep moving."

We hadn't gone far when a large stone block

crashed down in front of us, not quite sealing off the tunnel, but too large for us to crawl over it. My worst fear had been realized. We were trapped underground, and nobody knew where we were. I tried not to hyperventilate as my heart hammered my chest.

Banger looked through the narrow opening. "At least air can still get in from the other side."

"If we hadn't stopped because of my claustrophobia—" I choked on some dirt.

"Don't even think that. You're the last heir in a long line of Atlantean queens. If anyone can get us out of here, you can." He placed his hands on my shoulders and looked into my eyes. "Pull out one of your high-tech gadgets and fix this."

I hesitated and looked into his calm brown eyes. "Doesn't anything ever scare you?"

"Let's see, ever since I was called upon to deal with things involving you or your *realm*," he ticked the items off on his fingers, "I've encountered deadly ancient mechanisms, megalodons, krakens, an enormous snake, a pod of hippos, and a vicious crocodile, not to mention a burning airplane and bad guys bent on world domination." He smiled. "But every time I needed help you came through for me. I don't understand all your unusual abilities or the weird artifacts you've collected along the way, but I have faith in you. So, no, I'm not scared." He hesitated. "Maybe just a tiny bit worried."

FIFTEEN

Giza, Egypt

A full moon illuminated magnificent pyramids towering over the Giza plain while the Great Sphinx kept silent watch in the distance. Mike sat on the Range Rover's hood and focused his night-vision binoculars. "Nobody. They must still be inside."

Lance glanced at his watch. "They landed an hour and a half ago. I hope they're not trapped in there."

"What if they already moved to the Great Pyramid?" Bryce trained his binoculars on the huge monument that gleamed under the moon.

"How could they get there without being seen?" Lisa scanned the area.

"Maybe they found an underground passage."

Mike searched the barren plain between the silent beast and the trio of huge pyramids.

"That would have to be one heck of a long passage—at least a half-mile." Lance glanced over his shoulder. "Uh, team, we have company."

A Jeep carrying armed soldiers left a trail of dust as it pulled alongside their SUV.

Mike let the binoculars hang on a strap around his neck and aimed his cell phone at the Great Sphinx.

A soldier stepped out. "What are you doing here so late?"

Bryce answered in his polished British accent. "My mates and I wanted to get some pictures of the Giza monuments under a full moon."

"Mates? What about the woman?" The soldier looked at Lisa with contempt.

Bryce shrugged. "My sister—she insisted on coming. You know how it is."

Lisa crossed her arms and spoke in a British accent that matched Bryce's. "Don't you like women?"

"Are you drinking alcohol?" He studied the team.

"No, sir, we just want to enjoy the view and get some pictures." Mike held up his cell phone with a photo of the huge statue on it.

"Don't stay too long, and keep a good distance from the monuments." The soldier gave Lisa a parting glare and climbed into the Jeep.

The team waited until they drove away before speaking.

Mike stared at the departing vehicle. "Our tourist ploy might work for another twenty minutes, tops. Then those soldiers will insist we leave."

"When Sam and Banger surface, we'd better swoop in before the soldiers see them." Lisa checked her watch. "They'll be a lot harder to explain."

"Better keep scanning in every direction." Mike raised his binoculars. "Knowing my sister, they could pop up just about anywhere."

Underground Passage

Trapped in a secret tunnel with one of the bravest men I had ever known, I pulled the sphere out of my belly bag, ran my hands over it, and said, "Annihilate that big stone block with your laser."

Nothing happened.

"Maybe you need to say it in Atlantean." Banger took a step back. He looked ghostly, covered in pale dust.

"Okay, I'll try that." I spoke slowly, careful to pronounce the ancient words correctly as my claustrophobia escalated.

The silvery-blue globe hummed and vibrated, flew out of my hands, opened its portal, and zapped the obstruction with its laser. Rock chips flew at us, and the air clouded with tiny particles of stone debris during the continuous onslaught.

I yelled, "It's working," and then my throat went into a coughing spasm.

We ducked the sharp pellets and covered our faces with bandanas. The sphere kept firing until the huge stone was reduced to a much lower but longer pile of rubble. The portal closed, and the device landed back in my hands.

"Wow, I had no idea I could command it." I grinned, admiring the result of the laser's work. "This is great. I don't mind carrying it around now. I wonder what else it can do."

Banger chuckled. "That was awesome, my queen. Shall we continue?"

"I can't get out of this scary tunnel soon enough." My hands trembled as I placed the globe back in my belly pack. "Better keep your shield up and watch out for spears."

"What if the explosion damaged the ancient defense mechanisms?" He brushed some dirt out of my hair. "You could get killed."

"I'm willing to take the risk, rather than hiding behind you with spears constantly shooting at us." My voice sounded squeaky. "I really need to get out of here."

He pulled me in for a hug. "You're doing fine. Start out slowly while we test the tunnel."

We climbed over the rubble and eased down the dark passage, distancing ourselves from the cave-ins.

After ten minutes, I had to stop and catch my breath. My backpack was laden with heavy crystal pyramids, and my lungs were coated with dirt. Except for an occasional cough, Banger seemed unaffected, like he was out for a casual stroll.

"How do you keep so fit?" I asked, standing in front of his tree-trunk thighs.

He grinned. "It's the only way to survive missions with you."

"You're lucky your good looks make up for you being such a smartass."

"That's another thing all the girls tell me." He adjusted the straps on his backpack. "Ready?"

As he took a step past me, spears flew at his head. His quick reflexes and the shield saved him, the sharp pointed tips piercing the shield's thin metal cover and sticking into the wood. The frightening attack had occurred in mere seconds.

I stepped in front of him. "Whew, that was close. Better stay behind me."

"You think?" He yanked the spears out of the shield.

I swiped dirt off his cheek and planted a kiss before slowly moving forward, ever vigilant for traps. Thank god the security system built by the Atlanteans somehow sensed my unique energy pattern and withheld deadly spears as long as I remained in front of Banger. I prayed it wouldn't malfunction, but there was no way to know until it would be too late.

The nightmare passageway finally ended at a stone door. I located the lock, brushed away accumulated dirt, and inserted my key. The door opened to a five-by-eight-foot pumphouse beneath the Great Pyramid. I recognized the room because the low ceiling and rectangular design matched the diagram I'd studied earlier.

"According to the plans, we need to activate the hydrodynamic system before the crystals will generate electricity. It'll probably take a while for the water to flow in from the Nile and build up enough pressure to get the pump going," I said, looking around for the valve control. "I assume we'll have enough time to replace the components up in the electric corridor after we open the water valve."

"How do you know so much about mechanical engineering stuff?"

"I'm an airline pilot. We have to study schematics for every system on our airliners and fully understand how they operate."

"Makes sense, but weren't those ancient diagrams a lot more complex?" He arched a brow.

"I've had plenty of experience with complicated jet airliner systems, but you're right that Atlantean technology is different. They used the Earth's electromagnetic energy for most things, and they seem to have been overly fond of lasers."

He glanced around. "How are we going to open the water valve? I don't see any controls."

The walls appeared to be solid stone with no

markings. I closed my eyes a moment and tried to picture the diagrams from the room under the Great Sphinx. "I remember seeing a hand crank on one of the drawings. It has to be here."

"Ask the Eye where it is," Banger said. "Might save us time and effort."

"Sorry, I should've thought of that. My brain gets foggy after spending a long time in closed-in spaces." I pulled out the Eye of Atlantis and held it in my right hand.

A hologram appeared and showed the sphere zap a spot on a stone wall, opening a hatch that hid a hand crank. The image vanished, and I put the Eye back in the leather pouch.

"Looks like another job for my trusty little buddy." I pulled it out and spoke the command in Atlantean, "Open the water-valve hatch."

The sphere flew out of my hands and zapped a spot on the wall where dirt obscured a circular metal cover. I jumped back as sand and dirt fell away, and the hatch popped open with a loud clang, revealing a large-diameter handwheel.

"Amazing. I like this ancient tech." I bowed and pointed at the crank before putting the globe back inside my belly bag. "This looks like a job for you, my liege."

He glanced around. "I suggest you find a door into the pyramid before I open that valve, just in case a ten-thousand-year-old mechanism malfunctions and floods this chamber." He paused and smiled. "Not that stuff like that ever happens to *us*."

I ran my hands over the walls and felt an energy spike in a spot the size of my medallion. A little scraping exposed a gold slot. After a few minutes of careful dirt and dust removal, my key fit perfectly and triggered the door to open. Warmer air rushed in, and my flashlight revealed a slanted walkway leading upward into darkness.

I coughed again. "What if some of the dust we've encountered contains toxic mold? We could die from what anthropologists call the Pharaoh's Curse."

"A better time to worry about that would've been before we jumped out of the jet."

"*Really?*" I crossed my arms. "All right, Mr. Smartass, get cranking." I stood in the doorway so it wouldn't close.

He grasped the wheel with both hands and twisted.

Nothing happened.

He grunted and tried again. The crank groaned but remained stuck.

"Help me break it loose." He moved so I could grab one side of the wheel.

When I stepped away from the door, it dropped down and sealed the room.

"Oh boy, this had better work." I grasped the crank with both hands.

Slowly, and with much effort, Banger and I loosened the wheel and began turning it amidst loud creaking. After three complete turns, it reached its limit, and the stones seemed to moan.

"What's that weird sound?" He cocked his head. "I hope I didn't activate an ancient self-destruct mechanism built by vindictive Atlanteans."

"I'm hoping it's just the water pipes." I pressed my hand against the wall and felt a steady vibration. "But just in case there's a problem, we should probably leave now."

"You think?" Banger's sarcasm hadn't missed a beat.

I stuck my medallion key in the slot, and a small piece of gold broke off the inner lock and fell onto the floor.

"Uh oh, we might have a problem." The door wouldn't open. Frustrated, I pressed harder on the medallion. "Come on, already."

I reached down and picked up the gold chip. "I'm afraid the lock is broken. I hope we can reattach this."

He pulled out a butane lighter and held the flame to the spot on the lock where the gold chip had broken off. "Wait till it gets soft and stick that piece back on it."

My feet felt cold and wet. I glanced down.

Water had pooled around our ankles.

"The room's filling with water." I glanced around but couldn't see where it was flowing in.

"Great." He glanced at the floor and held the flame closer to the gold.

Water swirled around my shins as my voice shot up two octaves. "Is it soft yet?"

He touched the spot. "It's hot but not soft. This gold must be alloyed with a hard metal, and the water is rising fast. Better do something queenly."

I pulled out the sphere and commanded it to give the broken spot one quick zap with the laser. The little globe fired once and closed up shop. I replaced it in my belly bag and pressed the chip onto the hot gold. The molten heat welded it in place.

Banger splashed a handful of water onto it to cool the metal, and steam hissed out of the slot.

Meanwhile, the water in the pumphouse had risen almost to my hips. I pressed my key into the lock and prayed.

The stone door lifted, Banger slipped through it, and I followed. As usual, the door slammed shut behind me as we sloshed up the dark ramp in our wet boots. The crystals in my backpack felt like their weight had doubled since I'd begun the climb. It wasn't long before my heart hammered my chest, and my breath came in short spurts.

Banger tapped my shoulder. "Sam, stop and take a breather. We're probably high enough to avoid a flood."

"Okay, but just for a few seconds," I gasped. "We don't want these spare parts inside our packs when the pump starts."

"Why?"

"If the pyramid starts vibrating, we'll vibrate along with it, and the crystals we're carrying will produce electricity."

"And you think we'll get shocked—or worse?"

"It's possible, especially with our luck."

He lifted his shield and pointed ahead. "Then get your shapely ass up this ramp."

I hurried upward and prayed we'd get the components placed in their slots before the pump started. We rounded a sharp turn and found a door covered with electrical symbols printed in faded red paint.

"This must be it." I ran my hands over the door, felt an energy spike, and found a key slot hidden under ten millennia of dust. Mike's tool came in handy once again. After a little scraping, wiping, and blowing, a gold slot reflected the beam from my flashlight. I pushed my medallion into it, and the door opened inward.

Thank god!

"Sarcasm before beauty." I grinned and waved Banger in ahead of me.

A long, narrow corridor with nine copper-bottomed platforms loomed in front of us. The nearest end had a special slot for something else.

I pulled off my backpack and opened it. "This looks like it'll fit here." I pulled out a copper device I'd taken from the engineering room under the Sphinx and tried shoving it into the slot. It wouldn't slide in, so I turned it around and tried again.

That time, it fit perfectly.

"We'll place the ones you're carrying first." He pulled a crystal pyramid-shaped terminal out of my backpack and handed it to me. "Do your magic."

I set it on a square platform built for its exact size and shape. The crystal fit perfectly on the copper base. "One down, eight to go—but we have to hurry."

We moved to the next station and placed another sparkling pyramid.

"Good, keep going." He nudged me forward. "I've got six of these mothers in my pack."

I inserted my last crystal and rushed to the next station. Banger handed me one from his pack, and I locked it into place. Five to go.

A weak vibration stirred under my feet.

"Uh oh, the pump is starting." I rushed to the next station.

We placed four more with speed and efficiency as the vibrations grew more intense.

"One to go." I reached for it.

Just as I set the pyramid-shaped crystal on its base, it gave off a spark. "Ow!" I looked at the lighted component and spotted a number that hadn't been visible before. "Crap, they're in the wrong order." I yanked the pyramid off the base and rushed back to the second platform.

"How do you know that?" Banger followed me.

"They have numbers that weren't visible until they started to power up." I yanked out the one that had been on the number two base and replaced it with the ninth one from the far end.

Banger squinted. "That's a number?'

"Yeah, it's written in Atlantean. I have to put these in the right sequence."

The stone floor shook.

"How can I help?" Banger glanced down at his feet.

"Our wet leather boots might be a problem." I handed him the crystal I'd pulled out.

"You think?" He held the component like it was a live bomb. "You're the queen. Shouldn't you already know how to assemble this stuff?"

"Sorry, I never made it to queen school, but I know if we don't fix this fast, we're going to get fried." I yanked out the crystal in the first spot. "The one you're holding goes here, and this one goes on the final base." I rushed to place it as the vibrations grew even stronger.

"What about the other six?" Banger asked as he placed the crystal.

I checked slots three through eight. "They're all wrong. Hurry and help me replace these." I yanked one out and rushed to where it belonged, handing the other one to him. "This goes in spot number five."

We set about reordering the crystals as the vibrations intensified. The components filled with bright light and started to hum.

"This is the last one." I set the final pyramid in spot number seven just as the corridor began to buzz. "One more thing." I pulled another copper device from my pack and shoved it into its slot at the far end. The instant it locked into place a jolt of electricity knocked me onto my butt.

The entire pyramid hummed with deep vibrations, and intense blue-white mini bolts of lightning crackled from the nine power crystals.

"Oh, crap." Energy buzzed around me, stinging me like a hundred bees.

Banger pulled me to my feet. "Time to go. I hope there's another door at this end."

I ran my hands over the end wall. "I think it's here. Help me scrape off the dust."

Electrical sparks stung us as we worked to uncover a key slot.

"There it is." I shoved my medallion into it, and nothing happened. "It's dirty. I have to clean out all the dust." I pinched my nostrils shut as I blew hard into the slot.

Banger shouted, "Sam, we're running out of time here." He waved at the growing electrical storm.

My hand shook as I stuck my key into the lock. This time the door opened.

Bolts of blue lightning roared and flashed behind us as we rushed through the door.

"Whew, this is one time I'm grateful the door closed so fast." I shined my flashlight on him. "Did you get zapped?"

"Yeah, a little bit." He showed me a nasty burn on his right arm.

"This entire pyramid is humming with energy. I wonder if it's safe to stay inside a while and look around. What do you think?" My head tingled as I pulled on my backpack.

"Ah, Sam, nothing with you is ever safe. That's what makes working with you so exciting."

I sighed. "The Blue Dragon had better be here. We've been through enough already."

I headed up the corridor, trying to keep my balance on the shuddering stones. "Hurry, let's see where this goes."

Giza

Mike scanned the expanse between the Great Sphinx and the Great Pyramid—nothing but empty desert and clouds overhead moving in from the northeast. He glanced at his watch. "They'd better call or show up soon."

Lance nudged him. "Uh, the soldiers are coming back."

A Jeep pulled up, and two armed men jumped out, the pyramids silhouetted behind them.

One with a black, bushy mustache said, "Why are you still here? It's getting too cloudy for pictures of the moon over the monuments. Let me see your passports." He held out his hand.

Mike hesitated, trying to come up with a clever lie, when a mild vibration shook the ground beneath his feet. "What the hell was that?" His eyes wide, he took a few steps back and pointed behind the Egyptians.

"We're not falling for that." The officer opened his hand. "Passports, now."

Mike pointed again. "But it's not supposed to do that."

Lisa took her cue and screamed, "It's going to explode. We have to get away from here."

The soldiers turned around and froze, staring at the Great Pyramid. Jagged electrical sparks fired across the giant monument, deep humming grew louder, and the ground under them shook. The Egyptians jumped into the Jeep and sped toward the pyrotechnic display.

"I don't know what's happening, but you can bet Sam had something to do with it." Mike stared at the giant structure as thousands of blue lightning bolts danced across its surface.

Lance's eyes widened. "Whoa, what should we do?"

"If we get too close, the authorities will think we had something to do with this and arrest us." Bryce grabbed a handle on the SUV to steady himself on the pulsating ground.

"What about Sam and Banger?" Lisa focused her binoculars on the pyramid.

Mike clenched his fists. "I hope they aren't inside, because if they are, they're probably fried to a crisp by now."

"Think we should drive closer to the Sphinx and hope they'll come out there?" Lance focused his binoculars on the stone beast.

Mike checked his earbuds. "We'll wait a few more minutes and see if they contact us."

SIXTEEN

The Great Pyramid

We rounded a corner on the slanted ramp and faced a tall metal cage big enough for two people. I stared at it, trying to remember the diagrams I'd studied back in that room beneath the Sphinx. Meanwhile, the stones vibrated all around us and pulsated with energy.

"This is an odd place for a cage." Banger examined the unusual metal bars.

"There has to be a reason—" I snapped my fingers. "Of course, it's a Faraday cage. We need to get inside fast."

Banger tugged on it. "The door's locked, Sam."

"Let me try." I ran my hands up and down the cage bars, searching for a latch. There wasn't one.

"Better think of something fast, my queen."

Banger gripped the bars to steady himself on the shaking floor.

"Be the queen—maybe that's it." Speaking the ancient language, I commanded the cage door to open.

The jewel in my newly acquired bracelet illuminated, and the door swung open. I glanced at my wrist. "I wasn't expecting that to happen."

Banger dropped his shield and rushed in. I followed.

He grabbed the side bars as the door closed. "What exactly is a Faraday cage?"

"An English scientist named Michael Faraday invented it to shield the occupants from electric currents and EMFs." I glanced around, expecting something bad to happen outside the cage. "Looks like the Atlanteans built one several thousand years before he did."

Banger shined his flashlight on the metal bars. "Seems to be made of the same unobtainium as the sphere."

The cage shook as blue lightning bolts flashed on the outside, and the pyramid's vibrations became more intense. A deep rumbling like an earthquake preceded a shift in the blocks around us. The stone supporting the cage moved us into an opening created when adjacent blocks slid sideways, up, and down, like pieces in a 3-D puzzle, and enclosed us in a vertical shaft.

I looked up into the long passage, and a scary image popped into my head.

Uh oh.

I pulled Banger's paraglider and the harness we'd saved from my damaged chute out of my backpack and then donned my harness and empty backpack.

Handing him the chute, I said, "Uh, Banger, I think you'd better strap on your paraglider."

He shined his light up through the overhead bars into the vertical shaft. "What aren't you telling me, Sam? Is this cage about to launch us into the sky?"

"Maybe. Hurry and strap in so I can clip my harness to you, um, just in case."

He looked at me and shook his head. "Ah, my queen, you never disappoint."

While he rigged his paraglider, I double-tied the sphere's satchel to my harness and my belly pack in case I was right about what might happen next.

"Ready." He turned me around, tugged me backward, and clipped me to his harness in four places. "Now you're going wherever I'm going."

Blazing fingers of dancing light all around us made me see stars. My ears rang, and my head spun, dizzy from the strobe effect.

Banger handed me a section of the folded paraglider. "If we somehow launch into the sky, hold this close to us so it doesn't snag on anything on the way out."

I held the fabric against me. "Better hope we can get it open before we become dirt darts."

Deep humming increased to a high-pitched whine, and the Faraday cage shot straight up the shaft.

"Get ready," Banger said as he put his arms around me and held me against him.

"I hope the roof opens before we get there." I slid my hands over his and gripped them like a lifeline. He must've felt my body trembling, but he didn't say anything. Our super-charged ride was too scary for a sarcastic quip, even from him.

The stone ceiling loomed over us, threatening to smash us into a mess of broken bones and metal bars. When we were about fifty feet from the top, a stone slid aside, revealing a dark, cloud-covered sky.

Our cage increased in speed, and its metal top sprang open. I tightened my grip on Banger's hands.

We ascended so fast everything was a blur. When we reached the opening in the roof, the cage halted, but we didn't. We shot out of the pyramid like we'd been fired from a cannon.

When our vertical path upward arced into a descent, we flung out the black chute and waited for it to open. A sudden jerk confirmed it had filled with air.

Exhaling, I said, "My heart rate just broke a world record." Cool air swirled around me as my hearing and vision returned to normal. "Holy crap!

The pyramid is shooting energy beams out the shafts the Egyptians thought were air vents. Better steer clear."

"That'll be easier than avoiding all those soldiers." He pointed. "Good thing they're staring at the electric storm, but we're only five hundred feet above them, which means we have less than thirty seconds before touchdown."

"I have an idea." Speaking in Atlantean, I commanded the sphere to pull us to the airport.

The globe surged forward inside the satchel, yanking us away from the pyramids.

"What's happening, Sam? I can't see what you're doing."

"The sphere is towing us—probably flies using some kind of anti-gravity technology. I told it to take us to the airport."

It was a good thing our throat mikes and earbuds allowed us to communicate in whispers.

"We'd better inform the team," Banger said. "They're probably freaking out, wondering what's happening with us and the pyramid."

"You're right—I doubt they saw us with the clouds blocking the moon." I keyed my transmitter. "Mike, can you hear me?"

"Sam, where are you, and what's happening with the pyramid?"

"We're flying together in Banger's paraglider. The sphere is pulling us back to the airport. Meet us at the airplane. Hurry."

"Roger, team is RTB." Mike clicked off.

Next, I called our pilots. "Gulfstream, this is Sam."

Bill answered, "I read you, Sam."

"Plan wheels-up in fifteen minutes—could be exciting."

"Copy wheels up in fifteen. What's our destination?"

"Probably Ethiopia. File for somewhere outside Egypt and change it after we're airborne."

"Understood. Gulfstream out."

The device began pulling us so fast, our chute dragged behind us at a forty-five-degree angle. It wouldn't hold together much longer at that speed, so I commanded the sphere to slow down. In seconds, we were gliding along at about twenty knots with the rectangular canopy above us.

Banger said, "I'd feel better if I knew whether your little buddy could keep us airborne if the chute breaks."

"Let's hope we won't have to find out the hard way." I gulped in the crisp night air and pointed. "There's the airport about five miles away."

"The sooner we're back in the jet the better." He paused. "Mike won't be happy about the pyramid."

"Maybe not, but the Egyptians should be grateful. It could provide free electricity for their entire nation."

"Only if they figure out how to harness it." He

paused. "We could send an anonymous tip to look inside the room under the left paw."

"But then they'll discover someone recently blew up the room under the right paw. Can they trace the explosives back to America?"

He chuckled. "Come on, you think I'm an amateur? I used Chinese materials."

"Of course, you did. How could I doubt you?"

He nudged me. "See those flashing lights in the distance?"

"Looks like cops headed to the airport. I hope they aren't chasing our team."

Banger pointed to the right. "That's our jet over there. Deactivate the sphere, and I'll land behind the airplane. No one will see us in the dark with this black canopy."

I commanded the little guy to stop pulling us and shoved the satchel back inside my belly bag. "The sphere is secure."

"Ten seconds to touchdown, and there's the team walking to the airplane." Banger guided us to a gentle landing behind the jet.

"Perfect timing." I helped him gather the silk and roll it up.

We strolled around the tail as if we'd been doing the exterior preflight inspection. He opened the baggage compartment and tossed the chute inside along with our backpacks and my harness.

Mike trotted up to us. "Hey, Banger, good job keeping my sister in one piece. Come inside and tell us what happened." He hugged me and ushered us up the entry stairs.

I waited by the door until everyone was aboard and retracted the boarding steps.

"What are you doing?" Mike asked.

"Closing the door." I peeked out the side window. "Authorities are probably closing in. We need to leave now."

"We can't leave Egypt until you fix that giant safety hazard you created." Mike raised a brow. "What did you do to the Great Pyramid, sis?"

I closed the entry door, and Bill and Laura started the engines.

"We have to go while we still can." I elbowed Banger. "Tell him we can't afford to get stuck here."

"She's right, Mike." He glanced at Laura, who'd left the cockpit to get an update from us.

She asked, "Where to this time?"

"Take us to whichever airport is nearest to Hadar, Ethiopia. It's in the Awash Valley of the Afar Triangle," I said. "We'll need an SUV when we get there."

She glanced at Mike for confirmation.

Mike nodded. "Get us out of here as fast as possible."

"One more thing," I said to her. "Be careful to avoid the energy beams shooting out of the Great Pyramid."

"Energy beams? Seriously?" She glanced at the team to see if I was joking.

Banger nodded. "We're serious. You'll see them after takeoff."

She shook her head. "Who *are* you people?"

Banger moved closer to her. "Don't forget we have diplomatic immunity, so no matter what ATC says, get us airborne and the hell out of Egyptian airspace. Understand?"

"No, but we'll do it anyway." Laura turned and entered the cockpit.

As we taxied to the runway, I looked out a passenger window and spotted two police cars racing toward us with their lights flashing. The pilots must've seen them. Our jet increased speed, skidded onto the runway, and went to full takeoff power.

Our entire team was glued to the windows.

"It's going to be close," Lance said as we rocketed down the runway.

When the drivers realized the jet wasn't going to stop, they panicked and spun their cars, crashing into each other. They climbed out and shook their fists at us as we blasted past them.

"I knew we could count on Bill and Laura." I blew out a sigh and sat back as we accelerated away from Egypt and the chaotic lights over Giza. The Great Pyramid was still putting on a spectacular pyrotechnic show.

Lance leaned in and hugged me. "You okay, Sam?"

"We're good, just a couple of burns … hey, mine are gone." My jaw dropped as I held out my right hand and stared at the area where the copper device had burned me. My skin looked normal. I turned to Banger. "Do you still have that burn on your arm?"

He checked his right forearm, and his eyes widened. "It's gone. How'd that happen?"

"One of my devices must have healing technology. I wonder which one?" I glanced at the gold bracelet I'd taken from the engineering chamber. The diamond wasn't illuminated.

"Ooh, pretty bracelet." Lisa leaned closer. "Where'd you find it? That diamond's huge."

"It was in a chamber under the left paw of the Sphinx. I tried it on, and it attached itself to my arm. I can't take it off." I made a show of trying to remove it.

Mike perched beside me. "Did you find the Blue Dragon?"

I frowned. "No, sorry."

He slid onto a seat across from Banger and me. "All right, explain what you did and why you can't undo it." Mike crossed his arms.

Banger nudged me and said, "I'll start. Uh, remember that separate SEAL mission we were assigned?"

Mike hesitated, then his eyes widened. "You destroyed it?"

Banger nodded.

"Destroyed what?" Bryce looked at us.

Banger glanced sideways at me. "A WMD we

found under the Sphinx. The detonation caused a cave-in inside the tunnel that connected to the Great Pyramid."

"We were trapped until we discovered that the sphere obeys my commands as long as I speak Atlantean." I patted my belly pack. "It's my new best friend."

"Yeah, the little ball annihilated a huge stone that blocked our path, and later, it pulled us back to the airport in the paraglider." He grinned.

"It did other stuff too." I hugged the bag holding the sphere. "I really like it now."

"But what about the pyramid?" Lisa looked at me.

"We discovered a chamber under the Sphinx that had engineering diagrams carved onto the walls, indicating the Great Pyramid was a power plant. I thought maybe if we fired it up again, a hidden chamber would open and reveal the Blue Dragon." I shrugged. "No such luck."

"But why can't you shut it down?" Lance leaned forward.

"We barely escaped electrocution in a Faraday cage that launched us into the sky." Banger smiled at me.

"But the Egyptians must've had a way to turn on the power plant without getting fried." Lance looked from Banger to me.

I shook my head. "The Egyptians didn't have a clue—Atlanteans built the power plant. The normal way to activate it was in the pumphouse beneath the pyramid. That was back when the necessary components were already in place in the electrical corridor. Someone would open the valve to let in water from the Nile, and when the hydrodynamic pressure built to the point that it vibrated the pyramid, the crystals would produce electricity. By then, the operator had left the pumphouse and returned via the tunnel to the chamber under the Sphinx."

Banger nodded. "But we didn't have that option because the electrical devices in the pyramid had been stolen a long time ago. We found spare parts in the engineering chamber under the Sphinx and hauled nine heavy crystal pyramids all the way to the power plant."

I jumped back in. "I thought we'd have time to put them on their terminals before the pump created enough pressure to vibrate them into producing electricity. Plus, we didn't know we weren't supposed to be inside the pyramid when the power was on."

Banger glanced at me. "And we couldn't return through the connecting tunnel because it was blocked."

"We lucked out finding that Faraday cage, which was an escape device." I high-fived Banger.

Mike rubbed the back of his neck. "So now we're in deep shit with no way out."

"Wrong, brother dear. We did Egypt a huge favor, supplying them with free electricity." I shrugged. "The original plans showed the pyramid sending energy beams into obelisks strategically placed around the country, but several of those are missing now."

Banger nodded. "They should thank us—a few modifications and they'll be good to go."

"No way in hell are we admitting we did this." Mike glared at us.

"Relax, Mike." Banger nudged me. "Sam will send an anonymous message, explaining where to find the diagrams for the power plant, and Egyptian engineers can figure out how to harness the energy. Problem solved."

"The *problem* is not solved. It could take months or years to harness the power. Meanwhile, energy beams are shooting out of the pyramid. There has to be a way to turn it off."

I thought about the design. "If they shut off the water flowing in from the Nile, the hydrodynamic pressure will drop, the blocks will stop vibrating, and the crystals will stop producing electricity. The drawings in the room under the left paw will show where the pipe connects to the Nile." I looked at Mike. "Once their engineers see those diagrams, they'll realize that shutting off the water will turn off the powerplant."

"Maybe that will work, but what am I supposed to tell Commander Metz? He's expecting a report, and the man's not stupid. He'll know you did this." Mike shook his head.

240

"Tell him the truth." I shrugged. "Just don't put it in writing." I pulled out the Eye. "I'm going to try something simple." I said in Atlantean, "Show me where the Blue Dragon is hidden."

The Eye filled with light and projected a hologram of gold lettering written in the ancient language.

"Stupid hologram," I shouted, exasperated.

"What does it say?" Lisa stared at the strange words.

"It says an Atlantean queen must find the Blue Dragon where it's hidden in the Dark Continent, ensconced in an arid enigma and a primordial paradox, cloaked in eternal darkness."

"Well, bugger that." Lisa punched her seat, releasing her frustration.

Lance pointed at the Eye. "Ask it if we'll find anything important in Hadar."

I asked, and the Eye projected a new hologram that showed the entrance to a cave along a riverbank beneath a huge oak tree—the only tree in the vicinity.

"Oh, good." I rolled my eyes. "Another cave."

Banger crossed his arms. "There you go, stealing my lines again."

Mike sighed. "All right, everyone, get some sleep. Ethiopia isn't that far from here. We'll probably land in a couple hours." He reclined his seat and closed his eyes.

SEVENTEEN

Hadar, Ethiopia

The roaring of thrust reversers jolted me awake much too soon. I peered out a window as we landed in Ethiopia and taxied to the ramp. *I hope the Blue Dragon is in Hadar. I can't stand the thought of Sweet-water killing Ross if I don't find it.*

Mike tapped my back. "Any chance this'll be a quick in-and-out?"

I turned and yawned, covering my face with my hand to conceal my raw emotions. "Your guess is as good as mine."

"All right, here come the customs officials," Mike said to the team. "Pull out your diplomatic passports."

As soon as customs left, we sent our pilots to a hotel and closed the airplane's window shades.

Once again, I pulled out the Eye and said in the ancient language, "Show me where to go in Hadar."

Again, a hologram displayed a cave on a riverbank, directly beneath a lone oak tree.

Lisa paged through a guidebook for Africa. "That doesn't look like the cave complex for the Cradle of Humankind in Hadar."

I peered over her shoulder. "It's not, but that's a good thing—no guards."

"Good, maybe we'll have an easy go of it for a change." Bryce checked his weapon and shoved it inside his backpack.

Banger patted Bryce's back. "Nothing's ever easy when Sam's involved."

"Well then, we'd better take along those flashlights with the hundred-thousand-hour lithium batteries," I said as I raised a brow in Banger's direction.

He grinned. "My queen, I do believe you're getting the hang of SEAL banter."

"I might need years of therapy to undo all the terrors I've experienced with you." Forgetting what had happened last time, I socked his biceps. "Ow! Your arm feels like it's made of concrete."

"That's what you get for the love tap." Banger touched his index finger to his cheek. "Next time you feel the urge, try a pain-free kiss right here instead."

Lance grinned at us. "You two have developed an interesting relationship."

"A result of cheating death too many times with little Miss Danger Magnet." Banger patted my head.

Lance nodded. "Been there, done that."

"If you boys are done busting my chops, let's go find that giant diamond." I pushed past them, the hint of a grin on my lips. Their teasing, however annoying, helped distract me from worrying about Ross.

"Better bring some spelunking gear." Mike opened the inside door between the cabin and the baggage compartment.

"And plenty of bottled water." Bryce followed him. "It's like an oven here."

We loaded our backpacks with whatever we thought might be useful and headed for the airport terminal.

"We'll rent a vehicle and stop for some food before we start searching." Mike led us to the rental counter.

Thirty minutes later, we parked in front of a restaurant near the airport, and our meals were ready before we finished our first cups of coffee.

Mike took a bite of his omelet. "I hope it won't take long to find that lone oak tree."

"Can't be many trees in a desert." Banger sipped his coffee. "We'll stop in Hadar and ask a local."

After filling up on breakfast, Bryce drove us to

Ethiopia's Cradle of Humankind, which was two hours from the airport.

When we arrived in Hadar, we asked a villager where we could find a large oak tree beside a river. That turned out to be easier than we'd expected.

"Only one tree beside the river, and that one survived because a law protects it. Take that road," he said, pointing to his left.

We drove to the shallow river, and the oak tree was easy to spot in the sparse landscape.

I tapped Bryce's shoulder. "There it is, just like in the hologram."

Heat radiated over the barren land as he parked above the isolated riverbank.

"Alrighty, fingers crossed we find it this time." I jumped out of the SUV and pretended I was fine with entering another cave as I slipped on my spelunking harness and snugged it tight.

Mike tied a rope around the tree and clipped his harness to it. "We'll use this as a safety line, and Bryce will stay up here to cover our six." He backed down the ten-foot vertical bank.

Bryce leaned against the car, while the rest of us clipped ourselves to the line before dropping down.

I stopped next to my brother, wiped sweat from my forehead, and shined a light into the cave. "Looks like it slants down and goes deep underground." *Crap.*

"I'm right behind you." Banger tapped my shoulder. "Try not to disturb the bats."

My voice rose an octave. "What bats?"

"Geez, sis, when will you learn not to take his bait?" Mike shined his light on the earthen and rock ceiling. "See? No winged rodents."

I turned and glared at Banger.

"Don't give me the evil eye. They like to perch deep inside caves." He spun me around. "You'll see."

I walked slowly, scanning the walls and ceiling with my light, searching for anything that might indicate a hidden artifact.

And looking for creepy little winged creatures.

The deeper we went, the higher my heart rate climbed.

"What was that noise?" Lisa poked me and tilted her head.

"Probably the occasional flutter of wings." Banger chuckled and nudged us forward.

I turned and glared at him. "I don't like bats."

"Why not?" He looked at me as if I'd said I hated puppies.

"Because the little buggers like to dive at my blond hair." I smoothed my long ponytail.

Lance handed me his ballcap. "Here, wear this."

"Thank you." I kissed his cheek.

Fluttering sounds filtered through the passage as I stuffed my hair into the ballcap.

About sixty yards into the cave, it widened into a broad cavern. At least five hundred bats covered the high ceiling, sending my heart rate into the danger zone.

Banger nudged me. "Keep your voice low and maybe they won't swarm us."

Lance moved up beside me. "If they dive at us, stand close to a wall, and I'll get in front of you and block them."

"Thank you, Lance. Good to know there's at least one gentleman in the group." I lifted a brow at Banger, and he smirked at me.

Lisa stared at the critters hanging on the ceiling and whispered, "What makes you think we'll find something the locals missed?"

The men looked at her and laughed.

Mike shook his head. "Where have you been since we started this quest in Mogadishu?"

"Right, I'm forgetting the *Sam factor*. Of course, we'll find something." Lisa eased behind Banger.

"Alrighty, here we go." I ran my hands over the rock walls while my teammates searched the cave with their flashlights. And I kept glancing up at the winged rodents—couldn't help it.

No energy spikes were evident, and no symbols were carved into the rock.

Crap.

Crawling on my hands and knees, I checked the floor.

Nothing but dirt and bat dung. I didn't like getting it on my bare skin, but I couldn't wear gloves and still feel an energy spike.

"I hate this," I said, wiping my dirty hands on my jeans.

"What?" Mike looked at me. "Nothing here?"

I shined my light on the creepy critters. "Might be something in the ceiling, but they're blocking my view."

"Time to wake up the little dudes." Banger lifted his hands. "Start clapping."

Our claps echoed in the cavern, and bats scattered, confused by the noise. Their fluttering wings filled the air around me.

Ducking the diving demons, I stepped behind Lance. "Is there a way to shoo them outside?"

Banger waved his arms. "Go! Fly away and stop bothering our queen."

"*Funny*." Scanning the ceiling with my light, I spotted a glint of something gold, partially obscured by dirt.

"Banger, can you lift me up there?" Ignoring the circling creatures, I pointed at the place I needed to reach.

"Easy peasy." He squatted down and grasped my ankles.

With his long reach, I was able to get within inches of my goal. "A little higher?"

I ducked flapping wings and almost lost my balance.

"Keep your legs stiff." He tossed me up just enough to get his hands under my feet.

That was all it took to close the gap. "Got it.

Hold fast." Brushing away packed dirt, I uncovered a small gold trident.

When I grasped it, an energy spike shot through me, and I lost my grip. Banger must've felt it too because he let go of my feet, and I fell backward.

"Help!"

A second later, he caught me. "What happened, Sam?"

"A jolt of energy startled me, and I lost my balance." I hugged him. "Thanks for catching me."

"You're looking at the touchdown king for the Crimson Tide. I never dropped the ball." Banger set me down. "Sorry about letting go. That surge of energy surprised me. Ready for another lift?"

"Not until my heart calms down." I glanced at my brother. "Mike should lift me first so you can easily get your hands under my feet and raise me the rest of the way."

He stepped back as Mike grabbed my ankles and lifted. Then Banger's hands closed around my feet and raised me back up to the trident.

I looked down at my big friend. "Get ready for another jolt."

Bracing for the energy spike as I grabbed it, I squeezed hard and turned it ninety degrees. Vibrations in the ceiling indicated something was trying to move.

Dirt sprinkled onto my ballcap, and it took all my concentration not to jerk away.

Finally, a small slab of rock slid back, and a

foot-long metal canister dropped on my head from two feet above me.

"Ow." I grabbed it with one hand as it dropped onto my shoulder to stop it from falling to the floor.

Nothing happened when I held it—just a hint of energy.

"It looks like the same type of metal as the sphere. I need somebody to catch this so I can shine my light into the hole." I glanced down and dropped it into Mike's waiting hands.

My light revealed a glint of gold.

I hope there aren't any spiders in there.

I hesitated, reached in, and pulled out a gold ring with tridents curving around the band. It was set with a single diamond shaped like a pyramid. The stone had to be twenty carats and was set with the tip pointing up out of the ring.

I slipped it onto my right ring finger and shined my light into the hole for a final look. Nothing gleamed.

A careful examination of the ceiling convinced me I'd found everything meant to be found.

Or had I?

I sucked in a deep breath and reached back in. My fingers traced the dirt, searching for something with a firm, distinctive shape. A loose stone pulled free and bounced off my head on its way to the ground. Something light crawled across my hand and dropped onto my shoulder.

I glanced down and spotted a big spider crawling down my chest.

Arachnophobia took over, and I forgot about everything except getting the horrid beastie off me. I shrieked, swatted the spider, lost my balance, and fell.

Again.

Banger caught me and set me lightly on the ground. "What the hell, Sam?"

I stomped my eight-legged nemesis, then stood on tiptoe and kissed Banger's cheek. "Huge spider. Thanks for the save."

He looked at me and busted out laughing.

"*Really*, sis, a spider?" Mike handed me the silvery-blue canister. "Can you open it?"

"I'd rather wait until we get outside." I turned around, my heart still pounding. "Put it in my backpack, and I'll open it in the sunlight."

Mike zipped it inside, and we followed the team out of the dark cave.

The moment I stepped into the hot sun I felt the tension leave me.

That didn't last long.

We climbed up to the road, and Mike untied the line from the tree.

Bryce searched our faces. "Find anything?"

Before we could answer, two police vehicles roared up and slid to a stop. Four local cops jumped out.

"What you people doing?" one of them said in broken English. "This site protected."

Mike held the rope. "We didn't hurt the tree. Just took a brief tour of the cave. Lots of bats in there."

The policemen drew their weapons.

"Give backpacks." The lead officer held out his hand.

"Forget it. We don't have to give you anything." Bryce flashed his special passport. "We have diplomatic immunity."

"Not here." He waved his gun. "Give wallets, everything."

Bryce shoved his passport into a pocket. "What is this, a robbery? You're police officers."

The cop nodded. "Give us everything now or we shoot you."

Bryce slipped off his backpack and reached inside it for his weapon. One of the officers saw him do it and shot Bryce in his left shoulder. He dropped his backpack, fell backward off the steep bank, and rolled down to the river.

"No more shooting," I shouted. "I'll give you my treasure." I pulled out the silvery-blue globe and whispered instructions in Atlantean.

My little buddy flew up and lasered the weapons out of the cops' hands.

I glared at them. "You shot my friend. If you move, that thing will burn holes through you."

As the sphere hovered in front of them, the cops froze, their eyes radiating terror.

Mike took charge. "Banger and Lance, cuff them to their cars and toss their keys in the river while I help the women take care of Bryce."

As soon as the cops were cuffed, I put the sphere back in my belly bag and rushed down to Bryce.

Mike rigged the rope to the tree again and grabbed an extra harness. Lisa pulled a first aid kit from our SUV and followed us down to where our friend lay at the water's edge.

I ripped off my shirttail and pressed it over his wound with my right hand to stem the blood flow. The diamond in my bracelet illuminated, and I felt energy flow into my hand.

"Whoa, what's happening?" I lifted the fabric and checked his wound. The bleeding had stopped even though his wound was still open.

The diamond in my bracelet blazed with brilliant light as I placed my bare palm over his wound. In seconds, the bullet in his shoulder slid into my hand.

"Wow, look at this!" I showed the bullet to Bryce, Mike, and Lisa.

"The bracelet must be doing it," Mike said. "Let's see if it heals him now."

I dropped the bullet into Bryce's chest pocket and placed my palm over his wound again.

Bryce murmured, "Every time you touch me with your right hand, the pain stops."

As my hand buzzed with energy, his flesh mended in less than a minute, leaving no scar.

"Thanks, Sam, you fixed it." Bryce looked at his shoulder. "Good as new and no pain."

Mike slipped a harness over him. "Are you okay to go up?"

"Fine." Bryce sat up. "Well, maybe a little woozy from the blood loss."

"Let's get you up to the SUV." Mike clipped Bryce's harness to the rope and hauled him up the cliff. Banger met him at the top and helped him into the car.

Then Mike reached down and pulled me up the final two feet. "Check if that metal thing you found is safe to bring aboard the airplane." He reached for Lisa and helped her up. They waited in the SUV with our teammates.

I removed the canister from my backpack and stood with it outside the car.

Nothing happened.

My hands didn't tingle, and it didn't open.

The cops watched me. One must've felt brave again and yelled, "You not get away. We find you."

I turned my back to them and studied the metal container. It had a tiny triangular indentation in one end. The notch appeared to be the same size as the diamond in the ring I'd found in the cave.

Without taking off the ring, I stuck the gem's tip into the indent.

It fit perfectly.

The strange box sprang open, revealing a thick scroll secured to one side and several tiny vials strapped onto the other side.

"Mike, there's a scroll and some vials, but it's not a weapon. I'll figure it out on the airplane."

Lisa said, "Better stop on the way to the airport and buy Bryce a clean shirt. Airport officials will notice the blood."

"Good idea." Mike waited while everyone climbed in, then drove into town and stopped at a T-shirt vendor near the Hadar caves.

"I'll call the pilots while Bryce buys a new shirt," Mike said. He woke Bill and told him we were on our way back.

We drove to the airport and turned in the rental. Bryce wore a clean new T-shirt as we breezed through customs and security with our diplomatic passports.

Our pilots, Bill and Laura, weren't on the jet.

"Lance, will you do the walkaround while I do the interior preflight checks?" I dropped my backpack on a seat and slipped into the cockpit as he headed outside.

After firing up the auxiliary power unit and getting the electrical power and air conditioning operational, I ran through the preflight checks and called for a clearance to Somalia.

The pilots straggled in, looking exhausted.

Bill tapped my shoulder. "Sorry, thought we'd get here before you. Where to now?"

I turned to him. "Everything's set. I got a clearance for Mogadishu, which you will change to Camp Baledogle after we're airborne. Sorry we interrupted your rest, but you'll get plenty of sleep once we return to the base." I slipped out of his seat and eased past him.

He checked the panel. "Thanks for the setup. We'll get going after Laura does a quick walkaround inspection."

Lance poked his head through the door. "I just did it. Everything looks good."

I added, "Lance is a pilot with Luxury International Airlines."

"Right, I remember." Bill yawned. "Close the entry door and we'll go."

Laura slid into the copilot seat, and they began the engine start sequence.

I leaned in. "Uh, don't let anyone stop you from taking off."

He glanced back at me. "Are we in trouble again?"

"Maybe, but this time there won't be any energy beams to dodge."

He met Laura's eyes. "It's your turn to fly, but I'll take it if you'd rather not."

"No problem, boss, I've got this." She looked over her shoulder and flashed me a smile.

I nodded and left the cockpit.

A few minutes later, we taxied to the runway. I glanced out a passenger window and spotted two police cruisers racing toward us.

"Crap, I think it's the same cops who tried to rob us back at the riverbank. They're angling across to try and block us from taking off." I jumped up and ran to the cockpit.

EIGHTEEN

I burst into the cockpit. "Those cop cars are trying to intercept us. Don't let them." I pointed.

"Looks like a replay of Cairo," Bill said.

"Except these cops probably aren't smart enough to stop." I stared at the speeding cars.

Laura pushed up the throttles as we rounded the turn onto the runway. Our sleek jet's rapid acceleration pinned me against the cockpit door as the police cars angled toward us.

"It's going to be close, but my money is on our Gulfstream. Better buckle up," Laura said.

I pulled down the jumpseat and strapped in.

Laura waited until the last moment and hauled back on the yoke. "Gear up … flaps up."

We barely cleared the police cars, our main wheels almost brushing the vehicles' roofs.

Laura glanced back at me. "Flying you around is a lot more exciting than flying corporate executives."

"I'm glad you and Bill are such badass pilots. Good work. You'll get a much longer rest break at Camp Baledogle." I waved and left the cockpit.

Back at my seat, I pulled the canister out of my backpack and used my new ring to open it.

Mike leaned in. "Close call with those cops. What's in there?"

I held it open. "A thick scroll and some vials."

"Start reading and let us know if you discover anything important." Mike sat back and reclined his seat. The rest of the team followed his lead.

I pulled out the scroll and unrolled it. The text was in Atlantean—no surprise. I was fortunate the triplets had transferred all their knowledge of Atlantis—its language, history, and technology—to me via their advanced form of telepathy. In an instant they had saved me years of studying the scrolls I'd recovered from Atlantis's Hall of Records.

I slowly read the ancient scroll. The information shocked me. I read it again, thinking it could turn the world of anthropology upside down. Then I stared at the vials and wondered if I should tell anyone about this or just destroy everything and avoid the uproar it would cause. My mind raced as I rolled up the scroll and secured it inside its container.

Banger sat beside me. "Anything interesting in there?"

"Oh, yeah, but the scientific world won't like it."

"All right, my queen, let's have it." Banger sat back and looked into my eyes.

"For starters, Darwin's theory will be toast if this gets out. At least the part about human evolution." The evidence rested on my lap.

Banger sat up. "No kidding? What's on the scroll?"

"Atlanteans claim their civilization has been here for two hundred thousand years. They experimented with various types of apes to produce smarter, more capable animals with the end goal being domestication and servitude."

"Are you saying Africans descended from apes?" Banger arched a brow. "I thought that was what Darwin said."

"According to this, Darwin was wrong. Apes evolved from the many DNA experiments done on them by Atlanteans over millennia. The apes' DNA is very similar to ours because the Atlanteans injected their DNA into ape embryos." I glanced at the ancient container. "This refutes the theory that we evolved from apes. Neanderthals were examples of failed experiments, as were many others."

"Right, because if we evolved from apes, why are there still apes?"

I nodded. "My thoughts exactly."

Banger looked at me. "What are you going to do with the scroll and vials?"

"Well, the thing is, the DNA in the vials is Atlantean, which means if scientists get their hands on it, they might clone some new Atlanteans, and that might not be a good thing." I sighed.

"Besides the obvious moral issues, what concerns you?" Banger searched my eyes.

"Even though Atlanteans were super intelligent, they were also warmongers bent on world domination." I tapped the canister. "All they cared about were things that benefitted their people. Don't forget they planned to drown millions of people to regain control of the world."

"What about you? You're an Atlantean descendant, and you're not like that."

"I'm a descendant of a separate race worshipped by them because of our rare electromagnetic energy frequency and our telepathic and psychic abilities."

"Are you worried that breeding a new race of Atlanteans could end up destroying the world as we know it?"

"It's possible, not to mention the giant can of worms this scroll will open in the science of anthropology."

"What do you think Professor Armitage would do about this?" Banger nudged me. "Maybe you should discuss it with him."

"Ben will be blown away by this." I pulled out

my satellite phone. "And he has colleagues in the Anthropology Department at Harvard. I'll ask his advice."

Ben answered on the first ring. "Sam, glad you called. Harvard is buzzing about the Great Pyramid. Live video is playing on all the news networks. Did you do that?"

I gave him a brief recap about the engineering room under the Sphinx's left paw and what we'd done to fire up the power plant. "We had to leave in a hurry to avoid getting fried, and we didn't find the Blue Dragon."

"That's too bad," Ben said. "Did you find anything interesting?"

"That's why I'm calling." I gave him a description of what we found in the cave near Hadar. "I know scientists don't like having their life's work disproved. Do you think we should destroy the scroll and vials and forget we ever found them?"

"Never. You have something that might change history and anthropology as we know it. It's too important to be discarded." Ben paused. "Your little adventure in the Great Pyramid has already proven the Egyptians didn't build it. Not to mention everything we're learning from the Atlantean archives you recovered. It's high time the scientific community realizes just how profoundly Atlantis influenced the entire world for many thousands of years."

"It's just that I'm worried about what might be done with the DNA in the vials."

"Look, Sam, I understand you experienced the Atlanteans at their worst, but a lot of good might come from studying their DNA—medical cures, advances to the human race—the possibilities are endless." His tone radiated excitement.

"I don't know, Ben. I want to do the right thing. I guess I'll hand it over to our government and let them worry about what to do with it. They'll probably ask you for advice."

"I hope I can convince them to give a copy of the scroll and a vial or two to Harvard for further study." He paused. "What about the Blue Dragon? Where will you go next?"

"The Cradle of Humankind in Ethiopia had no clues to its location. Could be the same at the other site in South Africa. Any suggestions on where the Lost Sahara Civilization might be?"

Ben paused a few beats. "Try looking for a powerful intersection of ley lines in Tassili n'Ajjer."

"Tassili n'Ajjer? Where's that?" I pulled out my map of Africa.

"It's a huge national park and UNESCO World Heritage site in the southeast section of Algeria, near where it borders Libya, Niger, and Mali in the Sahara—looks like a weird lunar landscape. The area covers twenty-eight thousand square miles of rock forests made from eroded sandstone. That's why you need to find intersecting ley lines to narrow down your search grid."

"And what exactly am I looking for?" I asked, exasperated.

"An ancient civilization hidden somewhere under the Sahara Desert."

"But how can you be certain it's there? I can't afford to waste time with lives at stake."

"Fossils, cave paintings—some dating back twelve-thousand years, and ancient pottery have been found in a huge area covering all the way from Timbuktu in the west to Chad in the east. They prove that people lived in a lush tropical climate thousands of years ago. Satellite imagery shows a megalake once covered forty-two thousand square miles of the Sahara."

What Ben said didn't make sense. I asked, "Why did it become a huge desert?"

"The Earth's axis changed its tilt by two de-grees, triggering a climate shift that turned the area into an arid wasteland. That ancient civilization ex-isted, Sam. Find a way down to it, maybe inside one of those strange rock towers. The Blue Dragon might be hidden near one of the cities in a primor-dial lake or in a cave that connects to the lake. Look for an intersection of ley lines."

"Oh, *good*, sounds easy," I said, my frustration building.

"Sorry, but if it were easy, anyone could find the Blue Dragon, including Sweetwater."

"You're right, Ben, and I appreciate your help. It's just that I'm worried it'll take too long to find it.

There are only five days left after today, and then Ross and Derek will be killed."

"I'll research other possible sites while you're busy searching." Ben paused. "If you don't find it there, I'll have another location teed up for you."

"Thanks, Ben. I'll call as soon as we finish in Algeria, but first we'll need to get some sleep."

"Understood. Good luck, Sam. I hope you find it tomorrow."

An hour later, we landed at Camp Baledogle.

Mike tapped my shoulder. "Sam, you and I will meet first with Commander Metz and General Ryan while our team sleeps." Mike held the gold cylinder with the riddle inside from Thonis-Heracleion. He'd retrieved it from the wall in the airplane's lavatory. "We'll hand over this and the metal canister you found near Hadar, answer their questions, and then grab some sleep."

I nodded, yawning. "By the way, I discussed it with Ben, and our next stop is a weird section of Algeria known as Tassili n'Ajjer. Should be a lot more interesting than that cave in Hadar."

"Knowing you, it'll probably turn out to be the only place on Earth with living dinosaurs."

I grinned. "Good, then we can hitch a ride on a pterodactyl. I've always wanted to fly one." My tone matched his. I was getting the hang of SEAL banter.

Tassili n'Ajjer

It was day three in our one-week quest to find the Blue Dragon before Sweetwater's ultimatum expired. We passed a small area where, according to the sign, the live cypress trees were four thousand years old but were no longer able to reproduce. I studied the GPS as Bryce drove our military Humvee through an endless forest of strange stone towers bathed in bright sunlight.

Nature had eroded the sandstone into a sea of unusual shapes rising from the plateau's harsh wasteland. The reddish-brown-and-black landscape looked otherworldly and slightly distorted by rising heat waves. Our destination was a spot where multiple ley lines intersected.

"It looks like we're exploring another planet." I tapped Bryce's shoulder. "Just a little farther. It's probably near that tall formation that looks a little like a T-Rex."

Lisa fanned herself and sprinkled her neck with a few tiny splashes from her water bottle. "I hope we find a way in so we can escape this desert heat."

Lance leaned over and glanced at the GPS strapped to my left arm. "You're right. It can't be more than a hundred yards ahead."

"May as well park in the shade of that dinosaur rock." Mike looked back at me. "And if you find a secret passage, we're all going wherever you go, Sam."

Banger grinned. "Jealous about missing a chance to almost get fried in the pyramid?"

"Maybe if we stick together, like we did in the cave near Hadar, you and Sam will make better decisions, and nobody will almost get fried." When the Humvee stopped, Mike jumped out onto the hard-packed sand and pulled on his backpack.

Lance grabbed his gear and stood by Mike. "If you actually believe you can control the danger factor, you haven't spent enough time with your sister."

Lisa nudged Bryce. "How did we get roped into this weird mission?"

"What? You aren't enjoying our adventure with the crazy Americans?" Bryce smiled as he tightened the straps on his backpack.

Lisa sighed. "It's just that whenever I'm with Sam I feel like everything is out of my control, and I'm just along for the ride."

Banger laughed. "That's exactly what a mission with Sam is like."

I looked up at the massive sandstone tower rising almost three hundred feet into the bright sunshine. "Stop your whining and help me find a trident or some other symbol carved into that rock formation." I walked around the Hummer and ran my hands over the T-Rex shape from the ground up to as high as I could reach, starting at the rear of the imaginary beast. As usual, I had my medallion key hanging from my neck, the sphere in my belly bag, the Eye in its pouch tied to my belt loop, the healing bracelet on my right wrist, the pyramid ring on my right hand, and my backpack strapped to my back. Lucky me, a Sherpa for ancient artifacts.

"Anything?" Mike gazed up at the top as an eagle soared on the rising thermal air currents.

"Maybe." I looked around for Banger, who was right behind me.

He grinned. "Need a lift?"

"It's like you can read my mind."

"That's a scary prospect."

I poked Mike. "Better sling your climbing rope over my shoulder before Banger hoists me up."

Once I had the rope ready, Banger lifted me by my ankles. I ran my hands over the sandstone, feeling for electromagnetic energy.

"Move three feet to your right," I yelled down to Banger.

He did as I instructed, and my hands found the energy spike.

"Here." I pulled a scraper from my pocket and removed an inch of sandstone, revealing a gold hatch about half a foot in diameter. A notch in the center appeared to have the same dimensions as the pyramid-shaped diamond in my ring. The gem had opened the canister. Maybe it would work here too.

I turned my hand and shoved the jewel into the slot. The hatch shook for a moment, and then it popped open. Inside the shadowy interior, I spotted a gold lever shaped like a trident. Based on past experiences, I wasn't worried about pulling the lever.

My concern was for what might be lurking inside the dark space.

Just as I reached for the control, a black lizard leaped out at me. I jerked my head to the side so it wouldn't land on my face, but the sudden move made me lose my balance. I fell backward.

A second or two later, Banger caught me. Again.

"Woman, you're lucky I'm so good at catching you." He set me down. "What happened this time?"

"A lizard made me lose my balance. Sorry." I stood on tiptoe and kissed his cheek. "Thanks for another great save."

"Ready to try again?" He crouched down and grabbed my ankles.

"Up, please."

When I was once again in front of the open hatch, I pulled the lever toward me, and tumbling rock chips from above made me shield my eyes and glance up. The towering formation vibrated, and sand dropped on my head. An eagle soared over the rock tower as an opening in the solid stone appeared twenty feet above me.

"Now what?" Mike cupped his hands over his eyes and looked up at me. "You can't reach the door from there."

"I have an idea." I held one hand against my belly bag and spoke instructions in Atlantean.

The sphere lifted me up as I grasped the bag

with both hands to remain upright and yelled, "Let go, Banger."

My little friend lifted me straight up to the open door, and I stepped onto the landing. Now I knew it could carry me through the air without a paraglider.

"I'll look around for a place to fasten the rope." I shined my flashlight inside and spotted a strange black statue rising out of the interior. It had been carved deep into the solid interior wall, so I knew it wouldn't move. I couldn't reach it without stepping away from the door. Since I didn't see a way to open the door from the inside, I fashioned a loop and used it like a lasso.

I tossed the loop and missed.

"Dammit." My cowboy skills were lacking.

Banger looked up at me. "What the hell, Sam? I thought you grew up in Texas."

"I did, but I'm better at riding than roping." I flung the loop again, and it landed just short of the target.

Why does everything have to be so darn difficult?

It took five tries, but I finally got the loop over the statue. Once the rope was secure, I dropped the end down to my team.

"Okay, you can climb up now. I have to wait in the doorway so the door won't close."

Mike said, "I'll go first and check the rope."

Lance and Bryce followed him. They were able

to squeeze past me, but I knew Banger wouldn't fit with me in the way.

He stroked Lisa's skinny arm with his massive hand and glanced up at me. "Does that rope still look secure?"

"So far, it's not frayed, and it's looped around a statue that's part of this rock. Can Lisa make it up here?"

Banger turned to her. "She's coming up with me."

I watched while she climbed onto his back, and then he pulled himself up the rope like she was weightless.

I turned to Lance. "Hold my hand while I pull Lisa in." I grasped his hand and then took hold of Lisa's.

She stepped onto Banger's shoulders, and I drew her through the door.

"Banger, we'll do a modified version of what we did at the Sphinx so you can get in. Just don't step on my fingers this time." I eased down his back, keeping my head inside the door. "Move up slowly, while I lower myself behind you."

"Okay, steady as she goes." He inched up the rope.

As his body made it farther through the opening, I kept backing down so that just my head was inside. Once his upper legs cleared the door, I was able to grasp the rope and hold on. Hanging over the side with just my head and hands in the doorway, I waited until his feet cleared the door.

We must've been too close to a nest, because the golden eagle I'd spotted earlier swooped down and gouged my head with its powerful talons. Dizzy with pain, I lost my grip on the rope. As I fell backward, the stone door slammed shut with a loud thud, and the severed rope slapped against my bleeding head.

NINETEEN

R ealizing I had seconds to live, I commanded in Atlantean, "Stop my fall," as I wrapped the rope around me. The sphere's anti-gravity mechanism engaged and arrested my descent a foot or two before I would've smashed into the ground on my back. I reached down and touched the dirt, my heart thumping harder than a drum solo.

The eagle dived at me again.

My breath came in short spurts. There wasn't time to form a telepathic connection with the menacing bird. I commanded, "Fire the laser close enough to scare away the eagle without hurting it."

The laser ploy worked, but it burned a small hole in my belly bag, which still held the device and me securely.

"Lift me to the hatch," I commanded as I

hunched over the belly bag, clutching it with both hands.

Blood ran down my face as I hovered in front of the gold cover. I shoved my ring's jewel into the slot, opened the hatch, and pulled the door control. Then my new friend pulled me up to the open door, and Banger yanked me inside.

"Did you miss me?" I asked, pretending I hadn't been terrified.

Five flashlights shined into my face, and the door thudded shut behind me.

"Here's the rope." I tossed it to Mike, sat on the floor, and wiped blood from my face with my hand.

"Sam, you're hurt." Lance scooped me into his arms and held me on his lap. "Somebody, grab the dang first aid kit."

"Relax, I've got this." I placed my shaking right hand on my head. In an instant, my bracelet lit up, and the wounds healed quickly. "I just need something to clean off the blood."

Lance wet a cotton kerchief with his water bottle and gently wiped my face. He checked my head with his light. "The bleeding has stopped, and the wounds have healed." He sighed and hugged me. "Ross will never forgive me if I let anything happen to you."

"I'm okay. My spherical friend saved me, and the bracelet healed me. I just need a minute to catch my breath." I took a sip of water from

Lance's bottle. "My fall wasn't anyone's fault. That crazy eagle zapped me."

Mike squeezed my shoulder. "Glad you're back safe. I assume you told the sphere to pull you back up here before you hit the ground."

"Yeah, that little device is really coming in handy." I patted my belly bag.

"I didn't think about it until you fell, but we really depend on you and your artifacts," Bryce said. "We could've been trapped in here."

Banger patted his backpack. "That's why SEALs carry explosives. You never know when you might need them."

I stood and brushed sand off my chest and arms. "I'm recovered now, so let's get back on mission."

Stone steps led downward into utter blackness. "This looks a lot like those steps under the church in Lalibela. Ready?" I took the first step down, and my pulse quickened as the walls closed in on me.

"Lead on, my queen." Banger followed me with the rest of the team behind him.

Sweetwater's Hideout

Ross reclined with his eyes closed, trying to conserve his energy as the hot sun blazed through the bars of his cage. A vision of Sam invaded his head. She was holding a rope and dangling off the side of a cliff when a golden eagle dived on her and gouged her head with its powerful talons. She lost her grip on the rope and fell, blood flowing over her face.

"No!" Ross sprang up into a sitting position and opened his eyes.

Derek grasped his arm. "What's wrong?"

He glanced around and whispered, "I just saw Sam fall from a cliff. She must've been killed or seriously injured."

"Don't jump to conclusions." Derek squeezed his shoulder and whispered, "Call her."

Ross sucked in his breath. "I'll try." He closed his eyes and concentrated on calling Sam's name in his head.

Sweetwater paced in his air-conditioned hut as he responded to the caller on his satellite phone. "I want those vials of Atlantean DNA. They could be the key to eternal youth or intellectual superiority."

"I can't risk it. Navy Intelligence and the DIA are actively searching this base for your spy. I suggest you steal the two they promised to send to Harvard. Your people can break into a university, no problem."

Sweetwater clenched his fist. "You'd better be right about Harvard. I don't want to miss a chance to get that DNA. It would be far easier to snatch the tubes while they're still in Somalia."

"That's why Commander Metz sent them back to the States on a fast mover an hour ago."

"Bugger!" Sweetwater pounded a table. "Is Miss Starr responsible for powering up the Great Pyramid?"

"Yeah, she discovered engineering drawings and spare parts for the power plant. A SEAL helped her restart it. Too bad the Blue Dragon wasn't there."

"What about the gold cylinder, the bracelet, and the ring she recovered? Can you get them?"

"The gold cylinder was sent to the States along with a metal canister containing the scroll and vials. Miss Starr is still wearing the jewelry. She claims she needs it for the mission. She's also keeping whatever's in that little leather pouch and a small metal sphere with a laser."

"No matter. I'll get it all when I get her. Where is she now?"

"She took the team to Tassili n'Ajjer in Algeria to search for a lost civilization under the Sahara."

"So far, she hasn't looked in any of the places my researchers wanted to search, and yet she's already recovered several important ancient artifacts. Good thing I have a way to force her to work for me." He paused and checked the monitor that showed his two prisoners caged inside the lion pen. "Keep me informed on her progress."

Tassili n'Ajjer

"Sam! Sam! Sam!" Ross's voice blasted inside my head.

I held up my hand, stopped on the steps, and closed my eyes. *"Ross, it's me. Are you okay?"*

"Thank God you're alive, Sam. I saw you fall off a cliff. Did I imagine that?"

"No, but I'm fine. My team is in Algeria, looking for the Blue Dragon. I promise we'll do everything we can to find it and rescue you and Derek."

"Sam, I don't want you risking your life to save me. Focus on helping the military find us."

"The military is giving our mission priority now that they believe the Blue Dragon might be another weapon of mass destruction. If I find it, they'll never hand it over to Sweetwater, but he'll have to give me delivery instructions, and then we'll know where you are."

"Just as long as you don't come here. Let the SAS rescue us."

"Okay, but in the meantime, do whatever's necessary to stay alive. I love you, Ross."

"I love you too, Sam. Be careful."

His voice vanished from my head.

Banger put his hands on my shoulders. "Another call from Ross?"

I nodded. "He saw me fall and panicked."

"Your psychic connection is getting stronger." He turned me around.

Surprised, Mike said, "You talked to Ross?"

I nodded. "This was our second conversation. The first one was inside the Great Sphinx. So much has happened since then, I forgot to tell you. Sorry."

"That's all right." Mike looked over his shoulder at Lisa, Lance, and Bryce. "Keep Sam's telepathic communications with Ross a secret. We can't risk Sweetwater finding out about it." He looked at me. "Let's get going."

I shined my mag light down the winding staircase and noticed strange drawings. Tall, slender people, like Atlanteans, adorned the walls. They were depicted in various scenes with lush landscapes and domestic animals.

I rounded a corner, and the stairs abruptly ended on a landing at the edge of a dark void with no bottom in sight. "Halt!" I yelled, panicked my team would accidentally push me over the edge.

Banger eased up behind me and held my waist. "I'll pop a flare and see what's down there."

"Use this one," Mike said as he pulled one out of his backpack.

Banger activated the flare and dropped it into the pitch-black pit. A bright circle of light descended for at least a minute, becoming smaller and fainter as the distance increased. It ended as a tiny pinpoint at the bottom of what might be nothing more than a hole to nowhere.

"Looks deep." Banger eased me around and

looked into my eyes. "You're trembling. Is the claustrophobia kicking in again?"

I planted my face in his manly chest. "Maybe just a little, my liege."

He hugged me. "I've got you, my queen, but there's one question you need to answer for us."

I looked up at him, my heart pounding. "What's that?"

He arched a brow. "What would the Queen of Atlantis do in this situation?"

I paused. "She'd use the sphere to carry her down so she could investigate."

Banger squeezed my waist. "And she'd take me with her, because a queen needs her mighty warrior."

"What if that thing can't fly with the weight of both of you?" Mike peered into the pit.

Banger replied with his snarky tone, "We're not amateurs. Obviously, we'll test it first."

He rigged a harness and secured us together with me in front of him, facing forward. "Tell it to lift us straight up two feet off the ground and hold us there."

I gave the commands, and it responded instantly. We hung two feet above the landing like we were welded in place. The problem was the sphere was lifting us from inside my belly bag, which made us hang horizontally and strained my back. I grunted a command, "Lower us two feet to the floor."

"That was not a comfortable maneuver," Banger said as he stood up.

The team snickered despite the tense situation.

After Banger untied us, I placed the sphere inside my backpack so it could lift us vertically. He tied us together again, and we tested it one more time.

My little friend easily held us above the landing. "Okay, we're good to go."

Banger gave me a squeeze. "If it can hold you and me, that means it can hold you and anyone else on the team. Fly us down, my queen."

I glanced over my shoulder at Mike. "If we find a place worth exploring, I'll come back for everyone." My next words were in Atlantean, and the sphere took us down at a slow, steady pace so I'd know it was in control of the descent.

By the time we reached the bottom, which was approximately fifteen hundred feet down, the flare on the ground had burned out, and my blood pressure had shot up. We shined our flashlights around and found a dark tunnel branching out from one side of the chasm.

"Think we should take a look in there?" I pointed at the tunnel, hoping he'd say no.

"Give me a minute to untether us so we can walk."

Stealing a line from him, I said, "It's not like I have somewhere else to be."

"Funny, Sam. I'll make a SEAL of you yet." He

draped the rope over my shoulder. "The harness must remain on you for obvious reasons."

"Alrighty." I sucked in a deep breath, took a step toward the tunnel, and resisted the urge to grab his hand. *Claustrophobia sucks.* I struggled to keep from panicking as goosebumps prickled my skin. "Think bats might be in there?"

He laughed. "*That's* what you're worried about —*bats*?"

Our lights only stabbed maybe twelve feet into the endless blackness, and the smooth, dank walls magnified every sound we made.

I swung the beam along the right wall. "Huh, since somebody took the time to decorate this passage with all these paintings, it could mean it goes somewhere important."

"Good. We don't want to waste time on boring stuff." He urged me forward. "Admire the art later."

"I can't recall any boring stuff since we first landed in Somalia." I paused. "Could be a welcome change." I was trying to distract myself from the growing claustrophobia nagging at my brain as I eased deeper into the dark tunnel. Cool, moist air enveloped me.

"Surely you don't want boredom, my queen." Banger chuckled. "Adrenaline is your friend."

"All right, but let's get one thing straight." I stopped and faced him. "If we encounter any snakes or spiders, it's *your* job to deal with them."

He laughed. "You tamed a giant crocodile. The least I can do is wrangle a few spiders and snakes."

"Good, because I don't react well to creepy critters. You should've seen the enormous bird-eating spider Lance and I encountered in South America." I shivered at the memory.

"Yeah? What did you do?"

"I climbed up Lance, like a frightened cat scaling a tree. Not one of my finer moments."

A strange sound filtered into the cave. It was too distant to discern the origin.

I grabbed Banger's arm. "Was that a growl?"

"Way down here?" He shook his head. "Unlikely."

I hesitated as an icy chill shot down my spine. "Did you feel that?"

"Feel what?" He looked around.

TWENTY

"Wind. A cold, light breeze." I paused. "There it is again. The air smells wet, like after it rains."

"You're right. It feels like it's coming toward us. We must be near the end of this tunnel."

We covered another forty feet, and the tunnel opened into a vast cavern with a ceiling that rose at least three hundred feet. A large lake dominated the central landscape, and dimly lighted crystals revealed shadowy structures throughout the vast subterranean city. The eerie metropolis extended for miles.

"Definitely worth the trip." I paused and took in the panoramic view.

"Time to gather the team." Banger put a hand on my shoulder. "Want me to walk back with you?"

"Would you mind?" I didn't want to face that dark tunnel alone.

"I live to serve you, my queen." He grinned, handsome as ever, even in the dim light.

"Tiesha is a lucky woman." I sucked in my breath. "Let's go."

We covered the distance more quickly on the return, knowing what to expect. Soon we had reached the bottom of the deep chasm.

"Ready to fly up and get our team?" Banger looked up.

"I wonder if I can bring back two at a time. Then I'd only need two trips instead of four."

"Test it with Lance and Mike, like you tested it with me. If it holds all three of you, go for it." He saluted me.

I returned his salute. "Stay out of trouble while I'm gone."

I spoke commands to the sphere, and it lifted me up and carried me to the landing where my team waited.

Mike pulled me in. "What's down there?"

"We found a massive subterranean city with a big lake in the middle. Could be the Lost Sahara Civilization." I handed him the rope ends. "I'd like to test carrying two at a time with me, starting with you and Lance. We'll check the weight capacity first, like I did with Banger."

Mike and Lance secured themselves to the front

and back of me, sandwiching me and the sphere in the middle.

Mike tapped my shoulder. "All right, Sam, try a test lift."

I spoke the command for a short lift and hold. The sphere hoisted the three of us as easily as it had lifted Banger and me.

"Okay, Lisa and Bryce, I'll come back for you in a few minutes." My commands resulted in a swift trip to the bottom of the chasm with a soft landing.

Banger helped the men untie themselves from me, and then I slung the ropes over my shoulder and headed up again.

"Ready for your anti-gravity flight?" I asked Bryce and Lisa.

"I'll fasten myself behind you." Bryce began tying the ropes.

"Looks like you're stuck facing me." Lisa tied us together a little tighter than necessary.

"I would like to breathe on the way down." I tugged at the tight rope.

"You can breathe when we get there," she said in a higher pitch than normal.

"Alrighty, everyone ready?" I heard two affirmative grunts.

Lisa clamped her arms around me in a death grip as we made a quick flight down and another gentle landing.

I looked at her. "You can open your eyes now. We're on the ground."

Her eyes popped open as Banger and Mike untied us. She squeezed my shoulder. "Good flight."

"I think you'll enjoy seeing the city. The entrance is a hundred yards down that tunnel." I pointed.

"Yeah, the city is huge—covers several miles." Banger turned. "Follow me."

It wasn't long before we reached the end of the tunnel. I shined my light around the area, looking for symbols that might lead us in the right direction.

Mike pointed. "Is that rock shaped like a trident?" He shined his light on it.

"Yep, let's check it out." I followed a narrow path that led to the trident rock.

"There's dim light coming from these crystals." Lisa examined one. "Did you go in ahead of us and turn them all on?"

"No, they were like that when I got here." I studied the trident-shaped rock. A small crystal was mounted in the shaft below the three prongs. I touched it, and it filled with bright light. In seconds, all the crystals scattered throughout the city went from dim to bright, and we could see everything.

"I guess this is the master switch." I glanced around the vast landscape. "Wish I knew where to go next."

"Isn't that what the Eye is for?" Lisa pointed at my leather pouch.

I slapped my forehead. "Sorry, my brain's in a claustrophobic fog." I pulled out the Eye, and it projected the image of a circular, white marble building with nine spires evenly spaced around the roof's circumference.

"There." Banger peered through binoculars and pointed at a tall building on a hill beyond the other side of the lake. It appeared to be at least ten miles from us.

I slipped the Eye back into its leather pouch. "Oh, good, only ten miles away."

"There you go, stealing my lines again." Banger glanced around. "Looks like that path might take us there."

"Lead on, my liege." I followed my big buddy.

We weaved our way past unusual statues depicting tall, slender people with angular faces and long, spindly fingers. The statues ranged in height from seven to eight feet, like the Atlanteans I'd met in a secret enclave in the Himalayas.

Lance took in the scenery. "I'm beginning to wonder if there's any place on Earth the Atlanteans haven't been."

"Their influence does seem to have been far-reaching." Bryce peeked inside a nearby building. "Was this a jewelry store?"

Lisa stepped inside. "Ooh, look at the diamonds. Maybe I can find a healing bracelet like the one Sam has." She began trying on diamond rings, earrings, and bracelets. "Don't you want some of this, Sam?"

"I'm already loaded down with plenty of artifacts." I tightened my belly bag. "I should probably save room in case I have to wear more stuff that affects our mission. But the rest of you should grab a few things. It's not like there's anyone here to care."

The men shoved handfuls of diamond jewelry into their pockets.

"All right." Mike headed for the door. "This should make a lot of women happy. Let's get going."

Banger grinned. "Nothing like free diamond jewelry for my fiancée. May as well enjoy ourselves until the next deadly situation arises."

I nudged him. "You sound as though you expect bad things to happen when we're together."

He raised a brow. "History does tend to repeat itself with you."

Mike stuck his head in the door. "Sam, stop fooling around." He tapped his watch.

"Right, let's get going." I led Banger out the door and hurried to catch up with the rest of the team.

Sweetwater's Hideout

Sweetwater spoke into his satellite phone, "They disappeared in Tassili n'Ajjer?"

"Yes, sir, our team tracked them to abandoned Humvee in middle of stone forest."

"Good." Sweetwater checked the video screen showing Ross and Derek in their cage. "They must've found an entrance to the Lost Sahara Civilization under the desert. That means they're closing in on my Blue Dragon."

"Want us to wait here until they return?"

"No, Dmitri, I want you to follow them. They must've left footprints. If you find a spot where the footprints end, plant explosives, create an entrance hole, follow them to the Blue Dragon, and bring it and Samantha Starr to me."

"What about her team?"

"Should be easy. You have three times as many men. Kill them." Sweetwater disconnected and smiled.

Tassili n'Ajjer

Dmitri stood at the base of a huge sandstone formation. "Footprints end here." He looked up and spotted something shiny reflecting the sun fifteen feet above him. He took a few steps back and scanned the area with his binoculars. "Looks like small gold hatch with notch in center. Someone scraped off layer of rock to expose it."

Vasili, Dmitri's second-in-command, studied the tower. "I will shoot ballistic pitons into rock so we can climb up." He walked back to one of their Humvees and pulled out a special rifle. He loaded a piton with a rope connected to it and fired it into the area above the gold.

Dmitri tugged on the rope. "It's holding. Fire another one."

Vasili shot another piton with a rope attached. It stuck into the rock a foot from the first one.

Dmitri glanced at his men. "Who is our best climber?"

Rada Chugunkin, a young man in his mid-twenties, stepped forward.

"Ah, Rada, good man. Take small explosive charge with you and open hatch without damaging what may be inside."

Rada nodded. "*Da*." In moments, he had climbed up fifteen feet to it. He secured his harness to the second piton and studied the round gold device. After wiring a small charge into the center notch on it, he moved a few feet to the side and detonated the explosive.

The hatch popped open, revealing a gold lever shaped like a small trident. He pulled the lever, and sand dropped on him from above as a stone door rumbled open.

Dmitri looked up at the open door and shook his head. "How did her team get up there? Almost twelve meters—no piton holes, no ropes." He paused. "Last place she went, she began on Sphinx and escaped from Great Pyramid in paraglider. Maybe they have backpack motors." He turned and looked at his troops. "Strap on paraglider chutes and climb up to door."

Rada dropped down to gear up, while Vasili fired pitons with ropes above the open door. A soldier climbed up to the door and stepped inside. The instant he left the doorway, the door slammed shut with a loud thud.

Dmitri looked at Rada. "Climb to lever and open door for each man and then for yourself."

The men climbed to the door, one at a time. After each one entered, the door closed, and Rada opened it for the next man. Dmitri waited for Rada, who was the last to enter. They hurried to catch up to their sixteen teammates who had rushed down the stone steps.

Screams echoed below them, and they froze when Vasili yelled, "Pull D-rings." They eased around the corner to a landing where Vasili was crowded against ten of their comrades, all looking into a dark chasm.

Sam's Team

We followed the walkway along the lakeshore, passing beautiful buildings and statues of dolphins and various other mammals and sea creatures. We paused at a stone pier that extended a hundred feet over the lake. A statue of an Atlantean queen stood on a platform at the end.

I pointed. "That statue looks important. We should check it out."

I walked down the pier, and Banger followed me. Our team joined us.

Mike nudged me. "Why are we here?"

"I felt a strong pull toward this statue." I studied the marble face. She resembled me.

Banger reached up. "This crown looks like it's made of real gold and diamonds, but it won't come off." He grasped the gold and diamond scepter in the queen's hand. It wouldn't budge either.

Lance stroked the crown. "Maybe this is like Excalibur, but only a true queen can remove it."

Everyone looked at me.

"Fine, I'll try it." I reached up and easily lifted the crown off the statue's head. "Huh."

"Put it on and see if it fits." Lisa faced me.

I placed the crown on my head, and it fit perfectly.

"Whoa." Mike blurted, as everyone took a step back.

"What?" I touched the crown. It felt normal— no tingling or heat coming from it.

"The diamonds in the crown lit up after you put it on." Mike gingerly touched a diamond. "Feels okay."

Bryce pointed at the statue's right hand. "Try the scepter."

I grasped it, and the statue released it. A diamond pyramid mounted in the tip with the point facing outward filled with brilliant light.

At that moment, a huge crocodile raised its head and opened its mouth filled with razor-sharp teeth. It was only a few feet from me.

Startled, I pointed the scepter at it, and a powerful laser shot out and blasted a hole in the croc's head. "Wow, didn't expect that!"

"Just don't point it at us." Mike backed away.

More crocodile heads rose from the lake. The big reptiles surrounded the dead croc.

I waved at the feeding frenzy in the water. "Hurry and get off the pier while they're distracted."

We rushed back to the walkway and kept a watchful eye on the lake.

A faint boom behind us echoed in the distance.

I stopped. "Was that an explosion or my pounding heart?"

Banger looked back. "I heard it too. Sound carries well down here."

Mike stood, hands on hips. "Sweetwater's mercs must've followed us."

"But how did they find the entrance?" Lance looked behind us.

"The golden hatch." I sighed. "It would be noticeable if they happened to look up there."

"But how would they get through the door?" Bryce glanced at the path behind us.

"They probably used a mild explosive to open

the hatch and then pulled the lever." I looked at the lake where the feeding frenzy had ended.

"Yes, but you weren't there to keep the door open." Banger nudged me. "Hey, you'd better zap that croc before his buddies think it's a good idea to attack us."

I nailed it with my scepter laser, and a series of splashes told me the other crocs had gone back into the lake. "I've been thinking about that door. I assumed I needed to be in the opening to keep the door open, but that lever would've worked for anyone who pulled it, which means the door would remain open as long as someone stood in it." I shook my head at Banger. "Sorry, big guy, I guess I didn't need to climb down your back after all."

He shrugged. "I didn't mind the added excitement."

Mike squeezed my arm. "Was that a scream?"

I listened. Faint screams filtered through the vast cavern. Goosebumps erupted on my arms. "Sounds like it's coming from the tunnel."

"The mercs probably rushed down the stairs and fell into the chasm." Banger scanned the area behind us.

"We should hurry." Mike glanced around. "Sam, it's your job to zap crocs that sneak out of the lake. I want everyone's heads on swivels, looking for intruders and dangerous critters. We still have a lot of miles to cover to get to that round building on the hill. Move out."

We set out at a slow trot, constantly looking around us and listening to every sound.

My body hummed with adrenaline, expecting danger at every turn. Deadly creatures and Sweetwater's mercenaries distracted me from my claustrophobia, but that didn't help my jangled nerves. Something even scarier could be lurking ahead of us.

TWENTY-ONE

Sweetwater's Mercenary Team

D mitri waited a beat, then yelled, "Survivors, call out."

Four men responded.

One reported via his radio transmitter, "We lost Maxim and Alexi. Chutes opened too late."

Dmitri keyed his mike. "What did you find?"

"A tunnel. Her team must've gone through it. No one here except us and no obvious way to get back up from here. We'll need motorized lift ropes."

"I'll send team down," Dmitri said into his radio mike. "Rada will go with me and get equipment. Take men and secure Starr woman and Blue Dragon. Lift ropes will be ready when you return."

"Understood. Send men separately and tell them to deploy chutes immediately. Chasm is approximately five hundred meters deep. I'll light flare."

"Sending first man now." Dmitri waved to one of his men. "Jump and pull right away."

The soldier jumped and deployed his chute. Dmitri waited two minutes in order to avoid entanglements or collisions before he sent the next man.

After he received a report that all the men had landed safely, Dmitri turned and climbed the steps with Rada. When they reached the top, they faced a closed door.

"Help me look for door lever." Dmitri shined his flashlight on the walls.

"Other lever was behind hatch covered with sandstone." Rada pulled out his combat knife and chipped at stone near the door, looking for a gold hatch.

Dmitri pulled out his knife and joined in, chipping the rock.

Rada paused. "Did you hear that?"

The leader stopped and listened.

Faint screams and staccato blasts of gunfire filtered up the staircase.

Dmitri keyed his radio. "Vasili? What's happening?"

The radio remained silent.

"Should we go down steps for better reception?" Rada turned around.

"I'll go. You keep looking for door lever." Dmitri rushed down the steps.

When he reached the landing at the end of the staircase, he stood still, listening. Silence.

He keyed his mike. "Team, report. Can you hear me? Report."

Nothing.

He slowly ascended the steps. *What happened to them? No one on Samantha Starr's team could make my men scream like that. What is down there?*

Rada turned when Dmitri reached the top landing. "What happened?"

"No one answered when I called, and I heard nothing from below. Tunnel might be blocking radio reception." Dmitri waved toward the closed door. "Any luck finding lever?"

"*Nyet.*" Rada slipped off his backpack. "I have enough explosives to blow door."

"Do it. We've wasted enough time. Lord Sweetwater expects success, and he is not patient man."

Rada prepared the charges and set the detonator for ten seconds. He ducked down the steps with Dmitri and waited.

A loud boom echoed down the staircase, followed by a cloud of sand and dirt.

The men rushed up the steps and found a big hole where the door had been. The opening was taller and wider than the original door.

Dmitri looked out. "Where are climbing ropes?"

Rada stuck his head out and looked up. "Pitons blew out with door."

Dmitri was a problem-solver, which was what

made him a good leader. "Ropes above lever hatch are seven meters below us." He took off his paraglider pack. "We will fasten chute to this statue and use chute to climb down to ropes."

Rada assisted him. Once the chute was rigged to the statue, Dmitri climbed down to the outside door lever, and then switched to the ropes and continued to the ground.

As Rada climbed down the paraglider chute, Dmitri considered his options and made a decision. He drew his pistol and shot the young man in the back of his head. Rada fell the final twenty feet, landing in a crumpled heap, his dead eyes open in a glassy stare.

Dmitri holstered his weapon. "Sorry, Rada, but if I hadn't shot you, you would've been fed to Sweetwater's hungry lions. This mission is failing, and now my only option is to flee Africa and hope Sweetwater's search team never finds me."

He loaded everything of value from the other Humvees into the one he was driving. Then he took the batteries from the engine compartments and loaded them in his vehicle. "Good luck finding batteries out here," he said to no one.

Buzzards began to circle as he drove away, winding through the imposing stone towers carved by nature.

How much time before Sweetwater would send hunters? He had maybe twenty-four hours—less if locals came to investigate the circling buzzards.

Dmitri drove faster.

Sam's Team, Earlier

I glanced over my shoulder at Banger. "I just had a disturbing thought about those crocodiles. What have they been eating that allowed them to survive and grow so big?"

"Good question—I hope we never discover the answer."

I stopped. "Is that screaming?"

Faint screams were followed by staccato blasts from automatic weapons.

Banger keyed his radio. "Mike, we have company."

Mike led the team back to us. "Where?"

"We heard more screams and then gunfire coming from the direction of the tunnel," I said. "I wonder what's scaring them?"

"I doubt the crocs would wander that far from the lake." Lance glanced around. "Could be other dangerous critters down here."

I nodded. "Banger and I were just discussing what the crocs have been eating."

"Ooh, I didn't think about that." Lisa drew her weapon and checked it. "Could be loads of nasty creatures down here."

I thumbed at Mike. "My brother thinks dinosaurs might have their last habitat here."

"With you on the mission, nothing would surprise me." Lance looked around.

"Whoever is back there isn't making any noise now." Mike checked his rifle. "Let's get to that building on the hill. Maintain vigilance."

We rushed forward, listening to every sound, wary of every movement near us. Ahead, rock arches curved over the path, and strange stone formations depicting large, unknown animals flanked the walkway.

I glanced up and detected movement on the dark arches. "Everyone, stop and back away from the overhead rocks."

Spiders the size of small dogs dropped down. Mike batted one away from him as he turned and sprinted from under the arches. Lance and Bryce brushed off two before the spiders had a chance to bite them.

Lisa wasn't so lucky. She screamed as one dropped on her head, and another one landed on her back. She managed to swat off the spider on her head, but she couldn't reach the other one. It bit her, and seconds later, she fell unconscious.

Bryce pulled the spider off her and tossed it away as Mike scooped her up and carried her back to the rest of us.

Mike set her on the path in front of me. "Help her. Use your magic bracelet." He turned to the men. "Don't waste any ammo on spiders. Use your rifles like clubs and keep them away from the women."

I rolled Lisa onto her side and placed my right hand on her back where a large lump had formed. My bracelet lit up, and my palm filled with fluid. Spider toxin. I dumped the gooey liquid on the dirt path and wiped my hand on my pants. Then I placed my hand over the bite again.

Her back healed in a few moments, and she moaned and opened her eyes.

I helped her sit up. "How do you feel, Lisa?"

"A little dizzy." She stiffened and glanced around. "A big spider bit my back."

"You're okay now. My bracelet pulled out the poison."

Mike yelled, "Hey, sis, a little help?"

I turned and faced a horde of giant spiders attacking the men. The guys swung their rifles like bats, knocking away the arachnids. But their numbers were increasing.

I pulled the scepter out from where I'd shoved it under my belt. The diamond tip lit up and fired a laser into the closest spider, frying it instantly.

"Guys, get behind me so I can zap them without hitting you."

The men backed away, and the spiders rushed forward.

"God help me." This was my worst nightmare —hundreds of spiders the size of miniature dogs.

Banger lifted me from behind. "I keep my

promises. You concentrate with the laser while I hold you above them."

My hand trembled as I swept the scepter back and forth, zapping wave after wave of their relentless attacks. I missed one, but Banger stomped it.

"These suckers are too big to be squashed." He kicked a thick, hairy spider.

"Geez, how many more can there be?" The horde seemed endless, and I was on the edge of panic.

Lisa yelled, "Hey, Queen of Atlantis, you have the crown and scepter. Try commanding the spiders."

"That won't work," I said in an annoyed tone.

"Try it anyway, my queen." Banger kicked another huge spider.

I spoke forcefully in Atlantean, commanding the spiders to leave me and my people alone.

Instantly, the spiders retreated to their hiding places behind the arches. Burned spider carcasses littered the pathway.

"Huh, I never thought that would work." I looked at Banger as he put me down.

"Clearly, becoming the Queen of Atlantis involves a steep learning curve," he teased with a smirk.

I hugged him anyway. "Thanks for holding me above those awful spiders."

"My pleasure." He hugged me back.

"Uh, sis, is it safe to proceed now?" Mike searched the arches.

"God, I hope so." I checked the team. "Everybody okay?"

"I'm proud of you, Sam." Lance grinned. "Instead of climbing up Banger or me, you faced those eight-legged critters and gave them hell."

"Having the scepter helped," I said in a shaky voice. "Alrighty, let's roll."

The team scanned the arches again and hesitated.

I looked up at Banger. "You first, my liege."

He laughed. "I live to serve you, my queen."

I followed so close behind him I almost stepped on his heels. We passed under the arches without incident, and I breathed easier when the landscape opened up on either side of the path.

The white marble building with its nine spires gleamed on a hill behind the far side of the lake. It was at least six miles away. I couldn't stop thinking about the distant screams we'd heard and what kinds of animals the crocs had been eating all those years.

Sweetwater's Mercs

Vasili bandaged a gash in his arm. He edged up to a giant mound of fur lying in a pool of blood. "At least we got one of them."

"What is it, sir?" a soldier asked.

Vasili shined his light on the beast. "Looks like thousand-pound tiger, but is not possible."

"Could be many creatures down here that are not possible," another soldier said as he checked his fallen comrades. "We lost four more teammates."

"Leave them. We'll deal with the bodies when we return." Vasili checked the survivors. Ten left, counting himself. "Move out and stay sharp."

The team moved carefully through the tunnel to the end where it opened into an enormous cavern lit by crystals.

"What is this place?" A soldier gazed around.

"Legend claims it is Lost Sahara Civilization." Vasili pointed. "Follow path beside lake."

The men moved at a swift walk, wary of what might lie ahead. Ten minutes farther down the path, a soldier at the rear of the column screamed.

Vasili turned and spotted a twenty-foot crocodile dragging him into the lake. His men opened fire on the croc.

They killed the huge reptile, but it was too late to save their comrade.

"We're down to nine men." Vasili surveyed his team. "You two, keep watch behind us."

His team continued down the lakeside walkway.

TWENTY-TWO

Sam's Team

I poked Banger and stopped. "Automatic weapons firing again. What the heck are they shooting at back there?"

"Crocs, giant spiders, something equally unpleasant—take your pick."

Mike joined us. "If they're Sweetwater's mercs, they aren't conserving ammo."

"They'll regret that soon enough." Bryce checked his Sig.

"Sounds like the wildlife is taking out the mercs." Lance looked behind us.

"Good. Press on." Mike turned to Bryce. "Guard our six."

We began a slow trot toward the round building on the hill. I had no idea why the Eye had directed us there. It had made it clear it wouldn't tell me the exact location of the Blue Dragon.

The lakeside trail wound through some petrified trees. When we rounded a corner, a huge tiger blocked our path. He roared, bared his deadly fangs, and leaped at Banger.

No time for commands. I drew my scepter and sent a laser beam into its head between its glowing eyes, but the beast's momentum landed it on Banger's chest, pinning him with its dead body.

Mike and Lance rushed to pull it off Banger, who seemed to have had the wind knocked out of him.

Before I could help them, Bryce yelled, "Back here."

I turned around and spotted another tiger in mid-pounce. Bryce shot it in the chest, but that didn't even slow it down. The enormous tiger landed on him, ripped his neck open with its long fangs, and crushed him under its massive weight.

I destroyed the tiger's head with laser shots. "Guys, quick, help me get the tiger off Bryce." I ran to my friend, a pool of blood forming around his head.

Lisa kneeled beside him and pressed her kerchief against his neck wounds. "It's really bad," she said with a sob.

I held my right hand against the gaping wound that stretched across both carotid arteries. My bracelet didn't light up, and nothing happened.

Bryce was gone. I froze, staring at his glassy eyes, unable to accept his death.

Lisa poked me. "Hurry! They're closing in. Too many to shoot. Try commanding them."

Giant tigers snarled and bared their fangs as they formed a wide circle around us.

Still in shock, I stood on shaky legs and glanced at Lisa. "Are the diamonds in my crown still lit?"

"Yes. Do something fast!"

Shouting the ancient language, I commanded the tigers to leave us and attack the people following behind us.

Instantly, the tigers turned and left without making another sound.

I rushed to my big friend. "Banger, are you okay?" I searched his eyes.

"That sucker was heavy—it's bound to leave a few bruises, but I'm all right." He sat up and glanced over his shoulder. "What about Bryce?"

Mike and Lance shook their heads.

"The tiger ripped open his throat and crushed him." I choked back a sob. "He's dead."

"Like hell he is!" Banger grabbed my wrist. "Use your bracelet and save him."

"I already tried that, but it wouldn't work this time." I dropped to my knees, and my eyes flooded with tears.

Lisa held Bryce's hand as silent tears ran down her cheeks.

Banger pulled me against him and lifted my

chin. "There's no crying in combat. Stuff your emotions like you would if you were flying an airliner during an emergency—deal with your feelings later."

I swallowed hard, dried my eyes, and blew my nose into my sleeve.

"Good, now let's figure out what's wrong with your bracelet." Banger examined my right wrist. "It doesn't look broken."

Mike leaned down. "Maybe it only works on live people. Try healing Banger's bruised chest."

I placed my right hand over his chest, but the bracelet failed to light up. "See … nothing."

"It's only been about twenty minutes since you used it to save Lisa from the poison spider bite," Lance said. "Maybe it needs time to recharge after each use."

"Or it might be permanently used up now." I pulled on it, but it wouldn't come off my arm. I stifled a sob.

"Dang, those cats are big," Lance said, probably changing the subject to distract us from Bryce's death. He stared at the fallen beasts. "And their fangs are huge. What kind of tigers are they?"

Mike shrugged. "Could be saber-toothed tigers."

Lance's eyes widened. "That's good news."

"How could that possibly be good news?" I frowned.

"They might be the *primordial paradox* in the riddle."

"And we're under a desert, cloaked in eternal darkness." Banger tried to sound optimistic for my sake.

"Sorry to disappoint you guys, but those aren't saber-toothed tigers—just really big ones with fangs proportional to their size—not prehistoric and definitely not primordial." I glanced at Banger. "Are you able to walk?"

He stood. "Of course." He nudged Mike. "We'll take turns carrying Bryce—no man left behind."

Mike pulled a windbreaker out of Bryce's backpack and tied it over his head to cover the gaping wound. "We'd better take his weapons and ammo in case we get in a firefight with the mercs." He handed the extra pistol and mags to Banger, and put the extra flares and grenades in his backpack.

Lance stepped forward and slung Bryce over his shoulder. "I'll take the first shift."

"Lead on, Sam." Banger nudged me. "We don't want Sweetwater's soldiers to catch up with us."

I clutched my scepter and set off in a fast walk while constantly checking the area around us. After ten minutes had passed, my inner voice reminded me to do something people rarely remembered to do: look up.

At that moment, a huge bird dived at me, its sharp talons extended. I ducked, fried it with my laser weapon, and yelled, "Heads up, giant birds attacking."

The air filled with the strange birds. Their wingspans had to be at least ten feet, and their beaks were long and pointed.

My team opened fire on the winged predators.

I kept firing the laser scepter while commanding the birds to leave us and attack the people behind us. My nerves were just about shot, and I prayed the feathered predators would obey me.

Our airborne enemies suddenly pulled up and flew past us, zeroing in on something a few miles back—probably Sweetwater's mercs.

"What did you say?" Banger gazed at the departing birds.

"I told them to attack the people behind us. We need time to find the Blue Dragon and get the heck out of here." I zapped a bird flopping on the ground nearby. "Those are nasty-looking talons."

Lisa toed the dead bird. "We've repelled attacks from air, land, and sea. I hope we're done."

Mike sidled up to me and pointed at the nearest dead bird. "You know, sis, these birds look a lot like pterodactyls." I knew he was trying to distract me from thinking about Bryce.

I gave him an exaggerated eye roll. "Nice try, but they're way too small to be dinosaurs."

Lisa glanced around at the carnage. "Done and dusted. Let's crack on."

Mike took Bryce from Lance and slung him over his shoulder.

"Right." I turned and set off at a fast pace, my team close behind. I hoped they wouldn't notice I was shaking from jangled nerves and repressed grief. I might not be able to handle another terrifying beast.

As we neared the far end of the lake, the path wound behind the hill that supported our destination. The closer we approached, the larger the building appeared.

Automatic weapons fire echoed in the distance as we continued up the trail, climbing ever higher on a steeply slanted, curving path. I rounded the final turn and faced a gleaming white marble building.

Just as I said, "This part was too easy," the ground ahead of us seemed to shift. "Oh no—why did it have to be snakes?" I stopped, frozen with fear as countless serpents slithered closer.

Banger lifted me into his arms. "You zap them, and I'll stomp on them until you gain command."

His strength gave me renewed courage. I waved my laser scepter back and forth across hundreds of snakes as I commanded them to retreat and move away from the building.

After a few tense minutes, the sea of snakes parted and revealed a stone walkway leading to the building's front steps.

I breathed a sigh of relief as the snakes slithered away, out of sight.

"Let's find the Blue Dragon and get out of this nightmare." I jogged up the marble stairs.

A gold lock that matched my medallion key gleamed on the wall, and I inserted my key into the slot. Massive cedar double doors about fifteen feet high opened inward, revealing a shiny white marble floor in a circular white marble room. Crystal chandeliers hanging from a forty-foot ceiling bathed the interior in brilliant light. In the center of the round room a crystal tube six feet in diameter ran from the floor to the ceiling, and a gold throne with crystals embedded in the armrests faced the tube.

The rest of the room appeared to be empty.

I waited until my team entered ahead of me. As expected, the doors closed behind me.

Mike set Bryce's body down and peered through the tube. "What the hell is this?"

"I'll worry about whatever that is after I find the Blue Dragon." I ran my hands over the wall from the floor to as high as I could reach.

Nothing.

"Banger?"

He grasped my ankles and lifted me above his head. Again, I tried running my hands over the smooth marble as he slowly sidestepped along the curved wall.

When we completed the circle to where we'd started, he stopped. "Anything?"

"Nope. Put me down and I'll look in the throne."

He set me down, and I walked to the massive throne beside the crystal tube. The giant chair looked like it was made of solid gold.

I ran my hands over the gleaming metal but didn't feel an energy spike anywhere. I didn't know what would happen if I touched the large crystals embedded in the arms.

My team anticipated what I'd do next, and they moved behind the throne.

Mike said, "Go ahead and touch the crystals."

I placed my hands on the sparkling stones.

Nothing happened.

"Crap. I can't believe the Eye sent us here for no reason. What am I supposed to do now?" I eased up to the tube and noticed tiny gold tridents spaced about three feet apart at my eye level.

"Huh." I placed my hands over the tridents, and the crystal tube parted in front of me, leaving an opening from the floor to about eight feet high. Not certain what to do, I stepped inside and glanced straight up. A gold hatch covered the top of the tube.

The sphere in my backpack seemed to come alive. "Wait," I yelled in Atlantean, not wanting the sphere to blast its way out. I reached inside my pack and pulled it out. Then it flew above me, opened its little roof, and blasted the tube's gold cover with its laser.

The hatch swung up to the open position and locked against a marble beam. Then the sphere fired a laser straight up through the opening all the way to another metal cover embedded in the cavern ceiling. It opened, revealing a vertical tunnel. The laser fired once more, and a faint, distant clank told me another hatch had opened at the surface.

The little guy's roof closed, and in the next moment, it zoomed straight up the tube into the vertical tunnel and disappeared from view.

"Now what?" Mike looked around.

The door on the tube remained open when I stepped out. "This might be our only way out of here."

"But we haven't found the Blue Dragon yet." Lance surveyed the empty room. "It has to be here. The cavern fits the riddle, and the Eye led us here."

"I'll check again." I pulled the Eye out of its leather pouch and held it in my hand.

It beamed a hologram of the room we were standing in. The image showed me sitting on the throne with my hands resting on the crystal armrests, which were filled with light. My holographic team stood close together inside the crystal tube. In a flash, the team shot up the tube, continued up through the vertical tunnel, and ended up standing on the surface next to the open hatch.

No Blue Dragon.

The hologram vanished, and I placed the Eye back in its pouch.

"Well, that tube is our way out, but I don't understand why we had to come here in the first place." I shook my head, frowning.

"Maybe you need the crown and scepter to get the Blue Dragon," Lisa offered.

"Or maybe we lost Bryce for no good reason." Overcome with frustration, grief, and anger, I kicked the throne. "Ow."

Banger grabbed my shoulders and turned me around. He looked straight into my eyes. "What would the Queen of Atlantis do?"

I bit my lip and returned his gaze. "She'd send her people up out of this hellhole and keep looking for that damn Blue Dragon." I pointed. "Everyone, get in the tube."

My team entered the tube. Banger held Lisa against him, and Mike and Lance held Bryce's body between them. I sat on the throne and placed my hands on the crystals. In seconds, they blazed with energy, the tube door closed, and my team shot upward, riding an invisible energy beam that carried them to the surface.

Mike's voice barely registered in my earpiece. "We're safe topside. Come on up."

I left the throne and placed my hands over the tiny tridents to open the door again. When it opened, I glanced back at the throne. The crystals were dark. I stuck my hand into the tube. No energy.

Before I could think of what to do, an explosion

knocked me down. The cedar doors had flown open, and four men who looked like hardened soldiers burst into the room. They had numerous wounds under blood-soaked bandages.

I sat up against the tube and held out the scepter, pointing it away from them. "If you want to live and escape this nightmare, you'll do what I ask." I stood. Snakes tried to slither in behind them. "Move aside."

The men moved away from the door, and I blasted the snakes with my laser. Speaking Atlantean, I commanded the snakes to leave, and they did. That's when I noticed the men held knives, not guns. They'd run out of ammo like we thought they would. I could've easily killed them with my laser, but I decided to handle the situation with compassion instead.

A man in his forties with a nasty gash in his arm stood at the forefront, apparently their leader. I asked him, "Did Sweetwater send you after me?"

He nodded. "*Da*, he wants you and Blue Dragon. Where is your team?"

"I sent them to the surface. I'll do the same for you and your men if you cooperate."

"What do you want?" He looked pale and exhausted.

"Drop your weapons and kick them away from you." I waited while he thought it over, eyeing my laser weapon.

He glanced at his bleeding men. "Do what she says." He dropped his knife and kicked it away.

His men did the same.

"Now tie their hands behind their backs." I cut lengths of rope from a coil in my backpack, tossed them over to him, and watched while he tied their hands securely.

"Turn around and put your hands behind your back. One false move and my laser will burn a hole through you." I held the scepter in my mouth, pointing it at his head, while I tied his hands.

I took hold of the scepter and pointed it at him. "Turn around. What's your name?"

"I am Vasili," he answered in an arrogant tone.

"Which of you has the most serious injury?" I glanced at the men. They all looked pretty bad.

Vasili nodded at a man on his left who was bleeding more than the others.

I pulled the man forward. "You three, wait there." I placed my right hand over his chest wound just in case the bracelet might work again. It lit up, and the wound healed. Apparently, the bracelet had recharged itself from Earth's electromagnetic energy. "Are you okay now?"

He nodded, wide-eyed.

"Go stand inside that tube."

I waited until he was inside the tube and then pulled another man forward. He had a nasty gash on his thigh, claw marks on his left arm and across his chest, and a cut over his right eye. I put my right hand on his thigh, but the bracelet didn't work. Now I knew it needed about an hour to recharge after each use.

"Sorry, it needs to recharge. Join your comrade in the tube." I waved him in.

Soon, all four men were standing in the tube.

"I'm sending you up to my team. Cooperate, and they'll treat you fairly. They're good people."

I sat on the throne and activated the crystals. The door to the tube closed, and seconds later, the men shot upward and disappeared into the vertical tunnel.

As I sat in silence, a voice whispered inside my head, *"You have passed the final test, Queen of Atlantis. Find the Blue Dragon and save them."*

Once again, I opened the door to the tube. This time the crystals in the throne remained lit. I stepped inside, and the door closed. Seconds later, I rocketed to the surface, and the sphere zoomed out of the night sky and hovered in front of me. I grasped it and placed it inside my bag.

"Did you miss me, my liege?" I approached Banger and my team, standing under a full moon.

Banger grinned and hugged me. Then Mike took his turn.

"You had us worried, sis. A Black Hawk will pick us up in thirty minutes. Are we taking them with us?" He thumbed at the mercs.

"Yes, I have a plan." I walked up to Vasili. "You know Sweetwater will feed you to his lions if he catches you. I would like to offer you and your men a better alternative."

"I am listening." Vasili looked into my eyes.

"Your best chance for survival is to help us get Sweetwater. Lead us to him and let our soldiers dispose of him once and for all. You will be free to do as you wish after that. What do you say?"

"Is good plan, but I do not know where he is. Only our general knows location of Sweetwater's camp. Dmitri was supposed to bring motorized climbing ropes and meet us at chasm under entrance steps. Take us back there and I will convince him to help you. As it is, our mission failed, and Sweetwater will kill Dmitri too. He will want to help you."

I glanced at Mike, who said, "Good idea. I'll ask the pilot to fly us back there."

Forty-five minutes later, we landed near the Humvees and found a body at the base of the sandstone formation that housed the steps. The man had a bullet hole in the back of his head.

I looked at Vasili. "Dmitri?"

"*Nyet*." Vasili looked around. "One Humvee is missing. Looks like Dmitri made other plans."

TWENTY-THREE

Camp Baledogle

It was late at night when we arrived back at the base. We gathered in the conference room to debrief and report the loss of SAS Lieutenant Bryce Manning. The team's mood was somber as Mike related the circumstances that led to Bryce's death. I couldn't help feeling that it was partly my fault. If only I could've saved him.

When the base commander dismissed us and left the room, Lance stood and said, "I'd like the team to stay a few minutes." He glanced at his watch. "I really should've mentioned this before, Sam, but I kept thinking we'd have the Blue Dragon by now. I hate to bring this up so soon after losing Bryce. You need to fly home tonight."

"We've still got four days before Sweetwater's ultimatum expires." I glanced at my teammates.

Lance shook his head. "*We* still have four days, but today was the last day before *you* have to be home." He hesitated. "You really should leave now to get back in time. You can sleep on the airplane."

"What are you talking about?" I studied his face.

"Your captain job with Luxury International. You've missed too many flights over the past year."

"That couldn't be helped. Jeff wouldn't expect me to let Ross die just to fly an airline flight."

He shook his head. "It's not that simple. Jeff has to keep the airline's flights manned. If you don't show up for work tomorrow, he'll have to fire you and hire a replacement while our other captains take up the slack." He sighed. "Dang it, Sam, if he keeps covering for you, he'll lose *his* job."

"I feel terrible about this." I bit my lip. "I should've realized the awkward positions I've been putting him in. It's eight hours earlier there. I'll call him now and resign so he won't have to fire me."

"Dang it, Sam, everyone at LIA loves you." Lance hugged me. "We don't want to lose you. Can't you shoot home for your flight sequence and then rush back?"

"If I do that, by the time I get back here, Ross and Derek will be dead. They've saved my life more times than I can remember. I'm not about to desert them just to keep the job I love."

He turned to our team. "There has to be a way to save Sam's job."

"The military has 767s." Mike looked at me. "Since this is a top-priority mission, General Ryan could send an Air Force 767 pilot to replace you until this mission is completed."

I frowned. "It's not that simple. The FAA has strict training and currency regulations for airline pilots. And the military pilot would need an Airline Transport Pilot rating and pilot medical certificate. Military pilots don't have civilian licenses. It won't work."

"Could they borrow a captain from another airline?" Banger asked.

I shook my head. "I appreciate your concern, but I've been a problem for my airline long enough. I'll turn in my wings. Ross and Derek are my top priority."

I hugged my teammates and sent them to bed. Alone in the conference room, I called the chief pilot at Luxury International Airlines, my boss and friend, Captain Jeff Rowlin. I hated to resign, but it was the only way to ensure Jeff didn't take the blame for my many absences.

His deep Texan baritone greeted me. "Hey, Sam, it's good to hear your voice. Did you find Ross and Derek?"

"Jeff, it's good to hear you too. I wish this call was under better circumstances." My voice caught.

"What happened? Is Ross okay?" His tone conveyed deep concern.

"No, Sweetwater has him and Derek hidden somewhere in Africa. I've been given an ultimatum to find an artifact and deliver it to Sweetwater in the next four days or Ross and Derek will be killed."

"I'm sorry, Sam. Is there anything I can do to help?"

"No, my friend." I paused. "That's why I'm calling. You need a captain you can depend on to show up for flights. I've taken advantage of your kindness far too long. It's time I faced facts. My life keeps pulling me away from my job. I can't ever thank you enough for all you've done for me. Please accept my resignation so you can replace me with someone reliable. I hope we'll always be friends."

"Dang it, Sam, I hate to lose you." He hesitated. "I might be able to cover your flights this week."

"I appreciate the offer, but you've covered for me too many times already. I don't want to put your job at risk." I sucked in a deep breath and fought back tears. "I'm turning in my wings."

He sighed. "I'll miss you, Sam. Everyone will. Uh, Lance still has another week of vacation. Is he with you?"

"Yes, he's part of our small team. Mike and Banger are with me too."

"Sam, I wish you nothing but the best. Please stay in touch and let me know how things turn out. We can finalize the paperwork when you get back."

"Thanks, Jeff, and give my best to everyone at LIA." I hung up and cried like a baby.

The next morning, day four in my seven-day search for the Blue Dragon, I rubbed my sore, red eyes and met my team in the conference room.

We sat around the table, awaiting Commander Bob Metz and the base commander.

Mike looked at me. "What's wrong with your eyes? Have you been crying?"

I nodded, trying not to cry again. "Bryce's death and my resignation hit me hard—too much loss lately."

"Oh." Mike hugged me. "Sorry, sis."

Lance bit his lip. "Sorry, Sam. How did Jeff take it?"

"He understood and wished me well—you know how he is, always a gentleman."

Lisa sensed I was struggling and changed the subject. "Have you talked to Professor Armitage?"

"No, I'm waiting for his call." I checked my satellite phone.

Mike crossed his arms. "Do you have any idea why the Eye sent us into that hellhole?"

"I got the answer right before the tube sent me to the surface."

"Well?" Lance looked at me. "Spill it."

"I was meant to recover the crown and scepter,

but ultimately the entire adventure was a test, especially what happened last."

"What are you talking about?" Mike leaned forward.

"After I sent you guys to the surface, I tried to follow you, but the tube wouldn't work if I wasn't on the throne." I paused. "Since the sphere had deserted me, I had no way up."

Banger raised a brow. "I don't understand—you came up through the same hatch we did."

"That was after I'd sent the four mercenaries up, even though I could've easily killed them." I glanced at my teammates. "I thought maybe you could persuade them to help you find Sweetwater's camp." I shrugged. "It didn't look like I'd get out, and I wanted to save Ross and Derek." I sighed. "Besides, they were in bad shape at that point—I kind of felt sorry for them."

Mike squeezed my shoulder. "Saving your enemies was the final test?"

I nodded. "Right after I sent the mercs to the surface, a soft voice speaking Atlantean told me I'd passed the final test. It called me Queen of Atlantis and instructed me to find the Blue Dragon and save them."

"You entered the tube again, and that time it worked?" Lisa asked.

"Yep, it sent me up to the surface where the sphere returned to me, like it had all been planned by somebody. I don't know what to think about all this, and I'm not certain who the voice was referring to when it instructed me to *save them*."

My satellite phone rang, and I snatched it up. "Hello? Ben, thanks for calling. Our trip to Tassili n'Ajjer turned out to be my final test, but we didn't find the Blue Dragon. Any ideas?" I put the phone on speaker.

"Did you find any evidence of the lost civilization?" Ben asked.

"We found a vast cavern about fifteen hundred feet under the plateau. It had buildings, statues, a big lake, and lots of nasty critters trying to kill us."

"Any evidence it might've been an Atlantean community?" He sounded excited.

"It was definitely Atlantean." I paused. "Ben, we're on day four of our seven-day ultimatum. I'll tell you all about Tassili n'Ajjer later. Right now, we need help finding the Blue Dragon."

"I asked if you found anything under the desert because if you did, I'd know where to send you next. I have it all mapped out for you. Can you commandeer a Black Hawk?"

"Yes, our mission has been given military priority because we suspect the Blue Dragon might be another Atlantean WMD. What's our destination?" I felt a surge of hope.

"You'll follow a trail across the Sahara from Chad to Timbuktu, focusing on major ley-line intersections. Investigate each site that has a high EMF signature. The find in Tassili n'Ajjer proved you're on the right track."

"We really thought we'd found the right spot. The city and lake were beneath a desert—an arid enigma, they were cloaked in eternal darkness, and I thought maybe some of the weird critters down there might've checked the primordial paradox box."

"Oh, no, my dear, primordial creatures would have to have existed from almost the very beginning of Earth. The lake you found down there is much more likely to have been from primordial origins."

"I'll keep that in mind as we continue our search. Can you email me the track you mapped?"

"I already sent it to the base commander. He'll give it to you at your briefing. Call me if I can help with anything else, Sam."

"Thanks, Ben. I hope my next call will be good news. Bye now."

Bob and the base commander walked in and took seats at opposite ends of the conference table.

The base commander handed a map and papers to Mike. "This is your new mission track. I'm sending your team in a Black Hawk so you can land wherever you need to." He paused and glanced around the table. "The course covers several countries. I know your ultimatum only has three days left after today, but it could take a lot longer to search all the ley-line intersections. That WMD is a high priority."

Bob broke in, "Obviously, we intend to rescue Ross and Derek, but if our time runs out, you must still locate the Blue Dragon. It could be a threat to millions of people."

"I understand." I thought a moment. "So far, every time Sweetwater's mercs have failed, the survivors have been fed to lions at his secret camp. When you release the four men I rescued, have a team follow them. If Sweetwater's men capture them, your team can follow them back to the camp and rescue Ross and Derek."

Bob glanced at the base commander. "That's a good idea, Sam. I'll have a covert team tail them when they're released today."

Mike said, "It might not be that easy. If I were in their shoes, I'd have the men split up so they'd be harder to find."

"Good point, Mike," Bob agreed. "I'll order them to dog every man. We only need one to lead us back to Sweetwater."

The base commander pulled out a recording device. "Let's get started on a more detailed debrief than last night so you can begin your next search mission."

Two hours later, Bob and the base commander looked at us like we'd lost our minds.

"It all sounds too crazy to be lies," Bob said. "I could see by your faces as you relived the events that you were speaking from terrifying memories and grief over losing Bryce. Once this Blue Dragon thing is settled, I'd like to send a team down there for a thorough scientific exploration and recovery mission."

"Then you'd better plan for a safe way in and out because our entry path and unusual exit may not be available anymore. I definitely don't want to go back down there." I glanced at my team.

They all shook their heads.

"We'll worry about that some other time." Bob glanced at Mike. "Give me an equipment list of what you'll need on this mission, and I'll get everything loaded on the Black Hawk while your team gears up."

Mike handed Bob the list. "This should cover everything. After our previous adventures, we have a good idea of what we need now."

Bob examined the paper. "A C-17 loaded with replacement equipment landed this morning. We should have everything you need."

The base commander stood. "Team dismissed."

Mike stood. "Team, meet me outside in thirty minutes. A van will take us to the airport."

We nodded at the base commander, said our goodbyes to Bob, and filed out the door.

Sweetwater's Hideout

"Bloody hell!" Sweetwater yelled into his satellite phone. "Only four survived?"

"Miss Starr saved them. She tried to make them

tell her the location of your camp, but they didn't know where it is, and your new general is nowhere to be found."

"And the Blue Dragon?" Sweetwater paced in front of his office window.

"They're closing in on it. They'll probably find it today or tomorrow."

"Tell me where they're going and I'll can send another team to shadow them." Sweetwater glanced at the video screen showing Ross and Derek in their cage.

"You've got a bigger problem. Covert operatives are following the four survivors from your Tassili n'Ajjer team. They intend to track them back to your base if you bring them there for lion fodder."

He stopped pacing. "I'll order my men to kill them on sight instead."

"Bad idea. The covert team could follow or capture your assassins and use them to find you. A better plan would be to ignore the four men, play the long game, and deal with them a year from now when they think they're safe."

"Fine, then I'll send men after Samantha Starr's team."

"That hasn't worked out very well. I suggest you leave them alone and wait until they bring your prize back to Camp Baledogle. Then I'll steal it, and you won't lose more mercs."

"All right, but if you cross me—"

The man on the phone interrupted. "Relax, I'm

in this for the money, and I know you'll pay me a small fortune when I deliver Samantha Starr and the Blue Dragon to you."

"Keep me posted." Sweetwater ended the call and stared at his lion pen through the window.

Black Hawk Helicopter

We landed on the sand at the fourth intersection of ley lines on our track map. The first three had turned out to be false leads. My head tingled from the electromagnetic energy that was concentrated at the site.

Lance climbed out and glanced around. "Nothing but a whole lot of sand."

"Distract the pilots while I check the Eye." I walked behind the helicopter where the crew couldn't see me.

When I held the Eye, it projected an image of gold lettering that repeated the instructions to find the Blue Dragon in the Dark Continent, ensconced in an arid enigma and a primordial paradox, cloaked in eternal darkness.

"So, basically, no help at all." Banger kicked sand, sending it down a dune.

"Maybe it's trying to tell me we're on the wrong track." I turned to Mike. "I think we should RTB and fly down to Johannesburg and check out that other site for the Cradle of Humankind."

Mike glanced around at endless sand. "I agree."

He led us into the helicopter and stuck his head in the cockpit. "Return to base. New mission plan."

Our helicopter lifted off and turned back toward the east. We'd been in the sky fifteen minutes when one of its two engines exploded and burst into flames. Shrapnel from the engine hit a rotor blade, and our chopper shook with bone-jarring vibrations. The chipped blade sent violent spasms through the cabin as the severe imbalance triggered a rotor failure.

The pilot yelled, "Brace for impact!"

Banger reached over and yanked my seatbelt tight enough to stop circulation. Something in his facial expression told me he'd been through this before. We didn't try to speak in the midst of the mind-numbing noise and vibrations.

I glanced over at my brother and prayed for his safety. His seatbelt looked tight as he yanked on Lisa's.

We slammed into the desert at an angle, and the rotors broke off, stirring up a cloud of sand.

The last thing I saw before I lost consciousness was Banger's determined face as he carried me out of the wreckage.

TWENTY-FOUR

Sahara

I woke looking into Mike's worried eyes.

"What happened?" I rubbed my head and got a little dried blood on my left hand.

"We blew an engine and crashed." Mike checked my pulse. "You hit your head and got knocked out."

I looked around. "What about everyone else?"

"They're all injured." He looked around. "Your bracelet has a lot of work to do."

"What about you?" I noticed a wound on his right arm. "Any other injuries?"

"No, just my arm. I was lucky."

"Now that we know the bracelet has to recharge after each use, I'd better heal the most serious injury first."

I crawled a few feet on the sand to where Lisa lay. Her right femur was broken, and she looked pale from shock. Banger sat nearby. I checked him over and discovered his left wrist was bent at an odd angle, and his right ankle was swollen to three times its normal size.

"Banger, how did you carry me with your wrist and ankle broken?"

"I had to save you." He glanced back at the smoldering wreckage. "The chopper was about to blow."

I kissed his cheek. "Thank you. I'll heal you after I take care of critical patients."

"Better see to the pilots." Banger pointed. "Lance is trying to take care of them over there."

Both pilots appeared to be unconscious with head wounds, and Lance had a gash in his shoulder.

"Take care of them first, Sam." Lance moved aside. "I think the lieutenant is hurt the worst."

I checked for the lieutenant's pulse, but couldn't feel it. When I put my right hand on his wound, the bracelet remained dark. "Oh God, I think he's dead."

Lance leaned down and listened to his chest. "No heartbeat. He's gone. Try the other pilot."

When I put my hand on his head, he moaned and opened his eyes. The bracelet blazed with brilliant light, and soon his wound was healed, and the swelling was gone. "Sip this water." I handed him a bottle.

Just to check the bracelet, I placed my hand over Lance's shoulder wound. Nothing happened. The bracelet needed to recharge. "Sorry, we'll have to wait, and I should heal Lisa's broken bone first."

"No worries. I can wait my turn" He kissed my cheek.

"Has anyone called for our rescue?" I glanced around the group.

Mike held up his satellite phone. "I called. A chopper will be here in two hours."

"Yeah, that's the downside of searching out in the middle of the desert." Lance waved around at the vast expanse of sand dunes. "We're a long way from an airport."

I checked inside my large belly bag. The sphere looked undamaged, and my crown and scepter were safely tucked beside it inside a felt sack. The Eye was in its leather pouch tied to my belt loop, the gold medallion was safe around my neck, and the ring was still on my finger. "Looks like all my weird artifacts are safe."

"Good, because things are about to get a lot worse." Banger pointed behind us.

He was right. A huge sandstorm loomed on the horizon, rushing toward us like a thousand-foot tsunami made of dark sand.

"Oh, god." Horrified, I sucked in my breath,

staring at the monster storm. "Did any of our equipment survive the crash?"

Mike jumped up and grabbed two backpacks and two paraglider chutes that were still packed. "Lance, grab those other backpacks."

I pulled the D-ring on one of the chutes. "We can hunker down under this chute until the storm passes."

The pilot, Mike, Lance, and I snapped out of our post-crash stupor and scrambled to set up an emergency tent over Lisa and Banger, using the paraglider silk. We assembled the supplies that had been flung out of the baggage compartment in the violent crash, piling them on the windward side and tucking the silk edges under them.

Mike took command. "Sam, you and Lisa sit in the center, and the men will be the tent poles."

"Okay, but first bring in the lieutenant so he doesn't get buried in the sand. He deserves to go home to his family."

"Right—no man left behind." Mike helped the surviving copilot carry his pilot into the makeshift tent.

The guys made a circular human wall with the silk against their backs and the edges tucked under them, while Lisa and I hunkered down in the center.

"Get ready," Mike said. "It's almost here."

Moments later, the roaring wall of sand hit us, and the tent's interior became as black as a sackcloth. Shrieking like a banshee, the storm shot-gunned our silk shelter with an endless supply of ammo from the desert dunes. A fear of being buried alive held me on the edge of panic as I tried to control my breathing.

Banger must've sensed my terror. He reached out with his good hand and pulled me against him. His strength and steady demeanor calmed me.

I expected the storm to pass quickly, but it raged around us with no hint of dissipating. No one tried to speak in the midst the howling wind as sand battered the silk in a relentless attack. I remained still, listening and trying not to look as frightened as I felt. Eventually, my watch chimed. It was time to heal Lisa's broken femur.

Her swollen leg and pasty coloring soon returned to normal. "Thanks, Sam," she shouted above the roaring. "I was worried the pain would make me vomit. I feel good now."

I smiled and nodded. After resetting my watch alarm for another hour, I handed Lisa a bottle of water.

Every hour, I healed another person, starting with Banger. When I put my hand on his swollen broken ankle, the bracelet healed his ankle and broken wrist simultaneously. I hugged him and yelled over the storm, "You're back to normal, whatever that means."

He grinned and shouted into my ear, "That

means I can resume taunting you with SEAL banter."

Timing the bracelet's recharges and then healing Lance and Mike had helped distract me from feeling claustrophobic in the dark little tent. I intended to heal myself last, but I discovered my head had already healed. I assumed the same healing energy that had gone through me into my patients had healed me too.

When the storm finally stopped, we pushed against the caved-in silk and made a scary discovery.

"We're buried!" My chest tightened as claustrophobia took hold.

Banger pulled me to him again and hugged me. "Calm down, Sam. I'll handle this." He stood in the center and pushed up with his arms above his head, straining to overcome the weight of the sand. After a few tries, he managed to lift the fabric high enough to clear a small space in the center. Then he sliced through the silk with his combat knife.

Cool air, dim light, and a thin river of sand entered our tiny tent as I managed to slow my breathing.

Banger stuck his head outside. "The air is cool because it's night now. What happened to our rescue chopper?"

"They must've turned back when they saw the sandstorm." I stood. "How about lifting me out of here?"

"Still feeling a bit claustrophobic?" He grasped my waist and lifted me through the hole.

Cool, fresh air washed over my face, instantly soothing me. I scrambled out and used my cupped hands to pull sand away from the mound.

Lisa came out next and joined me in digging. Mike and Lance were hoisted out and helped us. It didn't take long before the opening was big enough for the pilot and Banger to climb out after passing the lieutenant's body and all the supplies to us.

A starry sky and almost-full moon lighted a vast sea of sand, curving like gentle rollers.

Mike took charge. "One of these paragliders will make a big enough bottom sheet for all of us, and we can use another one for a cover. May as well be comfortable while we wait for the rescue helicopter."

"And we'll cut enough silk off our partially buried tent to make a shroud for the lieutenant," Banger said.

Once we had everything set up, we gathered on top of the black chute. The clear night sky sparkled with billions of stars.

"This is a pleasant change from that scary sandstorm." I lay back and admired nature's brilliant tableau.

"It's unlikely anyone could sneak up on us out here, and we'll hear the chopper long before it gets here." Lance reclined on the silk. "Time to get caught up on our sleep." He pulled the top chute over us for warmth.

Sweetwater's Hideout

"They crashed in the Sahara?" Sweetwater said into his satellite phone. "Is Samantha Starr alive?"

"Her brother called for rescue and said everyone was alive, but injured."

"When will they be rescued?" Sweetwater paced in front of a window overlooking the lion pen.

"Uh, well, we've had a setback," the tense voice replied. "The rescue chopper had to turn back to avoid a huge sandstorm that lasted the rest of the day and into the night."

"But they're on their way now, right?" Sweetwater stopped pacing.

"Before the storm, the rescue helicopter was homing in on the wrecked chopper's emergency locator beacon." The man paused. "The signal should've been good for several days, but it stopped during the sandstorm."

Sweetwater clenched his fist. "Are you saying the military hasn't gone out looking for them again?"

"They flew around until they had to return for fuel. No trace of the downed team."

"Are they going back out?" Sweetwater stared at a map of the Sahara.

"We decided to wait a while and see if they call

us on their satellite phone." He paused. "They can give us exact GPS coordinates when they call—save us a lot of time and fuel."

"And if they don't call?" Sweetwater struggled to keep his tone even.

"We'll mount a massive SAR mission. We've already got our satellites looking for them."

"You have to find them fast," Sweetwater said. "They can't last long in the desert without water."

"We're doing everything we can. The Pentagon is well aware that the mission to locate the Blue Dragon will be impossible without Miss Starr."

"I want to hear the instant you know something." Sweetwater pounded the table, his frustration mounting.

My researchers are incompetent. That blond Yank is my last hope to get the power diamond.

Sahara

We woke under a searing sun heating our silk sailcloth. There wasn't a helicopter in sight. Nothing but miles and miles of empty sand.

I poked my brother. "Uh, Mike, shouldn't the SAR be here by now?"

He glanced at his watch. "They should've been here hours ago."

"Did you give them our GPS coordinates?" Banger searched the sky.

"They had our ELT signal, and the chopper homed in on that."

I scanned the sand. No wreckage. "We have a problem—no ELT. Everything's buried."

"It could be under tons of sand." Lance looked around. "No wonder they can't pick up the signal."

Lisa nudged Mike. "Call them on the SAT phone. They can get our location from the GPS signal."

He pulled out his phone, hit a button, and then shook the phone. "Battery's dead."

Lance turned to me. "Use your phone, Sam."

"I would, but it was in my backpack, and that never made it out of the crash." I glanced at the pilot. "How about you? Did you bring a satellite phone?"

"No, we weren't issued a SAT COMM." He frowned. "I suggest we check our water rations and come up with a survival plan."

"I've got that covered." Lisa pointed at a backpack. "We have ten eight-ounce bottles of water and a lot of salty beef jerky in there."

"We'd better remain under the paraglider for sun protection." Lance lifted it above his head for ventilation, and the other men did the same.

Banger edged beside me and smiled.

I looked into his eyes. "You don't look worried. Why?"

He lifted my chin. "I'm with Queen Samantha. Deal with this."

I considered my artifacts. Which one could help us? Suddenly, it came to me—the sphere.

I looked at the pilot. "Do you remember our crash coordinates?"

He nodded.

"Anybody have a piece of paper and a pen or pencil?" I glanced at the group.

The pilot pulled a small logbook out of his breast pocket.

"Tear out a blank piece of paper and write down our crash coordinates. Then give me the paper and pen."

He did what I asked, and I wrote a note to Commander Metz on the same paper.

"What are you going to do—send it by carrier pigeon?" Mike stared at the note.

I glanced at Banger and grinned. "Nope, I'm sending it in the sphere." I folded the paper and pulled my little buddy out of my belly bag.

In Atlantean, I commanded it to open its hatch and receive the note. After I slipped the paper inside, the roof closed, and I sent the silver-blue ball to Commander Metz in the conference room at Camp Baledogle.

"This could work—if it doesn't scare the crap out of them." Banger grinned at me.

"Commander Metz is super smart. He'll know what to do." I watched my tiny buddy zoom out of sight in an instant.

Camp Baledogle

General Ryan sat at the head of the conference table. The base commander sat at the other end, and Commander Metz sat on the side facing the window. Various support people with laptops and tablets filled the rest of the chairs.

"I'm not ready to give up on them." General Ryan glanced around. "Samantha Starr has many unique skills, and she always finds a way out."

The general's aide checked a laptop. "But, sir, there's nothing on satellite imaging, we haven't received a call from their SAT COMM, and their ELT stopped transmitting hours ago."

The base commander shook his head. "They were injured and could've been buried in that sandstorm."

"Or Miss Starr could've healed everyone with her bracelet," Commander Metz said.

Another aide said, "Maybe Sweetwater's mercenaries found them."

"If the U.S. military couldn't find them, I doubt Sweetwater's people did," said the base commander.

As soon as he finished speaking, the window shattered, jolting everyone at the table. Shards of glass covered the floor. Before anyone could react, a silver-blue globe about ten inches in diameter zoomed into the room and hovered in front of Commander Robert Metz.

Everyone froze.

The sphere rested lightly on the table in front of Metz.

The base commander stiffened. "Don't move. That thing has a powerful laser."

The tiny hatch opened, revealing a slip of paper wedged beside the vertically mounted blue marquise diamond.

Metz smiled. "Looks like Sam sent us a message. Everyone remain still while I retrieve it." He grasped the edge of the paper with his fingertips and gently pulled it out.

The instant he removed the paper, the hatch closed, and the silvery globe zoomed out the broken window.

Metz exhaled and unfolded the paper. "It's from Sam. She sent us the coordinates for their crash site. They lost one helicopter pilot. The rest of them are alive and healed, but they're short on water." He handed the note to General Ryan.

Ryan read it and handed the note to his aide. "Send the SAR helicopter."

TWENTY-FIVE

Sahara

The sphere sped toward me at blinding speed and stopped inches from my face.

I blew out a sigh. "That really got my heart pumping." I took hold of my little friend and commanded it to open its hatch. The paper was gone. When the roof closed, I placed the globe in its satchel in the belly bag.

Mike glanced at his watch. "Assuming that thing flies at supersonic speed, we can expect to be rescued in the next three hours, barring any sandstorms."

Banger hugged me. "Well done, my queen."

Exactly two and a half hours later, rotor blades thundered in the distance. Soon, the search and rescue helicopter came into view.

We waved the paraglider in the breeze like a huge flag, and the SAR chopper zeroed in on us.

It landed, and we ducked our heads against the blowing sand. We climbed in, carrying the lieutenant's body and what was left of our supplies.

What a relief to be airborne again. A crewmember passed around cool bottles of water, and we gulped it down.

Lance leaned in. "It'll be three hours back to the base after a fuel stop. That pretty much uses up this day, leaving us only two days to find the Blue Dragon."

"I hope we find it in South Africa in that other Cradle of Humankind." I bit my lip. "I couldn't bear it if I fail Ross and Derek."

Lance hugged me. "Don't worry. We'll save them."

It was dark by the time our helicopter landed back at Camp Baledogle. The team straggled into the conference room to plan our next move.

I studied a map of ley lines. "It has to be in one of those ancient caves near Johannesburg." I tapped a spot on the map. "This area has an intersection of three ley lines. That might be it."

Mike stretched. "Let's get cleaned up, regroup, and fly down there tonight so we can get an early start tomorrow."

Commander Metz walked in. "Welcome home. We're glad you made it back safe. Sorry you lost one of the pilots."

"Thanks, Bob. We're running out of time. I'm hoping the Blue Dragon is in one of the Sterkfontein Caves thirty miles northwest of Johannesburg. We'd like to fly down there tonight. Is the Starr Corporation's jet still here?"

"The pilots wouldn't leave without you, and the jet is ready when you are. Have you talked to Professor Armitage since your rescue?"

"No, not yet." I hesitated. "I lost my satellite phone in the crash, and Mike's battery died."

Bob handed me his satellite phone. "Fully charged and ready to go. Give him a call."

I handed the phone to Lisa. "Better check it first."

She took apart the phone and handed me a bug. "Good thing I looked inside." She reassembled the phone.

Bob's eyes widened when I handed him the tiny electronic listening device. "How did that bug get in there?" he asked no one in particular.

"Sweetwater has a mole in this base." Lisa handed the clean phone to me.

Bob frowned. "We'll check the phones from now on."

I dialed Ben's number and put the phone on speaker.

He answered on the first ring. "Did you find it?"

"No, we're hoping it's in that other Cradle of Humankind near Johannesburg."

"I've been giving this a lot of thought since your

adventure in that city under Tassili n'Ajjer." Ben paused. "The primordial part of the riddle has to be an underground lake—one undisturbed by time. Besides spelunking gear, you'd better bring plenty of full air tanks and dive gear."

"We have rebreather tanks. They're lighter and last longer, but where do we dive?"

"The South African Cradle of Humankind is a network of limestone caves. It covers a hundred and eighty square miles, but don't worry, there's an underground lake in the Sterkfontein Caves—probably primordial. It's in a chamber called Milner Hall. The lake's depth is unknown because they banned diving in 1984 after a diver got lost and died."

"Sounds like diving there is even more dangerous than most cave dives." I glanced at Mike, and he nodded.

Ben said, "The caves look like Swiss cheese with lots of side chambers, so be extra careful. The diver's body was found by rescue teams in an air chamber three weeks after he disappeared. That led to the discovery of another twenty-seven hundred feet of new passages—and more ways to get lost."

"Any chance we can get permission to dive there?" Mike asked.

"Oh, hi, Mike. The Sterkfontein Caves are owned by the University of Witwatersrand. You could try asking them, but then you'd run the risk of alerting them to your plans if they refuse permission."

"What are their hours of operation at the site?" I checked my watch.

"The caves are open to the public seven days a week with tours every half hour all day long. That means you'd have to sneak in late at night, lugging lots of dive gear."

"Nothing about this mission has been easy." I sighed. "Why should this part be any different?"

"You could look into whether our government has any leverage with South Africa, but time is running short, and going through proper channels takes days, possibly weeks. Use your best judgment."

"Thanks, Ben. That's good advice. Wish us luck." I ended the call not really knowing if we were on the right track, but we'd run out of options.

"Let's see what the Eye shows us." I pulled it out, and it projected a hologram of a cave marked by a sign that read Dinaledi Chamber (Chamber of Stars).

"Chamber of Stars—easy peasy." Banger grinned.

"Hold your horses, big guy." I Googled the cave. "There aren't any lakes in the Rising Star cave system, which is where that cave is located. And we already know the Eye won't lead me directly to the Blue Dragon. We should look in the underground lake Ben mentioned."

"Ah, but you're forgetting how late it is now and how long it takes to fly to Johannesburg from here." Banger checked his watch. "It'll be well into daylight by the time we reach the caves. We'll have all day to look around before we'll get a chance to sneak into the lake."

Sterkfontein Caves

We arrived at the site at nine in the morning local time, on day six of our seven-day quest. A sign for the tour instructed people to leave handbags and luggage behind due to tight passageways. I turned around and headed back to our two Range Rovers that were loaded full of dive gear and other luggage.

Mike caught up with me. "Why'd you do a one-eighty?"

"No bags allowed. I need a big shirt that'll cover my belly bag and leather pouch. I can't leave any of this stuff behind, so I'll wear the bag with the sphere under my shirt and they'll think I'm pregnant." I opened my suitcase.

"We'd better hide some spelunking gear under our clothes too." Mike keyed his hidden mike and recalled the team.

After spending a little time hiding ropes, mini lights, and small tools under our clothes, we headed back to the cave entrance and followed a tour group down several flights of stairs to narrow passageways carved into the limestone. We walked deep into the cave system, occasionally entering wide caverns with high ceilings and numerous stalagmites and stalactites.

Banger stuck close, checking me for signs of claustrophobia, bless him.

The farther down we went, the higher my heart rate soared.

When I spotted a sign for the passage to Milner Hall, I stopped in front of my team and whispered, "That way."

I ducked under a rope, and they followed me down a dark, narrow passage with many curves. After the fifth or sixth turn, my flashlight illuminated cobalt-blue water. It glistened between limestone walls covered with erosion marks and dark horizontal waves.

I spoke softly so my voice wouldn't carry too far. "Looks like limited access to the lake between honeycombs of limestone. It's easy to see how a diver could get lost down here."

"Are you feeling any ley lines or energy pockets?" Lance looked down at the water.

"No, but let me try something." I dropped to my knees and leaned down, dipping my fingertips into the water. "The water tingles and not just because it's cold. There's strong EME here."

"What if one of those chambers that only opens for you is somewhere along this rim?" Lance asked. "Might save a lot of time if I hold onto you while you run your hands along the side just under the water."

"It's worth a try, but nothing's ever that easy when Atlantis is involved." I had to rearrange my belly bag behind me before I assumed a prone position with Lance holding my ankles. Reaching over the edge, I stuck my right hand in the water and ran it over the stone side.

We'd just started our little experiment when a male voice said, "Everyone turn around and put your hands on your heads."

Lance helped me up, and I faced four security guards armed with handguns.

The leader asked, "What are you doing in this restricted area?"

I stepped forward. "It's my fault. I wanted to see the primordial lake, but then I dropped my phone into the water when I was taking pictures. My friends were just helping me try to retrieve it. Sorry."

"You violated the rules, and now we must escort you out," the lead guard said. "Come with us."

He and his men herded us down a passage, guarding us from the front and rear. We were deep inside the cave system, and it took two hours for us to reach the exit. Once outside, the guards led us to an office.

"Search them in case they took bones or relics from restricted areas," the site manager ordered.

It only took a minute for them to discover our

spelunking gear hidden under our clothes. When a guard reached for my belly bag and leather pouch, I stepped back.

"I'm sorry, but I can't let you touch those. You might get injured." I unzipped the belly bag. "Let me show you." I whispered commands to the sphere as I pulled it out.

The guards drew their weapons, and the sphere zapped their handguns with its laser. They dropped their superheated pistols onto the floor and raised their hands.

"I assure you, nothing we have is from your caves, and we have diplomatic immunity." I showed them my passport, and the team members pulled out theirs. "We apologize for any inconvenience we may have caused."

"Your immunity does not entitle you to ignore our laws. I'll call the police, and you'll be expelled from the country." The manager eyed the sphere, hovering in front of me. "Put that thing away."

I zipped it back in my bag. "I was just trying to protect you. No need to call the police. We'll leave right away. And again, my apologies."

My team followed me out the door, and I hoped the guards' fear of the sphere would prevent them from picking up their weapons and detaining us. We rushed to our vehicles.

"You know they called the cops the instant we left the building." Mike glanced back. "We need to disappear fast."

I glanced at my guidebook. "There's a back road that leads to another site. Maybe we can hide there."

"Lead the way. We might get a chance to come back here late tonight." Mike looked over his shoulder, scanning the road behind us.

By the time we arrived at the next site, the aroma of hot food reached our noses. A meal truck was parked nearby.

"Let's grab some lunch and decide what to do next." Banger sauntered toward the vendor.

We sat around a picnic table and studied the guidebooks while we munched on hot meals.

Mike glanced around. "May as well search this site, but keep your eyes peeled for local cops."

"Before we do that, let's switch our license plates with ones from other vehicles." I pulled out my multi-purpose tool and began unscrewing a plate on the Jeep parked to our left.

Soon we had replaced our plates with ones from nearby SUVs.

"Better drive to a different site so nobody will notice their plates are on our cars," Lisa said.

We drove to one of the many sites in the vast cave system. After several hours of fruitless searching and talking to anthropologists, we regrouped for another meeting.

"We may as well check out that Chamber of Stars the Eye showed us. It's dark now, almost eight —still a long time before we can dive in the underground lake." I pointed at a spot on the map. "The Rising Star Cave isn't far from here. It might be closed after dark, but we could sneak inside."

Thirty minutes later, Lance distracted the security guard, and the rest of us ducked inside the cave entrance. About a hundred feet in, I bumped into a fit man in his early thirties as he rounded a corner. He wore an ID badge that indicated he was an anthropologist. Perfect.

"Sorry." I smiled my best smile. "I guess I'm a little too eager."

He extended his hand. "Hi, I'm Dr. Phil Berger. What are you hoping to see here?" he said with a Boston accent.

I squeezed his hand. "Samantha Starr, and we're hoping to solve a vexing riddle."

He glanced at my wrist and hand. "That jewelry looks ancient. How old is it?"

"Probably twelve thousand years, maybe more." I looked into his eyes. "If you help us, I'll arrange for you to be the lead anthropologist on a huge find under Tassili n'Ajjer."

He furrowed his brow. "I haven't heard of a find there."

"That's because we just found it two days ago. It's part of the Lost Sahara Civilization."

His eyes lit up. "No kidding? Well, maybe I can help. What's the riddle?" He seemed genuinely interested, especially since I dangled our recent discovery under his nose.

I took a shot. "We're searching for an arid enigma and a primordial paradox cloaked in eternal darkness."

"Interesting. And if you find it, then what?" He seemed intrigued.

"Then we need to find an ancient artifact called the Blue Dragon and deliver it to a murderous man before noon tomorrow or he'll feed our friends to hungry lions." I blinked back a tear.

Phil tilted his head. "He'll really kill them?"

"Yes, the man is pure evil." I squeezed his arm. "Please, can you help us?"

"Wait—did you say the Blue Dragon?" He looked as if something had jogged his memory.

"Yes, the Blue Dragon. Is that familiar to you?" My voice rose in hope.

His face brightened as he said, "I hate to tell you this, but you're looking in the wrong country. Dragon's Breath Cave is in the Kalahari Desert."

TWENTY-SIX

"Are you saying that cave fits everything in the riddle?" My heart raced as I searched his eyes.

He nodded. "I've been there. It's hidden in the desert—an arid enigma because the cave leads down to a vast primordial lake under the sand, and it's cloaked in eternal darkness. The lake sends a mist to the surface—hence the name Dragon's Breath Cave."

"Oh my god, I could kiss you." And I did. On the lips. "Please, will you show us where it is? We're almost out of time."

"Out of time?" he asked, looking flummoxed from my enthusiastic kiss.

"It's a long story, but like I said, two lives depend on us finding something hidden in that cave before tomorrow afternoon." I gazed into his hazel eyes. "Will you please help us?"

"It's a really long drive from here." He paused. "I don't suppose you have access to a jet?"

I grinned. "We have a Gulfstream G650 waiting for us at Johannesburg International Airport. If you'll take us to the cave, we'll pay you and see to it you get a free ride home." I grabbed his hands and squeezed. "Please, we're desperate."

He glanced from me to my team. "How can I refuse a damsel in distress? Do you have any dive gear?"

"Yes, we have four rebreather units already filled and everything else we'll need for scuba diving and spelunking."

He hesitated. "I can't get off work until this weekend, but I can give you directions if you need to go now."

"Like I said, time is critical."

"Then you'll need to fly to Grootfontein Airport in Namibia and drive thirty miles northwest of the town to the cave entrance." He paused. "I hope you and your people are expert spelunkers and divers. You'll have to drag your tanks through a narrow system of caves with several drop offs that end in a final drop that's a hundred and twenty feet down to a lake three hundred and thirty feet beneath the desert. It's the largest non-subglacial underground lake in the world."

"But won't we need you to guide us? There must be lots of wrong turns."

"No, there's only one way down. There's a

guide rope installed, plus other ropes are in place to lower yourself down to each ledge that leads to the next cave and eventually to the last drop to the lake. There's a raft positioned at the bottom of the final rope. Use your ropes to lower the scuba tanks down onto the raft. Nobody knows how deep the lake is, but it's definitely more than four hundred and twenty feet."

I hugged him again. I couldn't help myself. It would be close, but we might succeed before the deadline. The Eye had steered us in the right direction after all.

Phil walked with us out of the cave. We stopped short when we spotted four police cars parked around our Range Rovers. Armed cops stood beside Lance, who was handcuffed.

I turned to Phil. "This is all a big misunderstanding. Some guards at the Sterkfontein Caves were frightened by my artifacts, especially the sphere." I unzipped my belly bag and pulled it out. "We don't want to harm anyone. We're just trying to save our friends. Please don't tell them where we're going."

I spoke commands in Atlantean, and the sphere lasered holes in all the tires of the police vehicles. Then it zoomed up high, out of sight.

The cops trained their guns on us.

I whispered to Phil, "We'll pretend we took you hostage. That way, you won't get in trouble." I slipped a tie-wrap over his wrists. "Stand in front of me."

He did as I asked, and Mike, Banger, and Lisa blocked the cops' view of us.

"Come out with your hands up!" a police officer yelled.

The cops held their hands outstretched in front of them, clutching their pistols.

Out of the dark sky, the sphere sent laser shots into each weapon, causing the cops to drop their handguns.

I led Phil to the police. "Uncuff my friend, and I'll trade this scientist for him."

The sphere hovered above the officers as one of them unlocked Lance's handcuffs.

I nodded to my team. "Cuff the cops to their steering wheels."

Once all the policemen were secured, I replaced the sphere in its sack, and we piled into our SUVs and brought Phil with us. About a mile down the road, we stopped.

"Phil, we're counting on you to wait as though we dropped you off several miles from here before you go back and free the cops. We need at least two hours to clear customs and fly out of Johannesburg. Will you help us, please?"

"Is your offer still good for that discovery in Algeria?" He held out his hands, and I sliced the plastic cuff with my knife.

"Absolutely." I squeezed his hand. "Expect to hear from Harvard Professor Ben Armitage."

His face brightened. "I know Ben. We have a deal. Good luck in Dragon's Breath Cave. I hope you save your friends." He waved as we drove away.

Sweetwater's Hideout

Sweetwater snatched up his satellite phone. "Where is she?"

"Her team just took off for Grootfontein Airport in Namibia. They're on their way to Dragon's Breath Cave in the Kalahari Desert. It leads down to the largest underground lake in the world." The man's tone radiated excitement.

"That has to be where the Blue Dragon is hidden. Ancient scrolls described a cave beside a body of water in Africa. Give me the details and I'll send a team."

Sweetwater jotted down the location and then called his new general.

My team is on the way. Soon, I'll have the Blue Dragon and Samantha Starr.

He poured a generous measure of Glenglassaugh, glanced out at the lion pen, and smiled.

Dragon's Breath Cave

We landed well before dawn, and I stopped by the cockpit while the team unloaded our gear into the vehicles we'd rented ahead of time. I looked from Bill to Laura. "Thank you for risking your necks to fly my team all over Africa."

Laura grinned. "I don't know about Bill, but this has been the most fun I've ever had on the job."

Bill nodded. "You do lead an exciting life."

"Yeah, well, sometimes it's a little too exciting, which brings me to my next request." I hesitated. "I need you both to promise me you'll fly back to Florida if you don't hear from us by ten this morning. I don't want you to end up in Sweetwater's crosshairs. That wouldn't help any of us. And don't stop at Camp Baledogle."

"But how will you get home?" Laura asked.

"There's always another way, and based on what we might find at Dragon's Breath Cave, we may be led in an unexpected direction that will take us far from this airport. That happened when we went to Lalibela, and it could happen again here. Also, we may end up in a combat situation with Sweetwater's mercenaries. You're not equipped or trained for that, so please don't stay. I can't bear to lose another friend."

They glanced at each other and nodded. I hugged them, said goodbye, and left the airplane.

Mike beckoned to me. "Come on, Sam. Time to go."

We drove thirty miles and pulled up to the site at dawn, our SUVs laden with everything we'd need. As promised, a mysterious mist rose from the harsh waterless landscape, marking the cave's entrance.

I faced the team. "Mike, I hate to pull rank on you, but we're almost out of time. The most efficient way to conduct this search is for you to come with me and leave the rest of the team to guard the cave entrance. Sweetwater is bound to know we're here."

"Why Mike and not me?" Banger crossed his arms.

"I have a gut feeling I'll need a blood relative for this." I shrugged. "Sorry, my liege."

"All right, what can we do to help?" Banger opened the rear hatch on one of our two SUVs.

Mike grabbed his wetsuit. "Help us unload the gear."

I pulled a wetsuit on over my shorts and T-shirt. "We'll each take two rebreather units, pushing one ahead and dragging one behind through the tight spots. And we'll need a few of those tactical lift bags along with the regular ones. The Blue Dragon Diamond is two feet long and probably heavy, and we'll need to tow our extra tanks." I shoved the leather pouch with the Eye into a pocket in my BC vest and secured the belly bag around the outside of the vest with extra clips. "I hope the cave is cold enough that I won't overheat in this neoprene."

Mike handed me two dive knives in sheaths. "Strap these to your calves. Do you want a speargun?"

"No, I've got the sphere and the scepter. They should be more than enough if Sweetwater's mercs manage to sneak down there."

"Just remember—wherever we go, we do it together. I'll lead until we reach the water." He clipped a Glock in a dry bag and his fins onto his BC vest and slung a ballistic speargun across his chest. "Let's go."

We had the dive tanks rigged with all the rope we'd need to lower them onto the raft one hundred and twenty feet beneath the final passage. I did another check of my gear. I had four extra lift bags, and so did Mike.

Banger checked me over. "Be careful down there, my queen." He handed me an extra mag light.

"You do the same up here, my liege. There's bound to be a battle with Sweetwater's mercs." I wrapped my arms around him.

Lance stepped in for a hug and so did Lisa.

It was go time. Mike and I slid down a rope into the misty hole and landed on a slanted cavern floor. The cavern ended in a small choke twenty feet in. Next came a low, narrow passage that required crawling to a twenty-five-foot vertical drop onto a ledge where we slid down another rope to a passage forty feet farther down.

"Oh, boy, this part looks even tighter. We'll have to crawl, shoving and dragging our tanks." I hitched one rebreather unit to my waist.

Mike checked my eyes. "How's the claustrophobia?"

"I'm okay, but if I never have to go in another cave, I won't be sorry." I dropped to my knees. "Lead on, big brother."

We crawled downward for what seemed like hours to my claustrophobic mind. Then Mike halted in front of me and peeked over a ledge.

"We've reached the last drop to the lake. It's a really long way down, and the lake is huge." He rigged his rebreather tanks and lowered them onto the raft. "Shove your tanks to me." He turned and rigged the ropes for mine. "Down they go."

Mike waved me forward. "You're next. When you reach the raft, secure our tanks to it in case it flips when I land on it."

"Okay, wish me luck." I grasped the down line with my gloved hands and backed over the ledge.

"You don't need luck, sis. You're Queen of Atlantis. Now let's get down there and kick ass." Mike's version of a SEAL motivational speech.

I was glad I'd worn neoprene booties as I wedged my feet against the rope and descended. I slid down as slowly as possible so I wouldn't tip the raft when I landed. A quick glance around with my night-vision gear revealed a vast cavern housing an enormous lake. The openness helped ease my discomfort with being so far underground.

I had descended the equivalent of a twelve-story building when my feet touched the raft. It felt tippy.

I maneuvered it with my toes until I was over the center, and then I gently eased myself all the way down onto it.

"I'm on the raft, securing the tanks," I said to Mike via my radio. "Start down slowly."

"Descending now," he replied.

I had no sooner tied off the tanks when my brother dropped into the raft without making a ripple.

"Wow, you SEALs really are agile. It seemed a lot more difficult when I did it."

"It's all about the training. I'll mount your tank on your BC, then you mount mine." He attached my rebreather pack to my buoyancy-compensator vest and switched on the air. "Looks good. Now do mine."

Our next task was securing the extra tanks to partially filled lift bags and tethering them to us so we could tow them behind us on our dive. I was grateful for our DARPA night-vision full facemasks —we'd be able to see in the pitch-black water and talk to each other.

Mike gazed at the immense lake. "Before we jump in, what's the plan?"

I thought for a moment. "We've arrived at the riddle's primordial lake, and I've passed all the tests and collected every Atlantean artifact we could possibly need for this mission. I think the sphere will take us to the Blue Dragon now. Hold onto my ankles once we're in the water, in case it starts pulling us."

"All right. It's worth a try. Give it the command." He dropped over the side and waited.

Cold water instantly cooled my hot skin under the wetsuit. The lake, undisturbed since the beginning of time, was crystal clear.

I commanded the metal globe to pull us slowly to the Blue Dragon once we were in the water. Mike grasped my ankles, and the sphere came alive inside the satchel clipped to me. It pulled us downward at an angle away from the raft. I prayed it wouldn't drag us too deep. Decompression would be an inconvenient delay we couldn't afford.

As we descended, we encountered a rare fish, the golden cave catfish. It glistened like twenty-four-carat gold, but it couldn't see us because the eternal darkness had made it blind.

Behind me, Mike cried out, "Sam!" and let go of my ankles.

I turned and spotted a dark cloud forming around him. Blood. His body was slowly sinking.

Two divers rushed at me from above. The sphere in the satchel kept pulling me away slowly. I telepathically commanded it to halt and pulled it out of its bag. When a diver waved his speargun at me, I distracted him by shoving the sphere into his hands.

It shocked him with a jolt of energy, and he dropped it and his weapon. I used that moment to slap a tactical lift bag on his ankle and lock it.

As he rocketed inverted to the surface, destined to suffer an embolism or the bends or both from this depth, the other diver shot me in the stomach. Blood clouded the water as I yanked out the spear. The enemy diver grabbed hold of the bracelet and tried to pull it off my wrist.

Dizzy and bleeding, I telepathically commanded the sphere to return and laser my attacker's head. It did, and the result was instant death for my enemy. As he dropped away, I looked around. Where was Mike? I couldn't bear to lose him.

I placed my little friend back in the satchel and commanded it to pull me to the speared diver. Mike was slowly disappearing into the depths when I reached him. A spear was embedded in his side, blood leaking out in a steady stream. That meant he was still alive.

I yanked out the spear and placed my right hand on his wound as I pulled him up slowly to a sixty-foot depth.

Dizzy, I prayed, "Dear God, please don't let my brother die."

The diamond in my bracelet blazed with brilliant light, and I saw stars again. I closed my eyes and prayed once more for my brother. I knew the same energy that was healing him would heal me, like it had in the Sahara.

"Hey, sis, what happened to those divers?" Mike's voice sounded strong.

I checked his side and my belly. "They're dead,

and your wound is healed." I hugged him and looked into his eyes. "How do you feel?"

"Fine." Mike smiled at me through his face-mask. "Let's go. We're burning daylight." He eased below me and grasped my ankles.

My head cleared now that my wound had healed. I commanded my little buddy to slowly pull us to the Blue Dragon.

An hour later, we reached the entrance to an underwater cave. The sphere pulled us inside and up to an air pocket.

I stuck my head above the water and gasped. "Wow, I never expected this."

TWENTY-SEVEN

"Awesome." Mike pulled himself up on the bank and tried the air outside his mask.

"Is the air good?" I asked as he pulled me onto the ledge.

"Yeah, you can take your mask off." He stood and slipped out of his vest and tanks.

"If this is what I think it is, we won't be leaving the way we came." I stood, slipped out of my dive gear, and pulled off my wetsuit. I removed the leather pouch with the Eye from my BC and tied it to a belt loop on my shorts. Then I cinched the belly bag around my waist and pulled out the sphere.

I stood before a giant version of my silver-blue buddy. It was at least thirty feet in diameter. "Open the door," I said in Atlantean.

The tiny sphere zapped a spot with its laser, and

an entry door opened where none had been apparent. Steps dropped down.

I turned my gaze above the large silver ball and spotted a huge metal cover in the cavern's ceiling. "Open the hatch," I commanded.

My little helper zapped the center with its laser, and the door swung open, revealing a vertical tunnel. Before I could say anything, it sent another laser straight up the tunnel, and a loud clunk indicated the surface hatch had opened. Sand and dirt rained down and slid off the giant globe.

Mike had removed his wetsuit and clipped his Glock to his shorts. We hadn't brought shoes, so we kept our neoprene booties on.

Mike edged closer to the strange craft. "Am I supposed to enter this first?"

I put the little sphere in my bag. "Yes, but I want to be holding onto you when you do, just in case it doesn't know you're supposed to be here." I grabbed his left hand. "Okay, go ahead."

He climbed the eight steps with me close on his heels. We emerged onto a flight deck with command seats, controls, perimeter seats, and two survival pods with people inside. An enormous blue marquise diamond was mounted vertically in the center of the interior. It had to be over two feet long. The Blue Dragon Diamond.

I glanced behind me. The stairs retracted, and the door closed.

I turned and stared at two unconscious people

lying under glass canopies—an elderly man and woman in separate pods. A control panel indicated the suspended animation function had failed, but the life support still had twenty minutes remaining.

"This is what the message meant when it said, 'Save them.' It was referring to this man and woman. They've been locked away for thousands of years and should've still been young when the time came for them to wake up. Too bad the system malfunctioned seventy years ago." I stared at their wrinkled faces in quiet repose, their eyes closed.

Mike stood beside me. "Are you going to wake them now?"

"Not yet. The divers who attacked us had to have made it past our team. That means our people need us. We should rescue them first."

Mike studied the analog readouts on the pods. "But, sis, they only have eighteen minutes until their life support runs out."

"Yes, but what if they're evil, super-powerful beings who immediately take control of the ship and prevent us from helping our team and rescuing Ross and Derek? I won't risk it." I turned away and sat in the command chair.

The instant I placed my hands on the crystal armrests, the machine powered up, emitting a low hum. I studied the strange instrument panel, trying to deduce how to control the sphere.

Mike peered over my shoulder. "I hope you know how to fly this thing."

"I've got ratings for all sorts of airplanes, sea-planes, gliders, jets, and helicopters, but I failed to earn my big round ball rating, so excuse me if the ride ends up being a little bumpy." I grabbed a crystal stick and pulled back.

"Whoa." Mike grabbed the back of my chair to keep from tumbling backward as we zoomed up the vertical tunnel and shot into the bright sunshine.

I wasn't expecting such an incredible rate of climb. We were at one hundred thousand feet in seconds.

"Crap, didn't mean to go so high." I eased forward on the stick, and we descended too fast.

"Careful, sis, we can't help our team if you kill us in this thing."

Even though we were inside a metal aircraft, the walls were transparent from the inside. I could see everything outside, including the ground rushing up at us.

"Do something!" Mike squeezed my shoulder.

I pulled back, instantly pushed forward, then neutralized the stick, narrowly averting disaster. We hovered a few feet above the ground near the Drag-on's Breath Cave entrance. I caught my breath and glanced around, looking for our team.

There were dead soldiers everywhere. Sweet-water must've sent a small army against our three teammates.

Just then, a bullet bounced off the sphere.

"I guess this unobtainium is bulletproof." Mike looked around.

I studied the panel, searching for a laser weapon trigger. *I wonder if this is it?* I grabbed a smaller stick with my left hand and squeezed.

Yep. A massive laser beam shot out and annihilated an enemy helicopter parked nearby. A big explosion was followed by tiny pieces of burning metal fluttering to the ground.

Mike tapped my shoulder. "Our team is crouched behind that Range Rover. Destroy those two Hummers and then hover in front of our people."

"Easier said than done. I'm learning as I go." I eased the control stick to one side, then stopped the turn and squeezed the trigger.

I hit one Humvee and missed the other, but the laser was so powerful, the explosion destroyed both vehicles.

Mike gently squeezed my shoulder. "Sam, you have to kill all the mercs or a survivor will call Sweetwater, and he'll kill Ross and Derek. Do it now. We don't have time to take prisoners."

"No, if we don't take prisoners, how will I find Sweetwater's secret camp?" I hovered the sphere in front of our team, and ten mercs dropped their weapons and kneeled with their hands on their heads.

"Our people are bleeding. They need help fast." Mike glanced back. "How do we open the door?"

"I don't know." Banger's voice replayed in my head. *"What would the Queen of Atlantis do?"*

I eased the ship onto the ground, never taking my eyes off the enemy, and shouted a command in Atlantean to open the door.

The door opened and the steps deployed. I took a quick peek as Mike rushed out to our team and led them back. He had to help Banger up the steps.

I commanded the sphere to remain on the ground and took my right hand off the control stick so I could heal my friends. "Mike, bring me the two with the most serious wounds first."

Banger sat in the chair beside me. His legs and arms were covered in blood from numerous bullet wounds. He pulled Lisa onto his lap. "What do you have in mind, Sam?"

"I think the bracelet will heal both of you if you stay pressed together while the energy passes through you." The bracelet blazed brightly and sent healing energy through my hand into them.

I looked outside and called to my brother, "Mike, come and put your hand over my left hand. If the mercs reach for a weapon, squeeze my hand. Otherwise, wait so we can get intel on Sweetwater's location."

One fool on the far left snatched up his weapon. Mike took aim and vaporized him. The rest of the soldiers immediately dived to prone positions with their hands on their heads.

Banger and Lisa healed simultaneously after a few minutes. "Are you both okay now?"

"I'm still a bit weak." Lisa rubbed her head.

"I'm good but really thirsty," Banger said as he turned and checked on Lance.

"Don't worry about me." Lance checked his bandages. "The bleeding stopped. I can wait until the bracelet recharges."

"Mike, get water bottles out of our SUVs. They all need to replace the fluids they lost."

Once our team had rehydrated, they felt better.

Mike glanced at the pods. "Sis, they're down to five minutes of life support."

"Hurry and find a soldier out there who knows where Ross and Derek are hidden."

Mike, Lisa, and Banger rushed outside, secured the prisoners, and found their commander, Sweetwater's new general. Mike brought him aboard and left the others prone on the ground. He glanced at the time indicators on the survival units. "One minute, sis."

I pulled the crown and scepter out of my belly bag and put the crown on my head. The crown's diamonds filled with light, as did the diamond tip on the scepter.

"Stay sharp, everyone. I don't know what to expect." I stood in front of the pods and spoke in Atlantean, commanding them to open.

The glass canopies lifted with a soft whoosh, IV needles retracted from the occupants' arms, and hy-

podermic syringes popped out of side compartments in each unit and injected something into the
man and woman.

I waited, searching their faces, expecting their
eyes to open any second. At almost the same instant, they inhaled deep breaths and exhaled slowly.
The woman opened her eyes first and sat up when
she saw me. Then the man did the same thing.
They turned their heads, looked at each other, and
gasped.

Tears ran down the woman's wrinkled cheeks.
She tried to speak and choked.

I opened two bottles of water and handed one
to each of them. They slowly sipped water and
stared at each other, alarm darkening their faces. I
spoke to them in Atlantean, "I am Samantha,
Queen of Atlantis. What are your names?"

The man said, "I am Zorel, and this is my wife,
Rona."

"Sorry, but there's a lot happening right now." I
waved at my team. "They are my warriors, and he's
our prisoner. Your suspended-animation systems
malfunctioned seventy years ago. The life-support
functions kept you alive but asleep while you aged.
How old were you when you entered the pods?"

Rona choked back tears as Zorel said, "We were
both twenty-eight the day we entered the Blue
Dragon. We expected to awaken to a new life in a
futuristic world ruled by Atlantis, but just in case a
worldwide catastrophe wiped out our population,

we would begin a new generation and carry on the legacy of our ancestors."

I glanced at my watch. "I have to handle a time-sensitive emergency first, and then we can talk at length. For now, lie back and regain your strength." I put the scepter in my belly bag.

They reached across and held hands as they reclined in their berths, their eyes wet with tears.

Mike had been interrogating Sweetwater's new general. "Sam, he says if he doesn't call in with a progress report in the next five minutes, his boss will assume the mission failed and feed Ross and Derek to the lions."

I looked at the general. "What's your name?"

"Ivan Baryshnikov," he answered in a deep Russian accent.

"You know what your boss does to those who fail him, Ivan. If you help us find Sweetwater, he'll be dead, and you'll be free. If you don't help us, he'll hunt you down and kill you." I moved closer. "Where is he?"

Sweat beaded on the general's face. "He has secret camp in Bwindi Impenetrable Forest near Uganda's southwest border with DRC." He paused. "I must call now or your friends will be killed."

Mike squeezed his shoulder. "Does this mean you're with us now?"

Ivan nodded, and Mike slit his plastic cuffs and handed him a satellite phone.

The general dialed Sweetwater, and Mike hit the speaker button.

"General, did you recover the Blue Dragon?" Sweetwater asked.

"I am standing inside it as we speak." He paused. "Kill SAS scum and run. They're coming for you."

Mike snatched the phone away as Banger squeezed Ivan's neck from behind.

Ivan choked out the words, "He has my wife and children."

"Wait," I yelled. "Don't kill him, just guard him. We're going to the Impenetrable Forest."

I pulled out the Eye of Atlantis as I sat at the controls. "Show me Ross and Derek."

A hologram of Ross and Derek hovered in front of me. Their hands were tied behind their backs, and their ankles were shackled. Soldiers held sharp knives and made shallow cuts all over their bare torsos. I held the Eye in my left hand so it would continue showing the real-time image.

"Banger, show me the map in your backpack."

He opened it, and I estimated a heading for the southwest corner of Uganda.

"Wait." Mike pointed at a gaping hole nearby. "Blast that tunnel first, and destroy the evidence of what we found."

I hovered the sphere and eased it above the tunnel. A few laser blasts caved it in and sand filled part of it, making it look like a small gully.

"Hang onto something, everyone. We're taking off." I pulled back on the stick and then eased it forward and around to the correct heading. My brief pullback had resulted in an altitude of fifty thousand feet.

Suddenly, the spaceship changed course, and in seconds, it shot straight up into outer space.

"Sam, what are you doing?" Mike grabbed my shoulder.

"I didn't do this." I looked back at the elderly couple. They were staring at the controls.

"Banger, slap them to break their concentration." I pointed at the Atlanteans.

He slapped them hard enough to leave welts, and I left my seat and joined him.

I spoke their language, "I am your queen, and I command you to relinquish control of this ship immediately or die." I glanced at Banger. "Wrap your hands around Rona's neck so you can snap it if they don't obey." I turned to my brother. "Mike, do the same with Zorel."

The spaceship stopped accelerating away from Earth and reversed direction.

I glared at the couple. "You'd better hope your interference didn't stop me from saving the man I love." I turned and took my seat at the command module.

Meanwhile, the Eye showed the soldiers had shoved Ross and Derek into the lion pen and were watching them from inside the cage as the lions crept closer.

"Oh, god, no!" I grabbed the stick, got us back on course, and glanced over my shoulder. "Lance, get over here and put your hand over my right hand and steer this thing while I concentrate on commanding the lions."

I tried with all my might to make contact with the lions in the pen.

Lance sat next to me and rested his left hand over my right hand. "I hope this thing isn't as squirrely as it looks."

The instant he exerted pressure on the stick, the ship zigzagged across several thousand feet of air space.

"Dang it! Sorry, team—steep learning curve here." Lance experimented with minute movements until he got the sphere stabilized in the right direction.

The hologram now showed the lions circling Ross and Derek, the big cats snarling and growling as they bared their fangs.

"No!" I stared at the real-time image and concentrated on the lions as we rocketed ever closer.

TWENTY-EIGHT

The holographic lions stopped growling. They crept closer, sniffing at the men. A lioness began licking Ross's wounds. Soon, all the lions were licking the blood off Ross and Derek.

The soldiers in the cage raised their rifles and took aim at the Scotsmen.

My gut twisted into a knot. "We're too far away for me to make a precise laser shot, and if I miss by just a little, I'll kill our guys."

Banger tapped my shoulder. "My queen, you're forgetting who you are. Command, and the laser will obey."

I commanded in Atlantean, "Laser the cage in the center of the lion pen shown in the hologram."

A brilliant flash beamed down from fifty thousand feet and vaporized the cage and the soldiers inside it. The lions ran to the far side of the pen and cowered. Ross and Derek collapsed.

I sent another laser into a portion of the fence enclosing the lion pen, then commanded the ship to home in on the location in the hologram.

When the small compound came into view in the middle of an incredibly dense forest that covered more than a hundred square miles, I took control and eased the sphere down to a hover position between our men and the only building. I shoved the Eye into its pouch.

"Anybody see Sweetwater?" I asked as I aimed the laser at the structure and pulled the trigger.

Instantly, the building became toast. Banger peered at the smoldering wreckage. "I don't see him, but if he was in there, he's fried now."

Lisa jumped up. "Sam, let us out so we can free Derek and Ross."

"Landing now." I eased us onto the ground and commanded the door to open.

I was about to rush outside to Ross when I spotted Sweetwater. He was running up some steps to a treetop platform with a helipad where a small Enstrom helicopter was parked. I glanced around to check on my team. They were behind the sphere, working to free our men from the shackles.

I had to lift off to get a good angle on the chopper. Sweetwater had reached the top step. It would be close, but there was no way I'd let that monster escape again. I was about to pull the trigger when I felt a blade against my neck.

"Take hand off trigger or you die with him. He has my family." Ivan gripped me from behind.

He must've found a knife in one of the back-packs the team had brought aboard.

I lifted my hand off the trigger stick as Sweet-water sprinted across the helipad. He pulled open the helicopter's door and turned around. A sound had apparently drawn his attention.

The male lion from the pen emerged from the steps. Snarling, the massive cat stared at his prey a moment and then rushed at him. The chubby little man drew a pistol, but before he could get off a shot, the lion leaped and landed on him, pinning him on the platform. The mighty beast bit off my enemy's head and spit it out.

Lord Edgar Sweetwater's bloody head rolled across the helipad and dropped into the jungle.

Live by the lion, die by the lion.

The general removed the blade from my neck and dropped to his knees, filled with despair. "My family—I'll never save them now."

I landed the sphere, pulled out the Eye, and spoke in Atlantean, "Show me Ivan Baryshnikov's family."

A hologram showed a woman and two children huddled in a windowless room.

"That's my family." Ivan jumped up and pointed at the hologram.

I commanded the Eye to give me a big-picture view, and it revealed that the room was inside a building on a river in Moscow, not far from the Kremlin.

"I recognize location. Please, allow me to rescue my family."

"You can rescue them after I save the man I love."

He handed me the knife. Before I rushed out to Ross, I commanded in Atlantean, "The systems and controls on this ship will obey only my commands and disregard any commands from Rona or Zorel."

Mike held a water bottle to Ross's mouth. Blood leaked from small cuts all over his torso, and his eyes looked dim from weakness.

"Lie down, darling. I'm going to try something that might heal you and Derek together." I re-arranged my belly bag behind me and instructed Derek to lie on his back alongside Ross.

I positioned myself over them with my right palm against Ross's heart, my right elbow on Derek's chest, and my body draped across them. My bracelet blazed with brilliant light, and the diamonds in my crown did the same.

"Whoa, sis, your bodies are glowing." Mike stared at us.

In minutes, their wounds were healed. I remained in place long enough to hopefully transfer some extra energy to them, revitalizing them a little.

Then I eased off their bodies and sat beside my man.

"Ross, I was so worried about you." I kissed him long and soft, over and over. "When I get you home to Scotland, I'll stay and nurse you back to health."

"I'll look forward to that," the love of my life said weakly. "Thanks for saving us, Sam." He sat up and hugged me. "I guess it was your turn." Glancing over at his best friend, Ross said, "Are you good, Derek?"

"Aye, thanks to your girlfriend." He reached for Lisa. Soon, he was smiling and joking in between Lisa's steamy kisses.

Ross thumbed at the huge sphere. "So, is that big ball the Blue Dragon?"

"Yep, it's a spaceship, and there are two Atlanteans on board who were in suspended animation for ten thousand years until the system partially failed. They're in their late nineties now." I stood. "Come on, guys. We'll show you our new toy." I helped Ross up the steps.

Everyone boarded the spaceship, and Ross and Derek smiled at the Atlanteans. I moved the elderly couple to side seats so our guys could recline in the pods. One more kiss for Ross and then I took my place in the command seat.

Mike nudged me. "Where to now, sis?"

I glanced back at Banger. "How are we fixed for weapons and ammo?"

"We used all our rounds on Ivan's strike team." Banger glared at the Russian.

"I've still got a full magazine in my Glock." Mike pulled out the handgun. "Why?"

"Ivan needs a weapon so he can rescue his family." I glanced back at him. "We're dropping him off in downtown Moscow." I pointed at the renewed hologram.

"Are you crazy?" Mike thrust his hands on his hips. "The Russians will shoot us down."

"We'll be in and out before they know what happened as long as he jumps out fast—right Ivan?" I raised a brow at him.

"*Da*, I will be fast. Thank you." He bowed.

I commanded the craft to proceed at maximum speed to the roof of the building in the hologram. We zoomed upward, the air outside darkened, and I realized we had taken an arced route up into the exosphere. Somehow, the ship managed to travel at tremendous speed without exposing us to powerful G-forces. I assumed it had something to do with anti-gravity technology. In moments, we arced back down toward Russia and arrived over the roof a few seconds later.

"Quick, Ivan, jump out, and good luck rescuing your family." I commanded the door to open.

He leaped onto the roof. At my command, we zipped back up into the exosphere the instant he was out and the door closed. The entire drop off and departure had taken less than five seconds. If

Russia had noticed us, which I doubted, even their missiles couldn't begin to match our speed. I replaced the Eye in its pouch.

Away from nosy satellites, I held the ship in a hover high above Earth and joined the Atlantean couple. "Where were you trying to go when you took control?" I asked in their native tongue.

"Our orders were to return to Atlanteas, our planet of origin, if we were unable to complete our mission." Zorel stole a glance at Rona. "No one has been back there since our forefathers came to Earth two hundred thousand years ago."

Stunned, I paused a moment to process this astounding revelation. "And as long as no one returns, they'll assume all is well here on Earth?"

"Yes, but we failed, and now our hearts are broken." Zorel squeezed Rona's hand.

Rona sobbed, "We wasted our lives for nothing. Our family and friends are long dead."

"How fares Atlantis?" Zorel looked at me with a hint of hope in his gray eyes.

"The last remnant of the continent lies under two thousand feet of water, and the enclave in the Himalayas was destroyed in a war." I paused. "I'm sorry, but you are the last remaining citizens of the once mighty nation of Atlantis."

"What about you, my queen?" Zorel focused on my crown.

"I am the last descendant of the queens of Atlantis, but I was raised in the United States of

America. It's a country on the landmass that borders the Atlantic Ocean, beyond what used to be the western side of the Atlantean continent."

"If only we could see our beautiful city one more time." Rona looked from Zorel to me.

"It's underwater, but I can show it to you. That is, assuming this sphere is waterproof." I pulled out the small one in my belly bag. "This little one is."

"Do you not know what this craft is, my queen?" Rona raised her brows.

"I saw it for the first time a little over an hour ago when I came to rescue you from the cave."

Zorel shared a meaningful glance with Rona, and she nodded.

"The Blue Dragon is the ship that brought our founding fathers to Earth many millennia ago." Zorel gazed around the spaceship, a faraway look in his eyes.

"It can take you anywhere in the universe." Rona smiled. "Perhaps you'd like to visit the home planet of your ancestors."

That revelation took me by surprise. "Uh, how is the ship powered?"

"The universe is charged with electromagnetic energy, and the sphere draws from that energy." Rona patted a sidewall. "It never runs out."

My team couldn't understand what we were saying, but the shocked look on my face clued them in to the fact that the conversation wasn't mundane.

I took a moment to bring them up to speed on what I'd learned.

Lisa squeezed Derek's hand. "Our grand adventure has gone on long enough, Sam. We want to go home—right, team?"

Mike glanced at the couple. "What are we supposed to do about them and this spaceship?"

"We have two elderly Atlanteans on board a two-hundred-thousand-year-old spaceship that still works perfectly." Banger glanced around the ship. "Apparently, unobtainium never rusts."

"Too bad we don't have that kind of metal here on Earth." I stroked the tiny sphere and placed it back in the bag.

"That would be why it's called unobtainium, my queen," Banger quipped.

"Apparently, your battle scars haven't diminished your proclivity to be a smartass, my liege." I grinned at my big friend.

The tall but frail Atlanteans sat beside my team, while Ross and Derek slept in the open pods, exhaustion having taken over their weakened bodies.

I looked at Rona and Zorel. "What do you want to do?"

"We want to go home." She squeezed her husband's hand.

I told the team what she'd said.

"Which home?" Lance crossed his arms. "The one underwater or the one on a distant planet?"

I asked them, and the submerged one was their answer.

I checked my watch and glanced at Lance. "I haven't forgotten you. The bracelet needs thirty minutes to finish recharging. In the meantime, we're going to Atlantis." I ensured everyone was seated and commanded the ship to take us there.

A few minutes later, the sphere dived into the Atlantic Ocean as smoothly as if the water had been air. On the way in, I spotted the USS *Leviathan* anchored nearby. *I hope Captain Rowlin doesn't shoot at us when we surface.*

As we descended through crystal-clear water, I turned to the Atlanteans. "Does this ship have bright exterior lights?"

Zorel nodded. "Yes, my queen, it has everything you need."

I commanded the ship to illuminate our surroundings. Instantly, bright spotlights revealed circular white marble buildings, some with giant statues as pillars. There were pyramids of varying sizes, some covered with semi-precious gems and gold. Giant sphinxes guarded the ancient city, and beautiful sculptures of sea life decorated public parks.

Zorel looked around, confusion clouding his face. "Where is the obsidian pyramid?"

"Sorry, it was destroyed." I pointed at a huge pile of black rubble.

Rona leaned into Zorel, tears rolling down her cheeks. "Poseidon's Sword failed to raise Atlantis."

I didn't know what to say to them as I relayed their comments to my team. It was hard to feel sorry that millions of people around the world hadn't drowned so their precious city could rise again. How could they be so heartless? My team must've been thinking the same thing.

Mike frowned. "They've seen their homeland, and frankly, I don't trust them. What now?"

Lance nudged my shoulder. "Holy mother—is that a giant squid?"

A hundred-sixty-foot kraken and its thirty-foot baby swam beside us, but unlike my past experiences with the giant squids, they made no attempt to attack us.

Rona said in Atlantean, "We're safe. They sense their queen is on board."

"This is a pleasant change from our previous encounters." Banger looked into the smart-car-sized right eye of the mother squid. "I wonder if she recognizes me."

"They can't see us." Mike tapped the side. "The ship looks like solid metal from the outside."

"Should we land on *Leviathan's* deck and hand this nifty spaceship over to our military or abscond to somewhere remote and regroup?" I looked from face to face. "Well?"

"What about them?" Lisa nodded in the direction of Rona and Zorel.

"They're ninety-eight and frail." I sighed. "Probably not a threat to national security. I kind of feel sorry for them, even though they were raised as heartless Atlanteans keen on world domination, and they tried to take us to a distant planet."

"They've lost everything." Lisa shrugged. "Not much we can do for them now, except give them a comfortable place to live for however much time they have left."

"So then, we're landing on *Leviathan*?" I glanced at my teammates, and they nodded.

Zorel asked in Atlantean, "My queen, Rona and I would like to join our ancestors in Atlantis. We're old and near death. Please allow us to take the escape pod and reside in our beautiful city until our air runs out and we die, entombed forevermore in our homeland."

"What escape pod?" I looked around.

He pointed at the floor beneath my feet. "It's under the command center."

I peeked under the command platform and spotted a small, two-person sphere.

"Will it launch underwater, or do you have to exit on the surface first?" I looked at him.

"It works in any environment." He squeezed his wife's hand. "Please, my queen, it is what we want. Will you grant us our last request?"

I told my teammates what Zorel had requested and asked for their opinions.

Mike shook his head. "I don't know, sis. They

could prove useful, helping us understand their technology. Our commanders would be angry if we let them go."

"They've had quite a shock." Lisa glanced at the couple. "Maybe they aren't thinking clearly."

"Put yourself in their shoes." Lance shook his head. "They're so old and disheartened, they've lost any desire to try and adapt to a completely unfamiliar world and its people."

Zorel and Rona dropped to their knees. "Please, Queen Samantha, we beg you."

I looked into their pleading eyes, and my heart melted. How could I refuse them? They were literally the last two citizens of Atlantis, and I was their queen.

I reached down and helped them stand. "You may take the escape pod and end your days in Atlantis. How may I help?"

"Open the hatch, help us inside, and command the *Blue Dragon* to launch us." Zorel helped Rona descend steps that appeared in the floor.

I turned to my teammates. "I have to let them go. It's the right thing to do."

In minutes, they were secure in their seats, the hatch closed, and I gave the launch command.

The little craft shot out through an opening that only appeared for a split second. Not a drop of water entered our spaceship. I watched them zoom toward a distant building.

"Well, that's that." I checked on Ross and

Derek, kissed Ross again, and then sat in the command chair. "Time to land on *Leviathan*."

I couldn't explain to the spaceship in Atlantean precisely where I wanted it to land, so I flew it manually. After three attempts to line it up exactly over the open deck, I finally managed it.

When we landed, we were surrounded by men with weapons trained on the sphere, as expected.

I glanced back at Banger. "My liege, the captain knows you best, and let's face it, you're instantly recognizable by the crew, so you should exit first."

"My queen, are you counting on my large stature to stop all the bullets?" He grinned.

"Yes, I am, so get your handsome self out there." I pointed at the open door.

He bowed. "Your wish is my command." Banger eased down the steps with his hands on his head as we watched from inside. When he reached the deck, he spotted the ship's captain, who was his commanding officer. "Hello, Captain Rowlin. Master Chief Ben Johnson reporting for duty. Mike and Samantha Starr are on board with a few other people you know."

Max smiled. "I should've known Samantha Starr would be involved." He turned to his men. "Hold your fire. The sphere is controlled by friendlies."

"Would you like the others to disembark, sir?" Banger asked.

Max strode up to his SEAL. "Permission to board my ship, Banger. Tell them to come out."

"Aye, aye, captain." Banger saluted and shouted for us to disembark.

The others walked out while Lisa and I woke Derek and Ross.

"Hi, guys, sorry for the short nap. We're on the deck of Max Rowlin's ship over Atlantis, and it's time to disembark." I helped Ross climb out of the unit where Zorel had spent so many years, and Lisa did the same for Derek in Rona's berth. "Can you walk okay?" I asked.

Ross yawned and kissed me. "I'm good."

Derek gave Lisa a sweeping kiss, leaning her over and back up. "I'm ready to roll."

"Let's get out of this weird ball." Lisa grabbed Derek's hand and led him down the steps.

"Sorry, darling," I said to Ross, "but I probably should leave last." I waved him ahead of me.

The instant I stepped onto the deck, the little escape pod breached the ocean's surface nearby and shot into the sky, disappearing at a high rate of speed.

Mike pointed. "Sis, they're running to their home planet to rat us out!"

TWENTY-NINE

C aptain Rowlin squinted at the fading silver ball. "Who—"

"Oh, crap!" I rushed back into the sphere and jumped into the command chair. The door closed behind me, and I hauled back on the stick.

In a flash, I was in outer space. I gave a command in Atlantean to catch up with the escape pod. When it came into view, I tried to shoot it with the laser, but the beam just bounced off it.

New strategy.

I commanded my ship to recover the escape pod and hold it on board.

In the blink of an eye, the smaller spacecraft appeared back in its bay beneath the command center. I looked down at the elderly couple.

Zorel and Rona stared up at me, alarm registering on their faces.

They can sit in there and contemplate the error of their ways until we land.

I commanded my spaceship to return to the deck of the ship it had just left.

My home planet morphed from a pinpoint of light to a beautiful blue globe in a matter of seconds. It wasn't long before *Leviathan* came into view. Moments later, the sphere landed on the open deck in the exact spot it had been before.

The crew and my friends were still where I'd left them. I descended to the escape pod and opened the hatch.

"Come with me—and no tricks or I'll snap you like twigs." I pulled Rona out first and then Zorel. "Put your hands on your heads like the disgraced prisoners you are." I led them outside and presented them to Max.

"Captain Rowlin, these are the last living citizens of Atlantis, Zorel and his wife, Rona." I stepped back. "Put them in cuffs. They're not to be trusted."

Max took a look at the thin, fragile-looking couple and raised a brow. "Cuffs? Really?"

"Don't let their age fool you." I glared at them. "Search them for weapons. They were on their way to their home planet to cause us a world of trouble."

Max turned to his Executive Officer, Vance Lowes. "Check them for weapons, take them to the brig, and see to it they get something to eat and drink."

"Aye, aye, Captain." Vance waved over a warrant officer and took charge of the prisoners.

Max peered up at the silvery blue sphere and shook his head. "So that's the *Blue Dragon?*"

"Yep, it's a two-hundred-thousand-year-old spaceship with a powerful laser weapon and an enormous blue diamond. Want a ride?" I grinned. "It's super-fast."

He sighed. "Where am I supposed to hide it? We can't let enemy satellites spot it."

"I can fly it into the water beneath your ship and surface in your moon pool in the ship's belly. Nobody can see it there."

Max nodded. "Take it into the water now and give me about thirty minutes before you enter the moon pool. We'll need to move the Scorpion subs to one side to make room for it." He glanced up at the sky. "Better hurry."

I rushed back into the spaceship and flew it into the ocean. While I waited, I took another tour of Atlantis. It really was quite magnificent. Too bad its inhabitants had been so evil.

A large, black cloud darkened the water—ink from the squids.

I guided the ship around it and found the kraken and her baby, or what was left of them, lying dead between two buildings. They had huge laser-blast burn holes in their bodies, which meant the escape pod must've had a laser weapon. Finally, all the monsters in underwater Atlantis, animals and humans, were gone forever.

I expected to be a little sad about this final chapter, but I actually felt relieved that such a huge responsibility had been lifted from my shoulders.

Time for the Queen of Atlantis to retire. I hope.

Max waited for me beside the moon pool in the ship's belly. He helped me disembark as the sphere floated near the edge of the pool. It was too big to fit beside the two thirty-foot Scorpion attack subs and the forty-two-foot research sub. We left the spaceship floating in the moon pool and closed the ship's belly doors.

I smiled. "Another crisis averted."

He frowned. "Unless that old couple managed to get off a message before you captured them."

"Oh, crap."

He raised his eyebrows. "Will they tell the truth if you ask them?"

"I doubt it." I spread my hands. "They have nothing to lose, so we don't have a way to threaten them into fessing up."

Max stood, hands on hips, thinking. "Let's ask anyway. Maybe we'll see something in their eyes that will show us the truth."

"It's worth a try." I took hold of his hand. "Sorry to dump all this on you, but it's good to see you again. I hope you'll still be able to attend my mother's wedding in Scotland."

"I'm planning on it, unless those giant squids decide to sink another ship." He sighed. "I thought I was finished with this place, but my 'expertise with the area' resulted in orders to oversee the site and protect the public."

"Then I have good news." I grinned. "The krakens are dead."

His eyes widened. "You killed them?"

"No, the elderly Atlanteans killed them with a laser weapon in their escape pod. I was cruising around Atlantis while I waited for you to clear the moon pool, and I found the carcasses."

Max's face brightened. "You're positive they're all dead?"

I shrugged. "About as certain as I can be of anything connected to this weird place."

Smiling, he hugged me. "I happen to have a few bottles of your favorite wine hidden in my state-room, just in case the Queen of Atlantis ever graced my ship again."

"Then we'd better pull the corks," I said, returning the grin, "because the queen is planning to retire very soon."

"All right, we'll take a stab at the old codgers and then gather your team in the wardroom for a good meal with some Opus One." He waved me forward. "Let's go."

When we entered their cell in the brig, the prisoners appeared to be sleeping. A closer examination revealed they were dead.

Max turned to the guard. "What happened to them?"

"Nothing, sir, they just sat there and closed their eyes. I thought they were asleep."

Shocked, I sucked in my breath. "Now I *really* need some wine."

Max shook his head. "We have no way of knowing if they sent a message." He paused. "That is, not unless a few thousand ships like the sphere descend on Earth with their lasers blasting us."

"I hope not because I've had it with Atlanteans. Thanks to them, I've lost my job, and my life's a mess. I'm loaded down with knowledge and abilities I never wanted, and I have no idea what I'm supposed to do now." I frowned at the ancient couple, now mocking me in death.

Max grasped my shoulders. "Sam, I'm sorry you lost your pilot job. I know you loved flying airliners, but now you're in a position to do a lot of good for your country."

"What do you mean?" I searched his eyes.

"You'd be a huge asset working in defense intelligence, and you already know several key players. I could arrange a meeting, set things up for you. Should I go ahead?"

"Let me think about it. My mother's wedding is coming up soon, and I need some time with Ross to help him recuperate from his ordeal with Sweetwater." I paused. "By the way, Sweetwater is dead, killed by one of his lions."

"Are you sure?" He cocked his head. "We've had plenty of false reports in the past."

"I saw the lion bite off his head." I grinned. "There's no coming back from that."

"Good. Think about my suggestion, Sam." He took my arm. "Let's head up for dinner."

We gathered in the wardroom for a sumptuous meal and plenty of Opus One. Ross and Derek looked so weak it broke my heart, but at least they'd live to recover and regain their strength.

My watch chimed. It was time to heal Lance. The bracelet lit up once again and healed his combat wounds as Max observed the process with a stunned look on his face.

Max pointed at my bracelet. "What—"

"It's an Atlantean artifact that heals injuries—I found it in a chamber under the Great Sphinx in Egypt."

Max shook his head. "Of course, you did."

Banger looked at Max. "Captain, what will you tell Washington about the spaceship?"

"No idea." He glanced around the table. "Any suggestions?"

Lance grinned. "Any chance we can keep it as our personal toy?"

"It's really fun to fly," I chimed in, "and it won't work for anyone but me anyway. We could bury the Atlanteans at sea here so you wouldn't have to put them in your report, and I can fly Ross, Derek, and Lisa home to Great Britain in the blink of an eye."

Mike nodded. "It would be a win-win for everyone. You can take credit for killing the krakens and get sent on a new mission more to your liking."

"And my woman won't get stuck demonstrating the sphere to the military for who-knows-how-long." Ross put his arm around me.

"What about the mercs we left in the Kalahari Desert?" Banger looked at me. "You know they'll tell somebody."

I thought about that for a moment, and a solution came to me. "Our military already knows about the small sphere I carry with me, and they know it has a laser weapon. We can say I used that, and the mercs must've hallucinated it being bigger because of the way heat waves bend the air in the desert."

"What will we say when they ask if we found the Blue Dragon?" Mike looked at me.

"We'll say we searched for it in Dragon's Breath Cave and didn't find it." I glanced at my team. "When we came out, we fought Sweetwater's soldiers and forced his general to tell us the secret camp's location and take us there."

"And if the Russian mercenary general mouths off to the Kremlin about the spaceship?" Banger raised a brow.

"He has no proof, and he wouldn't risk it anyway." I held up the leather pouch. "He knows I can use the Eye of Atlantis to find him anywhere."

Lisa nodded. "She's right. Ivan won't risk his family again."

Max glanced around the table. "My crew is pretty good at keeping secrets—God knows they've kept plenty about Atlantis. I think they'd keep quiet about a spaceship, especially if I tell them it's a national security issue, and Washington wants it kept under wraps." He turned to me. "But where would you hide it?"

"I'm thinking I'd hide it at the bottom of the North Sea away from oil rigs and shipping, and I'd use the escape pod to travel back and forth to it. The pod is small and easy to hide in a garage, barn, or wherever."

"The thing is, it would be a huge asset to our military in any battle situation." Banger glanced my way. "That unobtainium is bulletproof."

"It's also laser-proof—I know because I tried blasting the escape pod, and the beam bounced off it without leaving a mark." I faced Max. "I'm a loyal American, and if my country needed that weapon during wartime, I'd gladly fly it and blast the crap out of our enemy. What I don't want is to be chained to it for the foreseeable future because it only works for me. Our scientists wouldn't be able to reproduce it anyway. That metal isn't available on Earth, and I'm not willing to search outer space for it."

Mike came to my defense. "The plans for the lasers and maybe even for the spaceship are probably in the scrolls she recovered from Atlantis's Hall of Records. Let the scientists use that info to build advanced weapons and spacecraft. It wouldn't be fair to enslave Sam after all she's already given up to help our country."

Max looked at me. "Sam, I haven't forgotten that I owe you big for everything you've done for me and my crew, dealing with Poseidon's Sword and the Atlantis nightmare. I trust you, but what would happen if one of our enemies found the spaceship?"

I considered it. "They wouldn't be able to enter it, take it, or damage it—so nothing."

Banger jumped in. "It's true, Captain, it only opens or operates for Sam, the last Queen of Atlantis."

Max paused. "And if someone kidnapped you and forced you to operate it to save a loved one?"

"The instant I took control, I'd have it immobilize my kidnappers and blast the living crap out of everyone else involved. Then I'd rescue my loved one and hide the sphere again."

Max glanced around the table. "Sam may take the spaceship if everyone here agrees to keep it secret and also agrees that you never landed here."

We simultaneously said, "Agreed."

Max addressed Banger. "You're a member of my crew, but you'll have to leave with everyone else and return by other means."

Mike sighed. "There's still a big problem to

solve." He paused. "How do we explain to General Ryan, and the base commander in Somalia, and Commander Metz how we got from the Kalahari Desert to Ross and Derek and then to wherever it is Sam drops us off?"

Silence.

Lisa's eyes widened. "I know. We'll say we stole a Super Lynx from the mercs and destroyed the second one. We ordered our jet home and flew the chopper to Uganda to rescue Ross and Derek. Then we landed at Entebbe International and caught a series of commercial flights back to the UK for Sam, Ross, Derek, and me, and to airports in Florida for Mike, Lance, and Banger. I know how to insert us into all the flight manifests and document us avoiding customs using fake diplomatic passports."

Derek smiled. "I knew your spy skills with MI6 would come in handy."

"I have an untraceable laptop you can use in my stateroom." Max shrugged. "This *is* a spy ship."

"Uh, Lisa, don't forget that it's too soon for us to have traveled all the way from Uganda." I paused, trying to do some mental calculations. "Look up the flights and let me know when we can realistically get to our destinations, so I'll know when to drop everyone off. Great Britain is closer to Africa than America is, so I'll drop you three first and then return after I deliver Mike, Lance, and Banger."

Lisa stood. "I'll get cracking. In the meantime, Command will wonder why we haven't checked in."

"We'll tell them our satellite phones were destroyed." Mike looked at Max. "This will work, Captain."

"All right, everyone except Lisa remain in the wardroom and don't talk to the crew." Max stood. "I'll take you to my stateroom so you can start working on the flights." He led Lisa out.

I looked from Lance to Ross. "Hey, while I've got you both here, Lance said I should ask you why he's trying to redeem himself with you."

Ross looked at Lance. "You really want me to tell her?"

Lance's face reddened. "No, but she's bound to find out sooner or later, so go ahead."

I raised my brows. "Well, Ross? What happened?"

"As you know, Solraya masqueraded as you." He paused. "When she was in Key West, Lance had dinner with her, thinking she was you, and, uh, he spent the night with her." Ross shot a glance at Lance. "That's how we found out she wasn't you— no scars and some other clues."

"And Lance *told* you about it?" I was shocked. "You must've been pissed."

"He had to tell me to verify that she wasn't you." He paused. "I was bloody angry, but we agreed that if he helped save you, all would be forgiven. And he did risk his life to save you."

"Sooo, you guys are good now?" I glanced from Ross to Lance.

Ross narrowed his eyes. "Has he made any moves on you since then?"

"No, he's been a perfect gentleman, mainly just trying to keep me safe." I peeked at Lance. He was still red in the face.

Ross smiled. "Then we're good. Case closed."

"I need a nap." I kissed Ross, rested my head on his shoulder, and closed my eyes. When I awakened, an hour had passed, and Lisa and Max had returned with our fake flight itineraries.

Max gave us a hard look. "Don't make me regret this. I can't risk letting you stay here longer. I'll take you down to the moon pool, and you can depart in the sphere. If you have to kill some time before your phony arrivals, fly somewhere satellites and people can't see you." He hesitated. "Come to think of it, where are you going to let them off where they won't be seen?"

I glanced at my watch. "It'll be dark soon. I'll drop the UK three on the lawn of Duncan MacLeod's castle in Scotland. The others will be let out on rooftops close to their airport destinations, and they can take cabs or Ubers from there." I paused. "Then I'll land on the bottom of the North Sea in a remote area and fly the little escape pod back to Duncan's castle. He has plenty of places to hide it on the property."

Banger stood. "Just to give everyone a heads-up,

I intend to move up my wedding date to as soon as possible, assuming Tiesha is willing to change it." He looked at me. "Don't worry, Sam, it won't be too close to your mom's wedding. I've been thinking that life is short, and I want to be married sooner rather than later. I'll text everyone the new date so you can make plans."

Max shook Banger's hand. "Congratulations, Master Chief. I'll do whatever you need to get leave for your wedding, so let me know ASAP."

Banger grinned. "Thank you, Captain. I hope you'll be able to attend."

Max nodded. "All right, people, time to go." He led us to the moon pool.

We said our goodbyes to *Leviathan's* captain and boarded the shiny silver-blue spaceship.

I sat in the command chair, and Lisa handed me a paper.

"These are our fake flight itineraries. We need to kill four hours before you drop us in Scotland." She paused and pointed at a line on the paper. "Then you'll have to kill another five hours before you make the first drop off in Palm Beach. After that, you can take Mike to the international airport in Jacksonville, and then drop Banger off in Key West."

"Alrighty, anyone want to see the Arctic?" I eased us underwater away from the ship.

"Sure, why not?" Lance sat in the copilot seat.

Ross and Derek were already asleep in the open

survival pods when I dived the sphere and steered a circle around Atlantis. Max hadn't wasted any time disposing of the deceased Atlanteans. I spotted two weighted body bags descending into the sunken city.

"Well, they got their last wish to be buried in Atlantis." Mike pointed at the sinking bags.

Banger stared at the kraken carcasses. "That's enough of this place. Let's fly to the Arctic." He grinned. "What could possibly go wrong?"

I hauled back on the stick, and we shot into the exosphere in seconds. Easing forward on the control, we arced downward to the frozen North Pole.

"Nothing to see here but snow and ice. It's dark, and the polar bears are already asleep for the night." I glanced back at my teammates. "Let's have a look under the ice."

"Sounds like fun," Lance said. "Maybe we'll find another sunken city."

Banger shook his head. "I hope not. Nothing good ever comes from finding submerged civilizations, but at least we have a powerful laser to fry sea monsters."

The spaceship slid seamlessly into the ocean, and I commanded the floodlights to illuminate our path as we dived under the ice.

Mike tapped my shoulder. "Uh, sis, I think that's a Russian boomer."

An enormous nuclear submarine, the kind equipped with nuclear missiles, cruised slowly through the frigid water a thousand feet beneath the surface.

Lisa stared at the massive war machine. "Definitely Russian. I hope it doesn't detect us." As she spoke, a forward torpedo door opened and the tube flooded.

"Uh oh. Time to go." I dived the sphere and accelerated away in a flash.

Mike eased up beside me. "Since depth isn't an issue, let's have a look in the Mariana Trench."

"I don't know—we might not like what we find there." I frowned at Mike.

"And something we find might swallow us, ship and all," Banger said.

"Then we zap it with the laser." Mike looked at me. "Come on, don't you want to see what's down there?"

"Yeah, someday, but not tonight." I gazed back at Ross, peacefully sleeping. "My man needs rest, and an emergency situation might wake him. We'll save the trench for another time."

Lance turned to me. "Where do you want to go?"

"Let's check out sunken airplanes and battleships here in the Pacific." I steered us underwater toward Midway Island.

After scouring several underwater graveyards, it was

finally time to drop off the Brits. I zoomed us up to the exosphere again and arced down to Scotland, landing on Duncan's lawn. It was a clear night with lots of stars and a partial moon shining on the North Sea when I woke Ross and kissed him goodbye.

"Stay here tonight and I'll join you in a little over five hours." I waved as he left the spacecraft with Lisa and Derek.

I dived the ship into the North Sea and kept it on the bottom for five hours before dropping off Lance, Mike, and Banger in various parts of Florida. Then I returned to my hiding place. I commanded the craft to remain where I'd left it until receiving further instructions from me, and I departed in the escape pod.

It wasn't long before I slipped under the covers and snuggled against Ross's warm body. He was in deep slumber, and his steady breathing comforted me. I felt relaxed and safe with the man of my dreams, and although I'd lost my beloved airline career and had no idea what my future held, at least I had the one thing that was irreplaceable.

I enjoyed my first sound sleep since Ross had vanished in Africa.

The next day, I called my friend, Professor Ben Armitage. "Hi, Ben, just wanted to thank you for helping me find Ross and Derek. Everyone is home safe now."

"I'm glad you called. The U.S. government wants to organize a joint operation with Algeria to explore that underground city you found in Tassili n' Ajjer. They're asking archaeologists and anthropologists from Harvard to join the team."

"Do you know Dr. Phil Berger? He's an American with a PhD in anthropology working the Dinaledi Chamber, and he's the one who sent me to Dragon's Breath Cave."

Ben paused. "I do know Phil—he's a Harvard man. Why do you ask?"

"I promised him he could be the lead anthropologist on the Tassili n' Ajjer discovery. Think you can make that happen?"

"Well, you found the city, and Phil's a colleague, so yes, I can arrange it. Any chance you'd want to go with us?"

"Sorry, Ben, I've had enough of that hellhole. Warn the soldiers to bring plenty of ammo."

He sighed. "Maybe you'll change your mind when I see you at Loren's wedding in August."

Later that day, I attended Bryce's military funeral. Ross, Derek, Lisa, Duncan, and my mother came with me. Mike, Banger, and Lance weren't able to get there in time after having arrived in Florida the night before.

The somber ceremony reminded me just how much military personnel sacrificed for the rest of us. Bryce had served bravely in the UK's Special Air Service, their most elite Special Forces. And he had been my friend. Lisa gave his mother the diamond jewelry he'd taken from the underground city. It would never make up for her loss, but at least the valuable gems secured her financial independence.

I stared at his coffin and swallowed hard, trying not to cry. So many of my loved ones and friends served in dangerous military units. I prayed I'd never have to attend another funeral like this.

Rest in peace, Lieutenant Bryce Manning. You will be missed.

EPILOGUE

MacLeod Castle, Scotland

Summer in The Highlands was always lovely. I gazed out at the sun-kissed North Sea from my balcony in Duncan's castle on the cliff. It was the perfect day for a late-afternoon wedding—clear skies and warm breezes.

My mother, Loren Starr, had been a best-selling author for many years, writing medieval romance novels featuring handsome Highland chieftains on the covers. Today, she would marry Laird Duncan MacLeod, the spitting image of the last chieftain who graced her book cover. After losing her youngest child to murder and her husband to a plane crash, she deserved a second chance at happiness.

Mother walked into my room. "You look deep in thought. What's on your mind?"

"Lots of things, but most recently that you deserve a happy ending." I hugged her.

"You do too, Sam, especially after all you've been through the past year." She looked into my eyes. "I was so worried about you, but now you're here, safe and sound, and Ross has regained his strength, looking as handsome as ever, thanks to your tender loving care."

"Ah, yes, his deep blue eyes, thick black hair, handsome face, and tall, muscular build could qualify him for the cover of your next novel." I grinned. "He certainly takes my breath away."

"I feel the same about Duncan." She blushed. "His sky-blue eyes pierce straight into my heart, and he's wearing his dress kilt for the ceremony. That always gets my blood pumping." She paused. "Do you think you and Ross will ever get married?"

"I don't know—I love him, but he hasn't asked." I sighed. "Maybe he thinks I'm too much trouble."

"There aren't many men who would've put up with all the dangerous situations you managed to get yourself into, but Ross has hung in there." She paused. "He risked his life many times to save you. If he hadn't been there in the Himalayas—"

"But he was, and I'm safe now." I squeezed her hand. "All my enemies are dead, and we managed to fool the UK and America into thinking we never found the Blue Dragon."

"When you dropped off Ross and his friends on Duncan's front lawn, I never thought the plan would work." Mom shook her head. "Good thing Lisa is so good at hacking airline databases."

I nodded. "I managed to deliver everyone to their respective destinations at night without anyone ever spotting the spaceship. I wish I could use it all the time as my personal transportation. It's really fun to fly."

"Leave it on the bottom of the North Sea, dear. Your life would be miserable if the military knew about it." She glanced in a nearby mirror. "I hope I'll look as regal as Tiesha did at her wedding."

"I loved how the ballroom at The Breakers in Palm Beach was decorated like a palace. She really was a stunner in that fitted gown that flared at the bottom—sheer gold gossamer over white satin with a gold tiara and a matching gossamer veil that trailed to the floor." I smiled. "Tiesha looked like an African queen, and the gold stilettos were perfect."

"Didn't you tell me the natives in that under-ground city in the Amazon basin chose her as their Snake Queen?" She paused. "And their chief thought Banger was her warrior king?"

"Yep, they crowned her with an ancient gold and emerald crown that sold for thirty-five million at auction in New York." I replayed the crowning scene in my head. "Of course, she earned it, saving us from that enormous anaconda. She truly was the Snake Queen."

"And you and the other bridesmaids looked fabulous in those pink gossamer-over-satin gowns." She smiled dreamily. "It was a real fairytale wedding, and Banger was so handsome in his dress blues."

I hugged her again. "And now it's your turn. Your fitted ice-blue gown is perfect for a bride's second time at the altar, and you're the picture of elegance for your wedding to a Scottish nobleman."

"I hope so." She checked her blond hair in the mirror. "There will be a lot of dignitaries at the ceremony and reception. Rumor has it the queen might attend the wedding."

"She's at Balmoral for her summer vacation, so I guess it's possible she'll come." I stood beside Mom in front of the floor-length mirror. "I like my blue satin gown. It goes well with your wedding dress, which is good since I'll be standing right next to you."

"And Ross will be Duncan's best man." She glanced at me. "Will he be wearing a kilt too?"

"Oh, yes, he knows his kilt drives me wild—so sexy." I smiled. "Our handsome Highlanders."

Lisa tapped on the door and stuck her head in. "Ladies, it's time, and you won't believe who's sitting in the front row."

The ceremony took place on the castle lawn, overlooking the placid North Sea, and the queen and prince were seated in the front row. Afterward, the reception was held in the castle's great room, which was a bit larger than a basketball court. The royals didn't stay for the reception, but my twin brothers Mike and Matt were there with their dates, LIA flight attendants Barbi and Cindy. They shared a table with Lisa and Derek.

Recently returned from a week-long honeymoon, Tiesha and Banger shared a table with Lance Bowie, marine engineer Vicky Edwards, marine biologist Kip Peterson, Captain Jeff Rowlin, his son Max Rowlin, and Max's wife.

Sir Charlie Moncreiffe and his parents, and Dame Emily Brown and her parents, shared a table with Lord Colin and Lady Suzanne Covington.

Commander Robert Metz and a long list of friends, noblemen, and dignitaries were also at the reception.

Metz said, "I caught the mole at Camp Baledogle. Turned out it was the base commander. He's scheduled for a court martial with a possible life sentence for treason."

"Wow, Bob, I bet you were shocked it was him. I know I am." He nodded, and I excused myself to greet guests.

After a delicious dinner followed by chocolate wedding cake with white icing, and the traditional toasts, bouquet toss, and first dance, everyone enjoyed a festive evening of fine wine and dancing.

Ross took me into his arms for a slow dance,

and my heart rate bumped up as I melted into him. He held me close as we glided around the dance floor. When the music stopped, he took my hand and led me outside onto a cliffside terrace. A full moon illuminated the glistening North Sea below us.

He turned me to face him and dropped to one knee. "Sam, you're the love of my life, and I want you to be my wife." He pulled out a ring box and opened it. A round, six-carat solitaire heirloom ring in an antique gold setting sparkled in the moonlight.

He looked up at me. "Will you marry me, Sam?"

My breath caught as I gazed into the sincere eyes of the only man I had ever loved and gave him my answer.

"Yes," I said with a huge smile as I pulled him up and kissed him.

He slipped the ring on my finger and leaned me over in a long, romantic kiss.

Loud cheering interrupted us. Apparently, everyone had gathered at the doors and windows and witnessed the proposal.

In seconds, we were surrounded by well-wishers. Mom and Duncan pushed through the crowd and hugged us.

Mom grabbed my left hand and admired my ring. "I guess we'll be neighbors soon."

I smiled at Ross, Mom, and her husband. "A year ago, when I met Duncan on my first day in

Scotland, I never dreamed Mom would end up married to him, a handsome Highlander like the men in her romance novels. And now someday soon, I'll be married to a Highlander too. I guess this is one of those times when life really does imitate art."

My twin brothers, Mike and Matt, pushed in.

Matt asked, "Have you set a date?"

"Uh, no, he literally just asked me." I held my hand in front of my face and admired my ring sparkling in the moonlight. "Give me a minute to get used to being engaged."

"Maybe you should get hitched while we're all still here," Mike said, grinning.

"What's the hurry?" I playfully punched his arm. "I don't even have a wedding dress."

My mother stepped in. "Hold your horses, boys. Your sister deserves a special wedding day of her own, understand? Sam's wedding will *not* be rushed." She winked. "Besides, Duncan and I need time for our honeymoon first."

"Excuse me." Max took me aside and showed me a text message on his encrypted phone. It read: Silver sphere sighted over mountains in Peru. He leaned in. "Any chance that's the one you have?"

Frowning, I whispered, "I checked on it early this morning. It's right where I left it on the bottom of the North Sea." I gazed over at Ross, who was busy accepting congratulations and hadn't noticed our worried looks. "Don't tell my fiancé. I want him to enjoy this special night."

Banger sauntered up and noticed the look of concern on our faces. "What—"

I whispered, "Don't ask."

Max showed him the text.

He shook his head. "Ah, my queen, the adventure with you never ends."

AFTERWORD

All the places Sam visits in Africa are real except the subterranean city under Tassili n'Ajjer. The Lost Sahara Civilization is believed to have existed based on fossils recovered, ancient art picturing the pre-desert paradise, and satellite imagery showing evidence of a prehistoric megalake beneath the sand, but the civilization has not yet been found.

Camp Baledogle near Mogadishu in Somalia is a real American military base.

All the sites Sam visits in Egypt—Luxor, Thonis-Heracleion, the Great Sphinx, and the Great Pyramid—are real, and some experts believe (based on evidence) that both the Sphinx and the Pyramid are more than ten thousand years old. Some engineers believe the chamber beneath the Great Pyramid was a pumphouse, as described in this story, and that it was intended to operate the pyramid's power plant. An American Egyptologist used a seismograph to discover chambers beneath the front paws of the Great Sphinx (one was rumored by Plato to contain an Atlantean Hall of Records), but Egypt will not allow the chambers to be explored.

The eleven monolithic churches in Lalibela, Ethiopia, are real and are scientifically inexplicable, but King Lalibela's hidden tomb has not yet been discovered, and the passages Sam found beneath the churches probably exist only in the author's imagination. The Blue Nile Falls and Blue Nile River are real, and so are the hippos who inhabit the river.

The Cradle of Humankind near Hadar, Ethiopia is real, but the author invented the cave Sam's team explored. The other Cradle of Humankind, located primarily in the Sterkfontein Cave system northwest of Johannesburg, South Africa, is also real, as is the underground lake there in Milner Hall, and the nearby Dinaledi Chamber (Chamber of Stars) in the Rising Star Cave system.

Dragon's Breath Cave beneath the Kalahari Desert in Namibia is real and is as described in the story (including the enormous underground lake and the Golden Cave Catfish), but the underwater cave leading to the Blue Dragon is a figment of the author's imagination. Or is it?

Underwater Atlantis: An underwater city has been found near Cuba in three thousand feet of water. The city has a huge pyramid, but the site isn't Atlantis. The author created her version of Atlantis based partly on that discovery.

Bwindi Impenetrable Forest in Uganda is a real place.

The 1939 Bücker Jungmann biplane in the opening chapter and the Russian Antonov AN-2 cabin biplane mentioned later are real and are as described in the story. The author has owned and flown several Bücker Jungmanns and has also flown an Antonov AN-2.

Any factual errors in the story are the sole responsibility of the author.

MURDER ON BANYAN ISLE

JETT JORGENSEN MYSTERIES, BOOK ONE

As my flight approached Palm Beach International Airport, I spotted my family home on Banyan Isle. Named Valhalla by my Danish great-great grandfather, the home was built as a tribute to his Viking heritage. When it was passed down to my parents, the Norse theme seemed a bit out of place for my mother, a Cherokee shaman, but she loved it. Tall and slender with golden skin, high cheekbones, black hair, and golden eyes, my mother could've passed for royalty in any culture. Fortunately, I looked like her, except I had my father's light-blue eyes.

My lifelong best friend, Gwen Stuart, met me at the airport and drove me home. "It's good to have you back, Jett."

"I missed you too, Gwen."

When we turned between giant stone pillars and

followed the tree-lined drive to my family's home, I said, "Let's leave my luggage in the car until the rain stops." I held a huge umbrella over us as we navigated to my front door through an afternoon downpour.

She said, "Too bad your ancestor failed to include a porte cochère when he built this Nordic stronghold."

Heavy raindrops hammered puddles, splashing me with tepid water. "And stubborn Jorgensen descendants would rather get drenched than alter their patriarch's grand design for his South Florida home."

"Huh, typical Vikings," Gwen said. "Except you, Jett."

We rushed inside, and the heavy mahogany door closed behind us with a firm thud.

As I crossed the foyer, I caught a whiff of perfume and froze. Had I imagined it? It wasn't Gwen's or mine. It reminded me of my late mother's favorite fragrance. The weird thing was Mom hadn't been in the house since she and Dad had perished in a plane crash two years ago. The house was empty, yet the fragrance was real.

Gwen noticed my hesitation and stopped in front of one of the eight-foot winged Valkyrie statues flanking the twin staircases that curved up both sides of the two-story foyer. A brief image of Valkyries escorting my parents to Valhalla flashed through my mind. The fragrance I'd noticed seconds ago wafted past me again, jolting me back to reality.

"Are you okay, Jett? You haven't been home in almost two years, not since the funerals. Would you like to spend a few nights next door at my place?"

I bit my lip. "Something's wrong."

"Tell me."

"I'm not sure." A feeling of foreboding prickled my skin as I glanced around the dark foyer. Lightning flashed, reflecting on the white marble floor, marble stairs, and something else.

I gasped and dropped to one knee, tracing the moist marks with my fingertip.

Wet footprints, barely visible, glistened in the gray light cast by floor-to-ceiling windows and continued up the left staircase. Two sets, one from a man's shoes and the other from a woman's high heels.

Shoes like my parents had worn.

Thunder boomed, and I shivered as I pointed at the footprints. "My . . . my parents—"

Her jaw dropped when she spotted the faint trail leading upstairs. "No, it can't be."

"But—"

She interrupted, "Listen to me. I know your mom was a Cherokee shaman, but that doesn't mean your parents' spirits have returned. And ghosts don't leave footprints."

I gestured at the security panel. "The system is on, and the only way to enter without triggering an alarm is with the key and the code, so who—" I inhaled through my nose. "Is that cigar smoke? It smells a lot like Dad's favorite brand." My mouth went dry.

Gwen tilted her head, strands of her long red hair falling out of a hastily constructed French twist. "The odor seems to be coming from the second floor." She drew her police issued Glock 40. "Ghosts don't smoke." She transformed into her cop persona as she started up the steps. "Stay behind me."

We stopped at the second floor and followed the odor into the north hallway.

She hesitated. "Did you hear that? Sounded like a groan."

"Could be the wind." A humid breeze ruffled my hair. "The cigar smoke is coming from that guest room." I pointed at an open door.

We crept closer.

Gwen grabbed my elbow. "Wait here."

"But."

She gave me a look, and I nodded.

I waited a few moments. Indignant about the intrusion, I followed her anyway.

She eased up to the open door and peered inside. "The door to the balcony is open, and a cigar's smoldering in a dish on the nightstand." She glanced back at me. "Oh geez, there's also a whisky bottle and two glasses."

I peeked over her shoulder and scanned the

room. Curtains billowed in the fresh ocean breeze as I followed her through the door and caught another whiff of perfume. Goosebumps prickled my skin. "Is that a man's shoe sticking partway out from under the bed skirt?"

"Yep, he must've undressed and kicked his shoes under the bed. I'll check the bathroom." She moved to the inner door and peeked inside. "Nobody in there." She turned to me. "I'll search the closet while you check if the shoe is your uncle's size."

I eased up to the massive four-poster bed, leaned down, lifted the leather loafer, shrieked, and jerked my hand away like I'd just touched a tarantula. "There's, uh, there's a foot in it!"

Not the best reaction from a Navy Intelligence officer, but I was exhausted from the long sequence of flights from Afghanistan, and the foot had startled me.

Gwen rushed over, dropped to her knees, and lifted the lace bed skirt.

"Not just a foot—there's a body under here." She paused. "Make that *two* bodies. There's a woman beside him."

Available in Paperback and eBook from Your Favorite Bookstore or Online Retailer

ACKNOWLEDGMENTS

First and foremost, I'd like to thank my Lord and Savior, Jesus Christ, for the many blessings he has bestowed upon me.

As always, I'd like to thank my brilliant critique partners, mystery authors Fred Lichtenberg and George A. Bernstein, for their helpful insights and sage advice. Thanks, guys!

A big thank you to my expert beta readers, Suzanne Berglind, Kip Peterson, Virginia V. Guido, and Robert D. Krell. And additional thanks to Kip for his expertise on specialized dive gear.

Special thanks to my friends at the Singer Island Hilton for being so supportive of my work. They make the world a far better place, and the covered deck provides an ideal spot to dine while writing my books. The delicious food, friendly service, and fresh ocean air stimulate my creativity.

The Islander Grill inside the Palm Beach Shores Resort on Singer Island is my favorite night spot to stimulate my creativity while enjoying delicious food, live music, and superb service. Thank you to owners Niko and Meliodora Bujaj.

ALSO BY S.L. MENEAR

The Samantha Starr Thriller Series
Flight to Redemption

Flight to Destiny

Triple Threat

Stranded

Vanished

The Jett Jorgensen Cozy Mystery Series
Murder on Banyan Isle

Life, Love, & Laughter: 50 Short Stories

ABOUT THE AUTHOR

S.L. Menear is a retired airline pilot. US Airways hired Sharon in 1980 as their first female pilot, by-passing the flight engineer position. The men in her new-hire class gave her the nickname, Bombshell. She flew Boeing 727s and 737s, DC-9s, and BAC 1-11 airliners and was promoted to captain in her seventh year.

Before her pilot career, Sharon worked as a water-sports model and then traveled the world as a flight attendant with Pan American World Airways.

Sharon also enjoyed flying antique airplanes, experimental aircraft, and Third-World fighter airplanes. She has flown many of the airplanes in her Samantha Starr Series featuring a woman pilot, Flight to Redemption – Book One, Flight to Destiny – Book Two, Triple Threat – Book Three, Stranded – Book Four, and Vanished – Book Five. Samantha Starr will return after Sharon takes a short break to begin a new mystery series—The Jett Jorgensen Mysteries, starting with Murder on Banyan Isle. She also co-wrote Life, Love, & Laughter: 50 Short Stories, with her mother, D.M. (Dorothy) Littlefield.

Her beloved timber-shepherds, Pratt & Whitney, were her faithful companions for almost fourteen years, and she enjoyed riding her beautiful black and white paint stallion, Chief, who kept her mother's mares happy, fathering several adorable foals.

www.slmenear.com

 facebook.com/slmenear

Lightning Source UK Ltd.
Milton Keynes UK
UKHW021848161220
375343UK00003B/225